Dear Sally,
It was
you at Tu
you enjoy this
Journey!
Stacy B.

CORTHAN LEGACY BOOK 1

QUEST OF THE DREAMWALKER

STACY BENNETT

Published by Miramae Press
Second Edition 2018

ISBN: 978-0-9988086-0-4

Cover design by Ashley Fontainne
Author photo by Jaye Kogut Photography

OTHER BOOKS BY STACY BENNETT

CORTHAN LEGACY

Quest of the Dreamwalker

Call of the Huntress

Hound of Barakan (coming soon)

Tales of the Archer (prequel novella)

STAND ALONE BOOKS

Son of Anubis

Mi Carino (short story)

Mask of Innocence (spring 2022)

ACKNOWLEDGEMENTS

I had a veritable cast of helpers given the amount of time it has taken for this project to come to fruition. I suppose doling out thanks chronologically would make the most sense. So, thank you first of all to the boy I loved in high school, college and beyond, my first helper, editor and sounding board, someone who helped me grow this story from its tragically awkward beginnings to a much more presentable adolescence. And thank you to my friends Annie, and Audra who tolerated me talking about the story over and over and over again. I have nothing but love for Shelly, Joe, Mom, Dad, Valerie, and Amanda Makepeace.

Finally, thank you all of my writerly friends, for helping out with advice and editing and discussions, including Dorothy Sanders, Revo Boulanger, Ailsa Abrahams, Daniel Swensen, Ruth Long, Cara Michaels and James Whitworth Hazzard. And of course I have the fondest love for my beta readers: Steven Paul Watson, A.D. Trosper and Drea Damara who were unfailingly supportive and excited about the project. I couldn't have done it without your love, but honestly the butt-kicking was the most help.

~ Stacy B.

For my mom

who always wanted me
to follow my pipe dream.

And for my dad
who never quite managed to realize his own.

This one's for you, Dad.

CHAPTER 1
CARA

Beyond the walls that defined her world, the tundra burst to life in fierce swaths of lavender and white. The sorcerer's daughter both welcomed and dreaded that springtime awakening. It quickened in her a longing, an ache from deep in her bones that drew her to the highest parapet. Here, she could breathe in the heavy scents of saxifrage and moss. She longed to touch the greening scrub and walk the spongy lichen-covered rocks, but she was a creature of the Keep and that vibrant world was forbidden.

Tonight, the ache was particularly strong.

She often wished she could walk through the gate and roam the tundra. But such wishes were foolish, little wisps of thought without substance. She'd had opportunities to leave each time Father went south to get supplies, but had never even opened the main gate. Something held her back. Perhaps she feared she would fade beyond the black walls, like mist in the afternoon. Perhaps she lacked courage. She told herself it was loyalty—a daughter's loyalty to the complicated man who'd raised her. In darker moments though, she suspected something more insidious.

She'd always had a sense for the rightness of things. She knew when Father's sledge bears or message birds were unwell. She read his ever-changing humors as easily as he read his dusty tomes. Over the years, she had learned to trust her gift. And it was this intuition that told her long ago she was broken. Stunted. Crippled. She'd never possess the strength to cross that threshold.

Sighing with resignation, she turned her attention to the sky where wild hawks dove out of the wan sunlight to snag their unwary prey. She lingered like an errant child atop the western parapet. The arctic wind played in her long white hair and tugged playfully at her clothes. Though the days had begun to lengthen, a frigid breeze stung her bare fingers that roved the smooth hollows of the Keep's black stones. Winter's lingering chill seeped through her tattered cloak to prick at her skin. But the cold wasn't the reason her insides quivered.

The last blaze of sun sank below the horizon, setting the landscape on fire with gold and orange. She turned to find the moon, full and rosy pink, cradled in the peaks of the Black Mountains. The Keep was built at the foot of those dark summits. They loomed over her like hunched, somber old men, their craggy frowns admonishing her wayward thoughts. The time for lingering was past.

Turning away from the peaks, she wrapped thin arms around herself as if that could melt the ice that clutched her heart. She descended into the Keep, padding on soft slippers through the empty stronghold and climbed up the eastern staircase into the highest tower: Father's tower.

The circular room at the very top was dominated by a stone altar encircled by a ring of symbols carved into the floor. Blood-rimmed manacles hung from each corner of the altar. Braziers blazing with eerie blue-green flames sent stuttering shadows across the walls. On the pedestal at the foot of the altar waited her father's most prized scroll held open with crystals of green and amber. She paused at the threshold wishing there was another way.

"There you are," rasped a voice.

Startled, she turned to find Father standing behind her, his aged cheeks as craggy as the mountains. He was ill again. She sensed it in his bent frame, shriveled and gaunt inside his voluminous robes. The ebony damask brushed against her arm as he shuffled past, raising the hair on her neck like a cold draft. She shivered at the feeling of wrongness that surrounded him.

"Hurry now. Take your position, Daughter," he said, interrupting her thoughts.

"Daughter" was what he called her. It wasn't a real name, but he'd given her no other. She rubbed the chill from the back of her neck and walked to the table, her eyes following him to the pedestal.

That her gift said he was unwell made no sense to her. She couldn't see anything wrong with him. Nevertheless, she felt it, whatever it was. It gnawed at him, depleted him until he performed the ritual and returned to himself for a while.

Her heart pitied him sometimes, chained as he was to that scrap of paper on the pedestal.

He perused the scroll for the thousandth time, though she was sure he'd memorized the liturgy having repeated it so many times. However, the spell had to be recited precisely as written. How often had he muttered about the dangers of miscasting a spell? Not to her in particular but to himself as he checked off the requirements one by one each time in the same order: the sigils, the braziers, the stones, the scroll, and the subject. Tonight, the subject was her; other nights, when he had need, he would use one of his many guests.

She slid up onto the waiting altar, tucking her threadbare skirt around her legs. She ignored the bloody chains. Reluctant she might be, but he wouldn't need those. There wasn't a single drop of blood on the altar itself, only a thick layer of dust that coated her hands and clothes with the familiar scents of magic and death.

The dust of a hundred lives.

She quickly pushed the thought away. The others were not her concern. Wiping her hands on her clothes, she swung her feet up and laid herself down on the stone.

Her muscles tensed as his gravelly voice began the guttural singsong incantation. She didn't understand the words, but she could have repeated the sounds from memory.

Tendrils of fear curled in her belly as she prepared herself for the pain. Though her body was never marked, the scroll's magic stretched and twisted her inner being, tearing it away and funneling it into Father's unseen wound. Everything she was would pour into him, filling him and leaving nothing behind. She'd survive, waking in a day or so, but while she was in the grip of his spell, it felt like she was dying.

She stared at the vaulted ceiling, at the arches sweeping up into darkness. Heat gathered in the room. Beads of sweat prickled along her hairline and under her arms making her long for the stinging breeze of the tundra. Energy hummed between them. His need was a ravenous thing that sought her. In the end, she'd have no choice but to surrender to the spell and vanish into the darkness. But until then, she sought sanctuary inside her mind.

There was a lush woodland in her dreams. Whether it was a real place somewhere far away, or only a fear-induced delusion, she didn't know. But when she imagined herself there, the pain lessened. Calming her breath and closing her eyes, she painted the landscape in her mind, drawing it in meticulous detail. She focused on the sights and sounds of that place until she could no longer feel the stone slab beneath her. Instead of dust and death, she smelled damp earth and new growth. Her ragged linen robes became a leather vest and leggings. She inhaled deeply as she stood in her night-clad forest, its warm air caressing her cheek and night birds hooting in the trees. She knew this place as well as she knew the Keep, maybe better.

Father's chanting intensified, intruding on her peace. Her connection to the forest wavered; reality threatened to pull her back to the tower and that tearing pain. In fear, she pushed her mind back into the dream and ordered her legs to run. Each thudding footfall, each stinging branch kept her mind focused on the forest. She ran hard, her lungs working like bellows. Eventually, though, the magic was too strong and she tumbled, disappearing into the void.

CHAPTER 2
KHOURY

The sparse foam dissipated quickly from Captain Khoury's ale as he struggled to remember the last time a death had truly touched him. Today he'd been furious with that bastard Ranceforth and his cowardly tactics, but he felt no grief for those who'd died on the battlefield. Years of service as a Sword had numbed him to such losses, yet he found his apathy unsettling. When had he become a stone-cold killer?

He drank the quiet ale, letting the cool liquid soothe his roughened throat. The lull of day's end washed away his irritation until only the clenched muscles of his jaw hinted at his inner discontent. He leaned heavy elbows on the small table in the corner, watching his lieutenant sort coins with sure fingers.

An uncommon mercenary, Violet Meade was as good with money as she was with a blade. The coins slid and clinked on the polished wood surface without interruption even as she glanced at the wound on the side of his head.

"You should get that looked at," she said. Her voice was girlishly sweet though he'd heard her unleash a torrent of expletives that would blister a man's ears.

He touched light fingers to his temple and, seeing no blood on them, sniffed dismissively. The blow had knocked his helm from his head and left his ears ringing, but he'd been too angry to care. Besides, the ale had already taken the edge off the dull throb behind his eyes. Forcing a half-smile, he said, "I'm fine. Keep counting, Vi."

She pursed her lips in irritation but returned to her work. He watched her for a moment, her battle-smudged fingers flicking the coins to their respective piles. Her thick black hair, cropped unfashionably short, had been left in spiky disarray by her helm and a florid bruise temporarily marred her smooth fawn-colored cheek. He was lucky to have her in his corps but he didn't like her fretting over him. Archer was bad enough.

A gangly warrior, all elbows and knees, stumbled up to the table and saluted. "C-C-Captain Khoury, sir."

"What is it?" Khoury asked, looking up. Shocked by the warrior's youth, he found himself searching for a darkening of scruff on the smooth cheeks. Surely, he hadn't led this boy into battle today.

"Um, you wouldn't know me, Captain sir, but Ellis. Roger Ellis, that is. I mean, Lieutenant Ellis sent me to gather the coin. For the other Swords, that is." His head bobbed like a nervous goose as the youth's slender fingers twisted the edge of his stained cloak.

Khoury didn't ask the youth's name; he didn't want to know. "Did you fight today?"

The young warrior's eyes darted nervously. "Yes, yes sir, I did. Killed t-two of the bastards. All on my own."

Khoury's eyes narrowed.

"Well, actually. I did have a little help. With the one." The young man looked down at the twisted cloak in his hands.

Was I ever that young? Khoury marveled.

"Good work," was all he said, making the young man straighten with pride. "Tell Ellis I'll send the money when we're done counting."

The lad bobbed his head a few more times to take his leave and then scurried out the door. No doubt he'd be telling his drinking buddies how he'd met "the captain." Khoury sighed and finished his ale as his other companion returned.

The bulky Northerner with tawny eyes, a ginger beard, and auburn hair dropped heavily into the only other chair. Grinning, he slammed three brews down on the table, sloshing ale across the stained wood, the stacked coins, and Khoury's arm.

"Damned sloppy drunk." The captain scowled, shaking the ale from his hand.

The Northerner's name was Reid Tarhill, but he insisted everyone call him Archer. In a profession rife with haunted pasts and best-forgotten deeds, it was common enough for a man to choose a new name. Khoury knew that better than most.

"Better sloppy than morbid," Archer said, fixing the captain with a pointed stare. "Cheer up, you old sourpuss."

Violet stifled a chuckle, and the captain's scowl deepened.

Archer ignored Khoury's displeasure, sliding one mug to the captain and the other to Violet. "Anyone looking at you would think we got drubbed good and proper," he said. "But we got paid, didn't we?"

"That we did." Khoury eyed the gold glinting dully on the table. *Blood money,* he thought. *Nothing but blood money.* His ghosts would be ashamed.

"A quick battle it was, too," Violet said.

Not a battle—a slaughter, Khoury added to himself. The peasants' frightened faces as his horsemen bore down on them broke through the comfort of his alcoholic fog. *Damn Ranceforth! And damn the gold,* he thought. But if Khoury was angry at anyone, it was himself. Old Khoury had taught him better.

He chased his anger with more ale, drinking deeply from the new mug, his lip curling at its rancid taste. "Where'd you get this goat piss?"

"From the pens out back," Archer said with mock innocence. "It was cheaper."

Violet laughed out loud and put her ale down untouched. "Guess I'm done for the night."

"When I was someone's second," Khoury said, "I'd buy my captain the good stuff."

"Did you?" Archer asked. "Well, today I think you owe me the good stuff."

"How do you figure? I'm the one that bled Ranceforth."

"You'd never have gotten to him without me covering your reckless ass. What were you thinking?"

Archer had a point. Khoury had been reckless, but anger tended to blunt his common sense. "You saw their faces," he said. "They were just peasants."

"Rebelling against their lord. Who hired you, meaning us," Archer said, sweeping his finger to include all of them.

"That was no rebellion, Archer," Khoury spat. "A man fighting for his own freedom doesn't show that kind of fear. That was Ranceforth staging a coup."

"We'll never know for sure, boys," Violet said evenly, "since he's dead."

"If they were so ill-trained," Archer said in a rare flash of anger, "we could have taken them without losing a single man. And there'd be no need for you to race into the thick, leaving your guard—*and me*—behind."

"Let it go, Archer," Violet warned, giving the Northerner a hard stare. Then, she turned those eyes on Khoury. "Captain, you *were* hasty. And careless."

"Even Vi agrees with me on this." Archer leaned back and crossed his arms with a look of defiance.

"Don't get used to it, Northerner," she shot back.

"Enough," Khoury growled at them. He was tired of talking about the battle, tired of thinking about it. "It was my decision. I wanted to end it quickly. And I did. There's the door if you don't like it."

Violet and Archer looked at each other in the uncomfortable silence.

"Now, if you're done griping about my methods," the captain said, "you can take the money to Ellis at the Oak and Acorn." He pushed the largest of the leather purses toward Archer.

Khoury knew he should have been giving out the wages himself. There had been a time when he had crowed from the rafters as raucously as his men were doing right now. But he didn't feel like crowing anymore, and his irritation would only ruin their good time.

"I'm not gonna be the one to settle up with the innkeeper after that rowdy lot," Archer said, sliding the purse to Violet. "It's Vi's turn." He grinned at the dark-haired woman.

Vi stared at him for a long minute before she snorted with amusement. "Fine, coward." She swept the last of the coins into a purse, tied it closed and stood with a harsh scrape of her chair. "I'll see to the lads, but that makes the captain here your problem." She smirked, blew Archer an exaggerated kiss, and sauntered out of the inn.

Khoury heard Archer's long-suffering sigh though he pretended not to notice.

"I know you were doing what you thought best," Archer said, his voice low and rough, "but you've got to promise me, Khoury, promise you won't leave me behind like that again."

The captain looked up into tawny eyes that seemed as young as those of the unnamed youth. Eager, desperate eyes that weighed him down with the onus of Archer's loyalty.

It occurred to Khoury that he'd taken the Northerner on after that last battle he'd crowed about. Ultimately, the Barakan rebellion had failed but that battle had been a glorious rout. He never found out why Archer was fighting for the Barakan lords but it hadn't mattered. He'd been left behind, and Khoury's men found him half-crazed defending the body of his kinsman. After wounding three of Khoury's Swords, Archer had finally been subdued.

The depth of his loyalty and sorrow touched Khoury, and he had offered to let the Northerner swear fealty rather than face execution. Archer hadn't left his side since. Unless Khoury did something stupid, like today.

"Agreed," he murmured.

Archer smiled and raised his mug. "Then to victory, Captain."

The captain snagged Violet's abandoned mug and toasted with it. "Aye, victory," he said without enthusiasm, and they both drank.

They sat in silence for a while before Archer scrubbed his face, smoothed his beard, and struggled to his feet. "Piss time," he announced.

"Good idea." Khoury pushed his chair back and stood up. His vision darkened around the edges. *Pretty strong goat piss,* he thought.

Unsteadily, the two mercenaries weaved through the tables to the back door, alternately grunting apologies and returning threats. Khoury stumbled through the door first, and a cold breeze tried to rouse him with little effect. His mind was shrouded in fog, his thoughts clumsy and incoherent. *Must be the ale.* He tried to remember exactly how many he'd had as he leaned his forehead on the rough wood of the inn and relieved himself against the wall.

Over the patter of spilling water, a sound caught his clumsy attention. Was that a footstep? With reflexes honed over two decades, he whirled to block the strike, but his swing went wild. The world tilted sharply. Then, something heavy slammed into his temple sending him to the ground.

☙

Inner haste roused Khoury to semi-consciousness, though he didn't remember what had happened. His cheek bumped against a lurching floor that smelled of old wood and urine, making his head throb with each jarring bounce. The pain made him wish for oblivion again, while instinct urged him to leap up and fight. He leashed his instinct like an overeager hound so he could take stock of the situation.

Recognizing the familiar sounds of wheels and horses, he opened bleary eyes to the back of a box-wagon—spare and without seats. Small barred windows near the roof admitted a waning light. His lips were parched and stretched around a gag of rough cloth, his knees and wrists tightly bound. His sword and dagger were missing.

Captured. But why and by whom?

He had no answers, but he wasn't alone. Other men were sprawled over and around him, passed out and reeking of liquor. Among them, Archer bounced limply nearby. Gratefully, Khoury didn't see Vi.

Some good news then. Wherever they were, whatever had happened, she would eventually try to find them. He thought of his Swords sleeping off their drinking binge. A rescue might take a few days.

Closing his eyes against the daggers in his head, he herded his scattered thoughts to some semblance of order. He remembered Ranceforth and the battle at Balkridge Vale easily enough. He'd left his men celebrating at the Oak and Acorn in the nearby town of Telsedan, but he couldn't dredge up the name of the inn he'd gone to with Vi and Archer. He did remember that goat-piss excuse for ale. After that, though, he recalled nothing.

Eventually the others began to stir, untangling themselves with growls and grunts. When Archer woke, he squirmed close to the captain. Reading Khoury's mind, he turned back-to-back with the captain and they tried to undo their bonds. However, the knots were tight and their fingers numb. Khoury slumped back against the side of the wagon with a defeated shake of his head. Archer did the same, a hint of worry on the larger man's face.

When the pain in the captain's head subsided and the thinning light carried the burnished hues of evening, the wagon jerked to a stop. Khoury leaned on Archer, levering himself up to the barred window for a peek outside. His breath plumed in the frigid air that wafted in.

Outside pine trees studded a snowy landscape. An old tollhouse crouched near the road, all but abandoned. The stump of a broken gate, now useless, leaned into the road. Three dark-clothed men waited astride their horses just within sight, while a fourth dismounted. He knocked at the tollhouse door. The sharp sound of his bare knuckles reverberated in the cold air. When the door opened, the kidnapper disappeared into waiting darkness.

"It's a good haul, isn't it, Royce?" said an eager young man leaning over to nudge the second man.

"Five hundred a head between the four of us? It'll do," the man agreed gruffly.

"Assuming we get our money," said the third, reining his horse around to scan the road behind them.

We've been sold, Khoury thought with relief. It could have been worse. He and Archer could certainly survive hard labor until they escaped or Vi came with help. He pictured her smug amusement at having to purchase them back from whatever lord they'd been sold to.

"The poor sods," said the young man, eyeing the wagon with pity. "What do ya think he wants them for?"

"Hush, lad." The gruff one punched the boy's arm in reprimand and whispered hoarsely, "You don't ask an Islander what for."

An Islander! Khoury's mind whirled. *A sorcerer.*

Were they to be shipped to the Magus Academy on the barren rocks of the Far Isles? Khoury checked the sun's position and decided they had gone northeast rather than west. But then what was an Islander doing out here? And what sort of magic did they want them for? Usually a Far Isles master meant an unnatural death, a quick one if a man were lucky.

At that moment, the door opened and the fourth kidnapper returned followed by an old man in a shabby cloak. The newcomer's stooped gait was slow, and his hands were clasped casually behind his back.

Was this the Magus?

Khoury slid back down next to Archer as the rest of the men dismounted. He scanned the captives huddled in the cage, wondering what the sorcerer would need so many bodies for.

The locks slammed home and the door to the wagon opened. Three kidnappers climbed into the cramped space and without a word began untying the captives' legs. One by one, all the men in the wagon were handed down and led to a large cage. The cage perched on a waiting sledge harnessed to three enormous white bears. On all fours, the animals' shoulders nearly reached the captain's chin. The Clans of the Northlands, Archer's people, used sledges and beasts like these. Khoury noted the consternation on Archer's face as he watched the animals wait patiently.

Khoury's hands were untied before he was roughly thrust into the cage. He caught the cold iron bars and managed to stay upright though most of the others landed on the floor, weak-legged and staggering. They reminded him of spring lambs, their bleating complaints swelling as they removed their own gags. Some dared shouting for help. Khoury spat his gag out and scraped the pasty residue from his tongue with his teeth as he watched the cloaked man carefully. The man was heedless of their noise.

"Another ride," Archer said, testing his strength against the bars.

"We'll get our chance. Just be ready."

"I always am, Captain."

Khoury smiled grimly as the old man pulled tarps down over the cage. Shifting to where there was a small tear in the cloth, Khoury peered out. The man who had knocked on the door walked up to the old man a few feet from Khoury's vantage point.

"We did what you asked," the kidnapper said.

"You certainly surpassed my expectations," the older man replied.

"Well, your little potion did most of the work. You have our gold?"

"Of course." The old man pulled a hefty purse from beneath his robes and held it out to the kidnapper briefly, then drew it back. "Actually I'd like to retain your services against any...future needs."

"You know where to find me," the kidnapper said with steel in his voice, beckoning with his fingers expectantly.

"Indeed, I do." The old man dropped the gold into the waiting hand. Then he uttered something in a low voice and tossed some sort of powder into the kidnapper's face. Khoury watched as the kidnapper dropped to the ground, unconscious.

A chill gripped Khoury's spine. He was stunned at the speed with which the man had been subdued.

"What is it?" Archer asked, reading Khoury's concern.

"We've been sold. To an Islander," the captain said.

"A sorcerer?"

"So it would appear."

A sharp whistle pierced the air and the sledge lurched forward. Khoury settled on the cage floor close to Archer to keep warm in the increasing chill. They rode in silence, each lost in their own thoughts.

In the hours that followed, the weather changed drastically. A fierce wind began to blow, making the canvas dance with sharp snapping sounds. Frigid air invaded the cage. Beyond the flapping cloth, Khoury glimpsed driving snow. He and Archer remained close to each other, but their backs now pressed up against the others who huddled in the center of the cage. Every head was down; bare faces and hands tucked inside what little clothing they wore.

The storm's howl died to a distant shriek as the sledge came to a halt. When the tarp was released, it leapt from the cage and fluttered away like a giant bat. The arctic wind stung the captain's face as he looked around at a barren snow-covered bailey. Nearby, the severe lines of a stronghold rose darkly into the whirl of white flakes. It was unlike anything Khoury had ever seen. The Keep proper had been carved from the living rock of the mountains to the north and east. The unusual masonry gave the structure an alien aura. A thick curtain wall of black stones surrounded the bailey to the south and west. Two stories tall and strongly built, its ironbound doors were tall enough for fabled giants to pass through. The storm within the walls was mild compared to the howling winds he saw beyond the gate.

Khoury studied the battlements, but no one walked the walls; no one was stationed at the guard tower; no one manned the gate. There weren't even flags fluttering along the parapet. The Keep waited empty and quiet as a tomb. The whistling wind alone broke the eerie silence in the strange snowy half-night.

Archer's nudge drew the captain's attention to the sledge bears that, once released, lumbered quietly around the side of the building like well-behaved hounds.

"What?" Khoury wasn't sure what he should be looking at.

"Sledge bears are half-wild and ornery. We never let them roam."

"A spell, perhaps?" Khoury mused. Beyond Archer's shoulder, he noticed a second, smaller cage set on the sledge in front of the main one. In it were the men who had kidnapped them.

Double-crossed, he thought with a certain satisfaction.

"Gentlemen!" The old man's voice rang out clearly against the storm. "My name is Sidonius, and this is my Keep. Beyond these walls is a land of giants and of snow and a hundred other dangers. If you try to escape, you *will* die and not by my hand." He paced before the cage, his hands clasped behind his back. Rheumy eyes studied each man in turn. "I offer you simple accommodations, food and shelter. And in return I require your service…."

"Do you see any guards, Captain?" Archer whispered, scanning the battlements.

Khoury shook his head.

"There's just one of him by the looks of it," Archer continued softly. "We can take him."

If their captor had been an ordinary man perhaps. Even weaponless the two of them should have been able to overpower a much larger man or even a few regulars. But the memory of the driver falling to the ground with a few words and a handful of powder flitted through Khoury's mind.

"Patience."

The Northerner grunted with annoyance and turned back to what the sorcerer was saying.

"As you have no choice, please accept my hospitality until such time as I have need of you." Sidonius turned to the doors of the stronghold, which opened at a wave of his hand. Glowing firelight beckoned from within.

From where Khoury stood, the interior looked warm and inviting, making the cold wind even sharper on his skin. He detected a whiff of food, and his mouth watered. Next to him, Archer's stomach grumbled.

"You'll find a feast on the other side of these doors. Please eat your fill." The sorcerer gestured and the locks on the cages released of their own accord. As the old man headed up the stone steps, he called back over his shoulder. "Oh, and mind the steps. They're a bit slippery."

The men limped out of the cages on stiff legs and milled around, looking from the storm outside to the old man climbing the steps. Khoury was impressed by the sorcerer's show of power, but everyone had a weakness. He surveyed the yard, noting the Keep's layout as he stepped down out of the cage.

Sudden, angry voices erupted as two burly men charged Sidonius. Khoury recognized them as two of the kidnappers. They grabbed the hooded figure, one on each arm, and spun him around roughly.

"Listen, you stupid old sod. You got no guards, and you still think you can keep us?" The man spat on the stairs. "There won't be anything left of you when we're finished with ya."

Sidonius looked from one to the other. Then he threw his head back and cackled with gusto. The cowl slipped from his head, and his thinning shock of disheveled gray hair sprang to attention, adding to the demented picture he made. He stood on the icy steps in the snow, laughing. His wild eyes blazed.

And then his cloak did too.

At first, the flames were barely visible, just licking the hem of the fabric. But soon they grew, climbing his robes, enveloping his body. And still the old man laughed. The two men released him when they saw the fire, but it was too late. The flames jumped from the sorcerer to his attackers like pouncing cats. Screaming in pain, the men backed away, but the fire clung to their hands and crawled like a living thing up their arms and across their shoulders, igniting their hair and clothes.

Writhing in panic, they tried to beat out the flames. Twisting frantically, they slipped one after the other and tumbled to the bailey, human fireballs with clothes ablaze. In moments, high-pitched shrieks filled the air, grating on Khoury's ears.

"I told them to mind the steps," the sorcerer said.

Khoury looked up to see the old man enveloped by flames, yet untouched. Fear snaked through the captain as the sorcerer watched the men's death throes unperturbed.

"Such a waste," Sidonius said with a sigh as their screams turned to wet gurgles and finally silence. Then he snapped his fingers and the flames vanished, leaving only smoke and the smoldering bodies at the foot of the stairs. The stench of charred flesh filled Khoury's nostrils.

"Come along," the sorcerer commanded. He turned his back to the men once more and walked into the Keep.

A wide-eyed Archer met Khoury's look in shocked silence. As they climbed the steps, Khoury pushed the grisly scene from his mind. *What else was this sorcerer capable of?*

Sidonius hadn't lied. The banquet tables in the great hall were covered in a resplendent feast. Two roaring hearths provided cheery warmth and light, though the atmosphere was subdued as the captives sat down to eat. Khoury sniffed the food with suspicion, but Archer reached past him to grab a plate of roasted meat.

"Might as well eat, Captain," he said around a mouthful of crusty bread, crumbs dusting his thick beard. "Who wants to die on an empty stomach?"

"And if it's poisoned?"

"We'll be dead that much quicker." Archer tore meat from a drumstick and winked.

The captain chuckled sourly. *That might even be a blessing,* he thought.

Though he had little appetite, he ate the meat and fruit, washing it down with the weak ale that didn't begin to relieve his thirst.

"So," Archer said in low tones, "he controls fire. That's a problem."

"And I saw him knock a man out with a few words," the captain said. He looked over the other captives, hoping for allies. He wasn't impressed. Most of them looked like they hadn't had a decent meal, or bath, in weeks. His best bet for help would be the two remaining kidnappers, one of whom was no older than the Sword who had come to get the coin for Ellis.

"Think Vi knows we're gone yet?" Archer asked.

"Doubt it," Khoury replied. "Even if she's sober, no one else will be roadworthy for at least a day. But you know her; she won't rest until she gives us a good tongue-lashing for getting taken."

"Might prefer to stay kidnapped then," Archer joked. "Damn bastards took my bow. That one was my favorite."

"My blades as well," Khoury said.

"And our gold."

Khoury frowned. "Aye. At least Violet gave the men their pay."

"Think she'll be able to find us?" Archer asked.

"She's tenacious," the captain said, surveying the room. There were only two sets of doors, the ones they had come in through and ones leading deeper into the stronghold. Sidonius had disappeared and all of the doors were shut and, no doubt, locked. On the bright side, the food was warm and satisfying.

By the time their stomachs were full and the ale steins had run dry, Khoury noticed other men slumped over their feast, snoring. He himself felt dull and slow-witted.

"Archer, are you feeling all right?" he asked as the room tilted a little.

"Sleepy," his friend mumbled, looking pale. Realizing they would soon be unconscious too, Khoury grabbed Archer by the arm and searched for somewhere to hide. They were too exposed at the table. Running out of time and with few options available, he finally led his companion behind a pillar out of sight of the others. Irresistible darkness claimed him as, throughout the hall, all of the prisoners slept.

CHAPTER 3
CARA

She hurried to the great hall door, her worn slippers whispering guiltily against the stone floor. She paused, pressed an ear to the cold planks, and then turned the handle. Pushing the door open a crack, a draft of wood smoke and spices filled her nostrils, cramping her stomach with renewed hunger. After a cursory glance, she entered the hall where men slept scattered about the long tables. She closed the door carefully before scurrying to the nearest table and ducking behind the odorous bulk of one of Father's guests.

She surveyed the room a final time. They were all sound asleep.

Then she let out a breath, smiled and stood up. Snatching pieces of food from the plates, she filled her tied-up skirt. Flitting from table to table, she looted bread and meat and fruit, pausing only a moment to stuff a hunk of warm, crumbly biscuit into her mouth, and then continued her gathering.

Unlike the rest of the Keep, the great hall was gloriously toasty and well-lit. When her skirt was full, she pilfered a leg of game bird and squatted down to rest her loot in her lap. She tore the still warm meat from bone. Warm juice dripped down her arms. She hadn't finished licking her fingers when she heard the thump of his staff.

"Daughter," echoed his graveled voice, "I know you're here. Again."

She sighed, brushed the crumbs off her bodice and stood up, hiding her guilt under downcast eyes. One hand still clutched the treasures hidden within her skirts. A peek from under her curtain of pale hair showed him standing near the hearth, dusky robes hanging loosely on his gaunt frame. His gnarled hands gripped his staff tightly, but his face was merely disappointed.

"I couldn't resist," she said. "It smelled so good."

"You are not starving, Daughter," he admonished. "And you know I don't like you bothering the guests."

The girl nearly rolled her eyes. She knew nothing would wake these men. She'd made a game of it when she was younger. They were beyond her capacity to bother.

"I don't think I'm bothering them," she said with unusual contrariness. "I'm just, you know, cleaning up a bit." She grabbed an overripe sun-fruit from the nearby table and bit into its juiciness with a loud slurp.

Father's brow clouded with annoyance and she cringed, expecting harsh words. But he only sighed. "Eat up, but be quick about it."

And with that, she was dismissed from his thoughts. As he shuffled between the tables, checking his new arrivals, she thought he seemed unusually tired. The wrongness in his body larger somehow.

"Remember not to drink the ale," he said for the thousandth time.

"I know." Irritation gave an edge to her voice that earned her a stern look. She humbly cast her eyes down avoiding his glare. She felt strangely peevish.

"And tomorrow night, the tower," he said.

"A full moon already?" she whined, fiddling with a plate on the table.

"None too soon if you ask me. Moonrise, girl. Don't be late."

A good daughter should have been glad to help him and usually she did feel a measure of pity. But tonight she felt unaccountably irritated. Whether she wanted to or not, she would be there tomorrow in the tower. She watched as he grabbed one of the men by the wrists and wrestled him with great effort through the door leading deeper into the Keep. She didn't offer to help since he had forbidden her to have any contact with his guests. It was bad enough she was standing in the same room with them.

When the door shut behind him, she turned back to the tables. Unrest marred her usual placid thoughts. Her skirt had enough food to last a while, but she didn't want to leave the warm hall just yet. The storm outside had abated, leaving a quiet so deep it had weight. It hung about her like a thick blanket. She didn't mind it. She had grown up with the stillness and, if truth be told, liked it. The storm's ferocity had its own allure, of course. That's how she knew the banquet would be here. It was always the same: storm, guests, food.

She thought it was her imagination at first when a whisper slithered through the stony silence. It was only a small, breathy sound, but it definitely didn't belong. She turned in surprise, scanning the area, but found nothing amiss. After a few minutes, she shrugged and turned to leave. Then she definitely heard a groan. It raised goose bumps on her arms. She followed the noise to a pillar near the corner. Behind it, two men slumped against each other, apparently unconscious like the others.

What are they doing over here? Nothing else seemed out of place. She studied them with abstract curiosity. The one was very different from her father's typical guest: larger than the others with striking red-gold hair. Thick and trimmed to shoulder length, it was the color of sunset on a clear evening. She thought it strange how, with such red hair, his beard was almost golden. Fascinated, she moved closer.

The second man's short black hair was not nearly as striking as the burnished mane that had caught her attention. But his bold, dark brows spoke of strength. It was a surprisingly pleasant face despite a faded tracing of scars and a nose had been broken at least once. A fresh wound crossed his right temple, scabbed over but still red.

What kind of man is this? She studied the face again as if looking for the answer there and found him more intriguing for the scars. Her fingers itched to trace the lines of violence and as she leaned closer, his breath mingled with hers. Her heart skipped with illicit tension. She'd never been this close to a guest before.

"Who are you?" Her cool whisper grazed his cheek and an answering warmth echoed back, brushing her face, tingling and ephemeral like magic. Not her Father's sharp sorcery, but a feeling that brought to mind sunshine and the greening tundra. An unearthly breeze lifted the hair off her neck sending a cold-heat down her spine. She felt a wrenching in her chest as if something had broken loose. Even the light in the room changed somehow, but she couldn't explain what was different. Her pulse went from skipping to pounding.

Then the red-haired man moaned, breaking the spell. She shot him a quick glance, but his eyes were still closed, his sleep merely restless. When she looked back at the dark-haired man, the uncanny feeling had passed. No warmth tingled between them. All was ordinary.

Even so, her curiosity grew. On impulse, she moved to touch the red-haired man's cheek. Just before her fingers landed on the coarse-looking beard, he murmured again and she jerked back in surprise, overbalancing and landing on her rump with a squeak. A few fuzzy sun-fruit rolled along the floor.

She hastily retrieved the fruit, watching him carefully. His eyes were still shut, but through barely parted lips she heard a single word: "Please."

Only Father had ever spoken to her. And though this guest wasn't actually talking to her, his unconscious request somehow stripped her of her usual invisibility. She was suddenly exposed, naked. His nearness was a palpable force as he continued to mumble. His brows knotted as if in pain. The words came faster, indecipherable and urgent.

As she gazed into his sturdy face, the strange feeling of change returned. She was moved by the man's distress.

It's none of your concern, the stern voice in her head reminded her. How often had Father told her that?

She pulled cool dispassion around her like a well-worn cloak though the feeling of having been touched remained.

A disapproving cluck startled her, and she scrambled backward with guilty fear.

"You know the rules," Father growled. "Do not disturb my guests." She looked up to see him peering down his hawkish nose with a fearsome scowl. "Now get back to your room." Angry, he nudged her none to gently out of the way with his foot and grabbed the red-haired man's wrists, dragging him away like the other.

When she was alone and the silence fell heavy around her again, she got shakily to her feet and brushed herself off. Her luscious loot once more secured in her skirts, she went to the door that led back to her tower. Standing in the doorway, she couldn't resist one more look back at the scarred man where he sat leaning against the pillar. A nameless longing curled up under her ribs where it stayed as she headed back to her room.

CHAPTER 4
ARCHER

Archer woke on the black-stoned floor of a windowless room. The only light came from torches in the hall beyond the barred door. He had no idea how long he'd been out, but he was starving. His breath fogged in the biting chill. Standing on sore legs, he grabbed the thin wool blanket from the cot pushed up against the back wall and pulled it around his shoulders, rubbing his arms briskly as he surveyed his prison. The door was sturdy, made of iron bars. At the bottom was a small slot where a plate with cold gruel had been pushed through. Next to it was a small bowl of frigid water.

"Dinner is served," he muttered, picking up the bowl and downing the water in three gulps. He took the plate and scooped the unsavory slop into his mouth as best he could. With a frown, Archer slid the bowl and plate back into the hall, hoping meal times were more than once a day.

He pressed his forehead against the bars, peering up and down the dim hallway. Other cell doors lined the corridor.

"Captain!"

His shout wasn't the booming echo Archer had expected. The sound fell flat, snuffed out like a flame. "Captain Khoury!" No answer. He rattled the door on its hinges but even those sounds were strangely muted.

Frustrated, he turned back to his cell. With nothing to do but wait, he stretched and walked, working out the stiffness and humming softly. He knew the captain would be working on an escape. If anyone could find a way out it would be him, and he'd never leave without Archer.

Archer had met Captain Khoury during, or rather at the end of, the Barakan War when the wounded left behind were taken to him as prisoners. They had been fools to fight under Barakan's flag, he and his older brother Connor. Archer had lost his last scrap of family that day, the same day the captain granted him freedom when any other Sword lord would have slain him outright. In the past seven years, he'd grown quite fond of the man who'd stepped unwittingly into the empty space left by Connor.

Once warm, Archer sat on the cot and amused himself with raucous tavern songs, his velvety baritone almost obscene in the brooding silence. Time ticked by with painful slowness. There was never movement in the hall, never any sound. And every so often, Archer would go to the door and call out without response. When he tired, he lay on the cot telling fireside tales of home to himself until he fell asleep. When he woke, there was gruel on the plate and water in the bowl. He ate and called out for the captain again. Still no answer.

Without windows, there was no way of knowing if it was day or night. So he counted each sleep as a day and after about a week by this reckoning, Archer's nerves were raw and taut. The quiet of the Keep permeated the cell like a thick, suffocating presence. A window, or even a small draft, would have made Archer feel less isolated. But there was nothing, nothing except cold black stones and silence. He longed for action, for something—anything—to happen. Time stretched out like the tundra, endless and empty. Briefly, Archer wondered if he was already dead, a ghost with no memory of his demise.

No sooner had he thought of ghosts than a pale figure flitted across the hall, just a smudge of brightness at the edge of his vision.

He froze, wondering if his mind was playing tricks. Turning his eyes toward the door without moving his head, he saw nothing. Quickly, he backed up to the wall out of sight of the door, and waited, ready to fight. Nothing happened. He listened carefully for footfalls, but there was only the interminable silence. Had Khoury found a way out or had the sorcerer come for him at last? Unable to contain his curiosity, he leaned to the door and peeked out.

A small woman stood beyond his door, staring straight at him, her hair a pure white curtain to her waist.

He blinked in surprise, and then said, "Hello there."

She stared at him in silence.

"Thought you were a ghost," he said.

"Sometimes I think so, too." Her voice was tiny.

He waited for her to say more, but she didn't. She radiated the same ancient stillness as the black stones and the weighty silence. But where they felt dark and heavy, she was light, her eyes such a startlingly pale blue they reminded him of ice on Manowa Lake in midwinter. A sapphire amulet hung from a silver chain at her throat, its precious glow out of place against her shabby clothes, which were scarcely more than rags. She took a step toward the door.

"Where are you from?" she asked.

"The Northlands west of here."

"Your hair is so red." Her hand rose up as if to touch it, but she pulled it back. "Are your people all like that?"

"Most of us have red hair."

"I've never seen its like."

"My name's Archer."

She said nothing.

"What do they call you?" he prompted.

She shuffled a little closer and lowered her voice. "Daughter."

"That's not a name."

"It's the only one I have," she said with a frown. Her eyes held him like the Keep did, suspended in limbo.

He shook himself. "So you live here?"

"Yes."

"With the old man?"

"He's my father."

Archer couldn't believe his ears. "Your father is Sidonius?"

"Yes, didn't I just say that?"

"And your mother?"

"Mother?" She rolled the word over her tongue like it was unfamiliar. "I don't remember a mother."

"Then how did you get here?"

"Father came from the Far Isles. They're across a sea. He said the men there were untrustworthy. Jealous. They didn't understand his work. So he came here." Her speech was so childlike he wondered how old she was.

"So you came with him?"

"I must have."

"You don't know?"

"I don't remember the islands he talks of, but I've seen pictures in the books in the library."

"So you read?"

"Oh, not the magical tomes. They're forbidden." She glanced up and down the hallway.

"You don't do magic?"

She smiled then, a bright momentary flash. "Don't be silly. You have to be strong to do magic."

She was making little sense, but she had to know what was going on. "Can you tell me why I'm here?"

"You're going to make Father young again."

Archer didn't like the sound of that. "Young? How?"

"The ritual," she said in hushed tones. "That's why you're all here."

Archer sucked in a breath. All the barred cells, all the men in the wagon, were they all going to die to keep this sorcerer young? It wasn't that startling a revelation given how casual the old man was about the men who burned to death. But the way she said it with those big wide eyes, innocent and yet without remorse, made it all the more foreboding. He raked a heavy hand through his hair, his nerves stretched to breaking. He needed to find Khoury and soon. "I came with a companion. Have you seen him?"

"We have many guests." She avoided his eyes.

"Dark hair, blue eyes and—"

"It's not allowed," she hissed sharply, checking the hallway again.

"I just want to know if he's okay."

"Assume what you like. It doesn't matter." The callousness of her reply sent a shock of anger through him.

"I won't assume he's dead."

"Then believe he is alive. It changes nothing." She had retreated behind a cold wall of indifference. Her smile's warm brightness was only a mirage after all.

"It changes everything." He grabbed the bars, shaking them and startling the girl, though her bland expression returned quickly.

"Time has forgotten this castle, Northerner. Life here is always the same. The guests come and they go."

"You mean he kills them."

"As you wish." She shrugged but refused to meet his gaze.

"And what about you?"

She swallowed hard as if tasting something unpleasant. "I go to the tower, too."

"But you survive."

Her brow furrowed. "I think it tries to kill me." She shook her head as if to shake loose bad memories. "But it's a daughter's duty to help her father, isn't it? Even if I did die. It's what a good daughter would do."

"That's your choice, though."

"What happens to us in life isn't choice. Our path lies not in our own planning but with fate."

Archer coughed a short laugh. "Maybe for you or me. But you

don't know the captain. Fate has yet to lay her hands on him."

The girl frowned. "No. Your fates have already been decided. You are here."

"Khoury has cheated death more times than I have fingers and toes. He will escape this place, too."

Her eyes got huge, and her white skin paled even further though he wouldn't have thought it possible. He could see her trembling. "No man escapes the Keep." Her words were vehement, but Archer sensed doubt and terror.

"If you truly believed that, then it wouldn't matter if you found him for me, now would it?"

"You don't understand. I cannot," she hissed, growing more agitated. "I'm not even supposed to be here."

"Maybe it was fate."

She backed away, fear in her eyes. "No."

"Fate that you met me."

"No. My fate is here with my father."

"Only time will tell." He knew he was being cruel, twisting her fear when she was little more than a girl, but he had to find the captain.

"Time has told me," she said. "Things don't change."

Desperate, he changed tactics. "Please, I need to know. His name is Mason Khoury. Dark hair, blue eyes, and a wound here." As Archer pointed to his temple, a look of recognition crossed her features.

She has seen him, he thought.

"The first sacrifice is tonight. I must go." She turned abruptly.

CHAPTER 5
CARA

"Daughter!" The call echoed down the stairway from the highest tower.

"I'm here!" she yelled, lifting her skirts to take the stairs two at a time. He was going to be furious that she'd forgotten to prepare the room. The candles and the scroll were still in the library.

"Where have you been?" Father asked brusquely as she slid to a halt in the doorway. She'd kept him waiting, and his mood was as black as his robes.

"I fell asleep. In the barn." She was amazed how easily the lie slipped past her lips. Blood pounded in her head as he peered closely at her, his face skeptical.

What am I thinking? He's going to know it's a lie.

"You spend too much time with those beasts. They're not pets." He glared and then waved her out. "No time now. Go get the scroll."

Relieved, she rushed back down the twisting stairs, retrieved the items from the library, and hurried back up to the tower room. She carefully set the scroll on the pedestal, holding the brittle, yellowed paper open with the crystals. Then, she lit the candles and the braziers.

The night's sacrifice had already been brought up. Despite her fear of discovery, curiosity drew her eyes to the man on the ground. He was unkempt and foul-smelling but had a shock of dark hair. In the dim light, she couldn't decipher the color of his eyes as they darted around the room. There was a scrape on his cheek, and she tried to remember exactly what the other man behind the pillar had looked like.

"Take his feet." Father's curt request interrupted her thoughts.

She hesitated, surprised by the request. "But you said…"

"Hurry, girl. The spell is wearing off because *you* were late. Unless of course you prefer to take his place."

She shook her head and reached down to grab the man's legs. Together, she and Father lifted him awkwardly to the altar, bumping him roughly against the stone. Then her fingers touched his bare skin where it peeked through his torn clothes. In that moment, her mind was awash in heart-pounding fear. Blinding in its intensity, the trembling terror weakened her arms. She leaned against the altar, her throat clenched with sudden tears, and shoved the man's legs away.

The fear dissipated somewhat, though an echo of it pulsed around her like a wave of cold air. Shaken, she stared at the man seeing him for the first time as something other than Father's tool.

The weight of Father's scrutiny prickled along her neck, and she looked up to find him studying her. Guilty, she tried to hide her discomfort. She couldn't trust her voice but managed to school her features into vapid serenity. Pinching her nose, she made a disgusted face as if she found the man's odor offensive. Her father scowled at her childishness but went back to his preparations.

Her chest felt strangely tight as Father affixed the manacles to the man's ankles and wrists. The spell was beginning to wear off, and the man wheezed in panicked gasps. As soon as he could control his arms, he struggled, leaving fresh blood on the metal binders.

"You can't do this!" he shouted when he found his voice.

Her nerves hummed with fear. No one yelled at Father.

"Who's going to stop me?" her father asked. "You? You're nothing but scum." He turned his back and went to the pedestal. She felt off-balance, and Father was irritable tonight. The wrongness in him pulsed with hunger.

The sudden need to be sure this wasn't the Northerner's friend goaded her to step forward while Father wasn't looking. She pretended to check the manacles and whispered, "Mason Khoury?"

The man's confused look told her that he wasn't who she sought, and her sigh of relief surprised her. Ducking her head, she retreated and headed for the door.

"Wait!" the man called after her, his eyes imploring. "My name is Carter, Reith Carter. Don't leave. You must help me!"

She averted her eyes but felt worse for knowing his name.

"Please!" he screamed. "Please, help me."

His pleading pulled her gaze to his and when their eyes met, a fresh wave of fear washed over her. He knew he faced his death, and it terrified him. She pitied him, remembering how frightened she'd been as a young girl, knowing what was coming.

Then, Father impatiently motioned for her to leave and she gratefully crossed the threshold, closing the door behind her. She could still hear Reith Carter's pleading shouts as she leaned against the door, squeezing her eyes shut against the unfamiliar tears that threatened.

What's happening to me?

She angrily wiped at her damp cheeks. Perhaps, it was just the unsettling wave of emotion that had caught her off guard and put this sickening weight in her stomach. She'd never given any thought to the men who spent the brief end of their lives in the Keep before. She understood Father's rules now. That brief meeting of skin to skin, eye to eye, had shattered the glass cocoon she lived in. It had been easier to ignore the dust on the altar when she didn't know they felt the same fear she did.

If she was upset now, it was her own fault. First, she disobeyed Father by finding the red-haired man and now she was feeling sorry for the others.

I shouldn't feel bad, *she reasoned.* I can't change his fate any more than my own.

But the words of the Northerner haunted her. What if his companion really wasn't ruled by fate? What if things actually could change? The world suddenly felt larger, her future unmoored from the certainties her life had rested on.

Behind her, she heard Father begin the ritual. Not wanting to be caught up in the spell, she fled down the stairs.

She didn't return to her room. A strange urgency had taken root in her. She had to find the red-haired man's friend now—before it was too late. Forcing her newfound guilt from her mind, she scurried back to the corridor of cells. This was her best chance to find the man who defied fate if she was going to.

She slipped down the hall, peeking into each cell. Some prisoners lay despondent on the floor, some chattered dementedly. Some had gray hair, some brown, but none of them fit the description. Then, she noted constant movement ahead, a complicated repeating pattern. Behind the next set of bars, a lean, muscular man battled with thin air. He lunged and stabbed with a piece of wood, kind of a makeshift sword. His movements flowed in a steady mesmerizing cadence, like a dance. His black hair was damp with sweat and clung to his neck and cheeks. It took her a few moments to realize he was the one she sought; the scarred man from the great hall.

She had forgotten the tracing of scars on his face until now, but again such roughness only enhanced his features. The last time she saw him he had been unconscious, now he was full of a power undimmed by his time here. Her father may have caged him, but he was far from caught.

The man was so intent on his invisible adversary he hadn't noticed her yet, and she was drawn in by the intricacy of his practice. She laid a small hand on the bars as an echo of the warmth she had felt the other night kissed her cheeks, making her feel flushed. He was dangerous. He was fascinating. He was a man strong enough to evade fate.

Then his eyes fell upon her during a turn, and he closed the distance between them in two sharp strides. His calloused hand trapped hers against the iron bars. In that instant, her world tilted as a flood of emotions washed over her, like they had in the tower room. Only this time, it wasn't fear but fury. Visions not her own tumbled through her mind: Battlefields drenched in blood and screams. Rage and pain and determination mixed with the jarring clang of swords.

She yanked her hand away as if his touch burned. And as she looked up into his face, she noted a fleeting moment of shock before his expression closed.

He felt it too, she thought, rubbing her hand where they had touched as if to scrub away the unsettling feelings. He glowered at her from beneath those dark brows, and she noted that the cut along his temple bore a dwindling scab, the bruise and swelling already faded. Her eyes met his and echoes of emotion shuddered through her again.

"Who are you?" It was a command, not a question.

"Are you Mason Khoury?"

Surprise showed on his face. "How did you know…?" Then realization hit. "Archer sent you." A hint of smile brightened his eyes.

"Yes."

"So he's alive."

She looked away.

"Ah, not for long I take it."

She bit her lip to stop its trembling as guilt nipped at her conscience.

"Well, well. We're both to die then," he said almost jovially, apparently reading her mind. She didn't expect him to be so at ease with the news, especially after Reith Carter's frantic pleading. When she finally dared look at him, his face was quiet.

"Yes," she admitted.

"So, where is he?" The question was casual, almost flippant. The scarred man backed further into the cell, looking down at the makeshift sword and his hands.

"He's down the other hall." She edged closer, curious now that his focus was elsewhere. The masculine planes of his face were hidden beneath a beard that was dark except for the few lines of pale scar that crossed it.

"So you've escaped your cell," he said.

"No."

"Servant, then?"

"What?"

"Concubine."

"No. This is my home." An unfamiliar indignation flared, buoyed by the wash of fury she'd felt when they touched.

"You expect me to believe that?" His eyes flicked over her tattered robes with disdain.

She pressed her lips together to forestall an angry retort.

"You look far more like a slave than a member of the household," he said.

Her composure broke. "I'm not a slave! If you must know, I am the sorcerer's daughter and these clothes are perfectly serviceable."

"Sorcerer? Really? That tired old man?" Khoury sat on the cot and wiped the sweat from his brow with the blanket.

"He may be old, but he's very powerful." She wasn't sure why she felt the need to defend Father, but something about this man's arrogance irritated her.

"Of course he is. That's why he's hiding here."

"He's not hiding."

The man lifted his eyebrow skeptically as he tossed the blanket to the cot.

"He just chooses to live away from prying eyes," she finished.

"I doubt anyone's watching."

"Oh, but they are. They want to steal his secrets."

"Secrets?"

"Magic power they've never even dreamed of. Some of his scrolls are from as far away as the Eastern Lands." Her face was almost to the bars. Without realizing it, she had pressed closer during the argument.

"Eastern magic? What does that do?" His voice dripped derision.

She opened her mouth to explain, and then snapped it shut. How had he prodded her into talking about Father's magic?

Ignoring her silence, Khoury shifted to his back on the cot, crossed his ankles and pillowed his head in his hands. "I suppose you want me to believe you're a sorceress now."

"I didn't say that."

"Then what is it that you do here?"

The question struck a nerve. "I…feed him."

That turned the man's head. "Feed him?"

She nodded.

"Ah, you're his cook."

"No, not like that." She put her hands on the bars, leaning her forehead against the cold metal. She felt drained.

"Then how?" His voice was soft in the dark cell. She suddenly wanted to tell him everything. She wanted to tell her story to someone, what little there was of it. But how could she? If she did, he'd hate her. She was even beginning to hate herself.

"How do you feed him?" he asked, even softer.

She was embarrassed how the words came out of their own accord. "He has a special scroll, very rare. With it, he uses me to recharge his magic."

"How?" Though the man hadn't moved, the girl could sense his attention sharpening. She kept her eyes closed so she didn't have to see his face.

"He takes my energy. My soul maybe. I don't know exactly."

"And that's what we're all here for?"

She nodded, not wanting to elaborate.

Just when the silence had settled back around her like a comforting blanket, he asked, "What's it like?" His voice was barely a whisper.

"Don't worry, Mason Khoury. You'll only see it once."

The futility of second-guessing fate walled her off from hope as even he paused in silence. Then, his anger washed through her like a hot wind and with a growl he said, "Tell him to bring plenty of help when he comes to get me."

"He won't need help. A simple spell, and you'll be useless." *Like me*, she thought.

The captain had no comment.

"I'm going to Archer now. I promised to tell him if you were well."

At that, the warrior laughed out loud, the sudden noise startling. "I'm being held captive and slated for death. You have a strange definition of being well."

"I…" She flinched under his sarcasm, feeling foolish.

He lifted his head, leaned on one elbow, and watched her. He seemed amused by her unease. Waving her away, he said, "Go on, girl. Tell him I'm still alive. At least it will ease his fears. And once you've told him of me, you will come back." His soft words were neither an entreaty nor an order. But he seemed certain of her future, the way Father always was. She shivered at the similarity.

She turned away from his cell and padded up the hall. In truth, it would be better never to see either man again, but she knew it was too late for that. Already things were different. She was different.

The Northerner was lying on the cot, apparently asleep.

"Archer," she whispered through the iron bars.

"So soon. Is he dead already?" His voice was flat, not like before.

"No," she said. *Not yet.*

"He's alive?" Archer jumped to his feet and came to the door.

"I just said that, didn't I?" It was nice to bring happy news, though she knew bad news was on its way.

"Did he say anything?"

"Only that he's…" She paused mid-sentence remembering the captain's cutting remarks. "Actually no, he didn't say anything. But he was glad to hear of you."

Archer smiled, and she saw relief in the set of his shoulders. "Thank you."

She bobbed her head but said nothing. She wasn't sure what would happen next, but the constant wash of emotions was beginning to wear on her. She longed to go back to her rooms and bathe in the quiet.

"By the way, I've a gift for you." He smiled like a man with a secret.

"A gift?" What could he have?

"A name."

"I told you, I have—"

"I know. But this is a real name."

"A real name?"

"Like in a book. Sort of a reward for finding the captain."

Who could have guessed that a name, of all things, would be much of a reward? After all, there would be no one to call her by it when Archer was gone. But when he offered it, an eager excitement burned within her. She raised a questioning brow.

"Cara," he said with an official tone to his voice.

"Cara," she repeated, trying it on like a new cloak.

"In the Northern tongue, it means 'friend.'"

Friend, she thought with a shy smile. *I've never had a human friend before.* "It's lovely, Archer. I'm flattered."

"And … are you?"

"Flattered? Yes, I said that."

"No. Are you my friend?"

"Of course." The words fell easily from her lips before she realized what he would ask next.

"But you'll let me die." His words dropped into the Keep's silence, carrying the weight of a responsibility she wasn't ready for. Understanding dawned with dreadful clarity. This gift wasn't free. She needed to earn it.

Couldn't they see she was helpless, caught in a trap that, in its own way, was as strong as their iron bars?

"I see your point, warrior. But I could no more stop Father from taking your life than a snowflake could stop the winter wind. It only rides the wind." She danced her fingers through the air, imitating gentle snowfall. "It cannot fly where it wills. It simply falls and is done."

When she looked up at him, his face was stunned and sad. But the pity in his tawny eyes wasn't for himself.

"You don't have to be a snowflake," he said. "You could choose."

"No. I can't." Tears gathered on her lashes.

"Then you choose to let your father take my life and the captain's."

She squeezed her eyes shut, not wanting to think about the inevitable. "You don't understand. We're all snowflakes: You, me, your captain. All slaves to circumstance. Even Father thinks he chooses, but he doesn't. He does what he must. As do we all." The words she had always believed sounded cowardly. These were men of action, men who defied fate. She turned away, ashamed.

Archer chuckled. "You don't know the captain."

"If your captain can bargain with fate, then I hope he wins you your lives. But I cannot help you." Without another word, she left to return to the sanctuary of her room.

☙

But Cara's quiet world had been shattered, broken perhaps beyond repair. Trapped in useless circles, her mind refused to let her sleep and so she wandered in the deep, silent night. Her steps took her to the library where she thought she could lose herself in a book. She started a small fire in the hearth and settled into a large chair inside the circle of its glow. But the flame's cheery warmth didn't chase away the chill inside her heart. Where was her detached calm?

She'd never been lonely before, but she knew she'd miss Archer's voice when Father finally took him. She imagined him, chained and struggling for his life. Morbid pictures of his captain tormented her, too. As fierce and full of life as he was, even he would turn to dust and coat her ragged skirts the next time she lay there. The visions were so real, so vivid, they brought a stabbing ache to her chest. She pressed her hands into fists and squeezed her eyes shut willing her mind clear.

When she opened her eyes, Father stood before her. Reith Carter's death had restored the old man's power. His face was fleshed out, his hands smooth, his height restored. And there was a dangerous gleam in his eye.

"What mischief have you done, girl?"

She shrank back in the chair, the book sliding from her lap as he leaned down with a cruel smile. She didn't need her gift to tell her Father was not himself. Sometimes the ritual did this. He would become another man for a time, often a violent one. And at such times, she feared him with good reason.

"What have I done?" she protested, stalling for time as her heart pounded like the wings of a bird against the cage of her ribs.

"Do you deny consorting with prisoners?"

She knew the question was a trap. Neither a confession nor a simple lie would placate him, and she froze.

"Well? Answer me."

"I don't know what you're talking about."

"You can do better than that. C'mon, lie to me," he hissed. With a flick of his finger a whip of flame lashed her arm, raising a blistered welt and making her cry out in shock.

"In the dining room, I heard a voice," she whispered, hoping to placate him with truth. "I was curious. You saw me. But I left when you told me to." Tears dripped from her lashes. His nearness was suffocating.

"That wasn't hard," he said, drawing back. "Was it?"

She shook her head slightly, not trusting his sudden ease.

"It was the red-haired one, wasn't it?" he said as if refreshing his memory, though she doubted he needed to. "A strong man, indeed. I'll enjoy killing him." Her father gripped the arms of the chair, trapping Cara in her seat. "But I think you've neglected a part of the story." Little angry curls of smoke rose from the fabric beneath his hands to dance between them.

"There's nothing more to tell," she said weakly.

He slapped her cheek and gripped her chin with hot fingers, forcing her to meet his glare. His breath was foul.

"No?" he asked. "Then who is Mason Khoury?"

"Mason Khoury?" She feigned ignorance, her mind scrambling for a way out.

"Yes. The last thing in that little thief's mind was you saying that name."

Cara couldn't breathe. This was impossible. "But how?"

"The ritual. You didn't suspect?"

She shook her head, speechless with shock.

"There are no secrets in my Keep. Whether you tell me now or during the ritual, eventually I will find this Mason Khoury." His finger traced the track of a wayward tear down her cheek, and his hand came to rest threateningly on her throat. "You know Carter was not a very nice man. He killed his wife, among others."

Was that who her father was now? Reith Carter, wife murderer. She wondered about all the men he had feasted on. How many had been like Archer and how many like Reith? Cara thought of Khoury's strength and forced a calm she didn't feel as she looked Father right in the eye. "I honestly don't remember saying anything to him."

He stared in surprise. Then his face contorted with rage. "How dare you."

Cara tried not to flinch.

"Have it your way. In two days, I will drain this Northerner while you watch. And believe me, I will make him suffer. Then, it will be your turn and I will discover the truth."

He stood up and went to the door but paused to turn and look at her. "Do not become attached to creatures whose only purpose is to serve me, girl. You'll end up regretting it." Father murmured a few words, waved his hand and the fire in the hearth went out. With a swish of ebony robes and the hard slam of the door, he disappeared.

Cara shivered with shock and sudden cold, despair drifting like snow around her heart. As her tears washed over her stinging chin, she pressed a cool hand to the welt on her arm. Cara had never questioned the nature of Father's dealings with other men. Why should she? But then, she'd never seen friendship or loyalty before either. Hadn't she tried to warn Archer that she couldn't help him? A snowflake cannot fight the heat of such cruelty.

But she couldn't let her new friend die. Trapped between her father and the men below, she wracked her mind for an answer.

And then, something stirred deep inside her. Something new. She found the barest hint of willfulness. In the bleak darkness, Cara came to a daring decision she never dreamed she could make.

CHAPTER 6
CARA

Cara sat on the bench beneath her window, leaning her elbows on the cold stone sill, and stared out across the Keep. The other towers were silhouetted in the slanting evening light, and the slate roofs of the lower halls glowed gray against the darkened swath of barren bailey. She shivered, feeling tattered and restless.

After making her decision last night, she hadn't slept well. She'd risen earlier than the sun and ensured the bears were well-fed. The great beasts were the only thing in the Keep she refused to part with. She had lingered in the barn as the sun rose, allowing their scent to calm her. Her fingers swam in the soft thickness of their coats as their hoarse chuffing assured her she was not alone.

Then she scoured the castle for extra blankets and clothes, stowing what little she found into two burlap sacks. A third sack contained hard cheese and bread, much less than she'd hoped for. Now, at the close of the day, the bears slept in harness; the two sledges were ready and waiting. It stunned her to think that only yesterday she had searched for the Northern warrior. So much had happened it felt as if it were a dream. A vision of her emerald forest floated unbidden to her mind.

"Maybe there really is such a place," she whispered into the night.

She had avoided the prisoners all day, not wanting to disturb the delicate balance of strength and fear that kept her moving. She was perched on the edge of a precipice. This one act would ruin forever the life she knew. There would be no going back. She couldn't imagine what waited beyond the walls that defined her world. The enormity of it was daunting.

Just get the keys, she told herself. *Don't think about anything else.*

She rested her head on her arms and waited for the light in Sidonius's tower to go out. The minutes ticked by, and her eyes grew heavy with sleep.

When she woke, a glance out the window showed no lights in the far tower or the rest of the Keep. All was darkness.

"It's time." The sound of her own voice was strangely comforting. It covered the pounding of her heart. Her plan raced through her mind and, for a moment, overwhelmed her. Her eyes fell on her cot. Indecision stalled her. She could go to bed like every night, and let life continue as before. It would be easy; all she had to do was nothing.

But if she did nothing, Archer would go to the tower. Archer would fight the chains, leaving his blood and dust for her. And that was something she couldn't bear.

No more death, she promised herself.

She stretched to relieve the ache in her back and padded through the dark halls to the library. The keys to the cells were there in Father's desk. She listened at the door—nothing. Turning the knob, she pulled it open.

The library walls were covered with shelves, both tall and short. They overflowed with books and scrolls and manuscripts. Stacks of paper covered every flat surface including the few chairs in the room. Two tall windows flanked the dark, empty fireplace. She didn't need more than the light of the moon to find Father's large wooden desk. She leaned over to open the lowest drawer on the left. It stuck a bit and then gave suddenly with a loud creak, its contents rattling in the stillness. She froze, waiting for the alarm. None came. She swallowed hard and forced herself to start breathing again.

He's not coming. Take them.

Such a simple task, yet it took all her might. She reached a trembling hand into the drawer and felt around, brushing the objects with timid fingers. Finally, she recognized the feel of keys. Gripping the cold metal ring, she lifted it slowly out of the drawer. The keys fell into line one soft clink at a time. Then she wrapped the keys in the folds of her skirt to muffle any further sounds as she stood and, leaving the drawer open, fled the room.

She ran to the lower levels, arriving breathless at Archer's door. The torches in the hallway still burned, and she could see his large form on the slender pallet.

"Archer," she whispered. "Wake up." The bulky man stirred but didn't wake. She unwrapped the ring. It held at least thirty keys all of which looked the same to her. Haste began to shiver in her limbs. She tried one key and then the next, looking for the right one. "Archer," she hissed louder. Her back tingled with dread and panic nipped at her heels. "Get up. We have to get out of here!"

The first three keys refused to even enter the lock, and she thought she would cry. Frustration made her clumsy and the ring clattered to the stone floor, shattering the silence. Archer sprang from his cot, weight balanced on his toes. When he saw her through the bars, he relaxed. His lips stretched into an easy smile. "Oh, it's just you, Snowflake."

Snowflake, she thought with irritation. *What happened to Cara?*

"Yes, just me," she snapped, retrieving the key ring and trying another in the lock. She was flustered and hurried, imagining her father standing behind her, arms crossed and that furious scowl on his face.

"What're you doing?" Archer came to the door watching her hands fumbling in the dim light.

"I've been found out." Her voice squeaked with panic. "Father knows. He's going to kill you at moonrise. I'm sorry. I'm so sorry. I should never have talked to you."

The Northerner was stunned into silence. "What about Khoury?"

She shook her head astonished that, even now, he asked about his captain first. "I don't think Father knows about him yet. But he will when I go to the tower after you. I'll survive the ritual." The key in her hand turned in the lock. "But you won't."

She yanked open the door and stared up at Archer's puzzled face. His large hand reached for her chin, but he didn't touch her. He drew his hand back as narrowed eyes traced the burns on her skin. "Why?" he whispered.

"I don't know," she admitted. "The ritual has never harmed me, yet everyone else has perished." She shut her eyes, ashamed that she never once thought about the lives that ended in dust.

"No. I meant why are you risking yourself now?"

She opened her eyes to see the warm glow of gratitude in his. "I am a snowflake. I can't fight Father. Then I thought maybe a simple thing. Like opening a door...." She let the words dangle between them.

Archer laid a steadying hand on her shoulder. "Only a very brave woman would have stolen the keys and opened the door."

Cara knew it wasn't enough, not for the countless lives that had been lost. She could never make it right. "But you must promise me. Promise you'll save the others, too." She pushed the ring of keys into his hand as the urgency that had kept her going drained away. She couldn't ask him to take her too, although she didn't want to spend another night in the Keep.

His tawny eyes glanced at her chin again, and he frowned. "What will happen to you?"

"Father can't afford to kill me."

"I won't leave you here to face him. You're coming with us."

His unexpected concern left her humble and speechless.

"Let's get Khoury," he said.

She nodded, relieved that he had offered to take her. But what if his captain disagreed?

CHAPTER 7
KHOURY

Khoury lay on his cot in the smothering silence trying to figure out how long it had been since they'd been captured. A week, perhaps. Maybe two. Time was impossible to measure. The torches always burned. There were no guards to change shifts. Gruel and water appeared whenever he slept and, though Khoury often pretended to sleep, he could never catch sight of whoever delivered it. His isolation was absolute.

Except for the girl.

He shifted on the hard cot to ease the ache in his stiff joints. He'd assumed from the start the sorcerer intended to kill them, so she'd only confirmed his suspicions. And though Sidonius's paranoia made him a canny opponent, what worried the captain most was how quickly the kidnapper had fallen at the tollhouse. Would Khoury even know he was next before he died?

He shook his head, refusing to consider it. He had to believe there would be some moment of inattention, some whiff of luck he'd be able to take advantage of, which brought him back to the girl.

She claimed to be the sorcerer's daughter, but he doubted it. More likely, she was a tool like the captured men. He would have dismissed her as an ally except for the spark of magic that had flashed between them. She had, of course, denied it. But he knew the truth the moment he felt it. And somehow, that sharp jolt had jarred loose memories he thought he'd buried for good. They surfaced now in the dark, rising with surprising power and haunting him in the fecund silence.

The sound of footsteps sent Khoury to his feet. He pressed against the wall near the door and waited.

"Captain." A familiar whisper brought a smile to his face.

"Archer!" He went to the barred door, relieved to see his grinning lieutenant. "How did you…?"

The small gray mouse of a girl stepped out from behind Archer.

"Ah, you bribed the help," Khoury said, briefly noting the irritated frown that creased her forehead.

"I beat you to it this time, old man," Archer said.

"You did indeed." Khoury chuckled as he executed an elaborate bow. He'd be hearing about this turnabout for a long time, but he'd rather be humbled than dead. "Now, let's get out of here."

Archer tried a few keys before the right one opened the door. Once the captain was in the corridor, Archer introduced the girl. "Captain, this is Cara. You two met yesterday."

She stared at the captain with wary eyes, pale as twin moons, but she said nothing.

"Well met," he said, hoping his genteel tone was enough to soothe her ruffled feathers. They needed her cooperation. She seemed younger and there was no hint of power now. "Which way?"

Archer looked down at the girl. "Cara? What's next?"

The escape was the girl's idea. Interesting.

"You promised to free the others." Her hushed whisper was thready with taut nerves.

"And we will," Archer reassured her.

As Khoury's mind flipped through what he remembered of the Keep, his stomach growled loudly. "Is there food? Warmer clothes?"

She shrank from the weight of his attention. "I…I put what I thought could be of use on the sledges, but there wasn't much to be had."

Her eyes kept sliding to Archer for reassurance. Khoury wondered how he'd gained her confidence so quickly.

"Sledges, huh?" Khoury wasn't sure that was wise, but he decided this wasn't the time to argue. "Let's get the others out. I presume we don't have much time." He took the keys from Archer and strode to the next cell without waiting for an answer.

When the lock on the door released, Khoury beckoned to the haggard man inside. He had grizzled hair and a scruffy beard as dingy as his clothes. "C'mon, we're getting out of here," he said. The man didn't need to be asked twice. Khoury moved to the next door, and the next. Soon, the clamor from the crowd of men grew to worrisome levels.

"Quiet," the captain snapped at them. Ten pairs of eyes, varying from surly to sheepish turned on him. "We're not out of this yet," he said, his voice low and taut. "Wait at the end of the hall, and keep it down if you value your lives." They shuffled to the end of the hall where it joined another hall of cells. Their murmurs continued though more subdued, at least for now.

He turned his attention to the remaining cells. *Truly an unsavory lot.* Sidonius wasn't very picky about his prey. Or perhaps, the disappearance of men like this wasn't as noticeable.

When the last cell had been opened, Khoury joined the men who waited under Archer's watchful presence. The girl stood behind the Northerner, keeping as far as possible from the men she herself requested they save.

Khoury raised his hands for quiet and met their expectant looks with carefully cultivated nonchalance. "We have a common enemy, and if you want to survive we need to work together. Agreed?"

"Agreed," Archer said. "We defend each other to the end." He eyed the others expectantly.

"But what about the sorcerer?" asked an older man with a patched eye and a paunch. "I don't want to burn." Murmurs of fearful dissent rumbled through the crowd.

Khoury laid a hand on the man's shoulder. "If we're quiet and smart, he won't even notice until we're long gone. Don't waste this opportunity."

The men looked at each other nervously. None of them were fighters, but they were out of options. One by one, they grumbled a grudging consent.

Khoury turned to the girl. "Lead us to the great hall."

She hesitated. Her mouth hung open as if to speak, then she turned without a word and headed down the hall to the right and up a flight of stairs. They turned left into yet another barren hallway. The dark stones were muted and infrequent torches sputtered their pale light. Archer and Khoury flanked Cara with the others trailing behind in a ragtag group. As they passed a stairway to the right, Khoury pointed up it. "Where does this go?"

"My tower." Her voice was brusque.

Stairs rose on their left. "And this?"

"The library."

"Does the wizard keep weapons?"

"He doesn't need any."

"What about once we're outside? Any guard buildings? Towns?"

"From the parapet, there's nothing for miles."

"The parapet?"

Without breaking stride, she shot him a look of cool disdain. "I've never left these walls." He kept his disbelief to himself as she continued, "The Black Mountains east and north are impassable. South and west is tundra as far as you can see."

Damn, he thought. *We're going to be easy to spot.*

"You said something about sledges," Archer said.

"We have two." Her tone warmed for the Northerner, her lips curving slightly up. "Three bears apiece. I readied them both."

"Could be risky," Khoury said to Archer over her head.

"I can handle them, Captain," Archer replied. "We'll lead one if need be. They'll certainly be faster than walking."

"I can drive, too," Cara murmured.

Khoury ignored her. "All right, Archer. I leave it to you."

"Aye, Captain."

They passed a wall of windows opening onto what might once have been a manicured inner courtyard. Now desiccated and abandoned, skeletal hedge bushes poked up from the cracked dusty ground like the contracted claws of a dying thing. The black stones of a fountain lay in tumbled disarray along uneven flagstones. No hint of green graced the dead yard. The entire stronghold was a tomb.

"How many guards in the bailey?" Khoury asked.

"None."

Impossible, the captain thought. The Keep had been deserted the night they arrived, but he'd assumed it was because of the storm. *How could Sidonius maintain control with no guards and so many prisoners?*

"Not a single guard?" His disbelief drew a frown from her thin lips.

"He doesn't like people much," she replied.

"So it would appear." To maintain a stronghold this size without any guard was an impressive feat. He'd be glad to see the last of this strange Keep and its formidable master.

The girl sped up, forestalling any further conversation until they arrived at a set of sturdy double doors. "Through here is the hall you ate in," she said, "but there's no food left."

Khoury watched her listen at the doors, then push one open and peek into the room. Apparently satisfied, she entered, waving them in behind. Khoury recognized the hall, but unlike the day they arrived, the hearths were cold and the room dimly lit. Dust had already gathered on the empty tables.

"You don't use this room?" Archer asked.

"It's only for guests."

"Guests?" Khoury said, "That's one way to put it."

She frowned again but didn't reply as she headed up three low steps to the front doors.

"They're probably locked," Khoury pointed out as he surveyed the empty hall.

"Worth checking," the girl muttered. She put pale hands against one of the heavy doors and leaned into it. Grunting with effort, she eventually pushed it open. A predawn glow, cold air, and a few tiny flakes of snow scurried in.

Khoury wanted a plan before the men scattered outside. He sternly called them to gather around one of the tables with a forced whisper, and then to the girl he said, "Cara, come draw me a map."

As she turned and let the door shut behind her, he thought he saw a blue light on her face, but by the time she joined the circle of men at the long, polished table, it had disappeared. Khoury fired off a stream of questions about the walls, gate mechanisms, barns, and roads.

The girl sighed with irritation as she traced lines on the gray, dusty surface. "I don't know anything about how the main gate works. Here is the outer wall, and this area, the outer courtyard, wraps around toward the mountains and the barn is here. I should get the bears by myself. They can be—"

Khoury didn't hear the rest as his attention was drawn to the handful of men who were heading toward the doors, talking in excited tones. "Wait!" he called after them as loudly as he dared. The lead man waved him off and went to push open the door.

The explosion shook the Keep to its foundations. A flash of fire burst inward, blowing the men nearest the door clean off their feet and throwing Khoury and Archer against the table. Cara was knocked to her knees.

The captain straightened, muscles taut and ears ringing. Anger roared through his head, bringing the room into sharp focus. His nose itched with the sharp tang of soot and spark. Ghostly curls of black smoke rolled languidly upward in the dim torchlight. The doors were intact though scorch marks darkened the wood and radiated out like a charred flower on the floor. The men who had tried to open it were scattered in bloody pieces across the hall.

Three dead. So, the tally begins. How many will return to their homes?

Realizing it had been magic, anger blossomed into rage. The same righteous fury that had sent him plunging recklessly into Ranceforth's army. The door wasn't locked; it had been warded.

He scanned the room for the bent old man but saw only prisoners. Prisoners and the girl on the ground rocking back and forth, moaning in denial. How had the men triggered it when the girl hadn't? Was there a secret only she knew?

He grabbed her arm roughly and hauled her to her feet. "What did you do?" His voice came out a roar, driven by the coiled fury within his chest.

Her face had a green tinge and her lip trembled as she shook her head. "N-nothing."

Her denial sounded muffled to his blasted ears. "Tell me how you opened it." He grabbed her other arm and gave her a shake.

Her arms were fragile in his iron grip, and he pictured snapping her like a twig. With a growl, he thrust her away. Guilt soured in his mouth as he watched her back away in fear, tripping over a disembodied arm. She fell to her knees again, retching as crimson gore darkened her gray skirt.

He paced in agitation, trying to find the calm within his anger. It was then he heard a sound like a muted drum. He turned to the white-haired woman. "That noise."

Cara's eyes wandered sideways as she listened. When she heard it, her eyes locked with his as she jumped to her feet. "The alarm!"

Khoury's hands fisted as he struggled to keep control. "What have you done?" His voice was low and dangerous.

Archer quickly stepped between them. "So much for stealth," he said in a cool voice, his steady eyes watching the captain. Could his lieutenant read the battle rage that screamed in Khoury's head?

"He knows," Cara wailed, clutching at Archer's arm in panic. "He knows. Please, get out. Now!"

Her fear infected the other men, and the hair on the captain's neck stood up. They were trapped: The sorcerer behind them, the magic doors ahead.

"The doors are warded," he reminded her in a tight voice.

"No." She turned from them and stumbled frantically up the steps. "No, they were fine a moment ago. We have to get out." He followed her staggering path to the door. Her whole body shook as she lifted a hand to the blackened wood. The nearest group of men backed away, frightened and uncertain.

"What are you doing?" Khoury was torn between stopping her and getting a safe distance from the door. When she glanced over her shoulder, the sorrow in her eyes was a bottomless pool that held him frozen where he stood. She leaned into the door but before her weight hit it, he snagged her hands and held her back. Her skin was cold, and a sharp sensation shot through his arms to his still-ringing head, bringing with it an ancient memory so vivid he thought he'd stepped back in time. He remembered flames in the thatch; smoke in his eyes and nose. His brother's blackened eye and battered cheek accused Khoury even as his last words were meant to save him: *Run, brother,* he'd said.

Khoury snatched his hands back as if burned, shaking his head to clear the troubling scene from his mind. The taste of old sorrow tamed his anger. And in that moment, Cara threw her weight against the charred wood. Instinctively he covered his face with his arms, not that it would have saved him. But no blast came. She stepped halfway through the open door.

"I don't understand," she said, her voice shaky.

Khoury was just as confused. Something wasn't right. Then he noticed it.

"It's safe, Captain?" Archer asked. The men gathered close around them.

Khoury pointed to the glow of the blue stone at her throat. "No. She's protected."

"Protected?" Archer asked.

The men murmured angrily, and Khoury could sense their rising panic.

The girl looked down, but the thick chain was so short she couldn't see the stone.

"It's glowing," Archer said.

She stared at him in shock. "Glowing? Then, it *is* my fault." Her features crumpled as she backed into the room, letting the door shut with a heavy thud. "I…I killed those men." She sank to her knees and stared at her soot-smudged hands.

Now that his rage had left, Khoury felt her remorse in the pit of his stomach. He pitied her. She was little more than a child, as much a victim as the men. But they were out of time. The drums' continued beat sent a frisson of tension up his back. He knelt down by her, hoping his anger hadn't ruined their chances. "Cara," his voice was urgent, "you can still save them."

CHAPTER 8
CARA

Cara heard them talking, but the words were lost beneath the thudding of her heart and the beat of Father's alarms. Her belly churned painfully. She wanted to disappear or to wake from this nightmare. Or better to fall into a deep insensate sleep and never waken. Anything to erase that horrible moment of flash and gore.

"Cara!" The captain's sharp bark cut through her fogged senses. A shock of fear shivered through her at his tone. When she looked up, his cobalt eyes were almost kind, kneeling in the blood and soot as if, a moment ago, it hadn't been … someone.

Her mind staggered drunkenly. "What?"

"You can save these men," he said.

Save them?

No. Not this snowflake. She couldn't save anyone.

Then she noticed the fearful faces all around her, waiting and watching. And her heart quailed.

Archer crouched next to her. "Just hold the door open," he said, "and maybe we can walk past."

She couldn't decipher the look he shared with the captain. Nor did she want to. She couldn't think about the door or the men she had meant to save. Her mind was full of the scent of charred meat, the sight of a bloody arm torn from its owner, the crimson-splotched lump of flesh visible near the captain's right knee.

Such violence.

Death was something she thought she knew, but all she'd ever seen was dust and silence, not this slick carnage. Her stomach roiled again, and she tasted hot bile.

"Cara, talk to me." The heavy comfort of Archer's hand warmed her shoulder.

"What if you're wrong?" Her words were smoky whispers.

"We're not wrong," the captain said, exuding a strangely alluring confidence.

"I'd bet my life on it." Archer smiled easily as he pulled her to standing.

How could he say such a thing after what just happened? She grabbed his arm in desperation.

"No! No, you can't." But, what was their alternative?

"Come on," the captain said. His hand was on her elbow, gentle this time, drawing her back to the door. "You open it, and I'll go through."

As if it were that simple.

"Captain—"

Khoury silenced Archer with a raised hand.

The burnt odor reminded her of Father and set her legs trembling again. Closing her eyes, she did as he asked and put her hands against the cool oak. She pushed against its solid weight though she feared shock had stolen what meager strength she had. But the door inched open as the men waited, their impatience lapping at the borders of her mind. She stopped when the opening was wide enough to allow the captain to slip past her without touching it or her.

She was surprised by the pity on his face as he stepped past her out into the cool dawn. And nothing happened. The breath she didn't know she'd been holding escaped with a soft whoosh.

"Bring them through, Archer," the captain called over her head.

Then, as if she didn't exist, he turned on his heel and headed for the gate.

Archer organized their exit. One by one, the disheveled, dirty men slipped past her, their steps lighter with newfound hope. Archer was the last man out and once beyond the doors, he held out a hand for her. "Come with us."

She'd never gone into the yard through this door. It looked strange as she stood at the top of the stairs, an unfamiliar landscape stretching before her and directly ahead was the door she could never pass through.

She hesitated. Archer waited, his hand poised in the cold air between them as if her Father wasn't coming. As if they had time to dawdle. Without thinking, she put her small hand in his and let him lead her down the steps.

"Now for your bears," he said as they crossed the empty bailey. The morning frost crunched lightly beneath her slippers. "Where are they kept?"

"They may not like strangers," she said, suddenly eager for the warmth of the barn and her friends. "You go help at the gate while I get them."

"You don't need help?" He seemed surprised.

She laughed at his strangeness. "Don't be silly," she said. "Now go." She hurried toward the barn. What did he think she was? A child? Of course she could handle the bears. She pulled morsels of food from her pockets as she went, ducking between the fence rails of the paddock that originally had been built for horses. As she entered the humble peace of the barn, the scent of hay and fur calmed her frayed nerves.

She greeted the bears one by one: Little Tem, Hahn who was cranky, the meek twins Lorae and Dorcha, bossy Shona, and her favorite, steadfast Gar. Even in her hurry, she counted on their good graces and that meant abiding by their rituals. When each head had been patted and each black tongue had a turn licking a morsel from her small hands, she walked up to Gar and laid a hand on his broad head.

"Come." She led him toward the sledges, her gaze lingering on his tattered left ear. As a child, she had stolen to the barn to see the new creatures her Father had brought home. They had been wild then and young, and she was just a tidbit. She never knew why Gar decided to save her instead of eat her that day, but he did. His ear had been torn beyond repair during the fight that followed.

The large bear lumbered to his place and waited patiently as she attached the traces to his harness. "Stay," she said, though the word was more a request than a command. The bears knew what the sledges meant, and they were eager for the work. She arranged the six bears in two groups of three, Gar leading one sledge and Shona the other. In minutes, they were ready to go.

"Stay," she repeated the request to Gar and Shona again, and then walked outside.

In the distance, the men hovered by the door, and she picked out Archer standing beneath the window of the gate's squat tower. The lock mechanisms were housed up there. Three shadows were visible through that window and even at this distance she knew one was the captain. Such an impulsive and angry man, a sharp contrast to her father's banked temper.

She dragged the corral gate open and then opened both barn doors. Stepping up onto the runners of Shona's sledge, she checked that Gar's lead was secured and whistled gently. The sledge jerked as the bears threw themselves against the traces and out they went, through the barn door, across the corral and into the yard. She crooned to the bears in a low voice to slow their pace as the men darted fearfully out of their path. She halted the bears just in front of the still-closed wall gate. Archer approached looking pleasantly surprised as she handed him the reins.

"That was fast," he said, then turned to the crowd. "All right, everyone on."

She hadn't put the cages on. Father would have had to help her with that. So the sledges were little more than planks the men could straddle. The score of men arranged themselves evenly between the two sledges as Cara took the driver's stand of the second one and waited nervously on the runners. Soon all the men were seated except the ones in the gate room.

"Khoury, let's go!" Archer yelled as loudly as he dared. The captain waved down through the window as gears groaned and the gate began to open.

Archer stepped up on the rails of his sledge. Shona's nose was pointed at the gate and Cara's sledge was angled behind. The doors were almost opened enough to escape when a ball of fire flew past and burst apart on the wall.

"Daughter!" Sidonius's roar sounded as if he were standing right behind her. Her head whipped around in time to see another flaming sphere race past. This one exploded on the half-open doors sending rock debris and flaming splinters flying. The men in the tower raced down the stairs as a third ball of fire flew into the window of the gatehouse. Shona roared in fear, her panic echoing through her sledge-mates. Archer could do nothing but grab the uprights as his team darted through the barely open door, careening dangerously out onto the snowy tundra. Cara grabbed her own reins as Gar started forward.

"No, Gar!" she shouted, her control on the large beast tenuous but intact.

"Foolish girl. You think to leave?" Cara turned to see Sidonius walking down the steps, another ball of fire growing in his raised hand. Khoury and the two others raced to her sledge and hopped on.

Go!" Khoury shouted just as the fireball hit the ground next to her, showering them with hot dirt and rocking the sledge dangerously onto one rail. She braced herself and whistled a signal for the bears, her mouth so dry it was barely more than a wheeze. But even steadfast Gar was frightened and with a roar he jerked hard against the harness.

"You will never escape me!" Sidonius called after her as they raced through the gate.

The bears tore over the snowy ground, running flat out. And she let them. Fear tingled up her back, but she didn't dare look back. She kept to the vague path that was the southbound road expecting to see the other sledge, but there was only tundra and the snow that had begun to fall.

They made good speed for a quarter of an hour with no sign of the other sledge. But it began snowing harder with each passing minute. Suddenly, a wailing howl erupted from Gar, echoed a second later by the other two bears. Her worry turned to panic as the animals slowed to a stop, pawing at their harnesses. Their usual calming aura now full of nagging fear.

"Gar, let's go!" she shouted, whistling for them to move on, but they ignored her.

"What's wrong with them?" She recognized the captain's voice and glanced back to find him sitting right behind her. His eyes were uncomfortably intent.

"Father." The word stuck in her throat.

Gar lumbered forward with a strange barking howl only to turn in a sweeping arc back in the direction of the Keep.

"No, Gar, no!" she yelled, yanking on the leather reins. As she fought for control of the team, the strain of the last two days engulfed her. Her mind reeled with visions of the man in chains begging for his life, Father's threats, and the severed arm in the hall. It was too much. She missed the simplicity of her life before, and her courage faltered.

So easy, she thought. *So easy to just give up.* The serene limbo of her former existence beckoned, and her hand loosened on the reins.

"Cara?" There was concern in the captain's voice. His arm brushed hers as he grabbed the upright next to her and stood behind her. The solid length of his body against her back warmed her tired bones and sent a soft energy whispering through her.

"Don't quit now." The words slid unwanted into her ear as the sledge began to pick up speed. She thought of the altar room and the forest. Her forest. In a memory of damp earth and rough leather, she found one last tiny bit of strength. Leaning against Khoury's solid frame, she grabbed one rein in both hands and yanked it hard enough to turn Gar's head, making him stumble and slow. Then she slipped under the captain's arm and leapt from the sled, running along the rein to the lead bear.

"Gar, stop!" she cried, dragging herself close enough to lay her hand flat against his broad head. "Please stop." A sharp static tingled up her arm and, in an instant, Gar calmed. He slid to a halt, forcing the other two to stop as well. He turned to her, breathing hard, and hid his face in her skirt trembling like a cub. The other two bears, confused and still yowling, crowded close.

"What's wrong with you?" She reached out to pet Hahn and Tem while Gar's head pressed against her belly. Touching them quieted their distress, but something was very wrong.

The captain approached, wary of the beasts. "What's the matter with them?"

"I don't know. It's strange." She put both hands on Gar's cheeks and gazed deep into his bottomless black eyes. After a moment of dizziness, a heavy wave of emotion slammed into her. Images of Sidonius and flames and pain assailed her mind. It was overwhelming, and she cried out with the bears' distress.

"Go home," she wailed in chorus with the whining bears. "Or burn."

Cara tore her hands from Gar's head, shaking in terror. That had never happened before. Their beast minds had always been her haven. Though she no longer felt the need to scream, an echo of their terror lashed at her. Their massive bodies pressed closer, seeking contact.

"It can't be," she said, denying what her heart told her was true.

"What?" the captain asked.

"He's calling them. And they're afraid he'll hurt them."

"Can he?" Khoury asked, his hawkish eyes pressing on her.

"I don't know." She petted the furry head, fingering the torn ear. She lowered her forehead to Gar's. "I won't let Father hurt you. I promise."

She looked up at the captain. "Maybe I can convince them to keep going."

Suddenly, other cries rang through the cold air, growing louder as the other sledge team appeared racing back toward the Keep. For the first time, Cara noted stones set in the harnesses and they were glowing.

"Stop!" she yelled. Alone on the sledge, Archer sawed on the reins with all his strength. But the team was panicked. Heedless of her own safety, she ran in front of the other team and grabbed for Shona. Her arm jerked with the sudden speed, but she hung onto the harness, managing to touch Shona's face. The bear quieted like Gar had, stopping so suddenly they tumbled, bears and sledge and snow ending up in a heap at Cara's feet.

Archer was tossed from the sledge, and Cara was relieved when he stood up unharmed, dusting snow from his clothes.

"What the blazes happened?" he asked. "One minute, we're running southward and the next we're headed back."

"I'm not sure yet," she said. Now she had six sledge bears trying to find a place to lay a nose on her.

"Where are the others?" Khoury asked his lieutenant.

"As soon as the bears turned, they jumped off. I guess they'd rather walk."

Khoury chuckled. "I'm starting to think walking's a good plan."

Archer edged up behind the bears. "Cara," he called, "are you okay?"

"I've never seen them so afraid. They say they must go back or else."

"Or else what?" Khoury asked.

"Fire," she said. A heavy silence fell over the men.

"But Sidonius isn't here," Khoury said, scanning the tundra.

"No," Cara said. "I didn't leave him a sledge. But their harnesses are glowing. Father isn't just a master of fire but stone, too."

"Like your protection amulet," Archer said.

Cara nodded.

And then, all the harness stones blazed red. A bonfire glow ignited in the center of the pack. Whining turned to shrieks as the animals thrashed in pain.

Cara screamed at the sudden pain of fire washing over her body.

"Cara!" Archer cried from beyond the circle of howling bears. "Cara, what's wrong?"

"The fire! Get it off!" Her eyes were shut against the pain, but she could feel tongues of heat crawling over her. The odor of burning flesh seared her nose and stung her eyes.

"What fire?" Archer's voice was barely audible over the squalling bears.

"Help!" she screamed and beat at her body, trying to put out the fire. "Help me!"

"Cara, listen to me," Khoury said. "It's not real. There's no fire." His voice cut through her panic. "You're not burning."

How could he not see it? The pain forced her to her knees, heedless of the thrashing beasts around her.

"Cara!" Khoury's voice was insistent. "Open your eyes." His words were sibilant and thick like honey. They dripped into her ears, and she felt compelled to do as he said. Unable to resist, she opened one eye and saw nothing but panicked bears and snow on her clothes. There was no fire. Confused between what she felt and what she saw, her mind reeled. Khoury was still talking to her, his voice strangely powerful. The words crawled down her neck like warm rain. She clung to that voice, trying to ignore the feeling of her skin peeling from her body.

"The stones," Cara said, panting. "He's burning them through the stones. Get them off." She reached out her mind to the beasts and instructed them to stand still and let the men help them, but they were crazed with fear and pain. She grabbed Gar's head and held him still, staring into his black eyes as the fire burned them both. He whined and cried but waited.

The men approached warily and tried to remove the glowing crystal from Gar's harness. But it was set deep in the hardened leather, and they had no tools. The bear grew agitated, snapping and snarling, and Cara knew she was losing him.

"Hurry," she urged.

"The stones are set too deep," Archer said.

"Take off the harnesses!" she snapped at him, her control of the beast and herself slipping.

"Let them go back to the Keep, Cara," Archer suggested, fear in his voice. "We can walk."

"No!" Desperate tears streamed down her face at the thought of what Sidonius might do to them. "Please, no. Don't let him have my bears! You have to free us."

"Archer, take off the harnesses," Khoury said sharply.

"But Captain, one bite—"

"Do it!" the captain commanded. Cara gratefully redoubled her efforts to keep Gar calm, pushing him back away from the other bears.

"Hold on to him, Cara," Khoury said. "I won't give up." His voice was soft as velvet, soothing her raw nerves. "Just one more minute."

They quickly unbuckled the harness. Archer tossed it in the snow. Like a burning ember, it emitted a hiss and a trail of smoke.

Gar sighed and butted Cara's hip with an apologetic whine.

"It's okay, boy," she crooned. "He can't get you now." Feeling stronger, she turned back to the others and held out her hands to them. She called them close in her mind. She pushed images of cool water running over their fur to them. With her mind, she showed them that they were going to be okay, but they had to let the men help. The whines began to quiet as the bears waited to be freed. Soon, all six bears lay in the snow around Cara, exhausted but safe. She slumped against Gar's comforting bulk, sliding to the ground at his feet.

Khoury came over and squatted down. "Good job."

"It's not over yet," she whispered, her throat tight and her body trembling. "When this doesn't work, he'll just try something else." She looked up expecting more anger, but his face was soft with an emotion she couldn't place.

"We'll get moving soon enough," was all he said.

CHAPTER 9
KHOURY

Khoury rummaged through the supplies on the sledges, his thoughts tumbling chaotically. They had saved the bears but only barely. He didn't know if she was a sorceress, or something else entirely, but he was certain the girl had power and plenty of it. But she didn't know how to harness it. Without Khoury's push, they'd be walking now.

And he had pushed her. His gut knotted at the thought of using his talent to Command her, but it had strengthened whatever connected her to the beasts. The Voice, as his father called it, ran strong in their family. But Khoury swore he'd never use it.

Yet standing there in the snow, he could think of no better solution to her desperate cries. Her fierce loyalty to the beasts tugged at him. And she had refused to give up on strangers she didn't even know in the hall. He was impressed, but that didn't make her an ally. The captain didn't trust anyone with power. Not even himself.

When he finally found some rope, he took it to Archer who was reorienting the sledge back south.

"Think this will work?" the captain asked.

Archer tested the rope with a tug. "It should do." He started making knots. "Looks like the rest of our company decided to walk, too."

Khoury hadn't even noticed the men leave. Looking around now, he saw six bears, two sledges, Archer, the girl, and snow. It might be selfish but he was glad they'd gone. He didn't want to be responsible for their fates. Or the girl's either, if he had a choice.

"I did say that once we were out, it was every man for himself," Khoury said casually.

Archer stopped mid-knot and eyed the captain with suspicion.

"That is what we agreed," Khoury repeated, pretending to scan the horizon.

"You better not be thinking what I think you are." Archer lowered his voice so it wouldn't carry.

Khoury's gaze drifted to the small huddle of gray fabric leaning against the largest bear. As admirable as her actions were, she was not his task. He was no savior. He simply survived and that was enough for him. He liked his life simple.

Archer shoved Khoury's shoulder, bringing the captain's focus back to him. "Oh, no you don't."

"What?" Khoury scowled. "Splitting up might be for the best. She can handle her own sled."

"Captain, she saved us."

"And now she's free to go."

Archer leaned close and growled. "He'd find her and you know it."

The burning men on the stairs flashed through the captain's mind bringing guilt with it as he watched her sleep, her head pillowed against her bear. Dark circles were painfully obvious on her pale face. "I don't know that," he hedged.

Taking her with them would be asking for trouble. Trouble they didn't need.

"I'm not leaving her." Archer crossed his brawny arms over his wide chest with a stubborn look.

"And are you captain now?" Khoury challenged, holding the Northerner's eyes with a stern glare until Archer looked away.

"You know it's not right."

Self-preservation warred with pity, and for a moment Khoury thought it might go the other way, but finally he said, "Fine, but let's get moving."

In silence, they fashioned six makeshift harnesses. Khoury loaded all the supplies from both sledges onto the one. Stowing the last sack, he watched as Archer cautiously sidled past the hulking animals to Cara.

"Cara." Archer touched her shoulder gently, keeping his eyes on Gar. The girl startled awake and was on her feet before her eyes were focused. "What?"

"We need to get moving. Can you help me get three bears harnessed? We'll lead the extra team."

The pale girl nodded and shakily dusted snow from her clothes. Then she went about the business of harnessing the bears. Khoury watched in fascination as the giant beasts followed her touch, calm as oxen. She had them harnessed in no time as Archer stood shaking his head in disbelief.

A strong arctic breeze nipped at Khoury's cheeks, drawing his attention to the darkening sky. The air smelled like snow. The girl was right about one thing: Something was coming.

He looked to where Cara and Archer stood by the uprights. The wind picked up her hair, streaming it sideways like a white flag. Catching his eye, her unguarded face told the captain all he needed to know.

"Let's go," he barked, climbing onto the sledge planks near the supplies. The girl stepped up to the runners, gesturing to Archer to get on.

"Maybe we can outrun it." Her heavy voice belied her doubt.

Once Archer was settled, she whistled sharply to the beasts and drove them south at a run. But the weather caught them. A full-blown blizzard roared across the tundra, limiting vision to a few feet. The horizon disappeared in featureless white as the storm swallowed them up. The puffy flakes turned to sharp ice, and the angry wind pushed against the sledge like a living thing. Their progress slowed to a crawl as the road led directly into the wind. The bears voiced their displeasure with yowls and grunts. Khoury sensed an impending mutiny. The beasts were tired, and the wind fierce.

It was no natural storm. The girl had mentioned powers of fire and stone, but Khoury wondered if he should add weather to the list. Perhaps Sidonius had sent the storm to slow them down, keep them from heading south.

"Cara," he shouted to be heard over the storm, "is this your Father's doing?"

She looked back at the men, her hair obscuring her face. "There is always a storm when he brings guests."

"He controls it?" Khoury pressed.

"I don't know," she shouted back.

"What're you thinking, Captain?" Archer asked.

"I think he's trying to keep us from going south."

"Slow us down?"

"Yes, but we don't have to go south anymore. The others have already gone."

"Where would we go?"

"West?"

Archer's frowned in thought, and then he smiled. "Bear Clan!"

Khoury nodded. "How far do you think it is?"

"Two days, maybe? Certainly worth a try. We could be leagues away before he realizes we've changed direction."

"That's what I thought," Khoury agreed.

"Cara!" Archer yelled. "Go west."

"West? Which way is west?" Her tone was as sharp as the ice. She was spent.

"Let Archer drive. You're exhausted," Khoury said.

She shook her head with determination. "My bears. Where's west?"

"Keep the wind over your left shoulder," Archer explained.

She nodded and stepped off the runners. The bears were struggling so hard, she could walk to Gar where he led the team. His head was down to his toes as he fought the gale wind. She grabbed a handful of his fur and pulled him to the right. As he took a few steps and found the going easier, he picked up speed, dragging the other bears and sledge in line behind. Khoury watched as the girl leaned into the bear's bulk, using it to shield her from the worst of the storm. Archer got up and went to the extra team of bears, using the lead line to pull them west. Khoury got up and guided the sledge behind the beasts, pushing it when the drifts got deep.

Time ceased to have any meaning as they trudged through the storm, hungry and frozen. It could have been ten minutes or ten hours. Eventually, the sky began to lighten. The clouds thinned. Khoury could make out a brighter spot above the horizon that should be the setting sun. They had walked all day. Finally, the winds lost their intensity, dropping as suddenly as they started. The snow stopped. They had reached the edge of the storm and not a moment too soon.

As if the storm had been keeping her upright, the white-haired girl collapsed. Gar stopped to nose her gently, bringing the caravan to a halt. Khoury grabbed a rough blanket from the sledge and went to where the girl lay face down in the snow. Rolling her over, he noted how raw and red her face and hands were. Her knuckles had patches of white among fresh scabs, and her nose had some concerning traces of white-blue skin. He wrapped her in the blankets and lifted her easily. Archer waited by the sledge as Khoury approached with the girl.

"You were right," Archer said, looking at the sky. "We're out. How is she?"

"She'll be fine. Can you drive?"

"The team is exhausted, Captain."

"I know, but we need to push."

"I'll trade them out and maybe we could get another mile or so. After that, we need to rest."

"Fine. I want as much distance between us and this sorcerer as I can get."

"Me too," Archer agreed. He touched the girl's white hair with concern. "Poor thing."

"Just a touch of frostbite," Khoury said. "We're lucky to get away with our lives."

"Get her warmed up while I trade the teams."

Archer went about moving the animals as Khoury settled onto the sledge. He sat and arranged the girl against his chest with his thighs flanking her to keep her from falling off. He draped a second thin blanket over her and closed his arms around her. In a few minutes, her body warmed enough to start shivering and, after a short while of Archer's driving, she warmed enough to stop. She was so exhausted she was completely oblivious to the world. He felt a twinge of guilt that he had considered sending her off on her own. But even now, he felt uneasy around her. Her presence stirred something in him, something he didn't want wakened.

CHAPTER 10
ARCHER

Archer rolled out of the meager nest of blankets tucked up against the sledge. The cold predawn air prickled along his skin making him thankful it was early spring—cold, but not deadly. The three of them would have frozen to death that first night if it had been true winter. He looked to the nearby cluster of shaggy humps; no snow covered them this morning. Still, he was hard-pressed to pick out Cara's tiny form under Gar's massive head. The bits of gray he could see might have been only shadows. For two nights, while he and Khoury huddled together in the freezing dark, the girl had chosen instead to sleep beneath the chin of the giant beast.

She was probably warmer than they were, but Archer could never have slept that close to its huge maw. As it was, the fact that the creatures were free to roam made him uneasy. Carnivorous and unpredictable, he had seen many a boy mauled by the long claws that lurked beneath the shaggy fur on their paws. The kinship she had with Sidonius's sledge bears, Gar in particular, was more than strange. The chieftain would be intrigued.

Archer stretched again and shook the chill from his limbs as the sun began to surface in the east. Scanning the terrain, he smiled. Home was close.

They'd had no sign of the sorcerer or his magic in the last two days, but he still hadn't felt truly safe. With Bear Clan so close, he hoped to put this adventure behind them.

He nudged the captain awake with his foot. "Sunrise, Captain."

Khoury woke with a growl to instant alertness as usual. His beard had grown in, but his nose was weather burnt and his cheeks gaunt. The captain pushed himself to standing and stretched with an audible pop of joints. "How close?"

"I bet we're there today." Archer smiled again. It would be good to be home for a bit.

"Good. I could use some real food," Khoury muttered as his stomach rumbled loudly. "And an ale."

"A bath wouldn't hurt." Archer pinched his nose for effect.

"Says the man whose stink kills dung flies at ten paces," the captain retorted.

They shook out the blankets and folded them back on the sledge. The coiled ropes that passed for gear were laid out in clean lines.

When they finished, Khoury sighed and rolled his stiff shoulders. "All right, Archer. Get her up." He gestured absently to where the bears slept, then turned to take his morning piss in relative privacy.

The captain had been distant about the girl from the start but at least he hadn't suggested they abandon her again. Archer had grown fond of her shy smile and unexpected courage. She would do well with Bear Clan. They'd look after her when he and the captain rejoined their Swords.

He walked over to the largest mound of white and carefully reached out to shake Cara's shoulder that was just barely visible under Gar's chin. "Cara, time to get up."

One large bearish eye shot open, and the massive head swiveled around. Archer froze as the black nostrils flared to catch his scent. The ears flattened, perked up, and then lay back again. He backed up to a more respectful distance as the girl yawned. She reached up to absently scratch the side of Gar's throat.

"It's okay, boy," she murmured to the bear and rubbed her face into its fur. Then sleepily she said, "Archer, will you do something for me?"

"Maybe."

She clambered to her feet and swayed against Gar for a moment, eyes closed. "Make friends with Gar," she said.

Of all the things she might ask, he never would have expected that. The first rule every bear driver learned was not to fool yourself into thinking they were your friends. They were more than half-wild and very unpredictable. "Thanks, but no," he deferred.

"Don't you like him?"

"I like him fine."

"Then come here." She reached out and tugged at his sleeve.

Archer pulled away. "Cara, stop. This is insane."

"Why?" One of her hands absently rubbed Gar's head like a dog.

"I've seen what they can do to a man, Cara. They're not pets."

She frowned, and the bear's rumble echoed her displeasure. "He's seen what men can do. Come show him that not all men are cruel."

She reached out and grabbed his sleeve again. This time Archer followed her gentle pull, not wanting to make a scene. She stood between him and the bear and laid his hand on top of Gar's head, and gestured for him to scratch as she had been.

He pushed his cold-roughened fingers into the warm soft fur and stroked the giant head, feeling very foolish. Gar's wide wet nose snuffled the length of his arm. The bear huffed softly and relaxed into Archer's hand.

He couldn't help smiling as she leaned down and whispered to Gar, "I told you he was okay. Now, get the others up."

Gar pushed to his feet and shook himself in a violent furry wave from nose to rump. Then, as unbelievable as it seemed, the bear ambled over to nudge its companions. Archer was convinced Sidonius had charmed the animals somehow. But as long as she had control of them, he wasn't going to argue.

"Thank you," she said, "Gar feels better now."

"Sure." Archer laughed, shaking his head. "I was making *him* nervous. So, who's pulling first today?"

"They're getting hungry," she said. "We need to let them eat."

"Don't worry. There's food at the Clan for them, and we should be there by nightfall."

She nodded, squeezing her lower lip between her teeth in thought. "They're gonna be grumpy. But I'll let them know. We should save Gar for later in the day. He's easier to control."

"You know them best."

She whistled to the bears and they ambled over to the sledge, allowing her to harness them with an ease that still fascinated Archer. He noticed Khoury from the corner of his eye, watching her, too. The captain's face was stony.

He caught Archer staring at him. "You have something to say?"

"Nope. I'm just gonna be glad to see home."

The small curve of a smile eased Khoury's face. He took a deep breath. "Me too." Khoury bent to climb onto the sledge.

Cara climbed on behind Khoury as Archer whistled to Shona to head out.

The weather held to a thin layer of overcast. Cara had been right; the beasts were unruly, and his arms were sore by the time Cara took her turn. The landscape grew more familiar every mile. By the time the sky began to darken, they had passed from desolate tundra to the pine-forested foothills of the White Mountains whose peaks Archer knew by heart.

Cara was driving when they crested a high ridge and startled a heard of pine elk. Archer and Khoury had to hold tight as Cara fought the now-hungry bears who wanted to give chase.

"Gar, no! Stop!" she scolded as she hauled on the reins. The bears slowed to a halt with a reluctant growl.

The hill's meadowed slope tilted down to a forested vale with a river cutting through the trees. It split into two smaller streams as it ran southward and at the junction of those two streams stood a rough gray stone taller than any man in the Clan. Archer knew that carved face. It was so ancient that even up close you couldn't make out anything but the flat wide nose of Borran the Spirit Bear. It was the edge of the Clan lands. Archer was home.

His troubles dissipated like mist. "We're here," he said, striding down the slope. Khoury followed, and Cara brought the sledge down after them. Standing at the edge of the easternmost stream, he let the strength of Borran's familiar shape sink in.

"What is that?" she asked.

He laughed with the lightness of his heart. "The Guardian of Bear Clan. Hop on. I'll take us the last little bit." He strode to the sledge and took the stand. Cara whispered something to Gar's ear before she climbed on the sledge. Khoury hopped on, too.

Archer guided the bears between the pines along a wet path of scented needles. The snow had melted here, and the bears had to work harder to pull the sledge on its thin snow blades. The path skirted the river before breaking off into the thickening trees. Then it widened and wove around until they came to a clearing. But it was more than just a clearing; it was the center of the Clan.

Over fifty thatched huts nestled among the trees that circled the open area. Near the center of the clearing stood the main gathering hall and the kitchens; to the west was the Gathering Place where stories were told around the firepit. To the east, the smithy crouched, spouting puffs of smoke as the smiths worked the bellows. But most of all Archer welcomed the sight of the crowds. People filled the clearing: men, women, and children, all laughing and talking.

Archer drew in a deep breath of pine smoke and sugar mead, and felt the warmth of homecoming energize him. Shouts circulated as he pulled the bears to a halt just beyond the trees.

"Aedan! Gwenna!" Archer shouted back, waving. Familiar smiles rushed to greet them. The men were similar to Archer in build and girth. Most of the beards were long, and all the heads were shades of gold and red, even the gray-streaked ones. By southern standards the women of Bear Clan would have been considered sturdy but their auburn braids, generous curves, and open smiles were as welcoming as a lit hearth.

Dropping the reins and stepping off the runners, Archer hugged them one by one, large thumping embraces as their loud, boisterous voices chased away the memory of the silent Keep. He laughed, ensconced in the affection of his Clan.

Khoury stood up and greeted the Northerners, too, getting lost amid their bulky height. Archer smiled at how his people welcomed Khoury as one of their own. The captain had made friends in the Clan over the last few years, and Archer saw him really laugh for the first time in months.

"Reid!" The familiar shout was almost a squeak and he turned, smiling so hard his cheeks ached.

"Maura!" He opened his arms to the pretty woman who launched herself at him with a gleeful squeal. He spun her around, remembering how perfectly she fit in his arms.

"I had no idea you'd come back so soon!" She trapped his bearded face in both hands and planted a passionate kiss on his mouth. The taste of sugar mead on her lips and the aroma of baking bread on her cheek squeezed his heart and made him wonder for the hundredth time why he kept leaving.

"Nice to see you too, Maura," Khoury called over Archer's shoulder with jovial sarcasm. Archer felt her wave hello without breaking their kiss.

Then Khoury nudged him in the ribs as an older man with a braided beard approached. Archer gently put the woman down but kept one hand possessively on her full hips.

"Chieftain Bradan, the Spirits smile on you." Archer raised his hand in formal greeting.

"Reid Tarhill, the hearth is lit." Bradan nodded to Khoury as well. "Well met again, Captain," he said. His raised hand revealed the symbol of power tattooed on his palm. Behind Archer, Gar huffed a greeting himself.

Archer turned to see the bear focused intently on the chieftain. Cara crouched on the far side of him, staring at the raucous scene with tears bright in her eyes. For the first time he realized how lonely her life must have been, if her story were true.

"Cara," he said, waving her over to him. "I'd like you to meet Maura. Maura, this is the girl who saved our lives."

Maura looked at Archer with surprise and then held out welcoming hands to Cara. The pale girl crept out from behind her bear, wide-eyed and trembling. "Thank you for bringing my Archer back," Maura said. Then unable to contain herself, she drew Cara into a hug, which the girl awkwardly tolerated.

"And Chieftain Bradan," Archer said. "Bradan, this is Cara."

Cara swallowed hard and then stammered a, "Hello, Sir." Then she turned back to Archer. "Where do you let the bears hunt? They're quite hungry." She kept her voice low and her eyes focused only on him, her hands nervously clutching each other.

"Hunt?" Archer was confused, and then he laughed. "We feed our bears."

Cara blushed with embarrassment.

Looking around, he recognized a tall youth leaning against a nearby cart. "Ewan, find a few boys to settle the bears in," he called. "They're hungry."

The boy approached, glancing down his hawkish nose at her. "The pens are pretty full, Archer." His face was surly, barely covering his adolescent aggravation at being asked to help.

"Then move some around and find these a place."

"The others are out hunting."

Cara tugged at his sleeve. "I don't need his help. Just tell me where they go."

"She takes care of your bears?" the boy asked with disbelief.

From the looks of it, Ewan's attitude had improved little over the winter. Archer wanted Cara to feel comfortable with the Clan so he drew himself up to tower over the boy.

"*Lady* Cara is a superior driver. She could show you boys a thing or two. She can handle the six by herself so just show her where the pens are. And get her whatever she needs." He grabbed the boy's arm, leaning close with a stern look. "And be polite."

"Fine." The boy remained petulant but bowed slightly to Cara. "My lady, bring your bears this way."

Bradan raised an eyebrow in her direction as she followed Ewan. "All six alone?"

"Her skill is unprecedented. But I suspect the bears are charmed."

"Charmed bears. A woman rescuer. It appears you have quite the tale. Come to the hall. You boys can tell me more while you eat."

"Now you're talking," Khoury piped up.

"I'll have the girl brought to us as soon as she finishes with the beasts," Bradan added. Archer's stomach rumbled, reminding him how little they had eaten in the past month. He and Khoury eagerly followed the chieftain across the center of the village.

CHAPTER 11
KHOURY

Tension drained from Khoury's neck and back. The village looked the same as ever and, if Khoury felt at home anywhere, it was here. Beside him, Archer held Maura's hand, radiating a youthful happiness as they followed Bradan across the center of the village. His lieutenant confused him. At times, he was so besotted that it was painful to watch and yet in a week or two he invariably would be itching to leave. Not paying close attention to where he was going, Khoury bumped someone, hard.

"Excuse you." The familiar voice brought a pair of warm eyes beneath silky auburn locks.

"Nalia?" Khoury was surprised to see her, though she was usually the one on his mind when they traveled north. Today, he'd forgotten all about her and, as alluring as she was, Nalia was the last person he wanted to deal with right now.

"My captain! What a delightful surprise." Her smile was hungry and her voice husky as she sidled up to him.

"You are lovely as ever." Khoury bowed slightly and smiled. The languid sensuality that radiated from her warmed him in ways that had nothing to do with the cold. "Unfortunately, I've business with Bradan. No time to talk." He flashed another smile and turned to catch up with the others, cutting off any response.

"I see Nalia remembers you," Archer said.

"And very fondly, too," Maura added with a knowing grin. Khoury sighed but didn't bother to respond. Ever since the Keep, he felt irritable, unsettled and plagued by dreams of his past. What he needed was to get back to work. He kept his face blank and focused on the building ahead of them.

The main hall was a sprawling one-story structure of rough-hewn wood with a common room large enough for the whole village to eat in at once. Its inner darkness, a stark contrast to the bright afternoon, made him temporarily blind so the first thing he noticed was the smell. The heavy fragrance of herbs and meat made his mouth water. As his eyes adjusted, the common room was exactly as he remembered: Warm, low-ceilinged and busy.

They sat at an empty table while a ruddy-faced woman brought bowls of thick stew and slabs of dark bread. Khoury scooped the stew into his mouth, reveling in its hearty flavor.

Then came large pints of mead, sweet and tart and cold.

"This is the good stuff," Khoury said. "My eternal thanks for the 'hospitality' of your hearth, Bradan." He toasted the chieftain with his drink, and Archer laughed as they both downed them with pleasure.

"And how are things here?" the captain asked the older man.

"Would be better if you'd stop stealing our best bard." The older man thumped Archer on the back with affection. "But the hunting was good this year. Trading will be very profitable."

"Glad to hear it."

"And, as usual, Captain, you're welcome to stay as long as you like. I hear there's a woman here that might put up with you." Humor tugged at Bradan's mouth hidden in his beard. "I mean, put you up."

"Nalia could be persuaded." Archer smiled.

"If we clean him up a bit." Maura frowned, judging him nearly inadequate. "Maybe," she hedged, and then chuckled warmly.

He shook his head at them. "I'll not be settled that easily, even if Nalia were interested, which you very well know she's not."

"Perhaps," Bradan said, chuckling, "but one of you should take himself a wife. The right woman won't wait forever." Bradan tried to fix Archer with a stern look, but the younger man was conveniently intent on his dinner.

The right woman, Khoury knew, was sitting right there—Maura, Bradan's daughter. Embarrassed by her father's dig, Khoury watched her press her lips together and hide them in her mead. Though Archer had been reticent about their story, the village gossip was that Archer and Maura had been promised to wed at one time. Then Archer's father died. Archer had called off the wedding and ventured south with his brother, ending up alone on the losing side of the Barakan War. Why Archer had deserted Maura remained a mystery, especially when it was obvious he still loved her. And Khoury could see she still loved him, too. Each time they visited, she was here waiting, affectionate and hopeful.

"Well then, what trouble brings you home in such poor condition?" Bradan asked.

Archer wiped his mouth and began the story of how he and Khoury had been kidnapped. Stories, as Khoury had discovered over the years, were Archer's hidden passion, making him about the best traveling companion Khoury ever had. The captain happily focused on his food as Archer detailed with true Northern flair how they had been taken to the stronghold at the foot of the Black Mountains. He described the fiery death of the kidnappers, the interminable waiting, and how Cara came to his cell. Beside him, Maura's face became paler at each new danger.

Khoury heard her hold her breath as Archer described the night Cara arrived with the keys, remorseful and shaken, the exploding doors, the bears' mutiny and the blizzard. Khoury realized in retrospect that the storm would certainly have claimed their lives if the girl hadn't insisted on saving the bears.

Bradan thoughtfully tugged on his beard braids in the deep silence that followed the story, his dark eyes unreadable. Maura hugged

Archer and laid her head on his shoulder, a single tear on her cheek.

Then a burst of brightness broke the spell, and all heads turned to stare at the woman standing in the doorway, pale hair shining in the sunlight.

Archer stood, and waved. "Cara!"

Her worried eyes found him but she still trembled as if ready to flee at the slightest provocation. Whatever courage Khoury had seen on the tundra seemed only a memory now. As she carefully picked her way toward them, his pity for her returned, bringing with it a strange desire to shelter her.

The small boy Bradan had sent to fetch her dragged her by the hand and then darted out the door once he'd handed her off to Archer. She sank to the bench between him and the chieftain, across from Khoury.

"You must be starving, too," Maura said, standing up. "Let me get you some stew." She squeezed Cara's shoulder affectionately as she headed toward the kitchen. Only Khoury noticed the girl flinch at her touch.

Bradan nodded kindly to her, and she gave him a grateful smile. "Thank you for your hospitality." Her speech was low and halting.

"Archer was just telling us a little of your story." The large man leaned closer. "But I think he left out some important parts."

The look that Cara gave Archer was heavy with guilt and secrets, piquing Khoury's curiosity.

"Who are you really?" The chieftain took her hand in his tattooed one and her nostrils flared at the touch.

"Nobody."

"Nobody? I hear you're the daughter of a sorcerer."

She lowered her head as if ashamed. "Well, yes that."

"Then again, maybe not." Bradan studied her closely.

Why would the chieftain challenge her claim? *Khoury wondered.*

She gasped. "I'm not lying." She looked to Archer, briefly to Khoury and then back to Bradan.

"Far Islanders are recruited, not bred, my dear," he said.

"What?" Her surprised face held no guile.

"Far Islanders don't have children. They are forbidden from intimacy with women," the chieftain explained. "They believe it weakens their magic."

Khoury had never heard that rumor before. Then again, he'd never been particularly interested in sorcerer lovemaking. Before Cara could say anything more, Maura arrived with a steaming bowl and placed it in front of the girl.

"Are you all right?" she asked, noting Cara's shocked look.

The girl looked up at Maura. "Father, I mean Sidonius, always called me Daughter," she explained.

Maura looked sternly at her father. "Are you upsetting her already? Give the girl a minute to warm up."

"I am simply asking her who she is."

Maura sniffed with disappointment. "Food first. By the ghost, she's skin and bones." Maura shook her head as she sat down next to Archer, glaring at her father as if daring him to start the conversation again.

"It wouldn't be a bad thing, Cara," Archer said. "Sidonius not being your father. It would mean you have real parents elsewhere."

As Cara looked sadly into her bowl, Khoury could hear her stomach rumble. Then she took a breath and set her jaw. "Why don't you ask me what you really want to know?"

"I have," the chieftain said.

"No, the other questions." Her words were stronger now. "The ones you don't know how to ask."

Bradan blinked in surprise. Khoury couldn't remember ever seeing Bradan off balance before.

"He can wait, Cara," Maura interjected.

"No," Cara said, turning to fully face the chieftain. "Now." Her palms cupped his weathered cheeks. Then she breathed out in one long slow exhale and closed her eyes. Her head tilted to the side.

"Yes, he's very powerful," she said.

Bradan hadn't said a word. Khoury looked to Archer questioningly, but the other man could only shrug.

"Too many to count," Cara said.

"What's she talking about?" Maura whispered.

Cara swallowed hard and said, "They all died."

As Khoury listened to the eerie one-sided conversation, the hair on the back of his neck stood up.

"As long as I can remember." A tear ran down her cheek. "I couldn't save them. I never tried."

Khoury shifted in his seat. He had the sudden urge to pull her hands away from Bradan and soothe the sadness he saw in her face. But he resisted.

Bradan raised his hands to cover hers on each side of his face, and he closed his eyes as well as she continued. "I heard him in the hall. No one ever spoke to me before."

Bradan opened his eyes and asked the next question aloud, Khoury presumed, so they could all hear her answer. "And why did you help them escape?"

"He was nice to me. He cared so much about the captain. I'd never seen that before. When Father said he'd make me watch them die, I couldn't bear it."

She opened her eyes and dropped her hands. The tension disappeared with a palpable whoosh of energy, releasing Khoury from his trance. "I'm so sorry for what I didn't do," she said, looking first at Bradan and then Archer. Khoury noticed she avoided his eyes. "I'm sorry for all the men who died. What kind of horrible person am I?"

"Someone who never knew anything else," Bradan reassured her, placing his large hand over one of hers. "You acted when the time was right. Nothing more could be expected."

Looking around the noisy hall, Khoury realized that no one else had noticed the strange conversation, or felt the power. The girl slid her hand out from under Bradan's and tucked it in her lap.

"What was that?" Archer asked, incredulous.

"It's how I talk to the bears," she said as if that explained everything.

"I meant, how did you do that?" Archer asked her.

"I don't know. When I touch the bears, I hear what's inside their head."

Archer's hand grabbed her forearm, startling her. "Tell me what I'm thinking," he said with a boyish look. Maura punched his arm, hard.

"I can't," Cara said, shrinking away from him, "unless *I* touch *your* skin with my hand. But I don't like to do it."

"How long have you been able to do this?" Bradan looked at her intently.

"I've talked with the bears as long as I can remember. But I didn't know it worked on people until…." Her voice faded, and her eyes flicked to Khoury for the briefest moment.

His mind raced back to the first day he saw her, the jolt of energy that passed through him when he touched her hand. The way she pulled away. Had she heard his thoughts then?

"An impressive talent," Bradan murmured, nodding his head at Maura and then looking at another table.

Maura stood, taking Cara's spoon and bowl from the table. "Come on. It'll be more peaceful over here." She led Cara to another table.

Pity filled Khoury as he watched Cara walk in a daze to sit by Maura. Soon enough though, Maura had her eating and by the look of her, she had been starving, too. *Had she really lived there her whole life?* he wondered. *And where did Sidonius find her? Who were her real parents?*

Bradan turned to Archer with a fatherly smile. "Go on, Reid. My daughter's missed you." Khoury thought he heard a hint of accusation. "We make the girl anxious, but she seems comfortable with you." Archer smiled and took his drink to the other table, settling in next to Maura.

In the silence, Khoury felt Bradan's weighty stare. When he turned to him, the chieftain's eyes held mischievous curiosity. "Something you wanted to talk to me about?" he asked the older man.

"Always a sharp one."

Khoury took another slow sip and waited for Bradan to speak.

"You feel it, don't you?"

Khoury's guard went up. "Feel what?"

Bradan gestured to Cara with his chin.

"I feel sorry for her," Khoury allowed.

"I know you're more than you appear, Captain."

Khoury hid the sudden flush of anxiety with a careless stretch as he leaned back in his chair. "I'm exactly what I appear to be: A landless mercenary."

Bradan looked unconvinced. "Did you know the gifted have always been drawn to others with power?"

Bradan could sense innate power? Certainly, Khoury's talent had been forced down long enough to remain hidden. Or had it? "Meaning?"

"I can feel her power. Even from here. She glows with it. The more powerful the magic, the stronger the attraction."

Bradan's revelation about sensing power was more concerning to the captain than whether the girl might be a sorceress. And though the older man's eyes were on Cara, Khoury sensed he was the real subject of the shaman's scrutiny. Deflection had always served Khoury well. He leaned over and eyed the chieftain. "She's far too young for you. And aren't you married?"

"What?" Bradan was taken aback, "No, it's not like that. I want to help her."

"And so you will," Khoury said. Was the pull he'd felt toward her that simple, just her power calling to his?

"Do I see something of that in your eyes, Captain?" Bradan pressed.

"No. Nothing like that." Khoury's voice was rough. He coughed once and continued, "If it weren't for her, we'd be dead. I owe her my life."

With a shake of his head, Bradan got up from the table. "I see. We'll put her in with Maura for the time being. You remember where the guest lodge is, don't you?"

Khoury cleared his throat. "I do, and I appreciate you letting me stay a while."

"I don't think you'll be staying too long, Captain. I believe you have a job to do." Khoury felt a queer shiver at the older man's words.

CHAPTER 12
CARA

Once Cara started in on the meaty stew, she forgot all about the measuring stares of the men and memories of dust in the altar room. Her world for the moment consisted of nothing more than the strange, salty dark meat, the savory roots and the thick gravy. Maura and Archer spoke quietly next to her, content to linger while she ate. Once sated, a multitude of pains intruded on Cara's awareness: her scraped knees and bruised arms, the painful skin of her nose, cheeks, and knuckles.

"If you're done, let's get you cleaned up," Maura said. "I have some balm for that frostbite."

"Thank you." Cara stood and stretched, feeling almost human again.

"For me, too?" Archer asked with a wink.

Maura laughed. "You can go to Ingrid," she teased. "And take a bath while you're at it."

Archer laughed and scooped Maura against him with one arm, kissing her soundly. Then he chucked Cara gently under the chin and went back to the table where Khoury sat alone.

"C'mon." Maura took Cara by the hand and led her out the door. At the touch, memories of Archer's warm laughter and surprisingly mellow singing voice played across Cara's mind along with less joyful things. A cramp of borrowed longing lodged under her ribs at Archer's face disappearing down the road. Cara was too tired to make sense of the conflicting emotions washing over her. She longed for peace and quiet.

Maura released her hand when they got to a small hut of rough-hewn wood daubed with earth. Cara rubbed the feel of Maura's mind off her palm as she followed her into the dwelling whose only room was small by Keep standards. It was homey though. Skins warmed the floors and blankets covered most of the low wooden furniture. Shelves and chests made a wall, turning the back corner into a bathing alcove.

"Do you have any gloves?" Cara asked, feeling awkward.

"Oh, no." Maura's face turned pink. "I'm so sorry, Cara. I forgot."

"It's okay. Maybe if I just keep my hands covered."

"Good idea." Maura lifted the heavy lid of a large trunk near the washroom and pawed through its contents. "There's fresh water in the basin and this balm will soothe that frostbite." She straightened and handed Cara a small ceramic pot of pungent grease. Then Maura turned her toward the alcove and gave her a soft shove. "Just get the dirt off. We can get you a hot bath tonight."

Cara put the little jar down on the shelf next to the basin and scooped up the water in her cupped hands, splashing her face and rubbing gritty dirt from her skin. The refreshing coolness was delightful though it stung Father's burns and her frostbitten skin. She reached for the small pot of balm and gingerly dabbed on the salve, sighing with relief. The skin smarted at first but soon her fingers traced gentle circles and a warm tingling relieved the ache.

A tall polished silver mirror hung behind the shelves. The face that stared back surprised her. The white curtain of her hair was longer than she realized. With her blonde eyebrows and pale skin, she looked faded like a painting hung in the sun. *No wonder Archer thought I was a ghost.*

She'd never realized how slovenly her gray robes looked until she compared them to Maura's prim dress. And the clean brilliance of the sparkling sapphire at her throat only made the rest of her that much grubbier. What Cara saw in the mirror was little more than a disheveled orphan.

"Cara," Maura poked her head around the shelves and pushed a bundle of clothes at her, "these should fit you and will certainly be warmer than what you've got on."

Cara took them as Maura returned to the other room, giving her some much-needed privacy. She stripped off the familiar dingy robes, ignoring the scent of dust that rose from them. After a quick swipe with the cool, wet towel, she slipped into the new shift and over tunic. She'd never worn anything cut for a girl before and was surprised how naked one could feel in so much fabric. The shift was nearly black with long sleeves that came down to her wrists, and she covered it with a leafy-green tunic, fitted in the chest and waist with wider sleeves that only reached her forearms.

"Do they fit?" Maura asked.

Cara tugged and twisted to settle the fabric more comfortably on her small frame. "I think."

A hand appeared around the shelf holding a wide embroidered belt. "Here. Take this, too."

Cara tied the embroidered sash just above her hips the way Maura's was. When she checked the mirror again, she felt taller though the skirt dragged on the ground. Her amulet was hidden by the dark shift's neckline. The deep green of the tunic emphasized her pale hair and reflected in her eyes, giving them a hint of teal. But the most fascinating thing to Cara was that she had a figure, a woman's figure. Not as ample as Maura's certainly, but she didn't look like a child anymore. She walked back out into the main room, flushing with pleasure at Maura's approving smile.

"You look lovely," the Northern girl said.

"Thank you."

"Here are the gloves." Maura handed Cara a pair of cream-colored kidskin gloves, thin enough not to be clumsy.

Cara slipped one on and grabbed Maura's hand, relieved that she felt nothing. "Perfect."

"Now sit." Maura pointed to a bench and, for the next half hour, she brushed and braided Cara's long hair. "Now you're presentable," she said.

Cara toured the village with Maura who introduced her to everyone. The sun had set by the time they were done, and Cara didn't think she'd remember even one name. Back at Maura's hut, a large tub occupied the middle of the big room filled with steaming water. Maura left Cara there to soak while she went to the kitchens to help prepare the feast celebrating Archer's return.

In less than an hour, Maura was dragging her to the small clearing near the dining hall where a large bonfire now raged, controlled by a circle of stones. The smoke reminded her of Father. A chill curled around her belly, but the warm press of smiling people kept the worst fears at bay.

Cara caught sight of Archer across the clearing. His face was freshly scrubbed, and his beard now had two small braids. Auburn curls clung damply to his neck. The leather rest of a worn fiddle was tucked under his chin as he conferred with three other men holding instruments. Cara saw a man point in their direction, and Archer's eyes lit up when he saw Maura.

Maura waved to him. "Come on," she said, pulling Cara after her.

They passed Bradan and an older woman sharing a seat near the hall, his arm draped with warm affection across her shoulders. When they reached Archer, he had put down the fiddle and caught Maura up into his arms, planting a kiss on his lips.

He lowered Maura to her feet and looked at Cara, feigning surprise. "Maura, I don't believe I know this enchanting creature. Good evening, lovely lady." Cara laughed as he took up her gloved hand and kissed the knuckles gently.

Khoury materialized from behind Archer, sending her heart

thumping for no apparent reason. He stopped and stared as well, his dark eyebrows rising in surprise. She blushed with pleasure. He inclined his head in an abbreviated bow. "Lady Cara."

"Are you playing tonight?" Maura asked.

"A few melodies, my love. No more." Archer wrapped a strong arm around her waist, tugging her tight against him. "After that, I'm all yours."

Maura's smile faded a little. "I have…chores tonight." They traded looks back and forth, and Maura glanced at Cara. It didn't take long for Cara to figure out that she was their dilemma.

Seeing their awkwardness, Khoury stepped forward and took Cara's gloved hand in his. "I'll entertain our guest, Maura. You two go…have fun." He winked broadly at Archer.

Maura was easily convinced and gave Cara's arm a brief squeeze as she joined the group of musicians with Archer. But Cara wasn't sure she wanted to be left alone with the brooding captain. He had an unsettling way of looking at her. Placing a light hand on her shoulder, he turned her toward the bonfire.

"I have just the seat for you," he murmured. She allowed him to guide her to where Bradan sat.

"Ah, Captain, Cara, come join us," Bradan said when he saw them.

"Thank you," Cara said as she perched on the bench next to Bradan. Khoury remained standing nearby.

"May I introduce my wife, Ealea," Bradan said, gesturing to the older woman.

"The spirits bless you, child." His wife's voice was gentle but vibrant. Her dark hair was streaked with gray and braided into multiple strands interwoven with leather and feathers. "You seem to be settling in well."

"Yes, Maura is very kind," Cara replied, not knowing what else to say.

Ealea smiled and turned back to the storyteller who was standing by the fire. Cara hadn't noticed him earlier. The foreign cadence of his speech was soothing and Cara listened intently to the story. She noted how Ealea's head dropped against Bradan's shoulder and such contentment wafted from the two of them, Cara could almost pretend she was sitting with her bears. Together, they listened to the stories and songs until late.

Cara didn't know exactly when Khoury slipped away but one moment he was there and the next he was gone. She shouldn't have felt slighted, but she did. By the time the bonfire had burned low and the villagers were heading home, Cara wanted nothing more than to find Gar and sleep. It had been an exhausting day. Bradan and Ealea escorted her to Maura's empty house where an extra cot had been set up. Cara told them she was fine there alone. But once they were out of sight, she slipped away down to the bear pens and Gar's furry company.

☙

Cara woke to the sweet scent of dew and the chirping of birds. Stretching in her straw nest next to Gar, she smiled. It had been nearly a week since they'd arrived at Bear Clan. Her nose, chin, and knuckles had completely healed. She continued to wear the gloves though spring had brought clear skies and mellow temperatures. She scrubbed Gar's shaggy head, trying not to notice how grizzled his fur was becoming, coarser, and thinning around his dark lips. Archer had said that Gar looked surprisingly young for his years. But he was definitely aging now, and Cara couldn't help but wonder if there had been something about the Keep that had kept them stagnant. Frozen. She even thought she could see a bit of age in her own face reflected in Maura's mirror.

Pushing the worries aside, she kissed Gar's head and stood, brushing a few tenacious bits of straw from her tunic. Then she tended the bears with a quick brushing, fresh water, and some fish from the nearby shed. The sun was just beginning to rise above the tall pines by the time she finished and headed to Maura's house.

The house was empty when she arrived, which was just how she liked it. She quickly changed into clean clothes, braided her messy hair, and set out for the village center. Since her arrival, Maura had worked tirelessly to help her fit into village life. But the thing Cara was most grateful for was her job. It felt good to be useful, and Cara loved working in the kitchens.

The village was just rousing as she passed through the creaky door. The kitchen occupied the back of the dining hall. It was a large, warm room with an enormous hearth at one end and a roasting pit at the other. The walls and shelves were hung with all manner of pots and pans and utensils. The other cooks hadn't arrived yet except, of course, for Ingrid the village herbalist. A kind woman with craggy cheeks and gray hair kinked with age sticking rebelliously out from her long thick plaits. She knew more about plants and tinctures and teas and potions than any book in Sidonius's library, and Cara was eager to learn it all—anyway she could.

"Good morning, Ingrid," she said, still feeling a bit awkward.

"Potatoes this morning, girl," Ingrid rasped, handing Cara a stiff brush and pointing to a full barrel in the corner. Cara already loved the old woman's gruffness, wry smile and sharp eyes that twinkled with secrets. Her hair was almost as white as Cara's.

"Okay." Cara fetched a bucket of water, tucked her gloves in her belt and perched on a stool in the corner where the potatoes waited. As she set to work with the brush, she found herself humming a tune she'd heard the night before and realized she was actually happy. What could be better than a toasty room, vegetables to cut, and the wise stories of aunts and mothers? She had learned a great deal, not only about food and medicine, but also about what passed between men and women. Frequently blushing, she found it hard not to think of the captain's piercing eyes as the women told their raunchy tales.

It was nearly mid-morning and the kitchens were full and bustling when the door screeched open. A woman rushed in, worry etched on her face. "Thomas is sick again," she blurted out, wringing her hands, breathless in the middle of the room. Work stopped as all heads turned to her. Cara's among them, her wet hands still holding the pot she'd been cleaning.

"He caught a fever in the night, Grandmother," the woman whined, craning her neck to find Ingrid, her pale face framed with disheveled russet curls.

Ingrid looked up from a stew pot hung over the fire and shuffled up to her. "Is he coughing, Siobhan?"

"Yes. Spitting blood."

"It's the lungs again." The gruff old woman shuffled to the pantry, tipping clay jars and poking around the shelves. "And I'm out of willow bark."

Siobhan wrung her hands in silence as Ingrid puttered with her jars. "I can brew a soothing tea for now. The willow tincture I'll make by nightfall." Ingrid tapped some dried herbs and flowers from her stock into two cups and pushed a pot of water over the fire's heat. "Have a seat," she gestured to the long workbench in the center of the room, "you look like you could use a bit of tea yourself, mother."

Cara remembered some of the cooks talking about Thomas. He had been born sickly and, though he had reached his eighth year, he had suffered three bouts of lung fever since winter began each one worse than the last. As the water warmed over the fire, Ingrid pulled Cara from the dish tub.

"Leave off washing, child. I need you to find me some willow bark. Do you know which tree it is?" Cara reached out a wet hand and touched Ingrid's arm. Images flooded her mind of drooping whip-like branches and red buds. She knew what the old woman needed and how to harvest it. Ingrid's eyes narrowed, but if she were upset about the intrusion, she never said.

"There's one beyond the bears, by the river," Cara said.

Ingrid nodded. "That's it. Bring me as much bark as you can, and some buds, too."

Cara nodded, swooped up a small reed basket, and headed out the door. Her new boots crunched in the shallow snow that still covered the shadiest parts of the forest. Following the river that flowed behind the bear pens, she reached the bend where a willow leaned far over the water, its branches trailing delicately along the glassy surface.

Cara laid her bare hand on the willow and felt a slight thrumming just at the edge of her awareness. The tree seemed very old, reminding her of a grandmother, reminding her of Ingrid.

Its bark peeled away from the thick trunk in large patches that she gently scraped into her basket wherever she could find it, remembering not to force the bark off. Looking in the small basket, the supply seemed rather pitiful. She closed her eyes and tried to remember Ingrid's memories. The dangling whip-like branches caught her attention as they dipped in the looking-glass river. She could take the ends with the rosy buds as well and peel the bark from the twigs when she returned to the kitchens. She started on the side farthest from the water but because of its leaning, most of what she needed hung in the river. Peering into the water, she saw some large stones just under the surface.

Stepping cautiously out onto the stones, Cara felt the flowing water seep through her boots, chilling her toes. She took a portion of twigs from the nearby branches, tossing them back to the shore to keep her hands free. She tempted fate by walking out a bit farther, and then farther still until her boot slipped and she toppled into the cold water with a splash.

CHAPTER 13
KHOURY

Khoury heard the splash before he saw her white head go under. It was a long moment before she surfaced. The stream was moving quickly, swollen from the spring thaw, and he knew from experience the placid-looking surface of the bend by the willow hid dangerously deep currents. The girl was either reckless or stupid. He watched as her head bobbed in the water, not high enough to get good air.

Damn it, she can't swim, he thought with irritation as he raced to the edge and slipped the wool cloak from his shoulders. In one fluid movement, he dove into the water, bracing himself against the shock of ice that pierced his bones. He loved to swim but not in early spring in the Northlands. With practiced strokes, he reached her quickly, fighting the cramping of his muscles against the cold. Grasping her bodice, he propped her on his shoulder, face out of the water, and dragged her toward the shore. She coughed against him, violently expelling water from her lungs. By the time he dragged her out of the water and stood her next to him, she was breathing hard but not coughing anymore. Shaking, water dripping down her face, she stared up at him in surprise as his arms drew her closer to his body for warmth.

"Are you all right?" he asked, trying to quell his own shivering.

She nodded, but he could feel the hammering of her heart, its pounding shuddered through her whole body.

"You sure?"

"Y-y-yes," she chattered.

"Good. Then what the blazes were you doing out there?" His voice came out harsher than he intended.

She pulled back from him, shy of his anger, hands splayed on his wet shirt. "Getting willow for Ingrid."

"Willow for Ingrid," he mimicked. "You're damn lucky I was here." He led her to where his woolen cloak lay crumpled in the brush, still dry and warm from his body. Lifting it, he wrapped it around her shivering frame. She snuggled her nose in the furred collar. He rubbed her arms vigorously to warm her up, using the activity to warm himself. He shook his head and felt a strange urge to smile.

"What?" she asked defensively, her lower lip still a bit blue and sticking out petulantly.

"You," he murmured. His need to keep her in sight still puzzled him but when he'd seen her leave for the woods, he'd followed her. And a good thing it was, too.

"What does that mean?" She snuggled deeper into the cloak, her eyes wide and moist.

"You just," he paused to look at her, "have a knack for getting in trouble." *And dragging me after you,* he thought. Bradan's comment about magic calling magic rolled around in his head. Was that why he'd had to follow her, or was she just young and pretty? She had a pleasant face, certainly, with large eyes, though pale, and long lashes. Her cheekbones were thin, her lips soft, but nothing special really. He couldn't fathom why she drew him so strongly, but even now, he could feel the pull. It was like standing with his feet in the ocean's outgoing tide.

"Thank you," she said quietly.

He shook his head dismissively.

"No, really. I don't know what I'd do without you, Captain."

He wasn't sure what to say, wasn't sure what he wanted. The intensity of her gaze drew him in, and his arms slipped around her small frame of their own accord. He tried to decide again if this was simply the call of magic blood or something else, something deeper.

When her eyes flickered to his mouth, he realized she felt the pull, too. It wasn't just him. The curious longing blossomed into desire and he lowered his mouth to hers, quickly before good sense got the better of him, pressing her lips with his, their breath mingling.

Khoury didn't have time to decide if her lips were soft or her breath sweet because with that kiss a buried memory burst upon his mind. A beautiful woman danced, spinning within a cloud of chestnut hair, laughing. He remembered that laugh. How he had loved it—that cherished sound shattered him with grief. The bittersweet memory froze the breath in his chest, suffocating him. Stung, he shoved Cara away from him and staggered back a step.

"Sorry," he muttered, turning to face the water with hands clenched and a tight knot of despair squeezing the core of him.

"Why?"

Her innocence aggravated the raw emotions that seethed in him. He needed distance from her softness and time to compose himself, to shove the memory back where it belonged—in the past. "It was wrong."

"Wrong?" He heard her disappointment.

"It's cold and we're wet," he snapped. "And you are…" He turned to see her wide doe-eyes staring at him. "Very young." Khoury picked up her basket of bark near the tree.

"Not that young," she murmured almost under her breath. "Boys kiss younger girls than me here."

He turned, startled. "How do you know that?"

"I've seen them. Down by the river, near the bear pens."

He wondered what else she had seen and then decided he didn't want to know. "I'm no boy and you're too young in experience if not in years. We should go."

"I still need more twigs." She pointed to the ends of the branches that swayed over the water.

"Is that what you were doing out there?" He picked up a long branch that had fallen nearby and used it to pull the wispy branches closer to shore. Chagrined, the girl retrieved enough to fill her basket.

"Enough?" he asked.

She nodded.

"Then come on," he commanded, taking the basket and striding down the path without a backward glance. They made the trip back in silence.

When they reached the edge of the village center, she took the basket from him. "Thanks for fishing me out of the river," she said stiffly.

He dipped his head, not trusting his voice. The memory had faded for now but he felt it, waiting in the back of his mind to haunt him. Through sheer willpower, he kept his face placid despite the ache in his heart. He waited, letting her take the path to the kitchens alone.

When the memories came wrapped up in sorrow, the rage was never far behind. And that rage would consume all of the Mason Khoury she thought she knew, leaving behind only a selfish monster. He needed to stay away from Cara. In fact, he decided it was time to leave the warm welcome of Bear Clan.

CHAPTER 14
CARA

When Cara reached the kitchens, Ingrid eyed her soaked clothes and borrowed cloak with amusement. She took the basket from Cara's dripping hands. "Decided it was a good day for a swim?"

"No," Cara grumbled, "I fell in."

Ingrid laughed out loud. "Go home and get dry, clumsy girl."

"I'll be right back to strip the bark," she offered.

"No, no. You go change and then find Bradan. He was asking for you."

Cara was about to open her mouth to argue that the willow bark needed to be done first, but Ingrid put the basket next to three women sitting at the long center table. They immediately set to stripping the bark and collecting the buds, as Ingrid waved Cara out the door.

Feeling dismissed, both by Ingrid and by Khoury, Cara ducked out of the kitchens and headed to Maura's house to change, her boots squishing. Once inside the door, she dropped the cloak on a chair and stood frozen for a moment, resisting the urge to press it to her nose and inhale Khoury's scent again. Her mind swirled in confusion. It happened so suddenly, the fall, the rescue, that kiss. Cara hadn't known she wanted him to kiss her until his lips were against hers. And when he did a dark-haired woman flashed through her mind like a ghost.

She raised her fingers to her lips. Something else had flared inside her, too, with that brief contact. She didn't understand any of it: his anger, the ghost, or her own heart. Shaking off her confusion, she stripped off her wet things, hung them by the fire, and changed into dry clothes. She left Khoury's cloak where it lay draped over the chair. *If he wants it back, he'll have to come get it,* she thought petulantly.

A warm fire was burning in Bradan's hearth when she arrived and the grizzled chieftain was sitting cross-legged, eyes closed.

"You wanted to see me?" She took a step farther into the room.

Bradan didn't stir. He seemed to be sleeping, sitting upright. Not sure what to do, Cara waited and wandered the room, fascinated by his collection of clutter. She cringed at the bear's foot, claws and all, that hung in a circular web of leather, tied with feathers and colored stone beads. Bits of nature adorned every surface from the rafters, where herbs and roots hung drying, to the floor covered with furs from creatures Cara didn't recognize, even from her books in the Keep's library.

With a sudden deep breath, the old man's eyes fluttered open. "There you are. Did you have a nice swim?"

"How'd you know about that?"

He laughed. "I have my ways. Come, sit by me." Cara walked over and sat on the woven mat he indicated. He didn't speak for a long moment as she basked in the fire's warmth. "Do you know what I am?" he asked finally.

"You're the village leader."

"Not who. What."

"You're a sorcerer," she said, hazarding a wild guess. Did she need to fear him, too?

"No," he said, chuckling. "I don't do sorcery."

She gave him a confused look. "But you do magic?"

"There are many types of magic. Sorcery changes what is, destroying life even as it transforms it. What I do is different. I'm a translator."

"I don't understand."

"I communicate between our world and the Otherworld. We are surrounded by spirits." He gestured all around them, and Cara felt the hairs on her neck stand on end. "They exist in the Otherworld and, even though they are close, most people can't see them. I talk to them like you talk to the bears."

Cara nodded. "Ingrid talks about spirits in the trees sometimes." The old woman hadn't actually *said* that, but Cara had picked it up from touching her.

"Exactly, but those are not the spirits I talk to. I talk to ancestors, those who went before us."

She wondered if she had any ancestors and what they might say about her. "So you and Ingrid both talk to spirits."

"Ingrid doesn't talk to them. It's more that she can sense the nature of things. She can't ask them what happened to you."

"Nothing happened to me," Cara said. *Nothing except meeting Archer and the captain.*

"The spirits tell me your soul is injured."

Cara was suddenly frightened. "There's nothing wrong with me," she protested.

"Nothing is *wrong* with you. But the spirits tell me something is missing."

"I thought you said you didn't know what was wrong?"

"I don't because I don't know what's missing."

"How would I know?"

"Sometimes when bad things happen, a person might abandon a part of their soul, the piece that causes them pain."

Cara didn't understand how one would go about hiding a piece of their soul. It wasn't like tucking an extra roll in your sleeve to save it for later.

"They might leave it behind or hide it in a safer place," he continued.

"The forest." The words slipped out like a spilled secret.

"Forest?"

"When I was at the Keep, I could close my eyes and go to a forest. Like a dream in my mind."

"You were sleeping when you saw it?"

"No, I was…unhappy." Cara hesitated, not knowing how much she should tell Bradan about the sorcerer's need of her.

"Was it somewhere you'd visited?"

"Before Khoury and Archer, I'd never been outside the Keep."

Bradan asked gently, "Can you tell me why you were unhappy?"

She swallowed hard, thinking back to the round room and the altar. The scent of dust and magic pressed on her, draining the light from Bradan's hearth. "Sidonius wanted—no needed—something from me. He took it whenever he pleased." Cara lacked the words to explain how she had felt: helpless, empty, insignificant. Memories came back, things she hadn't thought about since they'd arrived: Reith Carter begging for his life or the disembodied arm in the main hall. Sadness drained her. She just wanted to go to the kitchens, get warm, and listen to the women gossip. "Actually, Bradan, I don't want to talk about this." She stood up to leave.

"Cara, you finally said no to him. You saved not only Khoury and Archer but those other men, too. Isn't that enough?"

She remained silent, knowing in her heart nothing could erase the guilt she felt.

"I can help you find whatever this piece is that you're searching for," he said.

Am I searching for something? she wondered. She didn't think she was. Except maybe a place to call home. She sighed and rubbed the tiredness from her eyes. "What I really want is to forget the Keep." *And the dust and the fire and the death.* "Can you give me that?"

"I doubt it. But I can help make you whole again." Confidence radiated from him.

She wanted to say that she was whole, except that would be a lie. Certainly she was happier than she'd ever been. But hidden deep inside her, she knew something was missing. Hadn't she always known she was broken?

"How?"

"Come tonight at moonrise."

The familiar-sounding words drained the blood from her face. Suspicion flared as she stared at him, but the shaman had resumed his trance. She left him murmuring in front of his fire. Stunned, she retreated to the kitchens hoping the work would soothe her nerves.

Dinner preparations were in full swing when she arrived and Vanessa, a large, ruddy woman who was in charge of the dining room, set her to work delivering platters of food to the crowded tables. She happily accepted; glad to have something to occupy her bewildered mind.

She saw Archer and the captain sitting together near the door and she hurried to bring them drinks, eager to chat. Her lips still held the ghost of Khoury's kiss, and even the memory of it roused a tingling heat in her body.

Before Cara could get to them, a woman with short chestnut hair sashayed in and slipped a possessive arm around Khoury's neck. When he looked up at her, she kissed the lips Cara had just been daydreaming about with more passion than Cara thought appropriate. Stopping in the middle of the dining room, Cara stared at them stupidly as the woman slid onto in his lap and joined the conversation.

Maura was helping tonight as well and, being closer, she served Archer, Khoury, and the strange new woman, laughing as Archer joked and flirted. Khoury leaned close to the woman's neck and whispered something; a hungry grin bloomed on her lips.

"Hey, Cara!" shouted a man behind her. "Are you giving those out or saving them for yourself?"

Shaken from her stupor, she delivered the food to the nearby tables. She couldn't help staring at Khoury and the other woman. Her crimson tunic was low cut and accentuated every female curve. The woman radiated a primal sensuality that Cara couldn't begin to comprehend, but it reminded her of the heady volatility of Khoury's kiss.

As Maura walked by to get more drinks from the kitchen, Cara put a hand on her arm. "Who is that woman with Khoury?"

Maura turned to look and her brown eyes became guarded. "That's Nalia," she hesitated. "She and Khoury spent a lot of time together the last time he was here."

Cara's mouth made an "O" shape as she remembered the dark-haired ghost. Was this Nalia the woman Khoury cherished? The hair was shorter, but Cara couldn't tell if the face was the same.

She felt Maura's gentle hand on her shoulder, guiding her away from them, back toward the kitchen. "I know you don't have much experience with men. And you've never had a mother to tell you how things go."

There it was again—something missing. She was missing a mother. Perhaps that was what Bradan needed to find, her mother. She let Maura guide her to the relative privacy of the kitchen.

"And I know you're quite taken with Khoury."

"Meaning?" Cara asked.

"You like him but he's…"

"With her."

Maura relaxed at Cara's apparent understanding. "Yes."

Cara felt an ugly emotion spread across her chest and shoulders. Khoury and that woman belonged together; like Maura and Archer.

"So he loves her," Cara said, haltingly.

"Well, I'm not so sure I'd go that far."

Then why did he kiss me? The thick bitter taste of shame glued her tongue to the top of her mouth. Cara turned her face from Maura hoping to hide the heat rising to her cheeks.

"Will he marry her then?" Cara asked, trying to understand his contradictory behavior.

"Ha," Maura scoffed. "Khoury is not the marrying type."

"I see," Cara said, although she didn't. "So, I should leave him alone?"

"Yes," Maura said, obviously relieved. Cara took her serving tray and started back toward the dining area.

As she served baskets of warm dark bread, the sound of laughter, sharp and wicked, pierced her ear. She searched the room for its source and was surprised that it belonged to Khoury's companion. That wasn't the laugh of the woman from his kiss. The wrongness of it all itched beneath Cara's skin, needing to be scratched.

She placed her serving tray down on the nearest table and turned to where they all sat.

"Where are you going?" Maura asked, coming up behind her. "You don't want to make a scene."

Cara didn't answer though she felt Maura trailing her as she went to the table where the two mercenaries sat. Archer was the first to notice her.

"Cara! Done working already?"

"Yes, I think so." She forced a smile at him.

"There's my girl," he said, reaching around Cara to draw Maura closer.

Maura reached out a restraining hand to Cara, begging with her eyes for Cara to relent. Pulling out of Maura's grasp, she stood opposite Khoury and stared at him.

"Am I missing something?" Archer looked from Cara to Khoury, feeling the tension in the air.

At first, Khoury refused to meet her glare, drinking his ale with focused intent and casual slowness. Finally, he lifted eyes that were cold with indolent disdain. The closed insolence stung Cara and, out of the corner of her eye, she noted Nalia's scornful glare. The woman's shift had slipped down, exposing one creamy shoulder, and the arm around Khoury's neck tightened. The silence lengthened as Khoury tried to wait Cara out, implacable as stone and about as warm.

Uncomfortable in the silence, Archer was the first to speak. "Did I miss something?"

"No," Khoury murmured but his eyes never left Cara's.

Fatigue and anger steeled her voice. "I didn't know what you meant before. But now I see. You've found someone who is *old* enough for you."

Nalia's eyes flashed at the insult. "There's a difference between years and experience, girl."

"And apparently you have plenty of both," Cara retorted, surprising herself. The smile Archer hid in his ale gave her angry satisfaction. She turned back to Khoury. "You have what you really wanted now. Don't follow me anymore. I don't want your help." She turned to leave.

"You're not staying for stories?" Archer asked. "I had a good one lined up for tonight."

"No," Cara said. "I've had enough for one day." She squared her shoulders and left with as much dignity as she could muster, the squeezing in her chest making it hard to breathe.

"Poor girl," she heard Nalia behind her. "So young, just a child really."

Child? The word turned in her brain. She was a woman of at least twenty turns of the calendar, maybe more, though she couldn't be sure. *Why does everyone think I'm a child?*

The night air was chill against Cara's scowl as she strode out angrily. She gazed up into the sky and noted that the moon had already risen. Her stomach rumbled but, heartbroken, she couldn't bear to go back into the hall to eat. She stomped through the warming snow all the way to Bradan's.

Ealea sat on a small mat outside Bradan's tent. She was humming near a small pit fire and, before Cara could speak, she motioned her toward the hide tent that stood a little behind Bradan's hut. Maura had told Cara it was for special occasions.

The hair on Cara's neck stood up as she slipped into the dark, musky space that reminded her of somewhere underground. A spicy scent rose from a brazier, tickling her nose, and furs were spread on the floor. Bradan seemed trustworthy but the combination of men and magic worried her.

"Come in."

She looked around and found the chieftain sitting in a darkened corner, his eyes glazed and a cup in his hands. She came close, sitting on the furs at his feet. Her anger at Khoury's rejection was still fresh in her mind and part of her hoped Bradan could change her enough for Khoury to notice her.

"My spirit guides tell me you need my help. Come, drink with me," he said, holding out the cup.

"What is it?"

"Like one of Ingrid's teas. A potion, if you will." When he handed her the cup, she sniffed, making a face at its potent, noxious aroma. "Come, child, you can trust me."

"I'm not a child," she said, though her petulance was unconvincing.

He chuckled at her frustration and placed a hand on her head. A calming balm spread from his touch, and she felt her tension begin to unwind.

"Not by years, no. But you have a child's ways about you."

"That's what Khoury says, and Maura, and everyone else." She let go of another breath, releasing more of the angry tension she was carrying. A single tear escaped. *They're right about me. I don't know anything. Nothing in the Keep prepared me for any of this.*

The old man leaned closer to her, and she could smell the sharp bitter pungency of his breath. "I sense the spirit world close to you. It follows you about. There is something they want you to remember."

What could I possibly remember?

"You have power in the spirit world. Even you should know that by now."

Cara suspected the man was a bit drunk, and it made her feel more uneasy.

"I want you to journey with me when I go to find your lost piece of soul. You'll be safe with me," he assured her.

Before Cara could ask what journey he was talking about, Ealea came in holding a drum of stretched leather. She sat down opposite them. Her quiet serenity soothed Cara's nerves. If Ealea was here, she had nothing to fear.

"Drink," he urged. "It's the only way to let your spirit travel without your body."

Cara wanted to tell him that she already could do that, but her recent hurt feelings and frustration kept her tongue-tied.

"Drink. It's the only way to leave the child behind."

Goaded into action, Cara picked up the cup defiantly and drank the oily liquid in one gulp. Its bitterness coated her mouth, and her empty stomach rebelled.

Bradan told her to lie down on her back on the blanket and then laid himself on his back next to her, only their hips and shoulders touched. As soon as he was settled, Ealea began to drum softly. The beat was steady and incessant, like a heartbeat. Cara's head felt light from hunger and the noxious tea. Her eyelids drooped. She heard Bradan speaking to her but couldn't make out the words, and then she was falling. Like those evenings lying on the dusty altar, light and shadow whizzed past her mind's eye. She could smell the dust now, feel it coating her hands, her hair, her mouth. The ground dropped out from beneath her.

The forest of her dreams sprang to life around her. Ealea's distant drumming echoed through the trees. A small breeze lifted her hair, and the damp earth squished beneath her boots. A shimmering image of Bradan walked toward her out of the forest. His left hand rested on the back of an enormous brown bear, the guardian spirit of the Bear Clan.

Bradan pointed at her throat with a questioning look. She looked down and noted the pale blue glow emanating from her amulet. Forgotten since the day of the storm, she wondered in earnest at its true significance. Then Bradan asked his guides to show him where her lost soul was.

In answer, a wolf howled in the distance calling a ferocious wind that roared past her, twirling the world around her, spinning her into a new part of the forest. Bradan and the guardian were gone. She found herself on tiptoes, tense, waiting. She tasted salty sweat on her lips and felt the bowstring tautness of her muscles. Listening. She was listening for danger, and it was near. Then a dark shape flung itself at her.

To Cara's amazement, she didn't cry out in fear, but met its onslaught with confidence. She sidestepped and leapt up on a stump, turning lithely to face her adversary. She held a knife in her right hand, its weight balanced in her palm. It felt right there, waiting for action.

A small bag of skin hung around her neck and thumped her chest when she moved. Somehow, she knew it contained charms: A rough amethyst from the deep cave in the south, the feather of a rare hawk she had tracked for days, and the tooth of a wolf that had died over the winter.

The dark form slunk around her in a circle, losing itself in the shadows made by the moon overhead. Crouching down, she kept the knife out of sight. With a snarl, it leapt at her again and she spun out of the way with grace, slicing with her knife as the predator hurtled past her. The creature yowled in pain. When it turned to approach her again, she could see the outline of a large hunting cat and the moonlight showed her the dark smear that creased its shoulder. Instead of fear, the sight of the snarling feline gave her the incomprehensible urge to chuckle.

When it attacked again, the cat landed square on her, throwing her from the stump onto her back. Its claws bit into her shoulder and belly. But her knife found its way to the beast's throat and the creature gurgled. Pinned under its weight, she felt its lifeblood spilling over her hand and chest, bathing her in its ebbing warmth. The battle was over.

Her lips were drawn up in a snarl as she muscled herself out from under the now-limp carcass and wiped her knife on the shaggy pelt. Then she lifted her chin and howled at the moon. A chorus of wolves echoed her throaty cry. She grinned with unfamiliar ferocity.

But then, Bradan's bear appeared. She felt a pulling sensation, her head spun, and the forest vanished.

…to be replaced by Bradan's tent. Ealea was drumming a different rhythm now, strident and demanding, and her husband was no longer next to Cara but hovered over her, his face a worried mask.

"Cara, are you all right?" He shook her by the shoulders as if trying to awaken her. She cried out in pain and the drumming stopped.

"Borran's blood, you're all right." He scooped her up into his arms and held her tightly like a found child. The remnants of the dream began to fade, and the pain in her shoulder and belly flared. Cara pulled away to touch her left shoulder. Her hand came away bloody.

"I'm bleeding," she cried. Panic tinged her voice and she panted, confused.

"You are a dreamwalker, Cara of the Black Keep," Bradan said in awe. "I don't know where you went, but I couldn't follow you. I sent Borran; did you see him?"

"Yes." Cara's head felt fuzzy, and she felt sick. "I saw the bear and then suddenly I was back here. What happened?"

"Do you remember anything?" Bradan sat her up against a chair as Ealea brought a bowl of warm water with a cloth. "Try to think. How did you get these wounds?"

"What did you do to me?" Hysteria rose in her fuzzy mind. *Was that a dream? Or was that real?* She tried to speak, but her tongue refused to function. Her eyes refused to remain open as she fainted into a deep sleep.

CHAPTER 15
KHOURY

Lost in a tangle of blankets, Khoury could almost convince himself he was alone. Nalia lay sleeping nearby but only her mussed hair was visible from his vantage point. Guilt stabbed at him for treading so roughly on Cara's feelings. He shouldn't have kissed her in the first place, but it would have been crueler to let her assume it meant more than it did. He comforted himself with the notion that she was inexperienced and her attachment just a crush. Nalia, on the other hand, offered him a much-needed release without concern. He knew as well as any man in the village that she gave everything but her heart.

He had lingered in the hall for a few more drinks to make sure the girl would be long gone before he left with Nalia. Once they'd arrived back at her hearth, he gave himself over to those primitive urges he blamed for his misstep with Cara. What began as heated kisses soon turned to a passion that seared the memory of feminine laughter from his mind. Nalia was every bit the rousing bed partner he remembered, and in the press of willing flesh and primal rhythms, Cara and his memories were forgotten.

But Khoury woke in the deep of night from a nightmare that left him full of dread and searching for his blade. In his dream, Cara was lost and fighting for her life. The protective urge swelled, waking him with the almost irresistible urge to cross the village and make sure she was safe. But he didn't. He stayed under the blankets, frozen between the need to find her and the desire to be free of her.

This is silly, he chided himself. *She's probably with Gar.* No harm could come to her there but the dread lingered.

The furs were clenched in his hand, reminding him that he was weaponless. He'd liked his previous swords. Good weapons, well-balanced and sharp, but they'd been taken when he was captured in Telsedan. He was shocked that he'd been in Bear Clan a whole week and still hadn't replaced them. It wasn't like him to be so complacent, and he cursed himself for ignoring the possibility of pursuit. He wasn't usually so sloppy. In the morning, he'd visit the smithy and get a couple of blades for himself. And one for Archer. He needed a good sparring match. His unsettled mood was eager for battle, even a mock one.

His mind chattered on as he lay there, ruining any chance of sleep. He needed to get back to work. Work always settled his pains. Sitting still had never been good for him, physically or mentally. He'd been gone almost a month now: Nearly three weeks in the Keep and one more week here. Traveling south would take them a few more days without horses, and he could only hope he hadn't lost his best men to another captain.

But there was nothing to be done about that right now and since rest was impossible, Khoury rolled over to Nalia and woke her with gentle hands on her curves and kisses in her hollows. As usual, she awoke with an eager smile for him. But even as her legs wrapped around his hips, haunting laughter bubbled in the corners of his mind.

CHAPTER 16
CARA

The sounds of the day pierced Cara's awareness, clearing away the misty sensation in her head. Someone was moving around close by, but she couldn't focus. Her tongue felt as dry as shoe leather, and her body ached. Still groggy, she groaned and sat up to find she was naked.

"Ah, you're awake." The voice behind her sounded relieved.

She clasped the blanket to her chest and craned her head around to find Bradan puttering about the hide tent where she'd met him. *Was it only last night?* The details were still muddied in her mind.

"Do you remember the forest now?" he asked.

The shocking deluge of memories disoriented her and waves of nausea crashed against her throat. Unprepared, she could do little but lean over before she vomited on the floor. Breathing heavily through her mouth, she fought to keep from passing out again.

"Breathe easy." Bradan rushed to circle her with a strong arm, leaning her head on his chest. He caressed her face with a damp cloth, bringing back some semblance of balance. Ealea came in and, with a motherly glance at the mess, took the soiled fur outside for cleaning.

"I'm sorry," Cara mumbled, embarrassed.

"Hush. You've been through a lot," Bradan said softly.

"The journey. The fight. Where did you take me last night?"

"We never left this tent."

Cara's hand went to her shoulder and felt the bandage. "But this."

"That is something out of legend. What do you remember?" He settled in next to her and waited.

She tried to straighten the disjointed images in her head. "You asked to be shown my soul and a wind came, like a storm."

"I remember."

"It took me somewhere. It was night. I was hunting." Her mind rebelled at the idea.

"Hunting?"

"Yes. An animal, like a big cat." Darting shadows and moonlight flitted through her mind, unsettling her belly again. She shied away from the memories. "I don't really want to talk about this."

"You know how to hunt?"

"No. It wasn't me."

"What do you mean?"

"It was like a dream and I was someone else. My clothes were different. Somehow, I knew how to fight. The knife felt…good in my hand." She shuddered, disgusted with herself. *More death. Always more death.*

"And then?"

Cara's throat felt suddenly thick as she remembered the cat leaping and the pain. "It attacked." She remembered her knife slipping into the animal's throat and the warm blood running over her arm making her jubilant. Her hand went to her shoulder even as she hated herself for howling in victory.

Bradan whistled in amazement. "I've heard stories of dreamwalkers. Shaman so powerful they transport their bodies elsewhere. But Ealea said you didn't leave; the wounds just appeared."

"I'm not powerful," she whispered. Hadn't years of helplessness proved that?

"Oh, but you are."

Cara wasn't ready to take his word for it and let the matter drop.

"Did you find my missing piece?"

Bradan shook his head. "No. But something is definitely going on." Discouraged, she looked up with a frown. He smiled. "Don't worry. We'll figure it out. Those wounds are minor. Get dressed. Eat something. You'll feel better by afternoon."

Bradan stood up and handed her the clothes she'd worn the night before. Then he ducked out of the tent. Grateful for the privacy, she dressed, pulled on her gloves, and then ventured out to where Ealea crouched over a pot of what smelled like stew. Bradan whispered something to his wife and then, kissing her, left for the village.

"Here you go," said Ealea in her dulcet voice. She handed Cara a small bowl and spoon, pointing to a mat near the fire. "I'll fetch you some fresh water." Lifting a bucket, she walked off toward the river.

Cara sat on the mat in the soothing silence and stared absently at the bowl in her lap. The stew smelled good, and she lifted a tentative spoonful to her lips. It proved to be as hearty as it smelled and after a few slurps, she felt better. She nibbled the vegetables while running through the dream in her mind. It wasn't like any other dream she could recall. The details were so vivid, the smells, the sounds. They felt more like memories. She could almost believe that she had killed the beast with her own hands.

And I have the scratches to prove it. A strange feeling of power filled her and she rested cross-legged, eyes closed, her face lifted to the sun until Ealea returned.

"Here's the water. Would you like more stew?"

"Thank you, but no." She took a deep breath of the cool morning air. "I feel good. If you want me, I'll be at the kitchens."

"A return to routine is always good medicine," she said, nodding.

Cara stood and left Bradan's home, but her feet automatically turned toward the bear pens rather than the kitchens. Others would have tended her bears for her, but they were her family. Caring for them had been her job every morning for as long as she could remember. Gar was waiting for her at the gate. She fed them and brushed them and scratched each bear's itchy spots, lingering in the contentment she always felt with them. As the sun climbed higher, she reluctantly left for the kitchens stopping by Maura's hut to change clothes.

While there, she removed the bandages and inspected her wounds. Three scabbed tears ran over the front of her shoulder and four ran down the left side of her belly. Bradan was right, the cuts weren't deep. Her shoulder ached a little but it was nothing that would keep her from working with Ingrid. Feeling strangely buoyant, she took extra care with her appearance, choosing a pale blue shift that matched her amulet with a dark blue over tunic embroidered with delicate images of doves about the neckline. She brushed her hair until it gleamed, braiding her luminous mane into a thick cord, and tied it off with a dark blue ribbon. Satisfied, Cara left to find Ingrid and tell her all about what had happened.

The kitchen was bustling, even more so than usual, and Cara joined the round of activity with uncharacteristic ease. Archer and some of the other men had gone out hunting and had returned shortly before with two elk. The meat needed to be cured and stored, and Cara was so busy she didn't get a chance to speak with Ingrid before midafternoon.

During a lull, Cara steeped a small pot of chamomile tea and brought it and a cup to where the old woman rested before the fire. Setting the cup down on a nearby stool, she smiled at Ingrid.

"A lovely child you are," Ingrid said. She was pale, her eyes bloodshot.

"You looked like you could use it." Cara pulled a small afghan from near the hearth and laid it over Ingrid's legs. So much of the day had passed already, the urge to tell Ingrid about the journey had faded. Cara just sat staring into the fire, sharing a quiet moment in their busy day. "I meant to ask you, how is the little boy?"

"Thomas?"

"Did the tea help him?"

"Not enough. I was up with him through most of the night. The fever has him tightly. I don't think I'll be able to save him this time."

The brightness drained out of Cara's day. "You mean he'll die?"

The crone put a hand on Cara's sleek hair. "Sometimes even the best of us fail. Who can tell what is truly meant to be?"

"Meant to be," Cara echoed, remembering Archer's words in the Keep.

"No life lasts forever," the old woman sighed, sipping the hot tea. "You must be wise enough to know when nature should take its own course."

In her heart, Cara couldn't accept that. Death was the enemy. As she sat, staring into the fire, the years of feeling helpless welled up inside her. Whatever power had buoyed her through the day faded beneath the weight of those memories.

"Taking a rest, ladies?" The voice pulled Cara from her brooding. Bradan walked over and pulled up a chair, sitting on the other side of Cara from Ingrid. "Cara, I've been thinking over what we talked about this morning. How much do you know about the history of magic?"

"Nothing really." Again, she was daunted by how little she really knew about the world everyone else lived in.

"Those who have power like Sidonius are born with it. You cannot acquire it any other way."

Ingrid straightened in her chair, her eyes intently on Bradan, but she said nothing.

"Which means one or both of your parents had power," he said.

"Does that mean Sidonius really is—"

"Your father? No, but there must be power in your family somewhere."

A strange look passed between him and the herbalist, and Cara thought she saw the old woman nod.

"We believe that all powers originally came from the Far Isles," Bradan said. "Relations between men and women are forbidden but new apprentices are young and often hot-blooded. They wait upon their masters, the Magi who serve crowns across the continent. Undoubtedly these young lads would have found themselves the object of interest, being forbidden fruit, as it were."

Cara didn't understand what he meant exactly but refused to pursue that line of thought. "Then is your power also from forbidden fruit?"

He shifted uncomfortably.

Ingrid cleared her throat and answered for him. "Not directly. No Islander has ever come here. But the Clans travel great distances to trade for goods. Dowries of trade rights are commonplace and make solid alliances. We believe that Far Isle half-bloods have married into the Clans, giving us our talented bloodlines as well."

"Over time these powers could have become more commonplace," Bradan explained. "But generally they show up in nobility. The backlash of its misuse led to the violence of the Tangoran raids," Bradan continued as if Cara knew the history he spoke of, "driving us farther north and into isolation to preserve our way of life. No more marriage alliances were permitted. This isolation, however, has caused talent to run thin. I am one of the few with power left in the North," Bradan admitted as if it were something to be ashamed of.

Only a few Northerners had power? From what she had seen, their powers were nothing compared to what Father could do. She looked back and forth between Ingrid and Bradan, sensing something unseen. Then, she noticed a resemblance she hadn't before. "How many more are there, besides you two?"

Ingrid sighed. "Only two others. One in Seal Bay and the other in Eagle Falls."

Only two? Which meant Sidonius's magic was rare as well as strong. "And what does all this have to do with me?" Cara asked.

"If you have power, and after last night there can be no doubt…" Bradan said, pausing.

"Then you must come from one of these noble bloodlines," Ingrid finished, her piercing eyes resting on Cara.

"You're saying I have royal blood?"

"Yes," Bradan said.

Cara laughed. "No, that can't be right. I'm nobody."

"I'm sure that's exactly what Sidonius wanted you to think. Your heritage may be the reason the spirits are interested in you. Then again, maybe not. It's hard to say. Still, we can arrange for you to go south to search for your real parents if you want. But I warn you, you might not like what you find."

Cara stared at him, trying to digest what he was saying.

Bradan stood. "You don't need to decide right now. But I believe you're far more important than you've been led to believe, and in such situations, ignorance is dangerous." He strode out of the kitchen, leaving Cara shocked and wondering.

"What did he mean: I might not like what I find?"

Ingrid finished her tea and set the cup down. "Not all nations are honorable. Better to be orphaned than be from the bloody mountains of Barakan. Dunhadrar, we call them. Brother-slayers."

"Brother-slayers?" Cara didn't like the sound of that. "Why?"

"There are no ties the Dunhadrar respect in their search for power, not even those of blood."

"Why would he think I'm one of them?"

"He doesn't, but each familial line has only one type of talent. If Maura develops any magic, it would be talking to the spirits. Barakan nobles wield mind magic." Again, Ingrid's eyes seemed to see through to Cara's very soul. "The power to command others is very seductive."

Cara looked away. A guilty stone lay heavy in her belly. Thought-reading didn't necessarily make her a Dunhadrar, did it?

"I don't really know what power I have," she said defensively. "Bradan said I might be a dreamwalker."

"Your skills are ambiguous then, which is itself unusual." Ingrid's expression softened. "You have a good heart, child. Trust in that."

But in the silence, Cara's mind whirled with self-loathing. As if thinking Sidonius was her father wasn't bad enough, now she might be from a royal line of murderers. "Ingrid, what would you do? About finding out…"

"Where you're from?"

Cara nodded.

"Nothing," the old woman said gruffly. "Decide who you want to be and be that. Bloodlines and power be damned."

Then Ingrid took a deep breath and pushed to standing. "It's time we got back to work, girl. There's gathering to be done." She held out her hand for Cara to touch.

Cara hesitated, wondering if her power condemned her in Ingrid's eyes.

The old woman smiled reassuringly. "I'm weary of talk. Take my hand, and let me show you want I want. And no swimming this time, you hear?"

Cara smiled and did as she was asked. She spent the rest of the warm afternoon wandering the forest in search of the plants Ingrid had shown her: Arrowroot and savory and rosemary, wild onions and cabbage. On the way back, she noticed a group of young men gathered near the smithy. Shouts echoed through the fading light and the occasional clang of steel. She was curious but her sacks were full to bursting and she was late, so she didn't stop. If it was important, she was sure she'd hear about it during the dinner hour.

At dinner, Maura had taken the night off and was sitting with Archer. But unlike previous nights, when Cara would see them laughing, Archer was unusually serious and a bandage covered most of his left hand. She would have gone over to visit with them but Nalia was there, apparently waiting for Khoury. Cara decided she'd ask Maura about Archer before going to the bear pens for the night.

The hall was busier than usual or maybe the villagers were just restless, but Cara spent most of her time dodging bodies and trying to avoid spills. So it was inevitable that she would run into Khoury. Literally. Luckily, the four ales on her tray only sloshed, but the sharp jolt to her shoulder made her gasp.

Khoury froze at the sound. "Are you all right?" he asked. Strong hands wrapped around her biceps, steadying her.

"I'm fine." She pulled away from him still angry about the night before. But out of courtesy she schooled her features into a pleasant mask. He silently took the tray, allowing her a moment to wipe the ale from her arms with the towel that hung from her belt.

He must have recently bathed as the scent of soap wafted off him. His dark hair, that had lengthened since she first met him, curled wetly over his collar, and his beard was thick and dark. He waited, watching her with unreadable eyes.

"Thank you," she said, taking the tray back, balancing it on one hand and offering him an ale with the other. She decided not to mention the night before, either Nalia or her journey with Bradan, mainly because there was nothing to be said. As he took the ale from her, she noticed cuts on his hands, fresh and bright red.

"You're looking well this evening," he said, drawing her attention away from his hands and putting her on her guard.

"Nalia is waiting for you," she said coldly. He seemed about to say something, a retort perhaps, but then tilted his head in farewell and left, disappearing into the raucous crowd of young men who all chattered at him at once.

There was a bonfire that night, and she took her usual seat by Bradan and Ealea. They watched as Archer and the other men played a number of songs, and then Archer sat near Bradan and told scary stories to the gathered children. He was very good at it. Cara was enthralled. Then he and Maura danced with other young lovers round the bonfire before he tucked her into his shoulder and led her away. Cara found herself dreading and yet looking for Khoury and Nalia. But she didn't see them. She knew she shouldn't, but Cara closed her eyes and relived the memory of Khoury's lips on hers until her heart sped up and her cheeks felt hot. She remembered the feeling of love in the memory of the laughing woman and pretended it was for her.

As the fire burned low, she left the bonfire and went to Maura's house to wait. She waited and waited. But Maura didn't come. Finally, Cara fell asleep on the cot that had been prepared the night of her arrival. When Maura finally did return in the wee hours, it was with a sad face.

"What's wrong?" Cara asked, rubbing the sleep out of her eyes. Maura sat down on the edge of her bed and sighed.

When she didn't say anything, Cara picked up a brush and sat behind her on the bed. She undid Maura's braid and brushed her hair with long, soft strokes. "You can tell me, sister." She hoped the endearment would entice Maura to talk.

"It's nothing," the Northern girl murmured, staring into the low glow of the embers in the hearth.

"It doesn't look like nothing."

"Fine." Maura huffed with frustration. "Archer and Khoury are sparring."

"Fighting? I thought they were friends."

"Not fighting. Sparring. Practicing fighting."

"Why?"

"Because they're mercenaries," Maura snapped.

"Oh." Cara understood neither the importance of sparring nor why Maura was cross with her. And though she was hesitant to ask for another explanation, she was more tired of her own ignorance. "And that means what exactly?"

Maura growled in frustration and whirled on Cara. "Fighting is their job. Sparring is practice. If they're sparring, that means they'll be leaving soon."

Now, Cara understood. Archer was leaving. Leaving Maura here alone, again. And then Khoury would also leave. Maybe that's why he seemed different tonight. Cara wondered why neither had said anything to her about their leaving. Then she realized that they had probably assumed she'd stay here with Bear Clan. They had lives to go back to that didn't have anything to do with her. Unreasonably, she felt betrayed. "Archer always comes back though, right?" Cara asked, wondering if Khoury always accompanied him.

Maura set her teeth and tried to stem the tears that began to crawl down her cheeks. "If he survives."

"Survives?"

Now Maura was angry. "Don't you know anything? Mercenaries are paid to fight wars. Every time they go, they might die. And one day," her voice cracked with a stifled sob, "one day, he just won't come back." At that, Maura broke down, bawling in earnest. She turned away, covering her face with her hands.

Cara was shocked. *How could Archer do this to her?* She awkwardly put an arm around the other woman's shoulders, not knowing what to say. "It'll be all right," she murmured.

"I don't know how much longer I can wait, Cara." She stifled her sobs and wiped her runny nose on her sleeve. "Reid, I mean Archer, changed when his father died. Spirits forgive me, but Old Man Tarhill was a spiteful soul. I know he said something cruel to Reid, something that changed his mind about me. I know he loves me, and I just figured whatever his problem was, he'd get over it eventually." Maura sniffled wetly, her eyes already red and puffy. "But it has been seven lonely years."

Defeated, Maura wept again. Cara patted the other girl's arm gently. It didn't feel like enough but it was all she could do. They sat like that for a long while, until Maura cried herself dry.

Maura sniffled and withdrew, swallowing hard and steeling herself. "There's nothing for it. I've made my choice. But please don't tell him about my tears. It wouldn't do any good for him to know how much it hurts."

"I promise I won't."

The atmosphere in the hut was somber as they settled in for the night, and sleep was long in coming.

CHAPTER 17
KHOURY

Clanging steel and screams roused Khoury from a restless sleep. Battle-honed reflexes propelled him from his cot in spite of his aching muscles. Thrusting feet into boots, he scooped up his new blades in their scabbards and raced through the door, strapping them around his hips as he went. Whatever he'd expected, it wasn't the gruesome scene before him, a picture at once unbelievable and all too familiar. A preternatural snow was falling and the now-white ground was streaked with red, littered with a dozen bodies. Huts were in flames. Villagers raced past or stood in groups to fight invaders the likes of which the captain had never faced before, and he hoped never to see again. He had heard the tales told round the story fires at night but nothing could have prepared him for the awful truth. For the first time in over a generation, giants were invading Bear Clan.

Heavily built and bearded, they stood so tall the burly Northerners reached only to their chests. Heavy-knuckled hands swung hammer and axe as they strode with determined silence through the village. Rage flared in Khoury watching them hunt his friends like animals. He drew a sword, taking grim pleasure in its weight. Wading upstream through fleeing villagers, he bore down on the nearest invader. His anger-fueled swing sliced the giant's thigh to bone with a shuddering shock that Khoury felt all the way up his arm. The giant roared, whirling to face him but Khoury had already yanked his blade free and stabbed upwards two-handed, his steel penetrating leather and flesh. The giant toppled as Khoury withdrew the blade, letting the lifeless body crash to the ground.

A guttural cry rumbled behind him. Khoury turned, narrowly dodging the hammer aimed at his head. In one motion, the giant swung the hammer back up and around, bringing it down for another try. The captain blocked the strike on the flat of his raised blade supported between a hand on the hilt and the other under the flat. The sheer force of the blow sent him to one knee. The giant leaned in until Khoury's arms shook and his scarred chest spasmed with effort. Twisting, he lowered his left hand, letting the hammer race down to the ground, unbalancing his foe and giving him room to escape. With a backhanded slice he nicked the giant's leg, drawing a trickle of blood as he twirled away. Still, the breeze of the next swing lifted the hair off Khoury's neck. He scrambled away, seeking distance and some advantage.

As the giant advanced, a broken pole canting out from a ruined hut caught Khoury's eye. He ducked under the next hammer strike and raced to yank the pole from the ground. Khoury sheathed his sword and turned with the makeshift lance to finish the fight, but his opponent had found a new target—a young Northerner lad, inexpertly brandishing a sword. With a fierce cry, Khoury charged, thrusting the spear up into the giant's back. But he was too late. The giant gurgled and fell to the ground beside the shattered body of the village boy.

Khoury's teeth creaked as he ground them together, staring down at the dead boy. He was one of a group of kids who'd watched the captain sparring with Archer just yesterday. Khoury squelched sorrow beneath fiery hate. Anger suited him better, hardening and strengthening him. A snarl escaped him as he yanked the spear free and prowled the village looking for his next victim.

The giants were scattered rather than grouped into fighting units. They had no fear of the Northerners, but Khoury could see no reason for their presence. They ransacked like ill-mannered children, tossing things about, killing at random or when attacked. As he strode among the broken houses to the dining hall, he noted a few clusters of villagers had dug in and fought back, taking their opponents one a time. But the giants seemed unperturbed by the resistance and, after lighting huts on fire, moved away.

Khoury caught sight of Archer standing in the doorway to the main hall, bow in hand. Of the giants that lay dead in the open area, Khoury noted that most had arrows protruding from their eyes or necks, a sure sign of Archer's work. Khoury stepped up to the giant nearest him, thrusting the pole overhand to get into the "soft spot" beneath the arm. The mortal blow dropped the giant to his knees, his weight wrenching the pole out of Khoury's grip. The wood snapped beneath the giant as it keeled over.

A shout drew the captain's attention to the dead giant's comrade rushing toward him, axe raised. Khoury drew his sword and ran toward the dining hall, trying to reach Archer and his knot of men. Before he'd gone twenty feet, he heard a grunt behind him and swerved, barely avoiding the axe strike that popped up a divot at his feet. His foot caught the clod of packed dirt, and Khoury knew he was going down. Instead of falling face first though, he dove for the ground, rolling over with a younger man's agility despite the stiffness in his scars. He found his feet and turned as the giant brought his swing around.

Khoury hacked at the giant with all his might. His sword banged off the giant's armored forearm, stopping his opponent's strike. But the jarring hit nearly disarmed the captain. The giant paused to switch hands on his axe and in that moment, an arrow appeared in his eye. The warrior screamed in pain and Khoury thrust two-handed up under the ribs, popping through the leather armor and sending the giant backward to the ground.

Scraping ribs as he pulled his sword free, Khoury dashed the remaining distance to the shelter of the hall where Archer and Bradan greeted him. A handful of other men were ransacking the hall, gathering supplies.

"We have to leave the village," Bradan said.

"And go where?" Khoury asked, wiping blood from his sword.

"Seal Clan. Our cousins in the north at the edge of the sea." The chieftain donned a cloak and picked up a finished pack. "The sledges are being made ready and, by bear or on foot, we will meet the survivors at the northwest spring before heading out."

"Everyone knows to go there?" Khoury asked, as Bradan slipped a large hunting knife into his belt and took the flanged mace awaiting him on a nearby table.

"It's not the first raid we've survived," Archer murmured in a cold voice that didn't sound like the man Khoury knew.

The captain looked out at the nearly empty village. Empty, that is, except for the dead and dying. No wonder Archer's face was grim as he held the bowstring to his cheek watching the giants loot his home.

"And not the last either," Bradan added.

With a twang and a whoosh, another arrow found its mark, sending a giant tumbling into the building he had just set on fire. Angrily notching another, the Northerner resumed his stance, stoic and focused.

Bradan turned Khoury with a heavy hand on his shoulder. "Nalia's already fled," he assured him.

Khoury nodded absently and grabbed a pack himself. Nalia was the last thing on his mind. The fearful images of his nightmare came back full force. "Cara?" he asked.

"She and Maura are helping with the bears. They've probably left already," Bradan said. He laid a restraining hand on Archer's arm. "Reid, time to go. Nothing more you can do here."

His jaw set, Archer lowered his bow and made ready to travel. Khoury didn't like leaving a fight unfinished either, but he had to see for himself that Cara was unharmed. The group of men loaded themselves with packs and then ducked out the kitchen door and raced into the forest. Once under the cover of the pines, they settled into an easy ground-eating jog, heading northwest, Bradan leading the way.

CHAPTER 18
CARA

"Get up! We have to go."

Cara woke to a disheveled Maura shaking her roughly. The Northern girl's hair hung in loose auburn curls to her elbows. Still groggy, Maura yanked her to her feet, dropped her boots in her lap, and threw the cloak Khoury had never claimed over her shoulders. She'd barely finished slipping on her boots when Maura grabbed her hand and dragged her out the door without explanation. A world so foreign and terrible that Cara had no words to describe it awaited her. In the midst of a late spring snow, enormous bearded warriors strode through the little village, laying waste to the Clan home with iron and fire. Huts were ablaze. Bodies sprawled in the dirt. Cara felt her stomach heave.

"Come on," Maura urged. "We need you at the bear pens." Allowing the other woman to propel her through the surreal carnage at a dazed jog, Cara noticed a group of older villagers shuffling toward the pens, leaning on their canes and each other. Then, she understood. Their only chance of survival was the sledges. Her task clear, she picked up her pace, racing side by side with the taller woman. Cara could barely feel her feet hit the ground.

When she slid to a halt at the pens, the animals were in an uproar, bellowing and anxious. The smell of fire frightened them, and the handlers were having trouble. Focusing on her task, Cara counted the sledges and sent Maura to have the larger lads get all the sledges out in the open. Then, one by one, she assigned bears into teams starting with Shona, one of her own most reliable bears. She pressed a hand to the bear's forehead, easily connecting with her mind, and then slid the traces over the large, shaggy neck. Next, she selected a smaller Clan bear and, though his mind was foreign, he was amenable. She quickly slipped him into the traces behind Shona. Grabbing a nearby Northerner, she handed off the reins and moved on.

An older Clan bear was next. But the old-timer yowled anxiously, watching her approach with suspicion. As she reached out to touch it, the enormous maw stretched wide. Its furious roar sprayed saliva, but there was no time for subtlety. Her heart thudded in her chest, but she held her ground. She took a step forward and the mammoth head swung side to side in displeasure. Feeling the press of time, Cara stepped forward again. This time, the bear reared up, lifting one monstrous paw to strike.

A lumbering white form knocked it to the ground.

"Gar!" Cara rushed forward to press her face into the familiar furry neck. "Thank you." She ducked under his head and reached out to the bear that had tried to attack her. Once her small hand touched his head, he calmed enough to be led to a sledge, and she slipped the leather lines around him. She pointed to a driver she knew could handle the restless beast and moved on to the next. As she continued down the line, Gar hovered just behind her, his calming presence helping her tune out anything except the bears and sledges.

The work went quickly, Cara harnessing and assigning drivers, and Maura getting people loaded up. One by one, the sledges left. She was putting rigging on the last of the bears, with the exception of Gar, when a sudden clang of weapons startled her.

She'd been so intent on the animals, she'd completely blotted out the reason for the retreat. Now she noted the smoke that hung heavy across the yard. Only a few smaller sledges remained and they were nearly full. Maura waved to her from a sledge poised to leave. And nearby, Ealea helped Ingrid onto a two-bear sledge that already held the sickly Thomas and his mother.

Three giants burst into the yard and time slowed. In the first heartbeat, the tallest brought his hammer down on Ealea's lead bear, sending the beast to the ground with the sharp crack of broken bones. In the second, his battle-scarred companion swung at Ealea who stood protectively over Ingrid. With a deceptively soft thud, her limp body flew through the air to land in a lifeless heap. The next moment brought a third giant who battered the sledge into the ground. The occupants were either thrown clear or pummeled into the broken frame. Cara watched the small body of Thomas roll away limply and her heart broke.

"No!" Cara shouted as time reasserted itself and all around her panic broke loose. Harnessed bears lurched with their sledges into the forest. Stragglers bolted for cover. Gar moved protectively in front of her, and she could feel his rumbling growl beneath her trembling hands. She knew she should run, but she couldn't tear her eyes from the violence before her.

Still tethered to the broken sledge, the second bear retaliated, roaring its fear and lurching over its dead brethren. It latched strong jaws onto the giant's free arm and tore through the thick leather breastplate with deadly claws. The long tears seeped crimson, and Cara finally understood Archer's hesitance around the giant beasts. Her stomach roiled as the bear shook its head, breaking the giant's arm and sending droplets of blood flying. But the poor thing was outnumbered. The other giants came to their companion's rescue, crippling the beast with heavy blows to its shaggy flank. Cara cried out with the beast's pain as it fell forward, hind legs suddenly weak. Still struggling, it toppled the giant, reaching out with yellow teeth for his exposed throat. Cara hid her face in Gar's fur as a giant raised his axe to finish the bear. Spitefully, she was thankful he was too late to save the one who'd killed the first bear.

Out of the corner of her eye, she noted movement. Ingrid was crawling away from the broken sledge. Somehow, she had survived. Her hood blew back and disheveled gray-white hair fell to her shoulders catching the eye of one of the giants.

"Ingrid!" Cara screamed the warning, reaching over Gar's white-furred back. The giant reached down, grabbed Ingrid by an ankle and dragged her upside down into the air. She thrashed like a wild animal, swinging recklessly. He shook her, hard, quieting her struggles and his free hand caught a dangling braid.

Cara watched as the giant called to his companion, gesturing to the pale locks. The second warrior came close, puzzled, and inspected the herbalist closely. Ingrid had the gall to spit in his eye. Angry, the first giant shook her again. His companions said something in a harsh, guttural language, shaking his head. Then without warning, the giant holding Ingrid slammed her body to the ground, killing her instantly.

No longer interested in the broken sledge, the giants turned to the forest, sweeping the brush for other refugees. But as the trailing giant turned for a last look at the clearing, he caught sight of Cara peering over Gar's back. His eyes grew wide and he shouted to his cohort, pointing at her. Excited, both giants rushed toward her. Guilt twisted inside her as they finally said something she did understand. "White-haired woman!"

She knew Gar would protect her to the end but after what she had just seen she wouldn't risk his life against two of them. She grabbed a handful of fur and hauled herself up onto Gar's broad back.

"Run!" she commanded and, with a roar, he turned and ran to the nearest patch of forest. She heard the giants storming after her. Her fingers dug deep into his thick pelt as the bear plunged into the woods. Numb with horror, she could only duck her head and ride it out as Gar wove in and out of the trees. Branches scraped her arms and back, but she didn't let go or look up. The giant's words echoed in her ears. *White-haired woman.*

After what seemed like forever, the sounds of pursuit faded. Gar crested a snowy hillock and slowed to stop, sides heaving.

Cara slid off and crumpled to her knees in a shallow snowy drift, her body shaking. "No," she wailed into the frozen ground. "No, no, no." The image of Ealea and Ingrid's crumpled bodies was burned into her mind. "Not them. Please no." She wept into the snow.

Hunched over, she noticed a strange bluish glow radiating from inside the cloak. She sat back and tucked her chin down hard. A pulsing blue light came from her amulet, just as it had that night she journeyed and killed the cat in the spirit world. She placed a hand over the stone and suspicion twisted around her spine.

"What have I done?" The giant's words rang in her memory again. She knew he could only have meant her. A cold weight settled in her stomach.

I brought this on the Clan.

"Father!" She screamed into the frozen sky as furious tears streamed down her face.

Her hands searched the chain for a clasp but for the first time Cara noticed that there was none. She tried slipping the chain over her head but it was too short. She remembered the blazing red gem on Gar's harness and the feel of fire licking at her skin. Panicked, she grabbed the stone, trying to pry it out of its setting. Neither the chain nor the setting gave way despite broken bleeding nails.

As she cradled the stone in her palm wrapping her fingers around it, it warmed. When Cara tried to drop it, her hand refused to open. Terror gripped her as the heat increased, spreading to her hand and then her arm. There was no feeling of fire as there had been on the tundra but her breathing came in quick, fearful puffs. The world spun for a moment as she collapsed in a heap still clasping the gem.

☙

Cara descended into a dark void. A foul wind ruffled her hair and clothes and the faint mumbling of an incantation hissed in her ears. She looked around but saw nothing: No landmarks, no light, no point of reference. A robed figure, its face hooded, solidified out of the dark, gesturing toward her. She felt herself pulled closer until she stood face to face with the dark shape. Then it started to laugh. Flinging back his hood, Sidonius's cruel face leaned close. Close enough for her to smell the dust that permeated his very being.

"You thought you could escape me, Daughter?" He snarled the name with disdain, and she knew then he had never been her father. "This will teach you to run."

He raised a claw-like hand and gestured at her with a quick twisting movement. Pain ripped through her belly and she doubled over. The breath whooshed from her lungs. But even here, she could feel the bandages on the wounds she'd gotten in Bradan's tent and her mind spun.

Was this just a dream? Intuition told her that to some extent that was true. But when wounded in her dreams, she returned to waking life with real scars. What if she died?

Desperate, Cara reached into herself for the forest. Her forest. She'd left Bradan behind in the spirit world; maybe she could do it now. Her jangling nerves distracted her; pain throbbed through her middle. Sidonius's cackling echoed in her frayed mind. Then, her nose detected a whiff of something familiar, the scent of pine and dirt. She latched her attention to the smell and by force of will drew in the essence of nature.

When she opened her eyes, she could see the familiar forest around her, feel earth beneath her feet. Unfortunately, Sidonius was still standing in front of her. His face twisted into an angry mask.

"Do you think you can play this game with me?" he sneered as he stretched his arms to the sky.

Cara's heart thudded with fear as thunder rumbled above. She closed her eyes tightly but it didn't save her from the rippling energy that tore through her body accompanied by the smell of lightning.

She had to get away. The weight of the amulet, still clasped in her hand, drew her attention. She reached her mind deep within the gem, looking for the answer. It glowed in her mind's eye, and she welcomed the energy. Drawing strength from the stone, she focused her mind on one thought—freedom.

"That trinket is mine," Sidonius said with disdain. "It can't help you." The stone's glow dimmed and it began to feel cooler but still she tried to soak up what energy she could. The coolness turned to cold as if it were stealing heat.

"Now I have you." The sorcerer smiled as the flow of energy reversed. The stone was pulling at her. The sharpness of ice lanced her hand, circled her wrist, and crawled up her arm as spirit winds swirled around her.

Frightened, she tried again to drop the stone but the skin of her palm and fingers stuck to it. She tried to use her other hand to pull it from the stone, anticipating the pain of skin tearing but it was no use. Another crack of thunder and a shock of pain spun through her head and down to her legs.

She struggled with the amulet, pulling it away from her with both hands, her mind focused on nothing but getting free. Pressure, like a giant hand, clamped down on the back of her neck, bending her forward but she resisted. And still she pulled, tears gathering. Her arms went numb. Then air refused to enter her lungs. Her throat convulsed with hunger as the pressure clamped down the sides of her neck.

Another crack of lightning sizzled through her body. She would have screamed except her throat was closed. Sidonius was choking her.

Finally, she felt a slight give. Her hand was in icy agony, but by now her whole world was pain. She kept telling herself it was just a dream. She told herself to wait it out. But her chest ached for air and the pressure on her neck changed again, tearing at her throat like a hungry animal. She thrashed against the chain, fighting like a trapped animal. She grew light-headed, fearing the end. Then…

Cara awoke in the real world, her face in snow, gulping air like a drowning woman. She was dazed and coughing blood. A warm, wet nose nuzzled her shoulder. She could smell Gar's musky scent as he lay beside her giving warmth and support. Cara opened her eyes, blinking back tears from the blinding whiteness of the hillside. A patch of snow beneath her chin was red with blood. Her hands rested in the snow, her left palm throbbing with gut-wrenching pain. Her throat felt like it had been crushed, her breathing was ragged.

It was then she noticed the silver chain lying slightly buried in the snow beneath her burned hand. She lifted her head and weakly picked up the chain. Its circle was unbroken, smeared with blood. The brilliant blue gem that once dangled at the end of the necklace was now a dull black rock. She dropped to the snow in a dead faint.

CHAPTER 19
BRADAN

How many hours had it been since he'd awakened from violent dreams to find a reality more brutal than any nightmare? An hour, a day? Bradan couldn't have said except that it had been far too long since he'd set eyes on his wife. Ealea had kissed him before she'd gone to shepherd the sick and weak to the pens. Now, the memory of her lips was like a drop of water to a thirsty man, only intensifying his need.

He felt itchy in his skin, restless and anxious, and he chided himself for his lack of calm. He was Chieftain. His people needed him to be steady. But a rising dread dogged his steps, sucking the very strength of his heart. Even the spirits of the pines were unnaturally quiet, their murmurings and sighs drowned beneath the cacophony of the battle.

He glanced back quickly to make sure he hadn't lost anyone and was rewarded with the haunted faces of his Clansmen and the grim coldness of the two mercenaries. He barely recognized Archer as the dreamy-eyed boy he'd once known. He turned back to the forest ahead of him and tried not to wonder if there would be anything left to entice Reid home after this.

A small breeze roused him from his thoughts, playing across his neck like fingers. His hair stood on end and a ghostly chill climbed his back, but he kept running. Giants were scattered even this far out from the village, forcing Bradan to lead the men on a meandering path. He stopped in a tight stand of trees to catch his breath. The men crouched in what nearby cover they could find.

With his head tilted back against the rough bark, he rubbed at the twinge of pain in his neck and shoulder. What waited for them at the meeting place? How many would be left?

The wind swirled around him again, insistent, teasing him with tendrils of air along his neck and face, tugging at his beard braids. He looked up at the leaves and realized there was no earthly wind to stir them.

A calling, he thought. So the spirits *were* still with him.

The restless captain crept out from his hiding place, low among the budding brambles. The chieftain watched him survey the nearby pines but as the man raised no alarm, Bradan allowed himself a moment's rest.

The wind's strange insistence spurred him to seek out the spirit who so obviously wanted his attention. Calming his breath, he stared sightlessly ahead as his power shifted him half into the Otherworld.

There was a voice waiting for him in that wind, its dulcet tone so familiar that his heart shriveled in his chest. Only the tree behind him kept him upright. Steeling himself, he closed his eyes against the prick of tears and listened well. When his sight shifted back and the wind had faded away, he knew what he had to do. Cara needed them.

Khoury returned to the group and whispered, "It's like they're looking for something."

"They are," Bradan said. "They're looking for the girl."

"Cara?" Apprehension skittered across Khoury's usual stony scowl.

Bradan nodded.

The captain is still drawn to the girl, the shaman thought. *Good.*

Bradan shoved away from the tree with more strength than he felt. "Thowald," he said, "take the others to the meeting place. If we don't show up by midafternoon, make sure the Clan heads to Seal Bay."

"But Chieftain—" Thowald began even as Bradan raised a hand to stop him.

"I follow a different road. Archer and his captain will assist me, but there is a spirit matter I must attend to."

Thowald's jaw clenched with rebellion.

"At the Standing Stones," Bradan added. The invocation of the sacred hill silenced any further comment. They would not argue with a shaman's duty. When no giants were in sight, the Clansmen headed off northwest as a group, and Bradan sent his desperate prayers for safety with them.

Once they had left, Bradan's heart felt even heavier. The captain was watching him with eager tension, but Bradan had little to say by way of explanation other than, "Cara's in trouble. Follow me."

Without a word, the two warriors followed him south into the snowy woods.

Bradan felt the change in the air well before they crossed the line of sarsens that jutted from the frosty ground. Twenty-one enormous slabs of stone stood at attention in a ring around the top third of the hillock. Their rough surface was pale gray with captured snow though toward the ground they darkened to a deep mossy green as if drawing color from the earth they rested upon.

They were old friends, he and these stones, these silent protectors of his father's lore. The familiar peace of the sacred place seeped into his joints, like spring sunshine on a cool morn. The spirit whisperings had returned though the number of voices had multiplied, apparently drawn to Cara's distress like moths to the moon.

Bradan slowed to a walk as he crossed that invisible border and climbed the gentle slope of the meadowed hillock beyond. No giant would find them here.

"What is this place?" the captain asked, and Bradan sensed a hint of awe and suspicion in his voice.

"The Standing Stones," Archer answered, his face softening slightly. It was the first he'd spoken since he'd seen the giants in the village.

"Standing stones, huh." Khoury's gaze raked the pastoral scene as if expecting an ambush, but he was obviously affected by the energy of the place.

"This place is sacred," the chieftain said aloud, taking comfort in the voices only he could hear, "and safe. It belongs to the Old Ones. Here, their energy is strongest, their influence the greatest."

He led the men up to the crest of the hill and there in a bare coating of snow, they found a large hump of white fur, which wasn't quite what Bradan had expected. It rumbled and shifted at their approach. Enigmatic black eyes regarded them with uncanny knowing, and Bradan recognized the beast by its tattered ear.

"That's Cara's bear," Archer said with surprise.

As they neared, Bradan noticed the blue hem of Cara's dress fanned out over the pale ground the same time as the captain did. She was sprawled facedown near the great paws on snow splotched with disturbing patches of red.

"Cara." The captain said her name on a hoarse breath as he rushed forward. A strange noise from Gar stopped him in his tracks: Part whine, part growl. It sounded like the beast was worried for her and the spirits echoed its concern.

Archer stepped around his captain, crooning in a low voice, imitating the sounds Cara made to the beast. "Easy. Easy," he said gently as he slid forward a step or two. "Remember me?" He moved forward inch by inch until he could touch the shaggy head. Laying his hand on the large expanse between the dark eyes, he pressed his fingers into the deep fur. "It's okay, old boy. We're here to help."

The bear sniffed him and then relaxed. Archer stooped near the large head and touched Cara's neck.

"She's alive," he said and gently scooped the small woman up into his arms. The bear rumbled anxiously but remained passive. As her hand dangled limply, Bradan noted something silver drop and land in the snow.

"What's this?" He bent down and retrieved what looked like a silver chain from the frost.

Khoury peered over his shoulder. "That's Cara's amulet. But what happened to the stone?"

The gem was no longer blue, but black—charred like it had been burned. Bradan reached for her hand and turned it over. Underneath her tattered glove, an angry scarlet burn streaked across her palm. Its contours matched the pattern of the stone's setting. Then he swept back her unbound white hair. An ugly wound completely encircled her neck, its edges littered with ragged bits of torn skin.

"What happened?" Archer asked, shifting her in his arms so he could see better.

Khoury took the chain from Bradan and examined it more closely. "It's unbroken."

The three men stared at each other in shocked silence over the head of the small white-haired woman. She was more a mystery now than she had been that first day in the dining hall when she had read the questions from his mind.

"Is she a sorcerer then? His true daughter?" Khoury asked, his face hard once more.

Bradan rubbed weary eyes with thick fingers as the voices rushed to answer the captain's question though the man couldn't hear them. "No. She isn't a Far Islander. Her talents are…of a different sort."

Cara whimpered softly in Archer's arms.

"Give her to me," the captain said, his voice thick. "I'll carry her." Archer eyed his captain with consternation but obeyed and handed her to Khoury. Once she was cradled against his chest, Bradan could sense the subtle easing of tension in the man and the spirits murmured their encouragement.

"Okay, let's get going," Archer urged. "If we hurry we can catch up to the others."

Weakened by numbing weariness and grief, Bradan allowed himself to follow down the hill and back the way they had come. He was too tired to figure out right then what he needed to do to help the girl, and he craved the familiar faces of his Clan to ease his sorrow. Khoury followed close behind Archer, and Bradan followed them side by side with the bear that huffed softly and trailed after the girl of its own accord.

CHAPTER 20
KHOURY

Khoury blindly followed Archer, his mind spinning. Though giants had a history of attacking Bear Clan, those forays were rare. Was it simply bad luck or had they come for Cara as Bradan claimed? And how would the shaman know? Many of Archer's childhood tales had included Bradan's uncanny ability to pull information out of thin air, but Khoury hadn't believed it. Until now.

If they had come for her, the only reason Khoury could think of was that the sorcerer had sent them. It was far-fetched but the timing was right. Did Sidonius really possess enough power to have giants do his bidding? Khoury suppressed a shudder at the thought. And if he had ordered the attack, how had he found them? Khoury turned the puzzle over in his mind, trying to make sense of it: Cara's powers, the sudden giant attack, and now the mystery of her removing the amulet.

The amulet! Khoury cursed himself for not seeing it before. The blue stone, like the bears' harness stones, had forged a connection between the wearer and the sorcerer. Apparently, one he could track.

Khoury paused, letting Bradan pass him so he could prop Cara higher on his shoulder. Holding her with one arm, he reached into his pocket and drew out the amulet. Gar came up quietly and watched as he tossed the circlet one-handed into the woods, far away from their tracks. Khoury resettled her against his chest and started walking. Gar fell in behind him.

The captain's grim pleasure at Sidonius's irritation when the giants returned empty-handed faded with the realization that he should have anticipated this. They should have been prepared for another attempt. Not that he knew the sorcerer had giants in his arsenal but even so.

Damn, I'm getting soft, he thought. *What's next? We hide at Seal Bay until we can figure out how to stop the bastard?* Khoury slowed. It still bothered him that somehow, magical or otherwise, the girl had too tight a hold on his emotions. But enthralled or not, he couldn't allow the sorcerer to have her.

The Clan was the closest thing to family he'd had in a long time. The losses they suffered today angered him, fueling his hatred of the sorcerer. A few steps later, he realized he was about to put them in danger again.

"Wait," he said, stopping. "We can't go this way." Both Northerners turned to look at him.

"This is the way. It's safe," Bradan said.

"We can't … I can't take Cara to Seal Bay."

"What?" Archer was crestfallen.

"Whatever she is, Sidonius desperately wants her back. And this setback won't stop him."

"All the more reason to join up with the others," Archer argued.

"No. It's all the more reason *not* to," Khoury said. "Giants, Archer. Think about it. If he wants her this badly, anyone we involve will be threatened. I don't know how far his power can reach, but he found her here, and I can't risk leading him to Seal Bay next."

"You're right." The grizzled chieftain deflated a bit. Khoury heard the weariness in the older man's voice. "She can't go to the Bay."

"You two go ahead to meet them," Khoury said. "I'll send word when I find a safe place to hide her."

Archer stared at Khoury, shock blatant on his face. "You're not facing this alone, Captain. I swore to protect you. I don't return to the Clan until you do."

"You should see Maura and tell her you're okay," Khoury said.

"She'll understand," Archer said. "And besides, I won't risk her either."

Khoury noted Bradan's frown deepen at the mention of Maura. Nevertheless, he was relieved Archer was staying with him. There was no one he trusted more.

"Okay, what's your plan?" Bradan asked.

"We need a road that leads to allies, not family." In his mind, Khoury shuffled through the faces of men he'd risked much for, someone who owed him, someone close enough to reach on foot.

"What about Wallace at Iolair?" Archer said.

"He does owe me a favor or two, doesn't he?" Khoury grinned. *Iolair might do nicely.*

"More than that," Archer said. "Rumor is he has a Far Isles adviser."

"Does he? That sly fox."

"Maybe his sorcerer knows our friend in the Black Keep and can tell us why he wants Cara so badly."

"Excellent plan, Archer."

"Can you trust this Wallace?" Bradan asked.

"Usually," Khoury said making Archer chuckle. "Anyway, my gut tells me that the farther we get from the Keep the better."

"All right, boys," Bradan said. "Let's see what we can find out about this Sidonius fellow."

Archer put a hand on Bradan's shoulder. "You don't need to come, Bradan. The Clan needs you."

"The Clan will be fine without me at the Bay. Old Fynan can be a bastard, but he'll look after them. I have another task to do." The chieftain gestured to Cara. "The Old Ones want me to help her reclaim her power."

Khoury's stomach soured. "Are you sure that's wise?" he asked.

Bradan looked puzzled. "Why wouldn't it be?"

"Power is a double-edged sword," Khoury said. She had a kind heart now but how often had he seen power turn kindness to cruelty?

"This is her birthright," Bradan said. "Would you keep that from her?"

If it kept her safe.

"Just because it was given to her," Khoury said, "doesn't mean it's good for her."

The chieftain looked stunned. "You would keep her small? Keep her ignorant?"

"Power comes at a price. Always. Are you sure she will want to pay it?"

The shaman stared at him like he'd proclaimed blasphemy. Khoury didn't even want the power he had. Not that it hadn't come in handy but each time he used it was a risk. Few men could resist the seductive taint of domination.

But this wasn't an argument he could win standing in the pines. "We should get moving," he said.

"South it is," Archer said. He sidled past Khoury to lead them south. Shifting Cara to a more comfortable position, the captain let Bradan go ahead of him and trailed after the other men.

After an hour of hiking, a winded Bradan called for rest. They paused in a thick stand of pine trees, and Khoury noted the sun was past its peak. It had been over half a day and yet the comfort of Bear Clan already seemed years away.

"You know, the Southern road is east of here," Bradan gestured down the slight rise. The chieftain looked wan in the afternoon sun.

"Archer knows what he's doing," the captain said. "Sidonius is sure to have spies along every main route south. We won't be using the road."

Archer just smiled at his chieftain and shrugged; he knew the drill. Knew Khoury would want to go to ground.

"How could he possibly cover them all?" the chieftain asked.

"I don't know," Khoury said, "but it's what I'd do. Cross country will be safer."

"Through the Tangle?" Archer asked the captain but only for confirmation.

Khoury nodded. "I've done it before. With Ellis."

"But Foresthaven," Bradan said in shock. "We can't pass that way."

"Foresthaven is in the Tangle, but it's not all of it. We can avoid them and still stay off the road. From the stories, the barrier to the forest is obvious."

Bradan harrumphed, apparently unconvinced though he didn't argue further.

The three men hiked the remainder of the day, making camp in a low hollow surrounded on three sides by boulders. They had covered a lot of ground with no sign of pursuit, but Cara hadn't roused. Khoury felt confident they could risk a fire. Besides, he needed some warmth to combat the chill in his bones. He laid Cara near the small flames Archer coaxed to life.

"Do you think she made it?" Archer asked out of Bradan's earshot, staring up into the cold night.

Khoury recognized the longing in that stance. "Maura's a smart girl," he said. "She's probably about ready to skin you alive for not showing up."

Archer snorted in agreement, but the humor didn't last long. He had always been steadfast in battle, but Khoury could see that the attack on the Clan had hit him hard.

Bradan took the first watch and Archer left with his bow to find some food, leaving Khoury alone with Cara and the fire. He wrapped her in his cloak and hers but still she felt cool. He tucked a loose strand of her long white hair behind her ear just as a heavy footfall thumped behind him. It was Gar coming over to snuffle her face. The great beast was so unobtrusive Khoury had forgotten he was with them. Then the bear settled in gently near her, seeming to understand her need for warmth.

And so, Khoury was alone with his thoughts. Iolair was a good suggestion. It was well-fortified, and Wallace would give them shelter for at least a little while. Wallace had been Khoury's lieutenant before Archer. Steadfast and smart, he'd been a good second, at least until he decided to turn in his sword for a baron's crest and a citadel that Khoury helped him win. Yes, Jacob Wallace would do his best for them.

Khoury thought he'd never find a second as capable as Wallace, but fate had smiled and Archer appeared within the month.

Suddenly, Cara bolted upright with a shout. She looked around with unseeing eyes in a panic. Khoury rushed to her, grabbing her shoulders gently.

"Cara. It's me." He turned her to face him. When she recognized him, she collapsed into his arms and buried her face in his chest. "You're all right now." Her soft hair felt good against his cheek. He breathed in her scent, content just to hold her.

Shifting against him, she turned her palm toward her face, inspecting the burn across it.

"Does it hurt?"

"Yes," she croaked, swallowing hard. Her surprised hand flew to her throat, the pain sharp enough to bring tears. Khoury gently took her hand in his, careful to keep the shreds of glove between them. Shadows of the day's brutality lingered in her ice-blue gaze.

"Too bad Ingrid isn't around to mix a poultice for that burn," he said, hoping to cheer her. "And perhaps some tea."

She shook her head vigorously at his words, tears running down her cheeks.

"What?"

"She's dead," Cara's voice was little more than a croak. She swallowed hard. "And Ingrid and Siobhan and…where's Bradan?"

"On lookout."

"I…I need to see him. He needs to know."

"No." Khoury dreaded the confirmation.

"Ealea is…" Cara shook her head.

"Are you sure?" The news would devastate the old man.

She nodded. "Thomas, too. And his mother. I watched them all die. It's not fair." The broken words tumbled out of her like water over a burst dam.

"It's not," he agreed, holding her close, not sure what to say.

"And worse, it's all because of me. Don't you see? It's my fault." Abundant tears spilled down her cheeks.

"Your fault?" he asked, though he knew what she was going to say next.

"Sidonius." The word slithered out in an ugly whisper. A pink flush crept up her neck into her cheeks. "I saw him in a vision. He sent the giants. I never should have left him." She bawled then, hard and inconsolable, clutching his clothes in desperate hands. He wrapped his arms around her, feeling the sobs shudder through her frail frame.

"The amulet's gone now," he said. "He won't be able to track you so easily. We're going somewhere for help."

Cara pulled back to look up at him. "We? You mean you're going to help me?" she asked with a hiccup.

"Someone has to keep you from falling in the river, right?" He cursed himself for a fool even as the hope in her eyes pleased him.

"I thought you wanted to leave me there."

"I thought the Clan would be safe for you." And he would be guiltless and free of her. Though now he wondered if that was really what he wanted after all.

She sighed and leaned against him, her calm returning. "I should tell Bradan now," she said. "Before I can't."

Khoury nodded, his heart grim. They found Bradan sitting on a stump looking out into the darkened woods. He turned as Khoury walked up with Cara in tow. When Bradan caught her eyes, his face crumpled.

"I hoped I was mistaken, but it *is* true."

"I-I'm sorry, Bradan. She was trying to…."

"Stop!" he rasped, cutting her off with a raised hand. "I beg you not to haunt me with details my heart will never forget. Do not speak them."

The shaman's sorrow cut Khoury to the quick. He knew all too well what the chieftain meant. He had his own ghosts.

Cara moved to put a hand on Bradan's arm but paused, unsure. "What can I do?"

"Nothing, child. There is nothing to be done except honor her… memory." Bradan stood slowly as if the air was too heavy to move through. "I'll be back by sunrise, I promise."

Cara moved to follow as he disappeared into the dark woods.

"Let him grieve his own way," Khoury said, grabbing her hand to stop her. When their skin touched through the torn glove, the ghosts she'd previously resurrected reverberated in his mind with painful clarity. He almost couldn't breathe. He released her hand, but it was too late. He couldn't look at her without his memories pressing on him.

"But he'll be alone out there," she said plaintively.

"Sometimes a man needs to be alone," Khoury said. "I'll stand watch." He nudged her back toward the warmth and the light of the fire.

After she reluctantly returned to Gar, the captain stared blindly out into the forest. As much as he resisted, his mind replayed the memory he dreaded. He'd lost that first battle. Lost everything but the breath that kept him going. And he feared this attraction to Cara would end the same way. He didn't know if he could survive that again.

The snap of a stick roused him from his morbid imaginings as Archer stalked out of the forest, three large bush-rats slung over his shoulder. "Dinnertime," he said. "Where's Bradan?"

"Cara woke up." Khoury rose to accompany him back to the firelight. "The giants killed Ealea."

Archer stopped short, and Khoury could feel fear grip his friend. "And Maura?" The words were barely a whisper as if Archer was afraid to breathe.

"Cara didn't mention her. We have to assume she's okay," Khoury reassured the larger man. Archer only grunted.

When they reached the fire Cara had fallen asleep in its yellow glow, curled up against Gar. The two men cleaned and cooked the small animals, eating in silence. They left some of the meat wrapped in broad leaves and buried in the coals to dry for the next day.

"I can take first watch," Archer said as he sat, putting a large branch on the fire.

"I don't think the bear would let anything get near her or us. You should sleep if you can," Khoury said, and he settled up against a tree, exhausted and troubled.

CHAPTER 21
CARA

Cara woke to Khoury and Archer packing up camp. Her throat burned. Her palm ached. And as for her heart, it was too broken to shed any more tears. Refusing to face the day, she pulled her knees up and snuggled closer to Gar's shaggy bulk.

Her ragged glove snagged a bit of dried skin, sending a burning ache deep into her hand and up her arm. She bit her lip to stifle a whimper as she carefully peeled the tattered leather glove from raw flesh. The blister had broken and dead skin sloughed away leaving an open wound through the valley of her palm, a grim reminder of the father who hunted her. She studied the pattern of Sidonius's amulet forever melted into her palm while she absently traced the edge of healthy skin around the wound like a prisoner pacing the edges of her domain.

A trail of warmth tingled on her skin beneath her circling fingertip. Each circuit increased the heat until it felt like a sunbeam was shining on her aching hand, chasing away the pain. She lulled herself with the hypnotic circling of the soothing warmth, her eyes half-closed as she watched Archer dig leaf-wrapped meat out of cooling embers.

A haggard Bradan stumbled into view. The tear-streaked grime on his face saddened her. There was dirt on his clothes and grief written in every move. Cara thought he looked far older than she remembered, as old as Ingrid had been.

Noting Khoury's stare, Bradan forestalled any questions with a raised hand. "I know. Past time to be on our way."

Cara knew she couldn't hide behind Gar any longer. She slid the stiffened leather glove over her hand again and pushed herself to her feet. She swayed against Gar's bulk, weak and dizzy. A concerned nose snuffled her arm and in her mind echoed a promise to carry her when she had need. She threw an arm over his shaggy neck in gratitude.

The four of them headed south, breaking their fast on the cold scorched meat as they walked. Her appetite had deserted her. It all tasted like dust—and dust reminded her of the Keep—so Cara slipped the meat in pieces to Gar as they walked. He enjoyed it so much he took to nudging her hand with his nose as they walked. His eager nudges grew more persistent and soon her arm was flapping comically, making her smile.

About mid-morning, Archer dropped back and pulled Cara aside. His face was anxious. "Maura?" was all he could manage to say.

She slipped a gloved hand in his and squeezed reassuringly. "She was already on a sled when the bears bolted for the woods. I'm sure she's on her way to Seal Bay right now."

Archer brushed at his eyes. "Thank you." His voice was raw with emotion, and he slid his large arms around her shoulders and hugged her tight. When he let her go, much of the tension had left him though his eyes were still haunted. When he noticed her scrutiny, he flashed a smile and threw an impulsive arm around her, dropping a brotherly kiss on the top of her head. His eyes drifted toward her ruined glove. Tenderly, he took that hand in his and turned it palm up.

"It's healing fast." Shock was evident on his face.

Cara looked down at the angry red pattern of welts. The flesh was no longer the raw meat it had been when she woke. It had matured and toughened. Skin had begun closing over the wet pinkness. "Strange," she murmured, looking curiously at it, her other hand absently stroking the sides of the wound. With her glove on, there was no sensation of sunshine.

With an odd look, he chucked her gently under the chin, scratched Gar behind an ear, and fell back to check on Bradan.

As the day wore on, Cara tired quickly. In the end, she rode Gar like the day before. Her limbs weak with exhaustion, she had no strength or desire to keep up with the others. She rubbed thoughtlessly at the tatters of skin along her neck with bare fingers. A familiar heat developed and she basked in the warmth, the rhythmic swaying of the bear's back lulling her into mindlessness.

A sad gloom hovered over the four companions as they headed south and west throughout that day. And the next. By the end of the third day, they had reached the southern snowline, which seemed to please Khoury immensely. He said the climate would be more agreeable, but Archer explained that Gar had to stay behind.

"Bears are bred for the cold. Heat makes them sick."

"I can't just let him go," she argued, "who would take care of him?" Panic settled in her chest.

Archer laid a warm hand on her shoulder, which did nothing to ease the knot of tears in her throat. "He's a grown bear; he'll be fine."

"He'll be lonely," she whined, frantic for a valid excuse as a tear escaped her lashes. "He won't understand. I can't do that to him." There was no stopping the tears that coursed down her face. Tears that hadn't come for days despite the sorrow in her heart now tumbled freely at the thought of being parted from Gar. Just imagining his absence cut through the numbness that kept her bruised heart from breaking further. She couldn't let go, she needed him.

Khoury exchanged a parental look with Archer and tried his most reasonable tone. "Bears aren't allowed in cities, Cara. They're considered dangerous. The guards would kill him."

She felt her lip jut out as she clamped her teeth together trying to be brave, knowing she couldn't win this fight.

Khoury leaned closer, his face gentle. "He wouldn't be safe there.

Besides, you'll have us." He reached out a calloused finger to wipe a tear off her cheek.

In the end, she knew this wasn't a fight she could win. They camped early for the night. Cara sat apart from the others holding Gar's head in her lap. She leaned her forehead on his between the black eyes that always looked at her with love. Reaching along the connection she shared with him, she tried to explain that he shouldn't follow, couldn't follow. He rumbled his unhappiness and an image of a woman in pale armor breezed through her mind. Cara had never seen the woman before and had no idea what Gar meant by it. She tried again, picturing him free to do what he pleased. He responded with the warrior woman again, her armor shining like a silver sun.

Finally, Cara decided she needed to give him a job. She pictured Maura in her mind. Gar whined in recognition. Then she told Gar to find her. He had to find Maura. Gar seemed to understand though Cara felt his reluctance to leave her. She only hoped Seal Bay had arrangements for sledge bears. Surely Maura would recognize him and take him in. With that settled, Cara wrapped her arms around Gar's neck and buried her face in his coat for a long time, memorizing the musty smell of him. When she couldn't hold back the tears any longer, she released him.

"You should go now," she whispered. "But don't forget me." She scrubbed behind his scarred ear like a lap dog. He leaned into her with affection, then snuffled her face and ambled off. Cara laid down in her blankets, her back to the others and cried until she had no more tears left.

☙

Gar's absence sliced a hole in Cara's world. She couldn't remember a time without him. When their entourage slogged through the wilderness like a funeral procession, the bear's mind had been a haven untouched by their sorrow. But now she had nowhere to hide.

Without Ealea, Bradan was lost, a scowling shadow of his former self. His somber mood infected Archer despite Cara's assurance that her last view of Maura was on a sledge disappearing into the woods. And though Khoury remained his usual reserved self, it didn't relieve Cara's loneliness. He and Archer slipped into well-worn patterns of mercenary efficiency and had little need for words. They made sure everyone's needs were met, but Cara remained at the edge of the camaraderie. Or perhaps she was the center around which they all spun. Either way, there was a gulf between her and the men. Intuition told her they stayed out of duty or perhaps pity. Certainly not affection.

The first day without Gar was endless, and her feet tingled and ached even during the rests. They stopped for the night in a glade shadowed by trees so tall that the air cooled quickly with the setting sun. Cara's whole body ached and the unforgiving ground only made it worse. She did her best to relax, listening to the snapping fire and Archer's fitful snores. Bradan had slipped off again into the dark, and Khoury sat watch near the edge of the firelight behind her.

She could feel the captain's eyes on her. She had caught him watching her during the day with an odd intensity to his sternness. Still, he'd barely said three words to her. She shifted, seeking some comfort, but she was cold even wrapped in her cloak. She missed Gar's thick fur and affectionate mind. Curling into a ball, she drew her arms tightly around herself.

There was a soft footfall behind her. "Cold?" Khoury's low whisper was nevertheless loud and much too close in the silent night.

She sat up quickly, discomfited by how he stood darkly over her. "A bit," she admitted. "How funny. All those years, I never really felt the cold. Now I can't get warm."

"Here, this might help." He swept the cloak from his shoulders and stooped to give it to her.

"No, you need that," she deferred, remembering vividly another day he'd offered her his cloak.

"Fine, we'll share." Before she could refuse, he sat down, wrapped them both in the voluminous fabric, and pulled her close with a casual arm. She stiffened against him, embarrassed by his nearness. But as the moments lengthened and he stared into the fire saying nothing, she relaxed, letting his warmth drive away the cold.

A distant branch snapped, and her head jerked up. The captain pierced the darkness with narrowed eyes that swept the small camp; his warm breath brushed her forehead. She looked up memorizing the hard angles and lines of scar on his face. His gaze dropped to hers, surprised at her nearness.

A tingling heat, equal parts embarrassment and excitement, swept down her neck and across her chest. Her breath came shallow and fast as she remembered the river and wondered if he ever thought of that cold, wet embrace. The memory of his lips on hers made her dizzy, like she was falling toward him on a heady tide. Unconsciously his head tilted, their breath mingled drawing her closer. The mere inch between them was charged with a gravity that begged her to close it.

Then Archer coughed. The sound startled her and snapped the attraction like a too-tight bowstring. Khoury sat back, opening a chasm between them filled with cool regret. He turned his gaze back to the fire. And said nothing.

His silence was infuriating. Cara was dying to know what he thought—about the river, about that kiss, about the laughing woman. With nerves drawn tight and quivering, she finally blurted out, "Who is she?"

"She?" His eyes went sharp, suddenly guarded.

"The one you were thinking of when you…when we…"

Recognition flashed in his eyes. He knew who she meant. "No one you need to worry about."

That didn't really answer her question but his tone's clipped finality made her hesitate. She chewing her lower lip anxiously. "Do you love her?" she finally ventured, braving his anger.

The captain's jaw clenched and unclenched, but he remained silent.

"Do you?" she pressed.

"Why?" His cobalt eyes bored into her, full of anger and something indefinable. "What does it matter?"

Taken aback by his intensity, Cara turned away to hide the truth that announced itself in the heat from her cheeks. "I just wondered, you know, if that was what it felt like." The lie slipped easily from her lips and for a moment, he simply stared at her. Cara peeked at him sideways and watched pity march across his features, softening him until he regarded her once more as a foundling child, not as a woman.

"Yes," he finally said with a soft snort of laughter that surprised her. His eyes dropped to his hand that smoothed the rough wool over his thigh. "That's what love feels like." His words were rough as if they were difficult to say. Disappointment twisted Cara's heart as the chasm between them widened.

So, he has a love of his own. A Maura who waits patiently for his return in some southern city. *And yet here he was standing between her and Sidonius.*

A memory of blood-stained snow doused her with cold reality. If she cared for him at all, she'd send him away. And if the captain left, Archer would too. And then Bradan would return to his Clan, leaving her all alone at Father's mercy. The thought frightened her so much she couldn't breathe.

But if the men stayed, none of them were safe. Father would find them and make good on his promise to make her watch them die.

The more Cara thought about it, the more sure she was that she would see the Keep again. He'd punish her, of course, but then life would go back to what it was before. As horrible as that would be to face alone, it was better than watching Khoury turn to dust.

"Captain, you should leave," she said.

"What?" He stared in surprise.

"Go home." She tried to sound firm despite the tears that crept up the back of her throat. "You should go home." She pushed his arm from her shoulder.

"I promised to help you."

"I know but I want you to…I mean you should…go back…to her." *And Archer should return to Maura.*

"Cara—"

"No, now. Before Sidonius kills you, too." As the last words rushed out on her breaking voice, she was sorry she'd said them. Naming her fear only made it more real.

The captain's face shuttered closed like windows against a storm. "I can't," he said.

"I'll be okay," she lied, hoping her face didn't show how frightened she was. "I'm sure I can find somewhere he won't—"

"She's dead."

Dead. The word dropped between them with all the harsh finality of a crushed sled. Her first instinct was to touch him, soothe his pain. But there was no healing this wound. She was shocked how little she knew about the man next to her.

"Now get some sleep," he said, getting up and leaving the cloak draped around her shoulders. He moved to put new branches on the fire and turned the embers. Squatting close to its warmth, he refused to even look at her.

She felt dismissed. But really, what more needed to be said? She snuggled her nose into his cloak, taking comfort from his scent until sleep claimed her.

The next day consisted of more walking and all too-short rests in the mud for it had started to rain as well. She missed Gar. She missed the peace of her simple days in Bear Clan's kitchens, and she even entertained a brief longing for the quiet inertia of the Keep. She couldn't remember ever being so tired. She barely noticed when the hills changed to grassy lowlands. Exhausted, she felt numb, unable to focus on anything beyond the next step. She didn't notice the tall grass or the lack of trees or even the gray skies that hovered threateningly over the meadow.

Suddenly, she was standing in slick mud surprised by the swollen river that flowed across her path. Her feet stopped at the water's edge without her bidding them to, but her eyes continued on to find a wall of dark towering trees rising from the far side of the glassy water. Their leafy majesty stirred something inside her.

Far different from the pine forests of the Northlands, the underbrush here was thick and dark, the trees wide-boled and taller than any Cara had yet seen. Their bark was purple-black and clung in roughened slabs to the straight trunks that drew her eyes upward. At the very top along the canopy, green leaves as large as platters splayed out, veined in purple and black. A heavy floral scent clung to the damp air as the heavy branches swayed in the breeze, revealing glimpses of dagger-like spikes. But there was a deeper difference here. A haunting familiarity that chilled Cara's bones even as it warmed her with an unexpected sense of homecoming.

The men knelt down to fill the waterskins, eyeing the forest with suspicion. Cara herself couldn't keep her eyes from returning to the woods. But it wasn't suspicion she felt, it was more like nostalgia.

But how can that be?

She bent down to slurp cool water from her cupped hand as Bradan argued with the captain behind her.

"I thought you said we wouldn't end up here," Bradan whispered angrily.

"Just bad luck," Khoury said. "We'll swing east for a bit."

"We can follow the river and then climb to that ridge up there," Archer said pointing to where the river curved out of sight at the foot of a hill sparsely covered with more familiar kinds of trees. "With the hill and the river between us and the blackthorns, we should be fine."

"What's the problem?" Cara asked.

"Foresthaven." Bradan gestured at the purple forest as if that explained anything.

"We'll be fine. The Huntresses won't bother us this side of the river," Khoury said.

"You don't know that," Bradan began.

"I doubt they'll bother to step outside their thorny hideaway for a couple of ragged travelers."

"We can't risk it," Bradan whispered, trying to avoid Cara's gaze. "It's not safe."

"Nowhere is safe," Khoury snapped. "For any of us. We need to get her to Iolair before Sidonius finds us."

They all fell silent at the captain's outburst. But Bradan wasn't done. "You know what they'll do to us," he said in the hushed tones of a threat, "if they catch us."

Cara's eyes slid to Khoury. Immoveable as stone, he stared at the older man, his jaw set angrily. "They won't. We follow the ridge." The two men stared at each other in a duel of wills, and in the end, it was Bradan who stalked away.

"What will they do to us?" Cara whispered to Archer, watching Khoury walk toward the bend in the river, surveying the terrain.

"Don't worry. They won't do anything to you." His smile didn't quite reach his eyes.

Cara wanted to ask Bradan what he knew about the strange forest, but when she sat down near him her attention was snagged by the wind whistling through the leaves. It sounded like voices, women's voices. She listened in a daze as the forest whispered to her. Time ceased to have meaning.

When Khoury signaled for them to move on, it had started raining again in earnest. The rain came down by the bucketful, soaking Cara's hair and weighing down her skirts and the cloak she wore.

At least it's not cold, she thought sullenly. The temperatures had mellowed since they left Gar behind. She wondered briefly what he was doing at that moment. Then her foot hit a tight clump of meadow grass and she stumbled, bringing her mind back to the terrain.

They followed the flight of the rain-driven river for a while and then, as it veered away into a gully between the strange purple-black forest and the hillside, they began to climb. The rain worsened, sluicing down her face as well as the steep slope. She climbed almost on all fours, grabbing brush and trees to keep from falling, feet slipping on wet leaves and mud. Cara was grateful when the terrain evened out. She paused to look around and was surprised at how high up they had gotten. Their path now cut across the slope. Her skirts were muddy to her hips and her arms to the elbows.

It felt like hours before Khoury called a halt. He stopped at a small rocky outcropping just barely large enough for the four of them to wedge themselves in between stone and tree to rest.

The sapling behind her pressed uncomfortably into her back as she wrung a torrent of water from her heavy skirts. Across the gully, Foresthaven still beckoned, pulling her eyes to it. A little further on, the stream split sending an overflow into the dark trees, disappearing from sight. Cara thought she'd imagined the spikes on the trees, but they were real. Even high up, large forbidding daggers adorned every cleaving of new growth, angry barbed thorns of black and deepest purple, many of them as long as her arm. The forest was eerie and dark, and the scent of damp earth was strong.

Cara's eyes drifted shut as the haunting mix of greening trees and pungent undergrowth teased her nose. The soft susurration of the wind and rain whispered to her like voices of the past, urgent and secretive. The rhythmic ebb and flow rocked her weary mind, and then…

…she crept through the forest on silent feet, coming to a glade of large flat stones. The rain was light beneath the canopy though the sound of water striking the leaves above drowned out most of the forest noises. Settling cross-legged on a dry granite perch beneath a large branch, she took the whetstone from her belt pouch, unsheathed her sword and began to polish the edge with care, humming a simple tune in time to the rhythmic swish of stone on metal.

Bradan's grip on her shoulder woke Cara from her dreaming.

"Time to move on." His eyes fixed curiously on her.

She yawned, trying to clear the drowsiness. "Already?"

"What were you singing? I didn't recognize it." He helped her to her feet as Khoury started to climb.

Cara shrugged as she watched Archer climb out next. She didn't remember singing anything. The rain had softened though the clouds still threatened a further downpour. Cara climbed out next with Bradan behind her lending a supporting arm.

Still groggy, she caught her skirts on a protruding branch, and before she knew what was happening she lost her footing and tumbled down the wet slope. Rolling and sliding, she slammed into a tree, knocking the breath from her lungs as her body wrapped around its thick trunk. Up the hill, the others were out of sight and calling to her, but she couldn't answer. She gripped some small vines and tried to scramble up the slope, but the ground gave beneath her and she slid down further.

She was almost to the bottom when her forehead glanced off a rough-barked trunk, snapping her head back. The final ten feet were a sharp, blind drop into the shock of cold fast-moving water. Panicked, she flailed her arms and legs against the weight of her voluminous clothes, but within moments darkness closed over her mind…

…Tasting lake water, she cursed her panic and kicked out strongly for the surface. For a moment, she had actually forgotten how to swim. Mother's love, what nonsense. How she had even fallen in was a mystery, but she was grateful at least no one had seen it. She crawled out onto the flat rocks, angrily squeezing the water from her hair. She stood for a moment, ashamed by her sudden clumsiness. She felt disoriented, like a bent old woman who forgot her purpose the moment after she'd settled on it. She shook the water from herself as best she could and started for home.

Cara woke coughing to a worm's eye view of old brown leaves and protruding roots. She lay on her belly, her mouth tasting of dirty water. Still dazed, she shoved to her feet and looked down at the muddy edge of a small stream surrounded by the strange thorn trees. The deeply shadowed forest was eerie, and she heard ghostly murmurings wafting through the branches. She stood and staggered with the weight of her sodden clothes, eager to find Khoury.

A crash of breaking branches startled her. Fear pounded in her veins as the ghostly whispers rose in agitated alarm driving her to thoughtless action. Feeling trapped, she unclasped the heavy cloak and let it fall to the ground as she fled into the brush. Whatever she'd heard thundered after her. Her mind conjured up creatures like the hunting cat of her dreams, only this time she was no hunter. Fear muddled her already scattered thoughts as the forest's whispering spirits nipped at her heels. Then she tripped and landed hard on her knees just as her name echoed off the trees.

"Cara!"

It was Archer. She was safe. She felt foolish. Relief rushed to her head making the world tilt before she fainted.

She jerked to a stop, thinking she had tripped. But she was walking, not falling. A niggling disturbance flitted through the edges of her mind. Had she forgotten something?

Then a horn sounded urgently in the distance, a pattern of four that was repeated. Intruders in the wood! She unsheathed her sword in one sleek movement and ran toward the sound, death on her mind.

Cara's eyes shot open to find Khoury, Archer, and Bradan leaning over her.

"Why'd you run?" Archer's face was a mask of worry. "Didn't you hear us?"

"No. Well, yes. I mean, I…" Cara sat up and put a hand to her throbbing head as she swayed in confusion.

"No time for talk," Khoury said as he and Archer each grabbed an arm and lifted her to her feet. "We've got to get back across the river." Khoury's jaw was tight with tension. He turned and jogged back the way they had come, his hand clamped around her wrist, dragging her after him. She noticed her muddy cloak draped over Archer's shoulder.

As they raced through the forest, she kept expecting to cross the stream she'd woken up in, but they never did. Confused, she focused on moving her feet and following the captain.

Suddenly, a wall of the black-daggered trees blocked their way, so closely packed no light or color was visible between the dark trunks. The trees hadn't been there before, had they? She couldn't remember, but she knew they were on the wrong side of those thorns. Somehow she'd led them into Foresthaven.

When a horn sounded deep in the trees, she knew in her bones this was a very bad place to be.

They found another overflow stream, but the fat branches and daggered spines of the thorn trees were there too, closing over the water, blocking their escape. Without missing a beat, Khoury veered away from the water, following the wall of dagger thorns. Cara hoped there would be a break in the foliage soon. The whisperings were getting angrier by the minute.

A whirring noise made Cara duck. Behind her, Archer stumbled and went down with a grunt. She glanced back at him though Khoury still had her by the wrist and showed no sign of slowing. A cord was wrapped around Archer's torso and legs. Another whirring sound followed, and she heard Bradan hit the ground.

"Khoury!" she shouted, pulling him to a stop.

He turned and slid her behind him while his right hand rested on his still-sheathed sword. Archer and Bradan lay in the wet leaves not more than ten feet from each other, cords clamping their arms tightly to their sides and circling their legs. Then in the blink of an eye, they were surrounded by leather-clad warriors with drawn bows. All of them were women. Like soldiers, the women were dressed alike in hardened leather bodices with epaulets all the same cut. Their brown upper arms were bare and wooden bracers carved with a leafy motif ran from elbows to wrists. Measured aggression shone from their uniformly brown eyes, and they all had black hair knotted at their necks. Short swords hung at their waists.

No words were spoken in those first long minutes as the warriors took their measure of the men. But Cara noted the gathering tension in Khoury. Two of the warriors leaned over, cut the leg cords off Archer and Bradan, and hauled them roughly to their feet. Then the tallest spoke.

"My, my. Trespassers." Her voice was low and smooth, and she had an unpleasant smile. "Do you know what happens to those who trespass our Haven?" She turned to Khoury, looking him up and down with obvious disdain.

Khoury straightened with an almost lordly air and turned his palms toward her, arms away from his sides. A gesture of peace even Cara recognized.

"Well met, Huntress." He inclined his head at her warily. "Mason Khoury, Captain of Swords, at your service."

"I am Rebeka Danad, Chief Scout of the Haven. Your trespassing will not be tolerated."

"Our presence here is merely an unhappy accident."

"Unhappy indeed. For you."

It wasn't the words but the hate behind them that shocked Cara. Why would these women hate them?

"It was an accident," she explained. "I fell in the stream, and they came to find me."

The warrior's eyes narrowed as they roamed over Cara's face. Anger glinted in them. "Was it he who bloodied your face, sister?" She pointed to Cara's forehead.

"What?" Cara raised a hand to her head, her fingers coming away red. "No," she said. "This must have happened when I fell down the hill."

"Is that what he told you to say?" The woman's eyes were skeptical.

"Of course not," Khoury said, with growing irritation.

"Then let her speak," the woman dared.

"I did speak. You're not listening," Cara argued. "I hit a tree."

"Someone hunts her," Khoury said, "and we've been charged with her safety."

"And do you think you're safe here?" The Huntress laughed.

Their arguing made Cara's head throb worse. "Iolair is safe," she said. "I need to go to Iolair."

"Iolair?" The warrior woman's scowl deepened and she looked back at Khoury. "And you thought to use our roads?"

"No," Khoury's voice was even. "As the girl said, an accident brought her here. We ask only safe passage back to the Tangle, and you'll never see us again."

"There is no safe passage here for your kind." Her words dripped with loathing.

His kind? What did that mean? Then Cara remembered Archer's words: They won't do anything to you.

Not me but the others. It dawned on Cara that this warrior meant men, all men, not just Khoury.

The Huntress drew her sword in one slow, deliberate move. Khoury hand tightened on the hilt of his, but he refrained from baring the blade. Cara feared bloodshed was next.

Bradan cleared his throat. "There's an Islander who'll kill this girl if he catches her. If not for courtesy, then for a sister in need, let us pass in peace."

The tall warrior turned her deadly stare to Cara. "Is this true? A sorcerer seeks to claim you?"

"Yes." Cara's throat was dry with fear.

"Then the Sisters will take you to safety." She strode up to Cara and took her none too gently by the arm, pulling her away from Khoury.

Khoury's hand snaked out, grabbing the warrior's wrist, breaking her hold on Cara's arm. "She stays with us." The growl in his tone surprised Cara. The nearest archer drew her bow full back and pointed it at Khoury's face but he didn't flinch.

The leader yanked her arm from his grip with a frown. "Touch me again and you die, Outsider."

Cara trembled as the warrior put a guiding hand back on her shoulder and pushed her away from the captain, her insolent stare daring him to refuse again. Regardless of what she had said to Khoury in the night, Cara wasn't ready to give them up, especially not for these sullen warriors. "Wait," she pleaded. "I need them. Father will stop at nothing."

"Father?" The warrior turned back to Khoury and smiled with disbelief. "Her father is after you? Perhaps you should repent your crime, return the girl and beg his forgiveness."

Cara stepped between him and the warrior. "It's not like that. He saved me."

"More likely he stole you." The tall woman lifted her sword slowly past Cara's face and pressed it against Khoury's throat. "Shame on you, warrior," she said, "I should slay you right here for your sins."

"He hasn't done anything!" Cara yelled though the warrior ignored her. Determined, Cara stepped forward, lifted her shaking hand to the blade and pushed it away from the pulse in his neck. "Stop."

"Men are not trustworthy, little sister."

Bradan took half a step forward and was rewarded with a knife at his throat as well. "I beg the right to be heard by your Elders."

"You men have no rights here," said the leader, her eyes never leaving Khoury's.

"No, but she does." Bradan nodded his head at Cara.

"Yes," Cara leapt on the idea. "I wish to see your Elders."

The warrior woman hesitated, looking down at Cara's unguarded face and then back to Khoury. "Very well, the high priestess will decide your fates. But there will be no bargaining once she decides to dispose of you."

Before Cara could register the threat, a young woman ran up and skidded to a halt, sword drawn. The newcomer's blonde hair was striking in comparison to her black-haired sisters. Though knotted in a similar fashion, her hair was disheveled with curly wet strands, loose and dangling. She didn't wear the uniform armor of the others either, but her blade glinted dangerously.

"What are you doing here?" the tall warrior hissed with obvious hate. She stepped back from Khoury and sheathed her sword with an angry snap.

"The horn summoned. I am here."

The blonde woman's eyes were fierce, deep green and flecked with gold. When she looked at Cara, those eyes bored right through her, shifting something in the air. Or was it the light? Transfixed by the girl's ferocity, her stomach flip-flopped. This woman terrified her as much as Sidonius did—maybe more.

CHAPTER 22
FALIN

When Falin burst upon the scouts and their captives, she was surprised to find the three Outsiders still standing and unbloodied. Even more surprising was the small, pale wisp of a girl standing between Rebeka's sword and one man's throat. The girl was shaking in fear, but her defiance had certainly cost Rebeka respect. Falin smiled at her rival's embarrassment, knowing her own presence there only fanned the flames of the chief scout's anger.

"It was an error. All is well in hand," Rebeka pronounced in an imperious manner. "We don't need you, little sister."

The "little" irritated Falin almost as much as Rebeka's manner, but she would nurse the offense in silence as she always did until the next time they crossed blades in the sparring ring.

Falin sheathed her weapon and relaxed. "As you say, Rebeka," she said, purposely forgoing Rebeka's new title. She placed her hand over her heart and executed a cursory bow that barely met the requirements of protocol.

Ignoring the slights, Rebeka turned her attention back to the Outsiders which gave Falin a chance to study them. She was curious, having seen so few. Most travelers knew to avoid their woods, and she had only participated in a handful of Cullings herself. But when

Falin caught the gaze of the white-haired girl, it was like a knife to her bones. She felt reality waver for a moment.

The girl was slight and weak, her fear palpable. Falin felt a surprising tug of pity, something she'd never been prone to. Startled by the emotion, she steeled herself.

Ever a Huntress. There is no place for weakness here, hers or mine.

Of the men, the one who'd asked to see the Elders was older, his once-auburn beard braids now grizzled with gray. His carriage reminded her of Sorchia. There was also a younger red-haired warrior. Brawny and muscular, he had a well-worn bow slung across his back. And then there was the last man, the one the girl was trying to protect. Falin caught his eye for a mere moment but would never forget the intensity of blue that peered out from beneath his dark brows. Battle-scarred and muscular, he stood with confidence and a leader's dispassion. His strength made Falin smile. He would have been a challenge. Too bad he'd be culled like the rest.

Two of the men were already bolo-bound. Rebeka's scouts then bound the leader's hands behind him and confiscated their weapons. Only the girl was allowed to walk freely. Once the prisoners were secured, Rebeka and her scouts ushered the strangers toward the village, ignoring Falin completely. Falin watched them depart and then followed on curious cat feet.

CHAPTER 23
KHOURY

Khoury followed the Huntresses through the dark towering trees. Once the women had appeared, the woods brightened. The wall of thorns they'd been following seemed to disappear. Archer and Bradan were a few paces behind him, and Cara to his left, flanked by two warriors. And somewhere in the woods behind them, the captain's intuition told him the other warrior followed—her presence a cold draft on his neck.

The blonde warrior had looked disturbingly familiar, but he couldn't place her. And it wasn't just him. Archer had looked twice, and Bradan had studied her with more interest than he'd shown since the giant raid.

Glancing in Cara's direction, Khoury noted her watching him with a worried expression. She had surprised him when she stepped forward in his defense although he probably should have expected it. That protectiveness reminded him of the day on the tundra when she refused to give up her bears. A smile lurked beneath his beard at the thought of such misplaced affection.

After an hour or so, the group arrived at a large village clearing. He couldn't see much of it because they emerged from the dense woods at the door of a small mud hut that sat just at the edge of foliage. Still, the scents and sounds reminded him of Bear Clan. He saw no other villagers as they slipped between the guards and through the squat doorway into the darkened interior. Once inside, Khoury made a quick circuit of the room. There was only the one door, and the slit-like windows—of which there were two and only as wide as his hand—didn't face the village. A small hole in the roof for ventilation wasn't large enough for a small boy let alone a full-grown man. Rebeka pushed a cowed Cara in last. The door shut with a soft clunk, and he heard the latch drop. Rebeka's fading voice instructed the guards to watch the door.

"Untie us, Cara," said Archer softly, moving toward the center where there was the best light. Cara stood where Rebeka had left her.

"I can't," she said. "I promised."

"We need to make a run for it," Archer urged.

"They're coming right back with their high priestess. She said if you're untied, they'll kill you immediately."

"Cara, they're going to kill us anyway," Bradan said. "Help us."

"I can't," she whined. Cara was exhausted, obviously still shaken from her tumble and the confrontation in the woods. His heart went out to her.

"Leave her be." He stepped closer to her and was rewarded with a grateful ice-blue glance. "We'll get our chance. Be patient." Archer backed down, trusting in Khoury's timing just like he had at the Keep. But Bradan growled and angrily turned on his heel to pace the far side of the hut.

The girl had been right though, it was only a few minutes before the latch clicked and the door swung open. Rebeka stood outlined in the light from outside.

"Back up," she ordered, her sword pointed at the men. Everyone except Cara moved back a step.

A black-robed woman entered with soft footsteps. Her hood was down revealing black hair streaked with gray, arranged in multiple loops draped across her shoulders. Her face was sturdy and weathered. Her staff of red wood thumped on the ground with each step. She scanned their faces with dispassionate calm until her eyes fell on Cara and then she stared.

Was that surprise he read on the priestess's face? If so, it was gone in a moment.

"Welcome, trespassers." The woman's voice was soft but grim. "It's an unfortunate day for you as I'm afraid the Law forbids you to leave."

Cara stood her ground between the men and the priestess. Her gloves were tucked into her belt, and he wondered when she'd taken them off.

Khoury pressed his lips together in frustration. The whole thing was ridiculous. He cleared his throat. "Priestess, we want nothing from the Huntresses except to be returned to the Tangle."

The old woman stepped past Cara to stare up at him with a placid smile. The top of her head barely reached his chin. Cocking her head like a bird, she eyed him with curiosity. "So, you're the one."

"What one?"

The priestess chuckled softly with a shake of her head.

"Will you listen to our story?" He barely kept the frustration from his voice.

"I already know what you're going to say." She dismissed him with a wave of her hand as she paced a slow circle around him. "I see you still deny what you know."

Confused, he looked down at her. "Deny what?"

"You're only wasting time," she said. Then, she turned and circled Archer, the gentle smile never wavering. She stopped in front of the Northerner and lifted a gentle hand to his cheek. "You are not cursed, storyteller. Except by your own hesitation."

Then she walked to where Bradan eyed her with angry suspicion. "I do not fear death," he said.

Her face softened, and she laid a gentle hand over his heart. "Our hearts feel the weight of your tears, Brother. You have our sympathy."

"I'd rather have cooperation than sympathy," he said.

She didn't reply.

She turned to Cara and took her hand. "Little sister, I will speak with you in private though there may not be much I can do about your situation. I do not write the Laws. Your fate, the fate of all of you, rests in the Mothers' hands now." She drew the girl toward the door.

"No," Cara balked, though her hand stayed in the woman's. Khoury noted Cara's eyes glaze as if she was listening to something far away. "Promise you won't kill them when I'm gone."

"You don't trust us." The woman's voice was curious though her face was stern.

Cara swallowed hard. "I don't know what to think, but I need them."

The priestess smiled and patted Cara's hand. "I promise, child, no harm will come to them. For now. Come with me. There are fewer ears in my hall." Cara looked back at the men, offered a thin, rather bleak smile and followed the priestess out. The other warrior women followed and the door closed with a soft thud of the latch.

"Make peace with your gods if you have them, Southerner," Bradan said as he lowered himself to the ground and leaned against the wall. It was the closest the chieftain had come to insulting him in all the years since they first met.

"We're not dead yet," Khoury said.

"We should never have been this close," Bradan snapped.

"The closer we were to Foresthaven, the fewer eyes Sidonius was likely to have. It was just bad luck we ended up right at the Thorns."

"You rely far too much on luck. And it appears yours has run out."

"Don't be so sure about that yet," Khoury said. His gut told him he had been right to come this way. And his gut was more to be trusted than most men. An opportunity would come, like it always did. He settled himself down to the floor to relax as best he could before Cara came back and he found out how much trouble they were actually in.

Then, on to Iolair and, if all went well, they could sail out of Cortland. Khoury knew a barely honorable smuggler who owed him a favor.

CHAPTER 24
CARA

The high priestess led Cara across the center of the village, a collection of mud-coated huts scattered beneath the looming trees. Cara hadn't noticed any of the strange purple-black trees on their trip to the village but there was an enormous one standing in the center of the clearing encircled by carved stones, each the size of Gar's head, inscribed with a mark. Its trunk was as wide as she was tall. The branches hung with braziers of incense and a flock of ravens, all of whom squawked angrily at her as she passed.

The village itself was a lot like Bear Clan. Except she saw no men. Not a single one. No children either. The youngest of the girls looked to be about fourteen or so. To a woman, they were dark-skinned, black-haired and tall, and when she accidentally caught someone's eye, she was rewarded with a contemptuous sneer. Many of the women wore the same leather armor as the scouting party, though some did not. But everyone carried a weapon. There were sparring rings and more than one smithy visible.

They even had a stable and horses, which Cara recognized from illustrations in the histories she'd found in Sidonius's library. Their unfamiliar but warm animal scent wafting across the open area reminded her painfully of Gar.

With her bare hand in the high priestess's, Cara searched the woman's mind for the key that would keep them safe. Unfortunately, the old woman's mind was a calm pool too deep for Cara to plumb its depths. What she did find was that the woman had a warmth of heart that reminded her of Ealea. And so Cara could only hope for the best and put her trust in that.

The woman led her to a door set into the side of a small hill that rose abruptly at one end of the village. Following the priestess into the hillside sanctuary, she was surprised to find that the passageway led back a hundred yards or so and then opened up into a vaulted antechamber lit through vents in the roof as well as rows of hanging lanterns. The elegant upward sweep of the architecture inside gave it a sense of space. A hearth was set into the dirt wall at each compass point but only the fireplace in the east was ablaze, giving off heat and a soft golden light. Cara stood in the center of the room, her mouth agape in awe.

The woman gestured to a bench and Cara sat, her hands twiddling in her lap. The priestess leaned her staff against a nearby wall. She grabbed a cloth off a hook, dipped it in a barrel of water near the hearth, and then joined Cara. A raven, which had been hiding near the ceiling, startled Cara as it fluttered down with a squawk to perch near the bench.

The old woman smiled as she dabbed the cloth on the sore spot where Cara's forehead had grazed the tree. "Don't be afraid. We mean you no harm." The old woman gently wiped away dirt and blood from Cara's face.

Too nervous to smile back, Cara's voice trembled, "And what about my friends?"

"I hold no malice toward them either. But we do have rules."

The priestess sat down on the bench next to Cara. The raven joined her, strutting its way over her skirts as she absently stroked its sleek black head. "My name is Sorchia, High Priestess of the Haven, head of the Elders. What are you called?"

"Cara. Just Cara." Cara poked at the tender swelling on her hairline with fingers that tingled with familiar sunshine.

"Have you heard of Foresthaven before, child?"

"No. Should I have?"

"I daresay your captain knew the danger. Did he not warn you about wandering here?"

"I didn't wander here. I rolled down a hill into a river."

"That is unfortunate. Your friends seem quite loyal."

"They were only coming to find me. Why can't you just let us go on our way?" Cara couldn't keep the whine out of her voice as her fingers traced rhythmically over her forehead. The headache she'd had since her fall had finally dissipated.

"I have nothing against your friends. But I cannot speak for the Mothers."

"What mothers?"

"May I tell you a story?"

Cara nodded as the priestess reached for a goblet and flask that waited on a low table nearby. She poured clear amber liquid into the cup and handed it to Cara before pouring herself one as well. As she returned the flask to the table, Cara sniffed suspiciously at the goblet finding the familiar aromas of apples and sweet pears.

"We are the direct descendants of the druids of ancient Tangora, children of the refugees who fled King Chrostan's Guard, the last of our line." She glanced at Cara as if searching for some understanding of the history she referred to. When Cara shrugged, Sorchia sighed and continued.

"When Chrostan decided the old gods were no longer necessary, he instructed his Guard to seek out and eliminate their servants, the druids. They began executing any who possessed that magic, enslaving our children and forbidding them their power. Rebellion brewed and our hearts grew vengeful.

"There was a rebellion, a very bloody one. One we could not win and finally we were forced to flee. There is a lake near where you were found, at the end of the river on the eastern border. It is sacred.

There our men chose to stand and fight, allowing what women and children had escaped time to hide in the woods. We call it the Pool of Blood because Chrostan's Guard slaughtered every last one of them. The water that flows through that river is blessed by their sacrifice.

"With the men dead, the Guard pursued the women and children into the forest. In desperation the wise Mothers, the oldest druids among us, prayed to the old gods: the same gods Chrostan scorned. They prayed so passionately that the spirits of the elm and the blackthorn and the ivy took pity on them. In that hour, it is said, the Mothers were swallowed up by the woods. Their souls were absorbed into the spirit of the forest itself and in the same hour, the great blackthorns grew into an impenetrable wall of thorns. So angry was the forest at our plight, that it killed the men of the Guard. Not a single one returned to their arrogant king."

Cara remembered the angry whisperings that chased her through the woods. Were they the voice of the Mothers?

"We have lived in this thorny haven for a century now. The old gods ask only that we worship them and honor our lost Mothers. Men are not tolerated within the Thorn Gates and not since before the first Culling have any walked here in peace. The Forest has eyes, girl. And a very long memory. It hates men, especially men of the sword."

"But we mean no harm. We simply needed a safe road."

The priestess smiled indulgently. "A road you may need, but the road through Foresthaven is far from safe. The Thorns don't think, they only respond."

Desperate, Cara dropped to her knees in front of the old priestess. "Please, please don't kill them. So many have already died because of me." The scent of dust touched her nose. Faces flashed through her mind: Reith Carter and Ingrid and Ealea. Would Khoury, Archer, and Bradan join the ever-lengthening list of her sins? "I couldn't bear to be responsible for their deaths, too." A tear of frustration slid down her cheek.

"What others do is not your responsibility."

"I did nothing when I should have done something."

"You will grow into your power."

"I have no power. If I did, they wouldn't have died."

"You are wrong. You possess the power to change things."

"Nothing changes. I'm only a snowflake," she whispered, sitting back on her heels and letting her hands drop to her lap.

"But you've already changed things," the priestess whispered back with a knowing smile.

Cara thought back to the Keep, the tundra, the giants. She'd been blown around by events beyond her control at every turn. "No. I haven't."

"I've dreamed of you, child. I saw the keys you stole."

"Because I had to."

"No, you could have done nothing. You saved your bears from the fire. You braved a blizzard and faced down the sorcerer in the void."

The way Sorchia said those things felt like a lie. She made Cara's actions sound like more than they were. And even if what she said was true, Cara hadn't saved Ingrid or Ealea. And it looked like she wouldn't be able to save the men either. "Those things mean nothing if people around me keep dying."

"The sorcerer killed those people, not you."

"But it was because of me." Cara wished it could be different. "Why won't he let me go?"

"Your magic keeps him young. He's not a fool."

Her magic? She hadn't realized the truth. He didn't need her, only her magic. Bradan was right. Sidonius had known about her power all along. Cold certainty closed around her heart. "He'll never stop."

"Not while you're both living," the priestess agreed.

"I have to kill him?" Cara had sworn to herself that there would be no more death.

"Yes. And it will cost you dearly." Sadness pooled in those ancient eyes.

"The cost is already too high," Cara said feeling trapped.

"Some things must be done for the safety of all." The priestess peered closely at Cara. "Don't you agree?"

Cara nodded. What else could she say?

"The Mothers want to know, little one. Are you strong enough?"

Cara squeezed her eyes closed. Fear leached along her limbs at the memory of her failure at the Standing Stones. "Not without my friends."

"Then we must ask the Mothers for mercy." The priestess lifted the raven onto her hand and spoke to it in a language Cara didn't understand. She thrust the bird into the sky, and Cara watched it winging its way up through a skylight.

As they waited, the only sound was the crackling of the fire. After what seemed an eternity, the bird returned, fluttering out of the cold hearth in the west. It landed on the priestess's outstretched hand and deposited something on her palm, squawking angrily. Then, it fluttered back to the rafters.

The priestess picked up a small sprig of purple black leaves and fat black berries. "Four berries."

"What does that mean?" Cara's eyes danced between the berries and the priestess.

"Four berries. Four lives." The priestess pressed the sprig into Cara's hand. "The Mothers remember what it's like to be hunted. They wish to help you."

"You'll let us go?"

"It won't be as easy as that."

"But you won't kill them," Cara said, her voice trembling.

"No."

Cara hugged the priestess's knees. "Oh, thank you."

"You're not safe yet." She stroked Cara's hair softly. "Fate brought you to Foresthaven, and we must pray she can get you back out." The priestess rose, pulling Cara up gently to stand with her, then gathered her staff.

"I'll return you to your friends. Their weapons will be returned soon. But you must keep them calm and the blades sheathed. And above all, don't anger Rebeka."

Cara nodded eagerly and cupped the berries to her chest with gratitude as she followed the priestess out of the hillside and across the village.

Rebeka lounged on a bench at the door to the hut when they arrived. She jumped to her feet and saluted the high priestess.

"The Mothers have spoken, Rebeka. Keep these Outsiders safe until I speak with the Elders. No other Sisters can know."

"What about a Culling?" Cara noted disappointment on the warrior's face.

"At the Elders' discretion, as always, my daughter. Patience." Sorchia turned to hug Cara, and whispered, "Rest up and be ready in the hour before dawn. I will send a Huntress to guide you. Remember, no matter what, do exactly as she says."

CHAPTER 25
FALIN

After watching Rebeka's scouting party put the strangers in the prisoners' hut, Falin grabbed her bow and padded into he forest to hunt. She wondered if she'd have spared the Outsiders' lives had she found them first. A wry grin twisted her lips. Probably not. She didn't need that kind of complication.

Rebeka, on the other hand, had reputation to spare and probably thought a public Culling would increase her standing with the Elders. Even with Chief Scout under her belt, Rebeka was still currying favor. Mothers' love, she'd be vying for a seat on the Council next. Regardless, the men would be dead by morning. Not that Falin cared either way; they weren't her problem.

When she returned with a few fat rabbits strung over her shoulder, Rebeka accosted her the moment she stepped into the clearing. "The high priestess wants to see you."

"I'll see her when I've eaten," Falin said, avoiding Rebeka's eyes. The scout's imperious tone never failed to stir Falin's insolence.

"No, now." Rebeka's face reddened. "You'll go and mind your manners, dandelion." She spat the nickname like a curse, referring to Falin's yellow hair. "She is the high priestess, not some thornless hunter like you."

Refusing to rise to the bait, Falin walked away waving her hand dismissively. She enjoyed flaunting Rebeka's inability to force respect from her. All the same, Falin turned her steps for Sorchia's, catch still in hand. The priestess had always been kind to Falin. In fact, it had been her decision to adopt the blonde Outsider orphan all those years ago.

Falin approached the hill, undoing her braid one-handed. Then, with the rabbits dangling from a leather thong between her teeth, she quickly combed her hair with her fingers and knotted it again. She wiped most of the dirt and blood from her tunic and sauntered in.

"Well, hello," Sorchia said, not turning from the steaming pot over the fire.

"Priestess Sorchia." Falin placed her hand over her heart and bowed deeply with respect and love. "A gift of rabbits," she boasted.

"My favorite. As you well know." She peered intently at Falin. "Is this a bribe for some as yet undiscovered crime?"

"Sorchia, you wound me. I walk the straight and narrow every day," Falin said with a knowing smile.

Sorchia snorted with skepticism. "As you say. Why don't you clean them for us to share? I have something to ask you."

Falin chuckled as she threw a leg over the bench and dropped the carcasses on the seat in front of her.

Sorchia raised an eyebrow. "Is something amusing?"

"When you busy me with kitchen work, I know you're going to say something I won't like." Falin bent to her task, wielding her knife with sharp sure cuts.

Sorchia smiled wordlessly.

"I'm right, aren't I?" Falin's green eyes twinkled merrily.

"Perhaps it will be happy news."

"Oh Mothers' love, now I know it's bad. All right, out with it. Don't wait and ruin my dinner." Falin finished stripping the skins and stopped to stare expectantly at the older woman.

"I do have a job for someone. You might actually want it."

"Liar."

Sorchia sighed, the smile dropping from her weathered lips. "You're restless, daughter."

"That's nothing new." Falin sobered, chafing at the unseen chains that held her. "My feet were born to roam." She sliced the bellies and swept the innards onto a cloth on the floor and then hacked the meat into sections with vehemence. Gathering the chunks in her hands, she walked over to a shallow pan, dumped the pieces in, and pushed it into the hottest part of the fire where the meat sizzled angrily. "You know the Elders will never let me beyond the Gates."

"I know, and I supported that restriction. You were not ready."

Not wanting to hear another lecture about her failings, Falin plopped back down on the bench. She didn't want to argue with Sorchia again but the raw burn of injustice pressed at her. "They don't even trust me enough to let me fight as a mercenary. It's ridiculous. I could be useful."

Sorchia looked at her with motherly disapproval. "You are useful. Here."

Trapped between her pride and a Huntress's duty, the burn bubbled over. "Catching rabbits every night? Any weanling pup could do that. I'm wasting my time!" Falin angrily drove her knife, point down, into the bench.

As Sorchia nodded to herself, Falin realized she had revealed too much. The priestess took on her teaching tone as she rearranged the rabbit in the fry pan. "We don't seek to elevate ourselves above our Sisters, do we?"

"No," Falin murmured, pushing down an angry retort about Rebeka's faults.

"And even if we go beyond the Thorn Gates, we must remain true to our Mothers in all things."

"Ever a Huntress." The proper answer.

"That's what I want to know, Falin. Are you one of us?"

Falin paused. Was she one of them? She used to think it a stupid question, but now…

"I would have been," she whispered, "with all my heart." It was all she'd ever wanted. Until last summer.

Sorchia sighed and relaxed. Whatever answer the old woman was looking for she'd found though Falin still couldn't sense which way the wind was blowing.

"I didn't agree with that decision," the older woman said. "They were wrong to overlook you." Falin looked up to see Sorchia's eyes mist with sadness. She plucked her knife from the bench angrily. She didn't want Sorchia's pity. Pity was for the weak.

"Their loss," Falin tossed out on a careless huff of breath, her armor once more in place.

"And my gain." Sorchia stirred the rabbit again and then checked the stew pot before she sat on the bench and laid a hand on Falin's arm. "I believe, my fierce one, that only you can help me with my plan."

"Plan?"

"A very sensitive matter has just come to my attention."

"The strangers?" Now, it was getting interesting.

"How do you know about that?"

"One of Rebeka's new bloods sounded the horn."

"And of course you went to help."

"Of course." Falin's smile was ferocious.

"Then you've met them?"

"I saw them, no more. Rebeka doesn't share with me."

"No more than you share with her."

"True." Sorchia was always even-handed in her criticism of the two women, though Falin had never revealed the cruel depths of the lifelong feud between Rebeka and her. A feud which had come to a head at Summer Solstice when Rebeka was chosen as Chief Scout. Falin had worked hard to earn the right, and she was the better scout. But her uncompromising nature had won her more enemies than friends. Being passed over irked her like an itch she couldn't scratch.

"I've spoken with the white-haired girl," Sorchia continued. "She may be young, but she will grow into a power the likes of which we've not seen since the Mothers."

"That snip of a mouse tail? She's afraid of her own shadow."

"Nevertheless, the Mothers have shown her to me in dreams. They want her to claim her destiny." The priestess gently shook Falin's arm for emphasis. "And she can lead you to your own."

Falin yanked her arm away. "Lead me? The meek little rabbit?"

Sorchia sighed. "Don't be deceived by appearances, proud one. All the same, she will need your strength or she won't survive."

Falin sniffed with scorn. Still, despite her sharp words, she remembered the strange sympathy that had washed over her. "Okay," she relented, "so I'm to help the girl."

"And the men."

"The men?"

"Yes."

"What about the Culling?"

Sorchia shook her head. "She will need the men, too." The priestess's eyes bored into Falin's as if offering something unspoken.

"You're not telling the other Elders about them?"

"No." The hard word set Sorchia's jaw on edge. Unfailingly forthright, Falin had never known Sorchia to lie to the other Elders. The truth of what Sorchia was asking made Falin's heart pound.

"And so," Sorchia continued, her gaze wandering down to her hands, "your part in this won't be discussed. When you leave, they will certainly be upset."

And think I finally deserted, Falin thought.

Sorchia waited in silence, letting the Huntress come to her own conclusions.

I'd be banished. Forbidden to return. Falin surveyed her possibilities. If she refused to help and stayed with Rebeka and this Council, she'd always be the Outsider, a lowly hunter forever. But if she left with the strangers, she couldn't begin to guess where she'd end up. New lands sparkled in her imagination.

"If I go, I'd be leaving for good," Falin said, making sure she understood.

Sorchia clucked softly and embraced her, something she hadn't done since Falin was small. The Huntress felt some desperation in the gesture. "Only do this if it's what you want, Falin," Sorchia whispered.

"Oh, I want this." Excitement coursed through her. "I'll do whatever you ask."

Sorchia drew back, chagrined at Falin's enthusiasm. "You must lead the strangers, all of them, through the Thorn Gates." Her voice was little more than a whisper. "The Elders won't look kindly on this so you should go in secret before sunrise."

"Secret? But Rebeka and her scouts already know." The last thing Falin wanted was to leave Sorchia in shame.

"You must perform a false Culling," Sorchia whispered as if, even though she said them supposedly with the Mothers' blessing, the words were a sin.

Falin's heart hammered at the thought of such dangerous subterfuge. She was not as devout as most, but if they caught her lighting a false Culling, they'd slit her throat right there and scatter her ashes in the Outlands. Betrayal and blasphemy would be Falin's legacy. "Rebeka won't agree to this."

"Let me handle, Rebeka. She's devoted to the Mothers."

Falin didn't agree about Rebeka's devotion but soon it wouldn't matter. "Where exactly do they need to go, these strangers?"

"Lead them south. Use the Guide's Prayer if the Thorns get restless. Make sure Cara gets to Iolair safely."

"Iolair."

"South to the White Mountains and then east to the pass."

It was a long way, far past the Thorns. A smile lifted Falin's lips. "I promise they'll reach Iolair," she said, already going over in her mind all she'd need to do before morning.

Sorchia surprised Falin with a sniffle and rose from the bench, her face in shadow. She puttered to the hearth and cleared her throat with a cough. "Well, now that that's settled, I'm starving."

Sorchia stirred the rabbit until it was cooked through and then dumped the meat into the vegetable stew as Falin grabbed two clay bowls from a shelf. She filled them with the fragrant stew and handed one to Sorchia along with a spoon. The two women sat on the bench eating the savory meal, each lost in her own thoughts until Falin realized she didn't want to leave the priestess with this awkwardness between them.

She put down her bowl and fetched the wineskin from the pantry. Pouring the deep purple liquid into two goblets, she shared the bittersweet blackthorn wine with the priestess and then began regaling Sorchia with tales of shame from that morning's sparring and idle gossip from the smithy. Sorchia recounted familiar tales of what a terror Falin had been as a child. They ate their dinner of rabbit and hoar-nuts with laughter. It was a good last meal together. When Falin finally left, it was with a lingering hug for the only mother she'd ever known, but the outside world beckoned and Falin wasn't about to turn it down.

CHAPTER 26
BRADAN

Exhausted but unable to sleep, Bradan lay on the reed mat and listened to the ghostly whispers that had followed him since they'd entered Foresthaven, women's voices whose hum drowned out the familiar spirits that had accompanied him from the Standing Stones. He could sense their intent but they were not his kin and so their words were muddled.

Ealea's absence in particular sharpened his frustration. Although in his mind he knew she'd crossed over, her spirit lingered near, watching over him, easing his sorrow. She was as present in his heart now as when she'd shared his bed.

Now he burned with anger that the Druids could not only take his life but had subverted his power as well. He longed for his wife's sweet serenity.

When the high priestess had touched his chest, her power had felt so familiar it made his heart ache. Their village, what he had seen of it, reminded him greatly of home. In other circumstances, he might have been struck by the similarities between Bear Clan and Foresthaven rather than railing at the differences. But there was no denying that beyond the bounds of the village, the dark spiny trees hungered for vengeance.

If it weren't for Cara he might welcome death. But to have lost

Ealea and his Clan only to fail the girl as well would be a shame he could not bear. And though Cara had returned with heartening news, the anger that shrouded his heart refused to let him trust it. He rolled over, trying to settle his mind and body.

And then suddenly, a soft voice sang through the night. He heard it not with his ears but as a spirit song of peace that eased his ragged edges. And the weariness and sorrow he kept tied up in knots loosened, like spring's first deep breath. And with that loosening, his eyes slid shut sending him into darkness.

There he discovered that he did not truly sleep. He had been summoned. He recognized the Otherworld forest as the one where he'd met Cara not so long ago. Though he didn't see her now.

A large raven swooped in with a single raucous caw and settled herself on a low branch. Her blue-black feathers gleamed as brightly as the intelligence in her eyes. He knew her.

"Priestess Sorchia," he said.

"You see truly, Brother." The raven sounded pleased. "Forgive the spell, but we needed to speak in private."

"What can you have to say to one of 'my kind,'" he mused with derision.

"Our clans are not as different as you might think," she said.

"Forgive me if I beg to disagree. We don't execute travelers."

The raven shook her feathers with a frustrated flutter. "As I said before, I do not make the Law, and it is not my place to question it. But I did not summon you here to argue. What do you know of the girl?" she asked, hopping further down the branch.

"Cara?"

"Yes, the Mothers whisper to me that she is important."

"Is that what they are saying?" he murmured, unaware that he had spoken.

"You can hear them?" the raven asked in astonishment.

"I hear whisperings. What they say is not clear to me."

"It is unprecedented. They do not make themselves known…"

"…to men," he finished.

"It is a sign," the raven said, her voice strong and sure. "I am even more sure of my course now."

He didn't ask her meaning.

"Tell me what you know of her magic," the raven said.

"She came to us a few weeks back, a recently freed captive of a sorcerer named Sidonius. She reads thoughts, commands animals with a touch. She also dreamwalks. A strange combination."

"Yes, in my experience talents do not come mixed."

"The Old Ones want me to help her but Sidonius will go to great lengths to retrieve her."

"But Far Islanders do not keep women," the raven said.

"Yet he kept her for years. Do you know what he wants with her?"

"I get only glimpses. I know he is tainted with an ancient evil, and his attempts to use the girl to rid himself of it have only strengthened its hold on him."

"So we battle Sidonius and something more."

"Yes, his life cannot be saved now. You must slay him to return her to her power."

"The captain may not agree," Bradan informed her.

"His protective instincts are to our favor. Do not worry; he will not be able to keep her from her true self."

"I hope you are right," Bradan said.

"It is decided. My Huntress will take you to Iolair. Trust her, though she is not always kind."

He bowed to the raven, feeling more hopeful than he had in days. "I thank you for our lives, Sister."

"We once had men like you to warm our nights, Brother. I wish you well on your journey."

CHAPTER 27
FALIN

Falin returned to the hut she shared with two other Sisters. She slept until the dark hours and then woke, silently gathering the few possessions she cared about. She strapped on her sword, hid her boot knife, and pulled the small leather bag from beneath her tunic. Inside were her special treasures, each one a token of victory. The most recent was a hunting cat's claw. It was long and curved and still wickedly sharp. Kissing each one reverently for luck, Falin placed them back into the leather bag and slipped it around her neck under her tunic.

She didn't dwell on the leave-taking, the Haven held little allure for her now. She didn't think about how she might miss Sorchia's guidance. She only thought on what needed to be done, on her responsibility as a shepherd to the rabbit and her three boorish protectors. Throwing a heavy linen cloak over her shoulders, she packed her sleeping roll, cook pot, some rope, a flint, her whetstone, and her bow with a quiver full of black-feathered arrows. Then, she left for the deep darkness of the forest.

After making her preparations, she went to the kitchens and gathered up some food, two packs, three additional bedrolls, as well as waterskins for her new companions. It was still dark when she arrived at the prisoners' hut. She tucked the packs by the side of the hut before she approached the guard, cursing her luck that it was Rebeka.

"Good morning, Sister," Falin greeted Rebeka with her hand over her heart, bowing with all the deference her rank deserved.

"So, you can be nice," Rebeka said with venom.

"And I thought you'd be happy to see me."

"Happy to see you? Never."

"I'm supposed to relieve you so you can go do important chief scout stuff."

"Don't lie to me. Something's not right. No Culling yet, and it's almost dawn."

"There'll be a Culling," Falin lied. "Sorchia has it all in hand."

"And how long are we expected to suffer men beneath the Thorns?" Rebeka snarled her displeasure.

Falin worried that Sorchia wouldn't be able to keep the scout in hand, but she had to trust the priestess. "Relax. They've only been here a little while. No one even noticed them."

Rebeka stood up quickly. Her tall lankiness so close that Falin had to back up. "Our Laws, our traditions, they're all a joke to you, aren't they?"

Falin forced patience as Sorchia had asked. "That's not true, but there is more to life than rules."

"You *are* more Outsider than Sister, aren't you?"

Rebeka's words stung more than Falin would admit but now wasn't the time for a fight. "I'm not your problem anymore."

As she moved to pass Rebeka, the taller woman's hand shot out and snagged her arm whirling Falin around. Rebeka stared into her eyes, searching for some half-discovered truth.

"You're leaving."

Apparently, Sorchia hadn't shared the whole plan with Rebeka. Irritated at being trapped in a half-truth, Falin growled, dropping all pretense of camaraderie. "You've always said I'm an Outsider."

"And you always will be." Rebeka pointed at the door to the hut and leaned close to Falin's face. "Just make sure you do your job here before you scurry off with your tail between your legs, dandelion."

Rage flared and Falin's hand tightened on the hilt of her sword. She checked her anger but only barely. "I've always pulled my own weight around here and you know it."

"That doesn't make you a Sister. Sorchia was foolish to take you in. It was nothing but wasted charity."

Falin's clenched teeth creaked. "You'd better hope you don't need my charity someday."

"Hah," Rebeka barked a short laugh. "Everyone knows you have none, you ungrateful little bitch."

Falin's hand flew without thought, her fist slamming painfully into Rebeka's strong jaw. The other woman, caught by surprise, staggered back onto the bench. Falin froze, stunned by what she had done. Her heart slammed hard against her breastbone; she didn't want to lose this chance to get outside the Gates.

She offered her hand but the scout angrily slapped it out of the way. Standing on shaky legs, Rebeka rubbed her jaw and flexed it tentatively.

"You better leave before I lay eyes on you again. And if you do come crawling back, I'll kill you myself."

Falin pulled herself to her full height though she still had to look up at the other warrior. "I dare you to try."

"One day I will, dandelion. One day." Rebeka knocked her with a hard shoulder as she walked past her and around the hut.

Falin shook with anger as the truth of Rebeka's words burned inside her. It was a long moment before she remembered the task set before her. She clenched her teeth and swallowed whatever feelings were trying to stir.

Falin knew now that none of the other Sisters would have done this for Sorchia. *Only an Outsider like me would dare.*

She steadied herself with a few soft breaths then crept around the hut to make sure Rebeka had gone. All was quiet. No one was around. She came back to the door, unlatched it, and pushed it softly open.

The fire had burned low and only a subtle glow flickered over the sleeping figures in the dirt. She crept inside and just as she began to push the door shut, a heavy weight slammed into her nearly sending her to the dirt.

Her attacker moved behind her, long arms reaching around. Her shoulders shrugged, tucking her chin down instinctively as an arm slid across, searching for the choke hold. Bringing both hands to the elbow, she held tight and dropped her hips back against her attacker's body to unbalance them. Cold shock coursed up her spine as she realized her attacker was male.

The man stepped back, twisting away from her. With one arm still across her chest, he pushed down on her far shoulder, tipping her back across his outstretched leg. Losing her balance, Falin heard the dirt calling to her. She twirled in the loose grip of his pushing arm, barely settling her feet below her weight in time, and ducked away from his grasp.

By the time she was free of him, they were standing hip to hip, facing opposite directions. She lifted the leg nearest him and thrust her heel hard into the back of his knee, buckling the leg. At the same time, she jammed her elbow back into his ribs, pushing herself away from him.

Another form straightened up from the deeper shadows, too tall to be the girl. She noted the gleam of a blade on the floor. They had their weapons back already.

Blood must not be spilled or we are all lost, she thought frantically. Before she could turn, the warrior behind her shifted, rebalancing on his knee. She felt his hand latch heavily onto the back of her belt. With an angry grunt, he yanked her from her feet and threw her face first to the ground. Using his heavier bulk, he pinned her with a knee on her lower back, twisting her arm behind her.

"What do you want?" His whisper was harsh, angry. The hand on her wrist clamped tight. Boots came into view as the other man came to stand near.

Anger swelled inside her, a violence born of shame that desired nothing less than blood. But she had promised Sorchia to shepherd them and so she swallowed it down.

"Get off me, you great thorny ass," she growled. "I'm your guide, and we don't have time for this."

After a moment's pause, the weight across her back lifted, and he released her wrist. As he was getting to his feet, spite flared in her chest. She rolled to her back and swept his legs out from under him, dumping him unceremoniously on the hard ground. Then she rolled gracefully to her feet and brushed the dirt from her clothes. In the low torchlight, she recognized those blue eyes.

"You," he said with sudden recognition. She wasn't sure what he meant.

"Yeah, me. Now get everyone up. I have packs outside for you."

He pushed to his feet and extended a hand. "Name's Mason Khoury."

She eyed the hand warily, suspecting a trap. "Falin."

The girl approached, rubbing the sleep from her eyes. "I'm Cara." Falin was startled to find that she and the girl actually stood eye to eye. Somehow, the Huntress thought she'd be the taller one.

"Archer," said the young Northerner. "And that's Bradan." He jerked a thumb over his shoulder at the older man who eyed her suspiciously.

"Well met," Falin said formally. "Let's get moving." Falin ducked out the door while they gathered their weapons and followed. She shouldered her own pack and shoved a spare at each of the younger men. The older man and the girl were given the sleeping rolls to sling across their backs. They followed her wordlessly into the dark.

She said nothing more to them as they circled west. Her mind was running through the coming ritual. Sorchia had called for a false Culling and Falin knew the true ritual. But she had a better idea, one less deceitful. That's what she thought made it better. Still, her sweating palms revealed a distinct lack of confidence.

CHAPTER 28
KHOURY

Khoury gripped Cara's small, gloved hand in his as they weaved through the forest. Their guide set a grueling pace that Khoury hoped she didn't expect to keep up for long. Still, he was glad they were out of the village and back on the move. Cara hadn't been clear on whether they were going through Foresthaven or just back out the way they had come. Either way, he was content that they'd be able to stay off the roads. That meant no inns with spying eyes.

He was surprised when they stopped after little more than a quarter of an hour at a large bowl-shaped clearing. On one side stood a huge blackthorn tree, its roots like fingers digging into the ground. Two small torches cast dim shadows across the clearing, a stack of branches between them.

Khoury stopped short and pushed Cara behind him as he recognized the pyre. On it were old bones, a hastily butchered carcass, and a young buck tied down so tightly by feet and horns it didn't have enough leeway to thrash. The hairs on Khoury's neck tingled.

The Huntress didn't break stride but sauntered in, dropping her pack in the center of the clearing. She untied a large sack Khoury hadn't realized she was carrying and dropped it by the pyre. Then she retrieved a machete that was almost too large for her and a long thin dagger, both of which hung from the tree. The clean well-cared for blades glinted in the firelight.

"What are you doing?" Khoury called.

"Shh," the Huntress hissed, motioning for them to stay quiet. She double-checked the knots and the bones and the wood, and felt the sloshing weight of an earthen pitcher that sat nearby. Then, leaving the machete at the pyre, she walked back to their small group, dagger in hand. Khoury's hand went for his hilt.

"Stop," she said brusquely. "Spill no blood, or you all die."

Cara crept out from behind him, craning her head to see better. "The priestess said we could trust her," she whispered shakily.

Khoury released his sword.

Falin gestured to them. "Give me a piece of clothing, a shirt or cloak from each of you men."

"Why?" Archer asked, dropping his pack and removing the long vest he was wearing.

"No questions." The Huntress's clipped tones left little room for argument. She took the vest and held her hand out to Khoury and Bradan impatiently. Khoury dropped his pack and slipped out of his leather jerkin and shirt, handing her the white undershirt and keeping the heavier garment to wear. She turned to Bradan who separated the shorter hide cloak from the longer woven one he usually wore and handed her that.

She strode back to the pyre and covered the buck in the garments.

"Wait," Cara cried, rushing closer.

The Huntress turned, impatient anger looming on her brow.

"You're not going to kill it, are you?" Khoury could hear the futile tears in Cara's voice. He moved in behind Cara, careful not to upset their volatile guide.

"It's the buck or the boys, little rabbit," the Huntress said.

"What?" Cara looked confused, but Khoury's breath caught as the pieces fit together in his head.

Falin sighed. "I said, you can save your men or you can save the deer. I don't care which way it goes. Just decide."

He looked more carefully at the pyre. There was a second fresh carcass below the live buck. And now that he was close, he could tell the other bones, the older ones, were human. He was stunned. He hadn't really believed the worst of the rumors but here he stood facing gruesome truth. "Cara, let her work."

Falin caught his eye. "Keep her back."

He pulled Cara away, tucking her close to him. "Don't watch," he said, trying to save her soft heart from what he knew was coming.

The Huntress took a steadying breath, her face grim in the flickering lights, and then she struck with the swift violence of a true predator. She stabbed the long dagger through their clothes, straight to the buck's heart once, and again, so that the fabric quickly soaked with blood. Cara, who had been peeking through her fingers, cried out softly and he felt her sob into his chest. She didn't try to look again.

The Huntress moved swiftly and efficiently without sentiment. She dropped the dagger, threw the bloodied clothes to the side. Then she took the machete and lopped off the deer's head with a single powerful stroke. The feet came next. She dropped the feet and head in the sack and reached back in to pull out three skulls. Three human skulls smeared with fat and blood. It took her a moment to match jaws to crowns, but very quickly, there were three effigies on the pyre and a pile of bloody ruined clothes at the foot of it.

The counterfeit was impressive. There were enough real human bones and fresh flesh to convince anyone on a cursory examination. Bradan caught Khoury's eye and gestured to the pyre, his meaning clear. That could easily have been the three of them.

But Falin wasn't done. She cleaned the blades, quickly and efficiently and returned them to their places. And then, she began to sing. Her voice was low for a woman but surprisingly pleasant. It was obviously a prayer of some kind, the sweet melody in stark contrast to her grisly chore. She poured the oil from the earthen pitcher over the effigies.

She picked up a torch and then turned back to the four of them. The torch cast a flickering light and in the near-dark with blood spatters on her face, her hair wild and a strange earnest gleam in her eye, she looked almost mad.

"There's no turning back after this. I have made a promise to watch over you and get little Sister to Iolair. But while we are within the Thorn Gates you must do what I say, exactly as I say. No questions. Is that clear?"

The three men nodded, unable to find any words for the tenuous situation they found themselves in.

"The primary rule is no blades. Do not draw your swords or knives or bows for any reason. There is nothing in this forest I cannot defeat single-handed and your steel will only anger the Mothers. No bare blades. Ever."

"Understood," croaked Bradan, the first to find his voice. Cara had stopped weeping and turned her head to watch the Huntress with wide, fearful eyes.

"If you're considering slitting my throat, know that you cannot make it past any of the Gates without me. Go wait at the edge while I finish." She pointed to a small grassy path that opened from the clearing, leading to a trail. The four of them waited there as Falin finished whatever ritual was required and lit the pyre. The stench of hair and flesh filled the air. Then she took up the full sack and her pack and, using her cloak, whisked their footprints from the ground before her, leaving only her own.

"Single file," she murmured as she squeezed past them and started along the path.

ଔ

The sun had cleared the horizon by the time the Huntress offered to stop. They rested a short distance from a clear brook that gurgled placidly through the dense underbrush. The grisly nighttime offering seemed unreal in the morning light. Had Khoury believed the worst stories about Foresthaven, he would probably have risked the main road. Bradan was smug but had the grace not to rub it in too much. Still, they were on their way and Khoury was sure Sidonius had no way of knowing where they were.

The brutal pace was a push for the shaman and had worn Cara completely out. So much so that when Falin called a halt, she simply dropped in her tracks and leaned against the nearest tree. Khoury found the waterskins and took some to Cara. Falin disappeared into the foliage with the sack and returned with it empty.

As she walked up to them, Archer smiled in greeting and then tentatively pointed at her face. "You've still got a little something right there." He mirrored wiping his own face. In truth, there was blood spatter all over her.

She wiped her face and looked at her fingers which themselves were still brackish. Twisting her mouth with displeasure, she dropped the sack and her backpack, and headed back to the stream to wash. Khoury leaned up against the tree next to Cara and she drifted off to sleep with her head nestled in his shoulder. He was growing dangerously used to it.

Archer sat nearby. "How long before the White Mountains?"

"Can't be more than a week."

Archer nodded. "I'll be glad for a bed in Wallace's castle, I can tell you that."

Khoury chuckled. "Me, too. These old bones aren't what they used to be."

"Bah." Bradan snorted. "Wait twenty years, then talk to me about old bones."

Falin returned and stood awkwardly in their midst, her face still damp. She seemed to be waiting. Her jaw was tight and her fists slightly clenched. She almost looked as though the danger had not yet passed.

"Something wrong, Huntress?" he asked.

Her green eyes momentarily clouded with worry but she lifted her chin and answered with a confident, "No."

"If I may, what was that place?" Bradan hadn't shifted from his laconic slump against a tree, but Khoury knew the man well enough to know when his interest had been piqued.

"The Culling pit," she said with caution.

"Interesting tree," Bradan continued.

"Was it?"

"It had power."

She looked more closely at him, a faint admiration surfacing. "You noticed. That is the First Thorn. The oldest blackthorn in the wood."

"Why the pyre? I thought the Elders let us go," Khoury said.

"The false Culling was the high priestess's idea."

"You lied to your gods?" asked Bradan.

Affronted, Falin's face hardened. "Wake the girl. We should go now." She stood and resettled her pack on her shoulders.

Khoury gently shook Cara's shoulder.

"Already?" she groaned reluctantly, though her face was less pale. The rest had done her some good.

"Already," he said and helped her to her feet. Khoury slung his pack onto his shoulders and watched Bradan approach the Huntress. He shook his head at the old man's persistence and hoped she was more patient than she looked.

"Why would your priestess risk angering the spirits?" he asked in hushed tones.

The Huntress's nostrils flared with indignation. "If Sorchia told me to blaspheme, it was for your sake, Outsider.

"Are you godless as well as bloodthirsty?"

The Huntress's hand tightened on her sword hilt. "I kept the Mothers' Covenant." Her lowered voice held a warning.

"You just said…"

"That a false Culling was suggested. What you saw was a simple burnt offering." She shifted her pack on her back. "It just happened to be in the Culling pit."

"But—"

Her patience at an end, the Huntress grabbed the front of Bradan's tunic. Even with her slight build, her anger gave her enough strength to pull him off balance. "No more questions. Do as I tell you and you'll survive. I owe you nothing more." Then she shoved him away from her and started into the forest at a rapid pace.

CHAPTER 29
FALIN

The smoke from the Culling pit had certainly alerted the Sisters by now. Whether they'd believe the farce or not, it was hard to say. It was certain they'd never dreamed men might one day walk the paths of Foresthaven unscathed. Still, with a Sister gone rogue, they'd be thundering down the roads searching for justice. Though the southern wood would be a hard trek for Outsiders, Falin didn't want to risk the easy paths. If caught, the men would be slain on sight, and maybe the rabbit, too. Falin was fairly confident they hadn't been followed but history reminded her not to underestimate Rebeka.

Her mind wandered back to her last meeting with Sorchia, bringing a sadness Falin never expected. For years, she'd thought of little except leaving to see the world. But something inside ached when she realized she'd never see the priestess again. She sent out a soft prayer for Sorchia's safety. Though it was almost certain Rebeka would lay the blame on Falin, the chief scout liked trouble, and Falin didn't trust her.

Footsteps approached, and she glanced over her shoulder to see the captain.

"You have to slow down. We can't keep up this pace."

"Sure you can," she teased. "But if little Rabbit is tired, we can rest." As she stopped she noted his lips twist slightly at the nickname, though she wasn't sure he shared her humor.

"Thanks," he said and turned back to the group. "Time to rest," he called. She watched as Bradan lumbered to a halt, followed by an exhausted Cara. Archer slowed, grabbed the captain and pulled him toward the rear. Falin perched on a nearby fallen tree and watched them put their heads together. She turned her head to stare off into the trees, though she could still make out their mutterings.

"We're not making good time," Archer said.

"They can't go any faster." Khoury glanced at the girl and the old man slumped against the trees.

"Five days' walk to the mountains and then four more east to Iolair?"

"If we can't pick up the pace."

Archer sighed, looking up into the trees nervously. "But we are safe here."

The captain snorted. "Safe enough. Unfortunately, the more time we spend, the better Sidonius can set his net and then whatever comes after will be that much harder."

"And after Iolair?"

"Depends on what news Wallace's Islander can give us. If it's bad, head for Cortland and run out to the Eastern Isles."

Archer nodded thoughtfully. "As good as anywhere I suppose. Let's hope for good news."

"Always." The captain clapped a hand on the Northerner's shoulder, his face heavy with the weight of command. To Falin, he looked like he'd love to be anywhere but in the middle of this mess.

Then why is *he here?* He didn't seem like the kind to be easily swayed. He dropped his pack and dug out his waterskin for a drink. As he wiped his mouth with the back of his hand, Falin watched him scan the little group. There was a moment as his eyes lingered on the girl when a shadow rippled through the stormy blue, and Falin knew where his weakness lay.

Archer cast a surreptitious look at Falin who feigned interest in her own pack. "Thoughts on our guide?"

Falin kept her eyes focused on her hands.

"As brutal as any Huntress I've ever met."

He'd known other Huntresses? Shock and a twinge of jealousy thrummed through her. She'd never been even as far as the Nest since coming to the Haven.

"Why the interest?" Khoury's eyes narrowed.

Archer shrugged. "We're gonna need all the help we can get."

"We don't need her kind of help. That one's trouble."

Falin scowled. What was he talking about? She'd been absolutely saintly.

"How much farther?" Cara interrupted Falin's thoughts with a whine. She watched the captain bring her the waterskin.

"At least a week, girl. So get used to walking." Her lower lip pouted until he sighed indulgently and sat down next to her.

Falin considered the Outsiders for a moment longer. She'd been right about the old Northerner; he was their Sorchia, praying and whispering as he trudged through the brush. Archer and Khoury had the easy camaraderie of long-time companions she so envied among the Sisters. And the girl was soft, not just physically but mentally. She fawned over the captain like a foundling pup until Falin squirmed with embarrassment. Sure, he was handsome, in an overbearing sort of way, but he was only a man after all.

The wind shifted bringing strange unease, though she recognized no specific threat. She turned her face into the breeze that caressed her cheeks like an oncoming storm. She'd known Sorchia's task wouldn't be easy, and she was determined to succeed. She shrugged off the disquiet and got up intending to put more distance between her and Rebeka only to find the girl was fast asleep leaning against the captain's shoulder.

She's not his equal, she thought. *Not like I am.* The appalling thought surprised her, coming out of nowhere. But like any crazy flight of fancy the idea took root and she found herself studying him: Broad not bulky, battle-scarred, thick dark hair, calloused hands, and eyes that were deep and wild and proud. Irritated, she shook her head to clear it. *He's only a man. And I am ever a Huntress.*

Her sudden irritation with herself demanded action. "Get her up, Captain," she called. "Let's go." She hopped down from her perch and strolled south, letting the others scramble to catch up. *Ever the Huntress*, she repeated as she willed his stormy eyes from her mind.

She pushed the Outsiders as hard and fast as she could throughout the day. Rebeka would assume it was a race to the Last Gates, and would send Sisters to each. But the old man and the girl were in no condition to outrun them. Falin decided it was better to lead them over an indirect hard-to-track path that took them past the Nest. There she could gauge the heat of the Sisters' fury. If it died down enough, they could sneak out without notice. Aside from the Last Gates, the Nest was their only way into the Outsider's world.

She called a final halt in a small glade near a runoff streamlet that would disappear come midsummer. It was far from the beaten track. Falin wasn't happy with the distance they'd covered, and she resolved to push them harder tomorrow. She wouldn't lose to Rebeka this time; she couldn't afford to.

"We rest here tonight." She grabbed a sleeping roll off Cara's back and unrolled it, kicking stray branches out of the way.

The mercenaries dropped their packs and set about readying camp with smooth efficiency. Khoury gathered the fallen sticks she'd cleared and piled them in a dirt patch near the center of the glade. He drew out a flint, but Falin placed a hand over it, surprised at how delicate her hand looked next to his larger one.

"No fire."

She watched rebellion swell inside him. But her steady gaze convinced him. His jaw bunched, and he packed the flint away without argument. The Outsiders arranged their sleeping rolls with Cara between the two younger men and Bradan's a short way off. The group sat close together as Falin dug in her pack to retrieve the food she stole from the kitchens.

"Dried venison and dark bread." She handed portions to each of them. "After that, you can clean up at the stream but then I'd get some sleep. We start early tomorrow."

"Who's got first watch?" Archer asked, gnawing the salty jerky.

"You don't need to—" Falin started.

"You first, Archer," Khoury rumbled. His dark stare dared her to complain. "Then me and Bradan."

Irritation rose like hackles across Falin's shoulders. The ingrates didn't trust her—the one who risked everything for them. She shoved her curses behind clenched teeth. "Fine, but remember, no blades."

Then, she rose and strode off into the fading light. Let them think they were alone. She'd keep her promise to Sorchia no matter what. She circled the camp, ensuring that there were no natural threats, though this part of the wood had been quiet since she'd killed the cat that haunted it during the winter. After a full circuit around the camp, she climbed one of the taller trees into the warm night, letting the lighter air dry the sweat from her brow. Through the trees, the night was cloudless above her but below little moonlight pierced the heavy canopy. She heard the murmur of their voices but her mind was busy rambling through memories.

She had been like that girl down there once, though she scowled to think on it. She had wanted so badly to belong. Yet each time she achieved a milestone, each time she did what they asked, the bar was raised. The Sisters required a new and harder task before she could earn a place. She didn't know quite when she realized they'd never let her in. That youthful eagerness hardened and turned brittle inside her. And now, here she was—the blasphemer—leading men through the Mothers' garden.

CHAPTER 30
ARCHER

Archer stretched his back and sighed. It was midday and they had stopped to rest. Again. A few hours' hike was all Cara and Bradan tolerated—even after three days. Now, Cara was napping in Khoury's lap, and Falin had disappeared into the leafy ocean that was Foresthaven. And Iolair felt no closer. He paced through the brush not realizing his steps led him away from the others. Usually the one to hunt, he missed the daily solitude. Not to mention how degrading it was to be tended to like children: not allowed to hunt, told when to light fires and when not to. It wasn't Falin's fault; he knew she had her orders.

The Huntress was surprisingly likeable, still prickly—as they all were. But the occasional tiny flash of smile was a far cry from the stony disdain Huntresses were known for. She wasn't welcoming, but he sensed warmth in her. If you were worth it, that is.

In the last few years, he'd found a sense of stability as Khoury's second. It was a comfortable job, demanding his best effort, and he liked it that way. But, Khoury was changing. Archer paused, wrapping his large hand around a sapling as he brooded. He could say the Keep had changed Khoury, but it had started before that. Why else would they be in that dingy inn alone instead of with the Swords? Archer didn't understand the captain sometimes. It seemed the more handsomely they were paid, the more displeased he was.

Then again, Archer thought, *maybe it's just the threat of Sidonius.*

His mind flashed back to the morning the giants attacked and his grip on the unsuspecting sapling tightened, making it creak softly. His blood boiled with a vengeful longing to meet Sidonius head on with a blade. But Khoury was in a cautious mood. Archer knew he wouldn't move on the sorcerer until they had more information. They needed to get to Iolair and talk with Wallace's sorcerer. But at this rate Archer feared they'd never get there.

He shook the sapling with angry futility, staring at the way his hand wrapped around it. Then he had an idea. What Bradan and Cara needed was help with fatigue. He looked around, this time actually seeing his surroundings, and found himself standing in a grove of a dozen slender saplings, all of them the perfect size for walking sticks. Selecting his first target, straight and slender enough for Cara's tiny hand, the Northerner drew his sword. It was large even for a man his size and would make short work of the young plant. Winding up, he swung with all his pent up frustration and felt the metal edge bite into the woody flesh.

A banshee shriek erupted in the glade, rising to a painful wail that lanced his ears. Looking for the source, he saw nothing. The pain of the noise hurried his next chop, sending a sliver of wood into the air. The tree was tougher than it looked.

The wailing reverberated through his bones and rattled his teeth. Resting his sword against his leg, he covered both ears with his hands and scanned the glade again but there was nothing. A headache throbbed behind his eyes and he bent over with the pain. That's when he saw the blood-red sap oozing from the cut. Only then did he remember Falin's warning.

Dread cramped his insides as the eerie ululation reverberated inside his skull. He needed to get back to the others. When he stood, the glade seemed darker than a few minutes before. He watched carefully and could have sworn the branches were closing ranks as he watched. With the piercing screech sawing at his mind and one hand over an ear, he gripped his sword and tried to push through the foliage. Something had hold of his feet. He looked down to see slender tendrils of ivy arising from the earth, closing about his boots, his ankles, his calves. He heaved his leg up to take a step, ripping the vines from the ground. One foot, then the other. Skeletal branches plucked at his arms. Every leaf, every branch, every root was trying to stop him.

"Khoury!" he called though he couldn't even hear himself. "*Khoury!*"

"*Bíar tsíozhán en.*" The lilting words carried through the ringing in Archer's ears as Falin seemed to materialize in front of him.

"*Bíar tsíozhán en!*" she shouted, one hand latching onto his shoulder as she kicked the sword from his hand.

She took his face in her hands, forcing him to look at her. There were wads of moss stuffed in her ears and she was shouting something, but he couldn't hear it beyond the wailing of the woods. Guilty eyes darted to the wounded sapling, and she paled as her eyes followed his glance. She hurried to the sapling, dragging him along. Then she pushed him to his knees before it. For a moment, he feared her sword would find his throat.

Through watering eyes, he watched as she took dark leaves from her pouch and stuffed them in her cheek. Chewing quickly, she carefully pried a loose piece of bark off and spit the wad onto it. She yanked his hand to her. Her knife flashed brightly as she slashed across the palm. Squeezing his hand, blood dripped onto the leaves. Then she cut her own hand, and her blood joined his. She mixed the blood and leaves all the while crooning her strange song. Somehow, her deep voice carried through the screeching.

"*Mathinas. Igntigh eginn gae mathinas gae cruezh egus fohle.*" She knelt down and painted a symbol on the bark with the blood mixture. "*Duiher egus íobeirt zhun eppais.*"

She took the rest of the blood mixture and smeared it over the sapling's wound. "*Dul er-eis zhodhled ahz.*"

The shrieking faded as she chanted the words over and over. His ears throbbed, and his jaw was sore from clenching. The Huntress then painted him with the mixture, smearing it over his face and hands. Without a word, she grabbed the back of his head and shoved his face to the dirt, putting her forehead to the roots of the sapling as well. "*Dul er-eis zhodhled ahz, mathinas.*"

He felt tendrils reach out of the ground, reminding him of the ivy around his legs. Only her iron grip on his neck kept him from sitting up. The tendril poked gently at his blood-stained forehead and then retreated into the loam. Out of the corner of his eye, he could see the glade lightening. The branches were retreating and soon it was as if nothing had happened, except Archer's ears ached and his face was bloody. When Falin released him, he let out a relieved sigh and sat back on his ankles.

"Thank you." His voice trembled in his throat.

Falin glared at him. Then her hand shot out and struck him across the face, hard enough to snap his head around.

"Thornless man!" she swore at him, climbing to her feet. "Motherless cretin! I gave you one rule! One." Her neck muscles corded as she shouted though he could barely make out her words. Her face was hard as she retrieved his sword and stalked out of the glade with white-knuckled fists.

He scrambled after her, the pain subsiding and the world growing quieter. He lifted a hand to his ear and when it came away bloody, fear crusted on his heart. No birds sang. No footsteps sounded, even when a branch snapped under his stride. Regret roiled through him. He was no use to Khoury deaf.

When he and Falin found the others, the three of them stood in a tight knot, their faces pinched with concern. He couldn't meet the weight of their gazes, but the Huntress strode right up to the captain and threw the sword at his feet like a challenge.

Archer couldn't hear what she shouted at Khoury but Falin was brimming with fury. The captain's face was stony as she pointed to Archer and then poked her finger into Khoury's chest leaving no doubt where she placed the blame. Shame heated Archer's face as the argument escalated.

Khoury knocked Falin's hand away in angry dismissal and moved toward Archer. The blue eyes that held Archer's were filled with worry. Determined to make her point, the Huntress grabbed Khoury's elbow and spun him around to spew some other venomous comment. Archer could tell the moment the jibe hit its mark. Without missing a beat, the captain punched her. The solid blow to her cheek whipped her head to the side though to her credit she didn't go down.

Cara cringed behind her hands as Bradan lumbered forward to intervene, but not before Falin straightened up and caught the captain with a sharp left hook. Her hands were still clenched and there was murder in Khoury's eyes when Bradan stepped between them. The older man strained to keep them separate as more heated words were exchanged. Finally, the Huntress backed off, still glaring. She hissed something at the two men that Archer couldn't hear but the angry snarl that twisted her lip was easy to read. She pushed the sack she'd been carrying at Cara, who jumped as if stung. Then she headed to the nearby stream.

Bradan followed Khoury to Archer. The captain fired off questions as he approached but the younger man couldn't hear anything beyond a whispering buzz. He shook his head, ashamed.

Khoury pressed his lips together and clapped a heavy hand to the back of Archer's neck, pulling him close and thumping him like Connor might have done. The pang of that absence only made Archer feel worse. Unshed tears gathered in this throat. He pressed his eyes tight shut and tried to put his brother from his mind. With a final brief squeeze, the captain released him. Bradan pulled the captain aside with worried glances at Archer.

A small hand on his sleeve drew his attention down to Cara who offered him a gleaming yellow-green apple from the sack Falin had handed her. He offered her a weak smile in return but shook his head. She leaned her head against him in solidarity.

Falin appeared at his side, startling him. Her face was freshly cleaned and still damp. Holding aloft a wet cloth, she roughly snagged his chin and scrubbed the blood and grime from his face with hard, brisk strokes. He watched the vibrant green of her eyes. A shiny swelling had begun high on her left cheek and her left eye was watering, but she seemed oblivious. There was a sideways softness to her mouth and damp delicate curls along her temple.

When she was done with him, she offered a thin smile. Then she retrieved his sword and slid it into the sheath at his waist with a pointed look and a wry wag of her head.

"I know," he said. It felt strange to make words he couldn't hear.

The Huntress's lips pressed thin, and she gave his arm a squeeze before she turned to the others. Archer watched as everyone began stowing their gear and slinging on packs. He found his and settled it over his shoulders. They moved out keeping close together and following Falin along a deer path through the stand of trees.

Archer was happy to be on their way. The attack had shaken him to his core though he couldn't say they hadn't been warned. Eyes to the ground to avoid their pitying glances, he purposely trod on wayward sticks hoping to hear the snap. But there was nothing except the echo of whispers. At times, it sounded like the voices of old women but he knew it was just his imagination.

In about an hour, they came to a wall of blackthorns like the one that had trapped them that first day by the water. Falin was waiting for them next to a huge thorn tree, as big around as a wagon wheel. Its thorns were as long as Khoury's sword and purple-black. Archer felt a quiver of fear just looking at it. She waited until they were close and watched them as they considered the obstacle in front of them. She looked up and patted the large tree as one would caress a favored hound. The whisperings in his head crooned in chanted harmonies.

Falin was talking but he couldn't read the words from her lips.

When she turned to the large tree, she took out her knife and poked her thumb with the tip. A large drop of blood gathered on the pad and she leaned over putting her hand in a hollow on the side of the trunk. The whisperings grew more urgent. A vibrant purple light glowed from the hollow but suddenly went dark as the whisperings stopped and only stagnant silence filled his head. He felt, rather than heard, the groaning of the forest as it moved for them. It stretched and shifted and suddenly there was no wall before them, only a road leading into a forest, benign and quiescent.

The Huntress wiped her hand on her leggings and led them past the large thorns. After fifty yards or so, the blackthorns disappeared completely from the surrounding forest. They were beyond the Gate and Archer breathed a little easier.

Falin stopped them early for the night, for which he was glad. It was an ideal camp near a small pond and obviously well-used. There were stumps and logs surrounding a small firepit with a spit. Though Archer had been in a hurry to reach Iolair, he was content to sit and stare into the fire. Locked in silence, his isolation was complete. He didn't notice when Falin disappeared. Bradan and Khoury were hunched in conversation by the pond.

Cara was his only company. She sat in front of a log near him, her eyes on the fire, her thin knee brushing his leg. When he met her gaze, there was pity in her eyes. He wondered if his eyes had looked at her like that in the Keep. She gave him a tentative curve of her lips and patted her lap, offering it to him for a pillow. He shook his head, shame once again washing over him. But she was persistent and eventually his exhaustion convinced him.

Weary, he laid down on the soft ground, his head on her thigh. She stroked the hair back from his face. Tired sadness welled up. Maura used to do that in their early courtship. He would sprawl beneath the pines staring up through the branches—head pillowed in her lap—and weave her stories of their forevers. He had been young then. Now it was such a tangled mess, he didn't know if forever was possible.

Cara's soft fingers swirled around his temples, unwinding the tension coiled in his head, and his eyes drifted shut. The whisperings returned. If he listened closely he might understand what they were saying, but he didn't care enough to try. His weight sank into the cradle of loam beneath him. It seemed to welcome him, as if forgiving his earlier trespass. His mind drifted in the fog between sleep and wakefulness while half-remembered dreams danced with thoughts of Maura and, oddly enough, his father.

CHAPTER 31
FALIN

The Nest was a small village in the far west of Foresthaven, named so because it was a nursery of sorts. It had another name, an Outsider name, but Falin never remembered what it was. There was little worth remembering about her years there. The important lessons learned by blood and sweat were tattooed on her very bones and the rest was irrelevant.

She and the Outsiders had been on the road three days now and she had to choose which southern Gate to head for. She planned to infiltrate the small village to find out what traps Rebeka had set for them. It would be tricky, getting in and out again. The Sisters were undoubtedly looking for her, her blonde mane too distinctive to miss. But she had a plan.

She had gathered blackthorn berries yesterday, each one half as big as her palm. Now, a dozen of the fragrant fruit bounced in her belt pouch as she ran. Their juice would dye even her brilliant golden locks black instantly. It was a shame to use them like that. Blackthorn berries were a delicacy and weren't easy to come by. Not many Sisters would brave the daggered branches to climb up where the sun coaxed first the purple-blue blooms and then the night-black berries from the Thorns. But heights never bothered Falin, nor did the thorns. Besides, Sorchia was very fond of the taste of them.

Falin's feet drummed out a steady beat through the brush, and she lost herself in the mindless rhythm. There were no whispers now. Not like earlier. She used to wonder if the Mothers' voices were real or if perhaps only true daughters of the druids could hear them. But there had been no mistaking the ghostly whispers that found her when the Northerner had gotten in trouble. Her name had echoed in the wind, and there had been unseen hands on her back urging her to hurry.

But she hadn't been fast enough. She had saved him, but his life would never be the same. When she'd seen the knowing in his eyes, the realization of what he'd lost, her normally iron-bound heart cracked just a little. It was a small fissure, but an unfamiliar weakness nonetheless. Falin flexed her jaw, feeling again the tightness high up in her cheek where the captain had struck her. She'd wanted to be angry: Angry with Archer, angry with Khoury, angry with life. She didn't care about the target and he'd willingly obliged.

Through the thinning trees she saw late afternoon sun bouncing off flaxen roofs. Children's laughter bubbled through the branches. The Nest was just ahead. Stopping to let her breathing calm, Falin surveyed the canopy for a likely roost. She edged closer to the village and found a handful of thorn and oak trees clustered together. Shinnying up the rough trunks, she found a comfy perch in the elbow of two branches that overlooked the whole village clearing and showed her a short bit of the road leading to the harbor.

The Nest was far enough west that it sat at the foot of the White Peaks where they curved inland. A river started there, in the lake fed by mountain runoffs, and wended its way through steep cliffs out to the ocean midway between Seal Bay in the north and the southern cities. The mountains and the heavily guarded docks limited access to the town but should the Nest fall to attackers, two Thorn barriers and a Gate still separated it from the rest of Foresthaven.

Falin always thought the Mothers callous in their design—the Sisters' own children weren't cloistered within the protective Thorn circle. But, roughly half were male and would forever be Outsiders.

Not even in their infancy would these children know the safety of Haven. Never would they suspect that druid magic thickened their blood. Even some of the girl children wouldn't be chosen either, if they were sickly or had the wrong temperament for a Huntress.

Falin herself had been elevated from the Nest to Haven sooner than most. Rebeka had loudly blamed it on Sorchia's favoritism, but Falin knew she'd earned it. And with more blood than sweat.

Falin waited and watched, surveying the people below. There was no sense of alarm or wariness in the village. Guards changed in routine fashion. Children ran in packs. Her attention was snagged by two blond-haired boys, obviously twins, racing straight toward the tree where she perched. They were old enough that she knew they wouldn't be here much longer, but the sight tugged on her nonetheless. She knew what it was to be yellow-haired in the Nest. And she had been the only one back then.

Unfortunately for the boys, the gang pursuing them had split up and they were outflanked. A cadre of older kids stepped out from the brush beneath her hiding place just as the boys reached the safety of the trees. The brothers were surrounded and, as Falin well knew, about to get a thrashing.

The boys skidded to a halt, resigned to the battle they faced. They pressed their backs to each other and raised dirty fists, each one secure in the knowledge that his brother stood with him. Falin saw Archer and his captain in those stern young faces. Close as brothers, sharing a bond that went deeper than any she'd ever been graced with. Falin's grip on her bow tightened until her fingers ached. There was nothing she could do for them and besides, she wasn't about to give herself away over a scene that was all too commonplace.

Their dilemma was quickly forgotten when she saw Rebeka herself riding across the village. What was she doing here? It didn't make sense.

The chief scout barely gave the boys a glance as she rode past them beneath Falin's perch and down the road toward the port. Sliding her bow back over her shoulder, Falin crept through the branches, following as best she could without leaving the canopy. In her haste, a twig broke off and tumbled to the forest floor. Falin froze, listening to the silence.

In the distance, she could still see Rebeka but not for long. With more care than speed, Falin continued after her. Where the road started to curve north, the chief scout stopped and scanned the road behind and ahead of her before she dismounted and led her mount into the forest. Falin scrambled down to the brush and crept with cat-like stealth, circling wide of Rebeka's path. It wasn't long before she heard voices ahead.

"What are you doing here?" Rebeka's angry hiss reached Falin before she could see the scout's companion.

"The boss got impatient." Falin froze. The deep male voice was the last thing she expected to hear.

"I don't have her yet."

"Problems?"

Falin crawled closer, finally catching sight of a grubby man about Khoury's height though his middle ran to fat and his lanky hair hid much of his stubbled face. His features weren't important. What was significant was that Rebeka tolerated him.

"The Sisters gave up the search. Sorchia convinced them that Falin killed the Outsiders."

"Did she?"

"Not a chance."

"So when you gonna get me the white-haired girl?"

"I'll get her."

"When?"

"Soon." Rebeka's angry growl carried a threat the man didn't seem to understand.

"Flesh is my trade, girl, and so far you haven't given me any." He stepped closer and raised a hand to the scout's face.

Heat flooded Falin's cheeks as his thumb stroked Rebeka's chin with indecent intimacy.

Then, like a snake striking, Rebeka's blade was out. She thrust the man up against the nearest tree, hard. The sharp edge of her blade pressed into his jawline. "And I deal in blood." Rebeka twisted her wrist ever so slightly, shaving off a section of the man's bristly scruff. The bare skin winked in the light like a pale scar.

He smiled a crooked smile and chuckled. "Fair enough."

Unappeased, she pressed the blade harder against his face, her jaw muscles jumping with murder. A thin trickle of red glazed the blade's edge. "After this meeting, you are never to set foot here again. Am I clear?"

He nodded cautiously and she released him with a shove, stepping back. He wiped the blood from his jaw with the back of his hand and eyed her with caution. "Where will you deliver her then?"

"Bring your men to the eastern Tangle road. You can collect the white-haired girl and the three men."

"And the other?"

"Is mine."

He nodded. "We will be waiting at the Vine and Thorn."

"I know the place," she said.

Hearing more than enough already, Falin scooted backward, her heart pounding so loud she wondered how Rebeka didn't hear her. She needed to get the Outsiders out of Foresthaven and soon.

Clamping sense over the hurry that screamed in her head, Falin crept carefully south. As soon as she was sure Rebeka wouldn't hear her, she broke into a run. She'd let the Outsiders rest today. But tomorrow. Tomorrow, they had to travel in earnest. Surely with the threat of capture, they'd make better time. The captain's scowl swam in her head at the thought. She could picture it perfectly and reconsidered her plan. It wasn't fear that made her decide in the end not to tell him but something else.

It didn't matter anyway, she reasoned. With any luck, she wouldn't have to mention Rebeka or her unsavory guest at all.

CHAPTER 32
CARA

Cara's hand tingled where the Huntress bumped it, even though she'd had the gloves on. A spark like static lingered on her skin, and with that spark came an idea too wonderful to relinquish. The tingling spread up her arm and expanded until a rumbling ember of restlessness burned in her chest. She had nurtured her plan in silence as they walked. Now, she tilted back to peer through the trees, careful not to wake Archer snoring softly in her lap. The captain and Bradan were deep in discussion by the stream; she was forgotten. Though she hated feeling as inconsequential here as she'd been in the Keep, right now it was exactly the opportunity she needed.

She'd been rubbing the burn on her palm daily since the night she'd shared Khoury's cloak. The tingling warmth had returned each time and now the wound was merely a silvery band of mature scar. She smiled as the shaman's voice rose in argument, knowing her privacy was secure for a short time at least.

Cara surreptitiously stripped the gloves from her hands, hiding them in the folds of her skirt. Then she closed her eyes and pressed her palms gently to the sides of Archer's head. A weighty silence loomed in the space between her hands, and faces appeared in her head.

She frowned. The laughing woman was still a sore point between her and Khoury. She didn't want to ruin this friendship as well. She tried to push the images away, but as long as she touched Archer the visions came whether she wanted them or not. She took her hands away and stared down at the young Northerner's serene face. She so desperately wanted this to work. Deciding his healing was more important than her reservations, she pressed her hands to Archer's ears once more.

The injury she sensed was a dry, empty place and the warmth from her hands pushed at it gently. Images of Maura washed through her, and in those visions, Cara saw through Archer's eyes. She recognized the dress that fell from Maura's curves to the floor, and her cheeks burned with embarrassment. She wanted to pull her hands away, but she forced herself to continue. Ignoring the memories as best she could, she concentrated on the healing energy infiltrating the injury like water over thirsty ground, small rivulets of warmth dissolving the silence. As the glow spread between her hands, the images in her mind shifted.

This time a much younger Maura stood before her, tears of anger streaming down her face.

"I know he's your brother, but am I supposed to just wait around until you're done gallivanting?"

"No," Cara heard herself say in Archer's voice, a lump of emotion crushing her chest. "No. You shouldn't wait."

"Shouldn't wait?" Maura's eyes went huge and round. "Are you saying…?"

"I was wrong, Maura." She felt Archer's words choke her own throat. "It's not right, you and me."

"That's your father talking," Maura hissed.

"No. I don't want you to wait." Cara pulled her hands from his skin and wiped the tears from her cheeks. Her stomach roiled in distress. Archer's words had been a lie; Cara knew it. But why would he lie to Maura? Cara didn't want to see any more, but she knew her job wasn't done yet. She glanced at Bradan and Khoury. It seemed they'd settled their differences. She didn't have much time.

She placed her hands on the sides of Archer's face one last time. The warmth came quicker and the memory that followed was murky with age. She was in a dark room stagnant with sickness, kneeling by a low bed.

"I'm here, Tarhill," she/Archer said. The man's eyelids fluttered. When they opened, milky blue eyes stared out.

"Maclan," his weak voice quavered, "is that you?"

A pang shot through her. "It's Reid."

The wrinkled face twisted with disgust. "Come to see me off?"

Awkwardness held his words prisoner. Archer knew there was no response that would please the old man.

"Ha, and where's that silver tongue of yours now, boy?" the old man wheezed with venom.

"Did you want a song?" she asked through a tight throat.

"Song? Bah." The old man spit. "You may have charmed the chieftain's daughter to your bed with that foolishness but that doesn't give you the right. You're no leader." A clawed hand groped up her arm, latching on with surprising strength. "For the sake of the Clan, boy, set the girl aside."

"I *will* marry Maura." Her jaw set stubbornly.

The hand shot up and slapped her cheek. "I'm still your father, boy, and I say you won't." The milk-white eyes seemed to see right through her. "You are not worthy of that mantle. Disregard my dying wish at your peril. I curse you that all who follow you will suffer for it."

Archer's fear sliced through Cara like a frozen knife. She let go of his head, covering her mouth with both hands to stifle her sob. His anger and bitterness lay upon her heart like a stain. She wanted nothing more than to scrub it away.

Khoury interrupted her thoughts, coming over and dropping onto a nearby log. She quickly wiped her eyes a final time and schooled her features smooth. Hiding her bare hands under her legs, she wondered how best to retrieve her gloves without drawing notice. She needn't have bothered. His attention was elsewhere. Sadness deepened the blue of his eyes as he stole sidelong glances at Archer. Bradan stacked kindling and branches in the firepit.

"You're back," Bradan said as the Huntress strode out of the forest, her leathers dusty and an enormous brownish-black bird slung over her shoulder. Her left cheek was swollen, the skin tight and shiny and already a blotched blue-black.

"So I am," she said, dropping her pack across the firepit from where Cara sat. A distracted frown hardened her features as she perched on a convenient tree stump.

"Need help?" Bradan offered.

The Huntress gave a quick shake of her head, dismissing him. Then she slid her knife from her boot, and spread the poor bird over her thighs, wings outstretched. Cara turned away before the Huntress began to carve.

Bradan squatted next to Khoury, his eyes intent. "You need to order him to go."

"I've already told you. It's not my decision," Khoury murmured back.

"It's for his own good."

"You know it's impolite to talk about someone when they're right here," rumbled a voice from her lap.

Cara squeaked in surprise as all eyes flew to Archer. His gold-brown eyes stared up at her, shining with emotion. "I thought I was dreaming," he murmured, his relief obvious. He pushed himself to sitting.

"You can hear us?" Bradan asked with the first smile she'd seen on the old man since they left the Clan.

"I don't think you were trying to be all that quiet," Archer quipped.

The captain stood up and reached out a hand. Archer grabbed it and Khoury hauled him to his feet, thumping his shoulder with good-natured roughness. The captain's eyes were bright as he held Archer at arm's length. "Loafing again, were you? I'll have to dock your pay, boy."

"Didn't realize this was a paid tour, captain. But damn glad to hear it." He winked broadly.

Cara couldn't stop the smile that creased her cheeks. She took their distraction as an opportunity to fish for her gloves.

"But how did you…?" Bradan was about to ask, then looked down at Cara. He caught her arm and pulled her bare hand into view. "Was it you, child?"

Cara blushed at the accusation, if that was what it was, acutely aware that she was now the focus of attention. Everyone including Archer turned to stare. "I…I'm sorry," she stuttered at Archer. "I just wanted to help." Her voice was little more than a whisper, and she couldn't meet his gaze.

"Oh, you helped, Snowflake." Archer laughed. "You helped."

She squeaked as Archer suddenly lifted her to her feet, enveloping her in a bearish hug. His warm solidness felt good against her cheek. "Thank you," he said into her hair.

She couldn't stop smiling. When he released her, a sudden wash of dizziness had her teetering against him.

"Steady there," he said, lowering her back to the ground.

Bradan offered her water from the skin. "You have to be careful, child. Healing is tiring work. But what made you try it?" Bradan's eyes narrowed.

Cara swallowed hard and showed them her burned hand, the scar across the palm silvery and flat. Without hesitation, Bradan grasped it and inspected it closely. As if the time spent working on Archer had intensified her senses, Bradan's sorrow hit her the moment her hand touched skin. Ealea's death had left a hole inside him, but there was something else there as well. Something she hadn't noticed that day in the dining hall. A web of golden strands surrounded him, each one humming with a different voice.

"You healed this?" He gestured to her hand.

"While we walked."

"I say again, Cara of the Black Keep, you have power, make no mistake."

Cara dipped her head to avoid the intensity of his face and quickly slipped on her gloves. Strangely, she felt a chuckle bubble up from somewhere deep inside.

"It's good to hear you laugh," Archer said, taking the waterskin next and drinking deeply.

"I'm just happy," she said, treasuring the warm kernel of pride in her heart. "After talking with Ingrid, I was so worried I was a Dunhadrar."

"Not much chance of that now." Bradan chuckled and patted her head.

"Dunhadrar?" Khoury's voice was rough and angry, his delight of a moment before gone. "Who told you about that?"

"I believe Ingrid mentioned it," Bradan said coolly before Cara could respond.

"And what does she know of it?" Khoury challenged.

"Only what anyone would."

"Meaning?"

"Barakan brutality is well-known. And that of the Dunhadrar, legend." He fixed the captain with a more measuring stare.

"It's an unflattering term and not one to use lightly." Khoury growled, fingering the hilt of his sword.

"Cara will be careful, I'm sure." Bradan lit the kindling with a few strikes of the flint, coaxing the tiny flames to life with patience.

The tense undercurrents made no sense to Cara so she was relieved when Khoury let the matter drop. He turned, snatched up the waterskins, and headed toward the stream.

Bradan watched the captain for a moment and then settled himself at the foot of a nearby tree. With an exaggerated yawn, he winked at Cara before closing his eyes.

"Archer," the Huntress called with a small cough. Cara had quite forgotten she was there. She turned to see the girl holding the severed wings out to the Northerner. Luckily for Cara, the carcass already looked less like a bird and more like dinner. "Start plucking," she commanded.

Archer took the grisly gift and sat down next to the Huntress, examining the long black feathers with skilled fingers. He smiled broadly. "Very strong. They'd make excellent fletching."

Falin shook her quiver of black-feathered arrows. "Better than yours by a long shot," she boasted. "You can have them if you do the plucking."

"Deal," Archer said, firmly grabbing a long wing feather at its base and pulling it with some effort from the wing. "But only if you cut the wood for shafts." He eyed the forest with exaggerated apprehension and a visible shudder, which drew an actual laugh from the Huntress.

Cara watched the two of them working in peace and shook her head. Maura had been right; Archer probably could charm the scales off a snake. He'd finished with one wing and handed it back to her to cook then began work on the other. It looked difficult, pulling the deep-set feathers out without damaging them.

"Huntress." He cleared his throat. "I…I wanted to thank you." His voice was low as he risked a glance in the direction of the stream.

Surprise lit the green eyes that glanced over at him, surprise and caution. "It's Falin. And you're welcome."

"I'm sorry—"

She cut him off with a dismissive wave of her hand. "I should have kept closer watch on you. You're obviously a troublesome man."

He raised a long-fingered hand to the burgeoning black of her cheek, hesitating before he would have touched it. "Khoury didn't…I mean, he shouldn't have." The Northerner lowered his hand and yanked another feather free, avoiding her gaze. "You have to understand. He's not a cruel man, he's just…."

She grabbed his arm roughly and gave him a firm shake. "Don't."

"What?"

"Don't apologize for your captain." Her reprimanding eyes bored into his.

"But he..."

"Is exactly as he should be." Her gaze wandered to the captain, a hint of admiration in her eyes. "What good is a hound with no teeth?" She smiled at Archer. Then she punched his arm hard and laughed.

Archer chuckled and shook his head. Any tension fled as they busied themselves with their appointed tasks.

Cara had to admit it was quite the feast that night. The groundhawk was roasted on a spit. And the Huntress had Cara help her dig up some tubers Sidonius's books called moss turnips. Wrapped in pungent purple leaves, they tucked them in the coals. Falin had even found time to harvest some of the large berry-flavored fruit of the Thorn trees. Sweetly sour but soft like a peach, Cara thought they were delicious. It was all-in-all the best meal she'd had since Bear Clan.

Though the Huntress still made Cara nervous, the good food and Archer's joking soothed much of the tension. At least until he tried to teach her a pub song. When he said her voice was low enough to be mannish, Cara thought Falin would give him a black eye.

Khoury was quiet all night. He hadn't commented on Cara's new ability or the Dunhadrar again, but he was edgy and sullen. He didn't join in the light-hearted conversation that Archer worked so hard for. Cara nervously noted how his fingers fiddled with the hilt of his weapon and how often he paced the edges of the campsite.

When the meal was over and Archer had regaled them with a song or two, Khoury stood and stretched. "Time to get some sleep. I'll take first watch, then Archer and then Bradan." He pointed to each man in turn, avoiding looking Cara or the Huntress. "And then wake me again a few hours before dawn."

"Yes, rest while you can," the Huntress said, standing to settle her sword belt lower on her hips. "We need to move faster tomorrow. Be ready." Then she slipped into the woods for the night.

Cara laid her head on her bent arm. The full belly and exhaustion made her feel like she could sleep for a week. She breathed deep, relaxed at last, taking in the earthy scent of loam and growing things. Night birds hooted. And suddenly she recognized where she was. She'd only ever seen it at night. The rush of the stream soothed her to sleep quickly, and the whispering of the woods followed her into her dreams…

…where she stood in moonlight bright enough to see by. Though alone, she felt the chill of unseen eyes. Her straining ears heard nothing as she walked. Still the sense of being followed increased until she could swear someone was right behind her. She whirled around, but there was no one there.

"Hello?" No answer.

Firelight glimmered nearby and she ventured toward it. A man sat there amidst a handful of blanketed shapes. Only one sleeping face was visible in the flickering light and it tugged at her mind. She fought to recognize the face but found herself teetering on the edge of a maelstrom that waited to swallow her up. Tearing her eyes away, she fled with her heart pounding in her ears. When her lungs ached, she stopped next to a still pond and bent down to drink. Before her lips touched water, the mirror-smooth surface showed her moonlit reflection. Startled, she scrambled away; the face that stared back hadn't been her own.

A howl sounded through the woods. Then a small black wolf stepped out of the brush, its tongue lolling out of a mouth that was drawn back in mock laughter. With a single sharp yip, the beast bounded off into the forest. She smiled. She knew this game.

She chased it to where the land sloped up. In a crevice between two huge stones was a den. The wolf flashed through the moonlight, darting into the hole.

As she moved to follow it, a strange light streamed from behind her, casting long shadows upon the stones. She turned to the luminous shine that was so bright she couldn't see anything except the outline of a woman in white armor.

"Welcome." A voice floated from the light, loving and eerie and multi-tonal

like many voices in harmony. "We've missed you."

"Who are you?" Her fingers tightened on the bone hilt of her knife.

"That matters less than who you are. Tell me, girl. Do you know?"

"Who I am? Of course, I do. I'm…" But whatever she was going to say flew right out of her head. Her mind cast about for the name, but it was lost.

"I see." Disappointment hardened the words. "As I feared. Listen hard, traveler. Greed has skewed your fate, tangling the skeins of destiny. You must go back to the beginning. Go back into the dark. There will you find your true name and the birthright set aside for you."

"The dark?" Though she didn't know what dark the apparition meant, she dreaded it to her bones.

"The Ironwood sword waits for you beyond the tide," the voice continued.

"What are you talking about?" she asked, but the woman was fading and the brightness with her. There was no answer as darkness closed in. After a moment, her eyes readjusted and the wolf den was gone. In its place was a tree. Moonlight silvered its multitude of tiny leaves and the white flowers shone like stars. A jagged dark line ran down the trunk where the tree had been split. Half was lying next to the stream like a solid reflection of the half that stretched up toward the moon.

Lightning, she thought. Lightning struck here.

She sat in the fork of the broken trunk, suddenly weary, and fell asleep beneath the wounded star-flowered tree.

CHAPTER 33
KHOURY

Dunhadrar. The word tumbled around Khoury's mind, yet another fragment of his past inadvertently exhumed by the white-haired woman. Though her innocence was genuine, she had an uncanny knack for unearthing things better left buried. Merely speaking that word was enough to earn a bloody necklace in some regions. Khoury consoled himself that Bradan's casual talk meant he didn't suspect the truth for all his probing comments about power and magic.

It was the captain's second shift of the night, but he wasn't the least bit drowsy. His churning thoughts had kept real sleep at bay. Archer shifted in his blankets, bringing Khoury's attention back to the present, and he realized with surprise that he'd been staring at Cara. Her small, ungloved hand pillowed her head; her thick white braid tucked neatly below her chin. She was so childlike at times he forgot what magic she carried within.

Life in the Keep had left her shy and easily frightened, yes. But that small stature hid real strength. A strength he'd misjudged. There was a cord of tenacity within her, humble and steady. And loyal. He'd seen it on the tundra, in the Keep, with the high priestess—and it always surprised him—but he was beginning to trust it. To trust her.

When that unearthly screech had echoed through the woods and they realized Archer was missing, Khoury had been far more worried than he was willing to admit. When Archer had returned, coated in blood and deaf, rage had consumed Khoury's reason. A rage that demanded violence. That the Huntress was spoiling for a fight as well was merely a convenience.

Khoury rubbed his cheek. It was definitely tender though not visibly bruised. His mouth curved in a half-smile. The warrior woman could throw a decent punch. Not to mention take one.

He breathed deeply with the gratitude of a man who'd survived a storm. Archer was fine now, thanks to Cara.

Healing was powerful magic and highly sought after. Sidonius's pursuit made more sense now that the captain knew her true nature. Of course, her value meant there were only two possible outcomes to this conflict, both of them lethal.

Even after Sidonius was taken care of, her skill would always make her something of a target. A wayward image of Cara ensconced in Khoury's own war camp, ministering to his company of Swords, flitted through his mind. He gave himself a mental shake. Did he really want her exposed to that? To let her see *him* at his worst? He thrust the daydream away. She'd be far safer returning to Seal Bay with Bradan.

Khoury stretched, stiff joints popping loudly, and paced the limits of the glade. Restlessness buzzed inside his head. He longed for action: A good sparring match, a hunt, even a run. Anything to calm the anxious waiting he felt.

The Huntress had said they needed to be ready early, so he woke Bradan and Archer as soon as he noted sunlight in the heights of the leafy canopy. Cara could afford to sleep until the last minute.

"Falin still gone?" Bradan asked when Archer returned from the stream, water dripping from the curled ends of his wet hair.

"She'll be back," Archer said with confidence. "I don't think she's used to traveling with company."

"Huntresses are loners," Khoury observed, taking the crusty bread

Bradan offered him.

"And you're not?" Archer challenged, helping himself to some bread as well. Khoury just shrugged, he wasn't about to debate the Huntress's suitability after yesterday's shouting match. The men waited for at least an hour, puttering around the camp and packing up what little they had.

Khoury was beginning to wonder if something had actually happened to the blonde warrior when a snapping branch sent him to his feet. The Huntress stumbled out of the brush, her eyes wild. Her hair, loose from its typical knot, lay tangled about her shoulders. She carried a newly fashioned walking stick of pale sturdy wood. Her eyes flitted over their faces, though Khoury had the impression she didn't really see them. She went to where Cara slept and squatted down, staring at the girl in silence. Then, she shook herself and stood, her eyes finally clearing.

"I'm late," she said, her voice hesitant. Then she frowned, pulling herself up straighter and brushing dirt from her tunic. She ran brutal fingers through her tangled locks, taming them and tying them back into a knot. Surveying the edge of camp, she turned in a circle and sniffed the wind like a dog.

"Something wrong?" Khoury asked.

"Not…yet."

Khoury felt a chill of foreboding.

The Huntress leaned down and shook Cara awake. "Get up."

Cara sat up with a yawn as the Huntress made a quick circuit of the camp, ensuring they'd left little trace of their presence.

Khoury offered the white-haired girl a hand. "Morning," he said. She beamed a smile, slipped on her gloves and let him help her to her feet. "Hope you're rested. Gonna be a long day."

Cara rolled her eyes, and he suppressed the urge to chuckle. However, there was no quelling the spark of desire that refused all reason. He thought suddenly of kissing her. Then the Huntress appeared at his elbow. With unusual awkwardness, she thrust the staff at Cara.

"It's witchwood," she said. "A rowan tree struck by lightning."

Cara's mouth hung slack, and she reached out a tentative hand to take it.

"I don't have time to teach you today but," the Huntress swallowed hard, "a Sister should never be weaponless."

The respectful title startled Khoury. Cara took the staff firmly, tears bright in her eyes. "Thank you," she whispered. "Thank you, Sister." Then she placed her right hand over her heart and bowed as the Sisters had done.

The Huntress returned the salute with slow grace. "Don't be afraid to lean on it today." She winked at Cara, casting an offhand glance at Khoury before slinging her pack onto one shoulder.

They broke camp and headed south. To say their pace was quicker would be an understatement. But what worried Khoury more than Bradan and Cara keeping up was that their guide seemed more than a little distracted. Her darting eyes had him nervously checking the undergrowth for something, though he couldn't imagine what.

There was no mid-morning break, and Cara suffered loudly for at least an hour before Archer had laughed and offered to carry her piggyback for a while. Khoury was glad to see the Northerner feeling so well. It was more than his hearing; whatever Cara had done had lightened Archer's heart as well. Even Bradan seemed less tired, though his breathing was labored and sweat ran down the braids of his beard.

When the sun was just past its zenith, the Huntress finally called a halt. Archer, Bradan, and Cara sat atop the soft mossy planes of the hillside glade but Khoury continued to pace, already feeling the stiffness in his scars. Falin passed around meat from the night before along with a few crumbs of cheese and green apples. Then she perched on a low branch, one leg swinging lazily.

"The border is close," she said, biting into her apple with a sharp, wet crunch.

"Then we're close to the White Mountains?" Archer asked.

Falin shook her head. "You probably have about a day of southern Tanglewood before you hit the foothills. But keep this pace and at least by tomorrow there will be no more Thorns."

The captain noticed that she said "you" and not "we." He glanced at his lieutenant. The furrowed brow and surreptitious pointing told him Archer had picked up on that, too. He groaned inwardly, dreading the impending discussion. Archer had a habit of taking on strays, but Khoury didn't want the blonde warrior along. The girl was hot-headed, untried, and as a Huntress would always have split loyalties. He shook his head at Archer and then turned away.

"Are there…are there wolves in this wood?" Cara asked, wiping her lips on her sleeve. Falin's foot froze mid-swing.

"What a strange thing to ask," Bradan said.

"I dreamed I saw one last night," Cara replied.

Interest brightened Falin's eyes. "There *are* wolves in Foresthaven," she agreed. "But they're not a threat." She gave Cara a stiff smile and dropped her eyes to the apple in her hand, then continued eating.

"Was it one of *those* dreams?" Bradan asked.

Cara nodded. "I don't remember much, but I do remember feeling like someone was following me."

Falin choked on her apple, slipping off the branch and landing neatly on her feet. Archer was closest. He stood and thumped her soundly on the back until she coughed and raised a hand for him to stop. A scowl furrowed her brow.

"Time to get moving," she croaked, tossing the core and wiping her hands on her leathers.

As usual, she scooped up her pack and left without preamble. Khoury followed with the others single file behind him. Archer brought up the rear. Either the Huntress had a gut feeling they were being followed, or she was hiding something. Regardless, he eyed the forest with suspicion, and his hands itched to draw his sword if only for the reassuring weight of it. Soon, he told himself. Soon, he'd have control of their group once more and the green-eyed Huntress would become one of Archer's tall tales.

CHAPTER 34
CARA

It was the second day after Archer's attack in the early afternoon. Cara stared in awe at the purple-black trees that blocked their path. They stood like soldiers, shoulder to shoulder, thorn-swords crossed. The impassable line continued into the forest on either side as solid as any wall of stone. Falin approached the largest, the hollow in its trunk as big as her head. Like before, she used her knife and let the crimson blood well up, then pressed her hand to the hollow.

The ghostly whisperings that had followed Cara daily rose like autumn leaves in the wind, whirling about her, agitated and yet forlorn. A glow of recognition briefly lit the hollow. Then, with a deep groaning, the trees obeyed. The thorny soldiers reluctantly drew back from their stations, revealing a path only wide enough for one.

Cara shifted her pack as Khoury took a step forward, obviously eager to continue their ground-eating pace. But the Huntress didn't move. Her hand lingered on the rough bark, stroking it gently as she gazed up, up, up into the waving purple leaves. She leaned forward, placing her other hand with reverence on the trunk, and then her forehead.

After a long awkward minute, the captain cleared his throat impatiently. Without looking at him, the Huntress sidled out of the way, keeping her hands on the tree. Khoury started through the tight corridor between the thorns. The Huntress stood quietly, her forehead to the bark as Archer went past and then Bradan stepped up to go next.

"Cara?" he said.

Cara waved him ahead. A knot of emotion held her breath prisoner.

"Don't be long," he said, then followed the others.

Cara stepped up to the path. As she got close, she heard the Huntress whispering. Though Cara couldn't make out the words, it sounded like a prayer. The men would be waiting but no one had said good-bye to their guide. Feeling like an eavesdropper, Cara lingered until finally the Huntress sighed, kissed the tree, and stood back. Her eyes fell on Cara, a challenge in their green depths.

"Are you coming?" Cara asked.

The Huntress nodded and then motioned for Cara to go first. The path was thin. Branches brushed at her skirts but the angry Thorns had receded. The Gate was deep, and it took longer than Cara expected to reach the other side. When she emerged, the whisperings that had followed her through Foresthaven stopped abruptly, leaving behind an eerie silence. Her eyes stung at the sun shining brightly on the hillside that was covered only sparsely with elm and oak. Her companions stood in a cluster a little beyond the Thorns, surveying the gentle slopes ahead.

The Huntress wasn't far behind, and Cara wondered what she must be thinking as she turned to watch the Gate close. A feeling of homesickness brushed at Cara's mind, reminding her painfully of Gar, though it disappeared as quickly as it came.

The Huntress raised her eyes to the vast expanse of blue, grinning like a child. "So bright," she whispered.

"What are you doing here?" Khoury asked brusquely.

Falin's smile evaporated. "What do you mean?"

"Outside Foresthaven. Your job is done."

"Captain—"Archer began, but Khoury stopped him with a raised hand.

"Isn't that right?" the captain said.

The Huntress's chin tilted up. "I promised Sorchia I would see Cara to Iolair," she said evenly. "So either I go with you, or I follow you. It makes no difference to me."

Archer grinned, and Bradan came up to stand next to him. "We'll need all the help we can get," the chieftain said. "Right, Captain?"

"You always say an extra blade is a blessing," Archer reminded him. Anger flattened Khoury's lips.

"I must admit," the Huntress said before Khoury could respond to Archer's prodding, "my expertise ends at the Gate. You'll have to lead us from here."

The captain considered the warrior with hooded eyes, then the lines of his mouth softened. "Fine," he said. "Archer, take point and bring us southwest and you, Huntress, guard the rear." Cara expected an argument at that, but the Huntress took the captain's clipped commands with little more than a nod of acknowledgement.

The group headed down the slope, their mood almost jovial in the brightness of the Tangle. The brush was thinner here, and a breeze played with Cara's hair. Bradan walked next to her, smiling and telling her about healers he'd known, techniques she might try. She nodded politely, but she knew in her heart that no amount of training would tame the unruly nature of her talent.

As the sun dipped behind the hills ahead of them, Khoury called a halt in a tilting glade, protected on one side by relatively thick trees and bordered on the other by a stream. Cara sank to the leafy ground and watched Bradan prepare and tend the fire. Archer had already left to hunt. The Huntress brushed by Cara and settled herself at the base of a tree. Cara had almost forgotten she was with them. If the men's indifference bothered her, it didn't show. She calmly honed her sword, as self-sufficient as she had been in her thorny home.

The meal was simple and once done, they settled in to listen to Archer's tall tales and songs. Bradan even surprised them all by joining his deep bass with Archer's familiar baritone while Khoury pulled his twin swords from their sheaths like lost loves. He inspected them carefully and then set to work with a whetstone in long, smooth strokes. Cara watched out of the corner of her eye as the rhythm calmed him, unwinding the tension he had been carrying with a slow swish, swish, swish.

The late spring night was pleasantly warm and peaceful. Cara couldn't help but think that they'd finally eluded Father. The life she'd had in the Keep seemed little more than a bad dream as she stared up at the tranquil stars.

The captain sheathed the blades and stretched. "I'll take first watch," he said. "Archer, you're up next. Then Bradan and then back to me." The men nodded agreement but Falin stood up.

"Captain, you don't need to take two watches." All heads turned in surprise as if they too had forgotten she was there. "I can take one."

"I don't—"

"Trust me?" Her hand settled comfortably on her sword. "After the last five days, you still can't bring yourself to trust me?"

"It's not that," he said.

"Then what, Captain?" She paced across the glade, her face relaxed though Cara noted the familiar challenge in her eye. "You know, you should let Cara take a watch, too. Or don't you trust her either?"

Cara's heart jumped at the thought. It was strangely appealing.

"She's not trained in a weapon," the captain said.

"She'd only have to wake you." The Huntress's tone was reasonable as she circled the camp.

"At least let the Huntress take a turn, Captain," Archer said. "She can handle herself."

Khoury looked like he wanted to say something but thought better of it. "Fine," he relented. "Archer can take first watch, then the Huntress, Bradan and then me."

"Thank you." The Huntress imitated a mock bow and retreated

back to her tree at the edge of the firelight.

Though Cara understood why Khoury hadn't included her, sharp disappointment dampened her mood. She was touched that the Huntress would even suggest it. Drowsy and tired, she slid down in her blanket and stretched out her tired legs. It felt good to be still, but the absence of the whispers was distracting. Even the ground felt different than the dark loam she had grown used to. She glanced at Falin who was propped up against her tree with the blanket pulled up to her chin. Her eyes were closed and her breathing even as if she had already fallen asleep. Apparently she trusted Khoury just fine.

As usual, Cara slipped easily into sleep but not for long. A rough shake jolted her awake.

"Wha—?"

A leather-bound hand clamped over her mouth. "Shh." Cara rolled her eyes and found Falin crouched over her, finger across her own lips urging silence. Cara nodded understanding, and Falin removed her hand.

"What's wrong?" Cara whispered.

"Nothing." Her mischievous smile gleamed in the firelight. "Don't you want a turn at watch?"

Cara blushed with trepidation. "But Khoury…"

"Won't even know." The Huntress held up a large branch as long as her forearm that had been hacked off at both ends but was fairly thick. "When this is gone, wake Bradan." She tossed the branch onto the top of the fire.

Cara watched with consternation as the flames licked it gently at first then sank hot teeth into the blackening ends. With a conspiratorial wink, Falin retreated to her tree and settled back in to sleep.

Cara almost called after her to say she couldn't take watch. But wasn't this what she wanted? To be taken seriously? Bradan certainly would have no qualms about it when she woke him. And by the time Khoury found out, it would already be done. She looked at Khoury's slumbering form—so close she could touch him. If she really felt worried, she could just wake him.

At first she sat cross-legged, nervously scanning wherever the light touched and peering intently into the shadows in fear. But soon, the playful dance of the crackling fire coaxed her to relax. The night was far from the quiet she expected. Bugs chirped and frogs peeped and as she listened she noticed a rhythm to the constant cacophony. Occasionally, a visitor flapped through the glade though she was never quick enough to decipher if it had been an owl or a bat.

When the branch had burned to half its size, Cara was startled from her musings by a rough grunt nearby. The captain thrashed, tangling in the folds of his blanket.

"Khoury, what's wrong?" she whispered.

He didn't answer but his head wagged back and forth and he growled again. Then she noticed his eyes were closed. He was still asleep.

It's just a nightmare, she told herself, shifting her stiff legs. But he continued to groan for what seemed like a long time. The longer he thrashed, the more she felt desperate to help him. Finally unable to resist, she reached out to soothe his brow, forgetting that she'd already removed her gloves for the night. His skin was warm beneath her cool fingers and in a heartbeat she was standing in the middle of a battlefield.

When she'd touched Archer, she had become him in the memories. Not this time.

She stood just behind and to the side of the blood-spattered captain, though she barely recognized him. Gone was the stony coolness. The network of tiny scars shone pale against his flushed face and his eyes blazed. The lips she had kissed ever so briefly were twisted in a vengeful smirk as he wielded two swords with deadly efficiency.

Where was the firm gentleness that had lifted her from the river? He hacked through the press of adversaries, indifferent to their screams. Her gut clenched at the bodies littering the ground, their individual humanity lost in a sea of ruined flesh. The captain himself bled from numerous wounds but showed no sign of tiring. She trembled. Overwhelmed by chaos, her only thought was to escape his nightmare. But, unlike before, simply deciding to leave didn't make it happen.

"Death!" Khoury roared, rousing the men who followed him to a pitched frenzy. He advanced on a young warrior with a trembling sword. An unseen tether dragged her along after him. The warrior blocked Khoury's first swing but the second blade caught him in the flank. She couldn't turn her eyes away as the captain's upward thrust pierced the thin leather armor, lifting the youth off his feet. The body jerked once then stilled, sinking to the ground. Khoury yanked his weapon free, turning to block another attacker in one fluid movement.

The callous violence made Cara shiver.

It's only a dream, she kept repeating to herself. *It's not really him.* Forced to follow, she closed her eyes and tried to fill her mind with other images of Khoury, kinder images. But his blood-spattered smile kept intruding.

Then feminine laughter echoed across the battlefield like clear water washing away the dust. Cara recognized the sound; it was the woman from his memories. At the joyful sound, the battlefield began to fade, and Cara wanted to laugh herself. But a furious Khoury whirled around, searching for the source of the noise. He didn't seem to see Cara but he definitely heard the laughter.

"No," he shouted to the sky. "No! You will not take me there!"

In a moment, the dead soldiers blew away like ashes from a cold hearth, and Cara was in a cozy loft looking down on a room filled with happy people. Music played and couples danced.

"I said *no*!" Khoury roared from somewhere out of sight and the dancers were wrenched away, leaving Cara standing on a hillside beside another boy. This time, she *was* Khoury, but a much younger version.

"Liar," the other boy scoffed. "That clump of feathers can't be trained."

"Maybe not by you," Cara heard herself say, feeling Khoury's pride in the fierce tawny bird gripping his wrist. Wild-caught and too small for hunting grouse, he loved her nonetheless.

The taller boy's face contorted with scorn. "Even my tiercel's bigger than that…sparrow."

Khoury stroked the downy breast with the back of a blunt finger, watching the amber eyes blink happily. "She's a good hunter."

"Prove it," the other boy challenged. "Have her find something."

"She's not hungry." Cara felt Khoury's wariness.

"Command her, cousin. Or has my mawkish uncle neglected your studies?"

"I can Command." Khoury huffed, but Cara felt his hesitation.

"Then let's see. Have her find…a mouse." The other boy elbowed Khoury roughly. "Or perhaps your mother's blood is too thin for real power."

His teeth creaked at the insult to his mother. Khoury drew in a deep breath, bringing with it a wash of angry magic. Cara felt it gather in her throat, hot and thick. The bird felt it, too. She flapped, pecking at his hand and resisting the jesses. At his bird's distress, Khoury's anger faded taking the magic with it. He didn't need the voice. She would do his bidding without Command. As the last wisp of power swirled in his throat, he leaned close to the feathered head and whispered a word—mouse.

Cara felt the magic flow into the word and ride his breath to the bird. Then ever so softly he said, "Please."

She squawked once as if understanding. Then he threw her into the air to catch the perpetual mountain breeze. With a loud cry, she circled his head once and then set out across the sloping meadow. The golden wings flashed in the bright sunlight. Khoury's heart soared with the graceful dips and turns, and Cara felt herself smile.

"You'll never Command men like that, coz," said a low voice in her ear. Khoury turned his head sharply to find the other boy too close for comfort and eyeing him with wicked intent. "You're too soft."

The hawk's cry drew Khoury's attention as she dove into the long grass. Then she rose to the sky, something clutched in her talons.

"Give me the bird," said a voice like thick honey, each word separate and full of power. Cara felt them press at Khoury's head, leaking down his neck like drips of fat rain. "Give it to me."

Before Cara could think, stone walls shot up from the floor of Khoury's mind, shuttering it closed, pushing her out along with the words. Then she was standing behind the boys. Khoury had turned to face his cousin, fists clenched in anger. "Not this time," he swore.

The other boy laughed. "Oh, so you've got some fight in you. But does your bird?" He turned to his own tiercel and with that same thick voice said, "Kill!" The dark red raptor launched off his wrist and headed straight for Khoury's bird.

"No!" Khoury shouted but in a heartbeat the birds had collided and fallen to the grass. Khoury raced down the hillside to where the tumble of screeching feathers flattened the grass. Drawn inexorably after him, Cara ran, too. When he reached the birds, he grabbed the darker bird and yanked, holding the tiercel aloft by its head. Ignoring the talons that raked his forearm, his eyes were fixed on the ground. Cara looked down and there was his lovely hawk, bloody feathers all akimbo, and one wing mangled beyond recognition. And she still clutched a mouse in her talons.

The other boy ran up and grabbed his bird from Khoury's dazed grip, soothing its ruffled feathers. He peered down, shaking his head with mock sorrow. "Your pride has cost you again, cousin. You should have given it to me when I asked."

Khoury spun around, his fist slamming into the other boy's cheek. His cousin staggered back, his bird flapping furiously.

The boy touched the side of his mouth and checked for blood, murder in his eyes. "You'll pay for that, Mason. And this time Uncle's not here to stop me." He turned and strode off, leaving Khoury to stare down at the shreds of his beloved bird.

Dropping to his knees, Khoury cradled the mess of feathers in gentle hands. "I'm sorry," he whispered as the feathered head leaned against him, mouth open in obvious distress. Then Cara saw his hand go for his dagger.

No, she thought. *No, you can't just kill her!*

She couldn't bear to watch him kill the golden bird. Her distress freed her from his dream and she sat up suddenly. The fire lit clearing was quiet, but Cara's mind whirled in a wild dance. Her hands shook, and she couldn't stop thinking about the hawk.

She looked over at where he slept, peacefully now, and she could make out the young boy's face beneath the beard and the scars. Who was he: the bloodthirsty warrior or the boy? She couldn't decide.

Just then, the fire popped, making her jump. The branch Falin had placed there was gone, burnt away. Cara wondered how long she had been trapped in Khoury's dreams. From the looks of the ashes, it was past time to wake Bradan. Cara calmed her trembling as best she could and went to rouse the shaman, though she didn't think she'd be able to sleep again that night.

CHAPTER 35
KHOURY

When Bradan woke Khoury the sky was already getting light. The Huntress's extra watch shouldn't have made that much difference, but the captain felt well-rested for the first time in days. His nightmare was fading, leaving only a subdued sadness. He admired the rose-colored sky. Not a dark Thorn anywhere. His scars complained tightly as he stretched and moved to the open end of the glade, his mind already focusing on the problems ahead. Sidonius's spies would be everywhere by now, including Iolair. If he were the sorcerer, he'd try to take Cara in the city, maybe use innocents to pressure Wallace into handing her over. Of course, the Tangle wasn't safe either. Sidonius's resources were extensive.

All the captain could really be sure of was his own skill and Archer's. He'd never seen the chieftain wield a weapon and the Huntress, though competent, was a dark horse he wouldn't care to bet on. Cara's healing power would be priceless—afterward. During the fight, she would be their weakest link. He and Archer alone could manage a handful of mercenaries, but more than that and there'd be trouble. Giants would be a death sentence. For now, the best thing would be to stay off the road as much as possible and make haste.

The captain inhaled the warm spring air and began his blade practice, using one sword at first. He'd missed his blades while under the Huntress's careful watch. Now, he danced with them. His unconventional forms had been perfected over many years, tailored to his body's particular needs. Performing each move slowly at first and then with more power and speed, he was soon moving with fluid precision. Khoury drew the second blade, altering the moves to match his weapons. The rhythm of his practice centered him, connected him to his blades, and relaxed his nerves. He felt more like himself than he had in days.

When he stopped, sheathed his blades and headed for the stream, the Huntress was already there and silent as stone. Her eyes followed his movements with a predator's intensity. He tilted his head at her, and she returned his cautious greeting. Then she splashed water on her face and returned to the camp to smother the embers.

He took his turn at the water, rinsing off and slurping the cool mountain runoff. When he returned to the others, the firepit was cold and damp and Falin was gearing up. Bradan was awake, too, rousing Archer with a rude toe in the back. Khoury found Cara still sleeping, her brow furrowed in her sleep. At his touch, she jerked awake with a startled cry.

"It's just me."

Wide-eyed and confused, she stared at him a moment. "Sorry. Nightmare," she said, shaking her head. "I wasn't myself. In the dream."

"I know what that's like."

"Do you?" She searched his face with icy-blue hope.

He didn't know what she was looking for but her steady gaze sparked a warmth in his chest he hadn't felt since that night after the giant raid. Looking at the curves of her face, he realized how much he counted on seeing her every day. He frowned at his weakness. It felt as if a knot inside him had come undone. He couldn't afford the mistakes he made at Bear Clan.

"Well, you seem like yourself now." He'd intended to brush her off, but she leaned against him, and he couldn't help but linger.

A stern voice interrupted the moment, "Captain, we need to go."

He looked up into the eyes of the Huntress, her impatient scowl making him feel like a boy caught mooning. Pulling away from Cara, he reminded himself to stay focused.

It didn't take long to get everyone moving. The underbrush was green with spring and not yet thick enough to hinder them. But when they stopped midday to rest and eat, his restless anxiety had returned. He drew one of his swords, hefting its comforting weight.

"Archer!" he called, assuming a stance.

The Northerner looked surprised but only for a moment. Then, he handed the waterskin to Cara, wiped his damp lips and drew his own weapon with a smile. "You wanna try me, old man?"

Khoury barked a sharp laugh. "I'll best you, boy." He lunged, slashing at Archer with measured power. The clang of metal made Cara squeak in surprise as Archer blocked and parried with a grin.

Khoury had sparred Archer so often, they knew each other's weaknesses. They pushed each other to the limit and beyond. And as with the morning practice, Khoury's world narrowed until it was nothing but the dance of steel. Sweat trickled into his beard and his ribs creaked. Nevertheless, here was contentment. His anxiety fled.

After nearly an hour of back and forth, Khoury disarmed the younger man.

"I let you have that one," Archer taunted with a wide grin, hands on knees and breathing like a bellows.

"No, I took that one," Khoury retorted, sheathing his blades. He scooped up the huge blade Archer favored and tossed it to him.

"Because I was taking it easy on you," Archer said, sheathing the blade with a cheeky snap.

"Right." Khoury took the waterskin Bradan offered and he drank deeply. He had all but forgotten their little group. Cara looked a little pale sitting next to Bradan who fingered his braids in thought. The Huntress's scrutiny, however, was full of challenge.

"Care for a match, Huntress?"

She smiled at that and he had a moment of eager anticipation when she stood and brushed the dirt from her backside. "Love to, Captain. But we should get moving."

He had Archer lead them southeast toward the Pass. They'd eventually have to use the road; but if his bearings were correct, they were far enough south that they wouldn't be on it for more than half a day before reaching the city. The Huntress took up rear guard without question which pleased him. He had to admit she was showing restraint and taking orders well. Then again, he hadn't asked her to do something she really didn't want to yet.

The sun hovered low in the sky when the trees finally gave way to meadows and the tops of the mountains could be seen in the south. Named for their perpetually snow-covered peaks, the White Mountains bordered the Tanglewood along its entire southern and western borders, stretching down into Barakan and northward to the Crown peaks. To the east, the peaks curved northward. The only way through the White Mountain range this far south was the Pass at Iolair, which lay to the east.

They stepped out of the trees into a warm afternoon breeze that foretold the coming of summer. Rolling hills dappled with tiny yellow flowers rose up on either side of them. Khoury hadn't gone forty feet out onto that meadow when the Huntress shouted.

"Riders!" She pointed up the hill. Almost a dozen armored riders crested the top and galloped toward them, swords aloft.

"Archer, look sharp!" Khoury called to his lieutenant who was still shadowing them from within the trees. He took a quick survey of the others: Bradan was behind him to the right, mace in hand, and the Huntress was dragging Cara back toward the relative safety of the trees on his left. She arranged Cara's hands on the staff so it crossed defensively in front of her body. Then, the Huntress stationed herself directly in front of Cara, dropped her pack, and unslung her bow.

"We meet them here," he said, scanning the trees for a glimpse of Archer. "Get them off the horses however you can." He drew his swords and turned to focus on the oncoming threat. Behind him, he heard the shaman begin to mutter.

As soon as the attackers entered shooting range, an arrow whistled from the cover of trees taking the first rider in the throat. Falin fired, catching another rider in the shoulder, making him drop his sword. Unbelievably, a second white-fletched arrow found another rider's chest before the Huntress had finished setting her second shot. Her next hurried shaft missed its target but lodged in the next horse's throat, sending the charger to the ground and pinning its rider. Archer stepped out of the trees and felled a third rider, then stowed his bow and drew his sword.

Khoury rushed into the remaining horses, swinging at the legs of the first one to reach him. He sent the animal crashing to the ground with a scream of pain. The rider was tossed into the nearby heather and Khoury rushed to the fallen man, laming another mount with a crude backhanded swing as he went. He slit the fallen rider's throat and turned to face the lamed horse's axe-wielding rider.

Terrified neighing echoed across the hills. Khoury and his opponent both turned at the sound. Bradan was calf deep in the yellow heather, a scowl etched on his face, and all around him fog rose from the ground. Khoury's skin crawled with a supernatural chill as the ghostly smoke writhed like a knot of snakes. Tendrils crept up the shaman's legs and out along the ground. The horses reared, snorting fear as their riders struggled vainly for control. Two of the warriors fell as their mounts galloped off into the heather. The third man clung to his horse's mane as it fled.

Khoury planted one sword in the ground and slipped the knife from his boot. Twisting, he heaved the blade after the retreating horseman, then turned back to his opponent just in time to block the swinging axe. The curve of the axe hooked Khoury's sword and the other warrior jerked it down, trying to disarm him. Following the movement of the locked blades, Khoury grabbed his second blade from the ground and then raised both swords parallel and hooked them into the head of the axe. He lunged sideways, grunting loudly at the tearing cramp in his side. He managed to unbalance the warrior who stumbled to one knee. Khoury untangled his shorter blade from the axe and stabbed the man in the hollow above the collarbone. Blood spurted and the warrior collapsed, catching Khoury's blade awkwardly beneath him.

Before the captain could shake the body loose, a thin sword pierced the meaty flesh of his upper arm. Pain shot up into Khoury's shoulder and a cold sweat broke out on his brow. He swung overhand with his other sword, catching his attacker with a glancing slash to the shoulder. The man laughed and twisted his sword making Khoury howl with pain. Leaning away, he lashed out at the man's knee with a booted foot. The joint crunched sideways under the kick and the man crumpled to the ground, taking his weapon with him. Khoury felt a gush of warm blood down his arm, pounding in time with his heartbeat.

He turned and hacked with his good arm. The blow nearly separated the man's head from his neck.

"Khoury, watch out!" Cara's voice rang out just as an arm snaked around his throat. Khoury couldn't lift his injured arm to break the hold as he was yanked backward off his feet. His throat closed as all his weight hung from the arm around his neck.

"Falin!" Cara cried. "Help him." But the Huntress had her own troubles, far larger and stronger than she.

The horror in Cara's face gave him purpose. He struggled to get a foot under him and dropped his sword, reaching behind with his hand, searching for a vulnerability—an eye or a throat, anything. He scanned the area, but Archer was fighting with his back to the captain and Bradan was struggling on the ground with one of the men he'd unhorsed.

Khoury's attacker jerked him back off his feet again, and he felt the claws of air hunger in his chest. His vision began to darken.

"Sister!" Cara begged.

With a distinctly unfeminine roar, the Huntress shoved her opponent hard enough that he stumbled backward a step. She backed up a step of her own as her hand went for her belt and retrieved a black bolo. In seconds, the spinning stones were only a blur. Then she twisted and hurled the weights at Khoury. He heard them whistle past his ear and strike his attacker in the head with a painful sounding thud. The pressure on his throat instantly released, and Khoury fell to his knees coughing.

He could only watch as the Huntress's opponent stepped in and leveled her with a punch to the temple.

Why she wasn't dead, he didn't know. She'd given the man a perfect opportunity to kill her but he hadn't. The captain sliced the throat of the man who'd tried to choke him then sized up the rest of the battlefield. Bradan was alone on his knees in the heather, relatively unhurt, and Archer was engaged with one opponent. The only other attacker standing was the one who'd knocked Falin out.

Khoury scooped up his blade, swaying on his feet. The blade had poked through the muscles in his arm without too much damage, but the pain hindered upward movement. The blood that dripped briskly from his elbow, however, hinted at a deeper problem. He had to finish this and fast.

He rushed Falin's attacker with a flurry of strikes that set the man on his heels. The attacker wasn't a skilled swordsman and even injured and woozy Khoury had him at a disadvantage. When Archer's opponent fell, the man flicked a fearful glance in that direction, providing a fatal moment of inattention. Khoury gutted him. Dizziness swarmed around Khoury's head, but a strangled cry from Cara told him they weren't done yet.

He and Archer turned to see a warrior with a black-feathered arrow in his shoulder, holding Cara by the root of her braid, his knife at her throat.

"Just a minute." Khoury took a step closer. "Let's talk this out."

"No talk," the man snapped.

Bradan staggered to his feet but when he tried to approach, the wounded man tugged Cara's hair back harder, making her whimper. "Don't move or she dies."

Khoury could see the indent of the knife in the soft flesh of her throat.

Bradan halted, hands in the air. Khoury surrendered his weapons to the ground and wondered if the shaman had any more ghosts. Just then the Huntress rolled over with a groan and pushed herself to her knees between Khoury and the kidnapper. There was a gash on her temple and a line of blood down her cheek. Sitting back on her heels, she shook her head drunkenly.

"I said don't move!" the man yelled down at her with desperation.

The Huntress raised her empty hands in surrender as she staggered to her feet.

The nervous warrior squeezed another squeal out of Cara. "I'll kill her," he insisted.

The Huntress stared at him for a moment. Then, as her mind cleared, she shifted into familiar nonchalance, stretching her back as if completely at ease. "So, kill her," she said flippantly. "But you better be sure you've got the right girl."

Khoury's gut clenched. What did she think she was doing?

The man looked momentarily confused. Then his face clouded with anger. "It's her. Look at the hair."

"Then you can't kill her, can you?"

The man looked at her then back at Khoury. "I will kill her anyway if you don't bring me a horse."

"No, you won't." Falin's blunt skepticism gave the man pause.

There was more desperation than anger in the face that turned to the Huntress, but the knife pressed deeper and a line of crimson appeared between the blade and Cara's white skin. "Try me," he hissed.

The Huntress stopped and turned to face him, hands on her hips. "You were told to retrieve her," she said slowly, "alive."

The Huntress's words obviously hit a nerve with the man, but how did the Huntress know what his orders were? Khoury's mind was fuzzy. He couldn't take his eyes from the gathering droplet of blood on Cara's throat. Blood dripped down his arm, too, pooling warmly in the crease of his elbow.

"But…"

"Don't do it," Falin warned the man. "You do *not* want to see him angry."

Does she know Sidonius? Khoury wondered, feeling edgy and off-balance.

A drop of blood broke loose from the blade at Cara's throat and trickled down to the neck of her dress, staining the fabric. Crimson soaked into the blue. Where had he seen that before? Khoury's mind wandered. A memory of fire tickled his nose as the Huntress stepped closer, her hand reaching out for the man, gentle persuasion on her face.

"I'll kill you, too," the man threatened weakly. "Even if it is against orders."

What orders was the man talking about? Suspicion flared in Khoury's murky brain. Was that why she wasn't dead yet?

"No, you won't do that either," the Huntress said. "Just give her to me."

Give her to me. The words echoed in the captain's head.

Give her to me. Dreams and reality clashed, and he felt the echoes of an ancient betrayal.

"What are you playing at?" he growled at the Huntress. "You swore to protect her."

Falin turned to Khoury, flicked a glance at the kidnapper and then back to Khoury. Then a sly smile flashed across her features, quickly replaced by her usual stony facade. "She's not worth risking my life for." Her haughty tone grated on Khoury's nerves.

"You lying traitor." He lunged at her, his hands clenched into fists and his head spinning.

She took a step back. And he advanced. Crimson-soaked blue silk. Broken feathers of gold. A burned-out house. His mind flitted with fragments of dreams.

The Huntress stopped retreating, chin tilted up and challenge in her eyes. "How many more will die for her, your little pet?"

And then it happened. The fury inside him broke through, overwhelming his flagging mind, dulling his pains and his fear. His hand was around Falin's throat before he knew it. Her eyes flew open in surprise and the rage delighted in it. He couldn't stop his fingers from tightening. She clawed at his hand. Blood thundered in his head drowning out the soft sound of an arrow strike. The man behind Cara gurgled as she shrieked in panic, shocking the captain back to his senses.

Archer and Bradan rushed him, each one taking an arm. His fingers unclenched as the anger faded. The Huntress fell to her knees in a crumpled heap.

It had been a ruse, all of it.

To give Archer time.

Cold shame snuffed the last of the madness out as Cara rushed to him. She pressed her face to his chest and his good arm closed around her shaking frame without thought.

Archer gripped the captain's shoulder tightly, his eyes boring into Khoury's. "Captain," he whispered urgently, "are you back?"

Khoury nodded, dropping his gaze. 'It's passed."

He heard Archer's soft breath of relief, and the hand that gripped his shoulder tightened briefly and then let go.

"Are you hurt?" Khoury whispered to Cara as Archer moved to where Falin crouched, her hand massaging her throat.

Cara shook her head.

"But you are," Bradan said, grabbing Khoury's arm. "We need to staunch that. And quickly." He tore a strip from his shirt and bound it tightly around the wound. "Cara, you'll need to tend this."

At the mention of healing work, Cara pulled back and stared into

Khoury's face. There was something she wanted to say, he could see it. But a rough hand whirled him around before she could.

"You thornless son of a rat! You tried to kill me!" Falin's eyes blazed. "What's the matter with you?" Her throat was just beginning to show the purple badge of his anger.

Then a voice from behind them interrupted. "I see your new friends don't like you any more than we did."

Falin blanched, and Khoury turned to see the rider who'd been pinned in the initial attack walking toward them. He'd forgotten about that one. Then the rider reached up and removed his dented helmet. Only it wasn't a man at all; it was a woman. A woman with long black hair.

"Hello, Sister," Rebeka said.

CHAPTER 36
FALIN

"You almost made it." Rebeka drew her sword, twirling it lazily. "But you never win this game, do you? I always find you."

Falin clenched her jaw until her teeth creaked. With the Final Gate behind her, she thought she'd finally escaped Rebeka.

"I haven't lost yet." Her voice was hoarse as she drew her blade.

"Yes, you have." Rebeka stalked closer, her eyes never leaving Falin's. "I'm here to finish this."

Khoury stepped up next to Falin, blade in hand. His bandage was soaked already, his left hip and leg darkly wet. With all that blood lost, no wonder he'd snapped.

"Stay out of this," she snarled at him. "This is personal. Take the others and go. I'll catch up."

"So sure of yourself, dandelion." Rebeka laughed, then she winked at Khoury. "Don't worry, Outsider. I'll save you a dance."

"Leave them be." Falin rushed Rebeka with a slashing attack, trying to keep the scout's attention off the captain and Cara who stood behind him, clinging to his arm.

Rebeka parried the strike easily. "I can't do that, Sister. The stain must be purged." The two Huntresses circled each other.

"What stain?"

"You and your kind. Bad enough an Outsider like you lived in Haven, now men have soiled our Mothers' sacred forest."

"That wasn't my idea. I'd have killed them in the Thorns. You took them to Sorchia."

"I had to honor the girl's request for safety," Rebeka sneered, "not that I wanted to."

"So you took them to Sorchia in hopes of a Culling. That didn't go as planned, did it?"

Anger reddened Rebeka's cheeks. "No, but bringing you back, dead or alive, will get me on the Council." She lunged, and Falin deflected the blow.

"You'll never be an Elder."

"Oh no?"

"Not when they find out what you've done."

"I've done nothing."

"I saw him." Her words hung in the air tauntingly.

Rebeka's knuckles whitened and eyes flashed with hooded fury seconds before she lashed out. Falin blocked the angry slash to her head, the jarring clang resounding up her arm.

"How long have you used the ships to make deals with men?" Falin asked, sparking a flurry of attacks.

"No one will believe you, Outsider."

"Sorchia will, and she has the Council's ear." Falin thrust at Rebeka and the clang of metal rang across the hillside.

"She has betrayed the Council and soon they will know," Rebeka threatened. "As for your tale, it seems I'd better take you back dead after all."

She leapt to the attack. The Huntresses fought in earnest with nothing held back on either side. Their blades met and sparked. Clanging steel, grunts and hate filled the air. Like Archer and his captain, the two sisters knew each other too well. Unlike the men, no quarter would be given.

Falin feinted, drawing Rebeka close. Then she ducked under

Rebeka's angry overextended lunge. In two strides she passed the scout, slicing through leather as she went.

"Damn you!" Rebeka whirled, blood oozing from her thigh.

Falin hadn't intended it to be deep. "First blood," she boasted. She intended to take her time. She wanted Rebeka to know she'd been bested, wanted her to feel the sting of her defeat. But in the flurry of the fight, she'd forgotten about their audience.

Rebeka, however, hadn't. She had angled back toward the tight knot of Outsiders and now the scout attacked the nearest of them, Archer. Falin was a half second behind and would have been too late again, except that Rebeka's blow fell against Khoury's deflecting blade. Even wounded as he was, his reflexes were quick.

Seeing her prideful mistake, Falin hurriedly tackled the black-haired Sister, and they hit the ground hard. Rebeka's sword spun off into the grass. Falin straddled the other woman, landing a solid left to Rebeka's jaw and then another. Rebeka grabbed for Falin's sword as Falin clung to it with both hands. Then Rebeka's fist slammed into her wounded temple and her vision blurred.

Rebeka shoved her off into the grass and scrambled to her feet. A swift kick at Falin's sword hand sent that blade to join the other and both women dove into the fragrant lushness looking for a weapon. Falin's fingers found metal first, and she eagerly wrapped her fingers around the cold edge. Rebeka saw the movement and dove for the weapon, too. Grabbing the hilt, she yanked the sword away.

Instinctively, Falin gripped the sword tighter. The sharp edges bit deeply into her palm and fingers. With a forceful twist, Rebeka slipped the blade through Falin's grasp. The edge scraped bone as it tore free, smeared with scarlet. Falin stifled her cry of pain and crawled to a crouch, blood dripping from her hand.

Rebeka was breathing hard, but she smiled arrogantly and examined the bloody sword. "My, my. Bet that hurts." She laughed and lunged at Falin, making her leap to her feet.

"You were never as good as you thought," Rebeka jeered. She

slashed again, keeping Falin moving.

Falin pressed her fist into her belly trying to quell the gut-wrenching pain. She felt sick. Falin scanned the hillside. She needed a blade but there was nothing.

"I'll never know what Sorchia saw in you," Rebeka said. She attacked again as she spoke, slicing the blade through the air.

Falin felt the breeze of it and knew it should have found its mark. But Rebeka was toying with her now. The other Huntress's arrogance was something Falin could use against her. After the next attack, Falin faked a stagger and dropped to one knee with a groan. As she clutched her leg with her bloodied hand, she retrieved the small dagger from her boot.

"Khoury, do something!" Cara's plaintive cry grated on Falin's ears.

Rebeka barked a short confident laugh and turned on Cara. "Save your worry for yourself, little sister. I've seen what hunts you."

Khoury pushed the girl behind him, sword at the ready.

No, Falin thought, *this is my kill.*

She launched from the ground and charged. One hand grabbed the knot of hair at Rebeka's neck, dragging her backward and down to her knees. The other hand pressed her blade to Rebeka's neck. Falin's wounded hand throbbed, but she held the blade steady.

"Drop it," she rasped through gritted teeth, shaking Rebeka roughly. The Sister dropped the sword on the ground.

"You're a disgrace to my people," Rebeka said angrily.

"They're my people, too."

"We were never your people," Rebeka shot back.

Rebeka's words cut Falin to the bone, sickening her. She bent Rebeka's head back to look her in the eye. "I warned you once not to depend on my charity, Sister." Falin brought the bright blade to the other woman's throat with lethal intent.

"No!" Cara raced around Khoury's bulk and grabbed Falin's arm.

Her hand was bare and the moment their skin touched, Falin's head filled with visions. Bloody manacles and the scent of dust trapped her in a waking dream that stank of nightmarish fear.

"Let go," Falin snarled. Her head spun, and her hands tingled. She forced the emotion down, stilling herself for the kill. One swift sure strike. But her arm refused to listen. Her blade quivered hesitantly over Rebeka's neck.

"Sister, please," Cara urged softly. "Stop this."

Cara didn't know what she was asking. There was no telling what Rebeka would do. Leaving her alive would only end badly. Falin squeezed the knife more tightly, but she couldn't command the final cut. A fog crept into her mind, robbing her of her strength.

She looked to the men hoping for an ally, but not one of them made a move.

"Tie her to a horse and send her away," Cara said with unexpected confidence.

Falin's eyes sought Khoury's. Surely, the captain understood.

The captain was pale, blood still dripping from his bandaged arm. Wearily, he said to Archer, "Get some rope."

Defeated, Falin dropped her gaze to the ground. She hated Cara in that moment, but she hated herself more. She kept her knife at Rebeka's throat until the others took her and tied her well. Only then did Cara step away, slipping her hand once more into her glove.

Letting Rebeka live was foolish, but worse, Sorchia would be in danger. Falin refused to say it out loud, fearing that would make it come true, but the thought weighed heavy in her gut.

Bradan pulled Cara away to help with Khoury's wound while Archer collected horses and weapons from their fallen attackers. Falin seethed inside, refusing to mention her wounded hand.

How had Cara forced me to show mercy? she wondered, but could find no answer.

"I thought you were stronger than that," Rebeka said.

Falin refused to even look at her. Tears shamefully burned in her eyes. She was weaker than she'd ever been, and she despised herself.

"I thought you'd at least do some damage," Rebeka continued.

"But it seems you've crippled yourself only to watch me go free."

The scout's astute observation only inflamed Falin's shame further but there was still a mote of rebellion left. "Don't think you've escaped unscathed," she warned.

"Oh, but I have," Rebeka replied, haughty once more.

Falin's knife snaked out, slashing the dark-haired woman's cheek from hairline to chin. Rebeka cried out in pain, but no one noticed.

"You can't hide now," Falin hissed. "When the Elders ask about that, and believe me they will, give them my regards." She stood and replaced her knife into her boot. "If you cross me again, I *will* kill you, even if I have to kill her first." Then she stalked off across the hillside.

Six horses grazed in a patch of sun where Archer and Bradan rummaged through packs and saddlebags. Cara stood amidst the animals, the head of a sleek chestnut gelding pressed to her chest, the picture of calm. Jealousy rumbled inside Falin.

Not watching where she was going, she nearly bumped into Khoury. The bandage on his arm was fresh and without stain. His color looked better. Apparently, Cara had already worked on him.

"Huntress, I..."

She held up a hand for him to stop. She was in no mood to listen.

He sighed and held out his hand. Her bolo dangled from one finger.

She'd completely forgotten about it. She snagged the swinging weights with her left hand. "Thank you," she muttered.

His fingers tightened before she could pull the bolo away, forcing her to look at him. "No, thank you." His lowered voice rumbled in his chest. "For...everything."

She snorted a chuckle. "Is that supposed to be an apology, Captain?"

He tilted his head with wry acknowledgement, then said, "How's that hand?"

"Fine," she lied.

"Have Cara look at it."

"I'd rather lose it than have that woman touch me again," she said with spite.

He paused at her vehemence but there was understanding in his blue eyes. "I must insist." His voice was low enough that no one else could hear, sparing her a spectacle for which she was grateful, but she would not cave this time.

"Please, Captain."

"It's Khoury."

"Captain," she whispered firmly, "leave me some shred of dignity."

"Dignity? Or pride?"

She had to smile at that. "It's the same thing, isn't it…for people like us?"

He scrubbed his disheveled hair. "I see I must defer to your judgment. Archer says there's a stream a hundred yards back." He jerked a thumb at the trees. "Take care of it, Huntress. I can't have you slowing us down." His tone was formal but there was a hint of sympathy that she didn't expect.

"I will," she murmured. Falin grabbed her pack where she'd dropped it and hurried into the woods. Following the scent of damp earth and sounds of gurgling, she quickly located the stream and knelt in the cool mud to face her worst fears.

She plunged her hand into the cool running water to clean off the clots and blood, gasping at the pain. Then, she inspected it carefully. Revulsion tightened her throat at the sight of the long slash across the palm and each of her four fingers. White glistening bone was visible in the base of the wounds and they gaped widely. Grabbing a clean cloth, she scrubbed the hand under the water. Curls of fresh blood floated downstream and the cloth was stained deep red. She brought her hand up and inspected it again. Dread curled in her stomach as she tried to move the fingers, she had a little motion but… She quelled the morbid thoughts with practicality. Since the injury had no inclination to stay closed, she'd have to stitch it.

She dug in her pack for some willow and chewed the bitter bark as she worked. Then she retrieved a small bone needle and some sinew and set to the grisly task. She had to pause a few times as her stomach heaved rebelliously but soon it was done. Her palm burned with the rough treatment. She ran a soothing finger over the ruined planes of her hand and wondered absently if it would end up clawed and useless.

"Falin!" Archer's voice rang through the woods.

"Here," she shouted, quickly wrapping her hand in clean bandages and shoving her supplies hastily in her sack.

Archer rode up towing a small gelding behind. "Thought you might like this guy." He tossed her the reins.

She shrugged. She knew how to ride but never really had an affinity for the beasts. She stroked the sturdy neck by way of introduction and was surprised when a kind of peace settled over her. The whiskered lips tickled her good hand, nudging her with equine affection as the bottomless brown eyes offered unspoken sympathy. She felt strangely soothed by the animal. Too exhausted to walk another step, she gratefully swung a tired leg over the saddle and settled in with a sigh. "Let's go."

CHAPTER 37
CARA

Somewhere in her heart, Cara knew she should be sorry but she wasn't. She had stopped death—if only this once. She watched with pride as they sent Rebeka, bound to a surefooted pony, off across the foothills. The disfiguring gash across Rebeka's cheek had been Falin's bitter justice, and Cara could live with that. The scout still had her life.

And for the first time ever, Cara felt powerful. It was intoxicating.

She tightened up her mare's girth and was just about to shove her foot in the stirrup when a touch on her shoulder stopped her.

"What did you do to her?" Khoury asked, his face stony.

He could only mean Falin. "Nothing," she said calmly though inside something tightened, preparing for a storm.

He stepped closer, keeping his voice low. "Was it…memories?"

"No," she said. And it hadn't been. She couldn't see into the Huntress at all. "I saw the knife at Rebeka's throat and all I could think of was the knife at my own." She rubbed at the thin scab on her neck wondering at her own half-truth, wondering how much of her he saw clearly. "I really don't know what made her stop."

He studied her, weighing her answer. He was good at that—judging. Especially considering who he really was.

But he only said, "It was unwise to let Rebeka go."

"Falin was going to kill her."

"We all killed today," he said softly.

Not me, Cara thought with some pride. "That was during a fight," she said. "She'd already stopped Rebeka." There was a difference in Cara's mind that she couldn't explain.

Khoury remained unconvinced.

"So you would have…I mean, would you have killed her?" she asked.

"Yes," he said.

Perhaps his dreams were closer to the truth than she wanted to know. Visions of him on the battlefield floated in her mind. She turned back to her horse, suddenly angry.

Before she could mount up, Khoury leaned over to whisper in her ear, his body disturbingly close. "Before we go any farther I need to know something, Cara."

His voice was low as if the words were meant only for her. Energy snapped between them. Ever since the battle, she felt more alive than ever and his husky tones made her forget what they were talking about. Anticipation heated her blood. She pressed back against his hard chest. "What?"

"When the time comes, I need to know that you won't try to stop me from killing Sidonius."

She turned, surprised by the question. But she knew he was right. Hadn't the priestess said Sidonius would only stop if they made him?

"I won't try to stop you," she whispered, meeting his gaze. His nearness pulled her, made her want to fall into him. She loved the blue of his eyes.

"Good," he said. As his eyes roved down her face to her lips, her heart sped up.

But instead of satisfying her want, he stepped back. She nearly toppled forward into the cool space.

"You'd do well to remember the lesson of the Dunhadrar," he said coldly.

Dunhadrar? She was confused.

His eyes bored into hers. "The power to Command does not give you the right to." Then he turned on his heel and mounted up.

Why would he think her a brother-killer when she'd just saved a life? And what did he know of the Dunhadrar anyway?

Angrily, Cara pushed the questions away. She didn't have to answer to him. She swung herself up into the saddle just as the Huntress and Archer rode out of the forest.

Falin slid a sideways glance in her direction then pulled her gelding to the far side of Bradan. Cara was surprised at the haunted expression on the warrior's face. Her eyes were puffy as if she'd been crying. It was obvious that the others were upset about Rebeka, too. But Cara refused to feel bad. She raised her chin defiantly as she rode beside Khoury who led them at a comfortable trot, east toward the Pass.

After a few long hours in the saddle, Khoury called a halt at the edge of the foothills where a screen of large boulders jutted out of the hill protecting a small thicket of thin white poplars that glowed luminously in the setting sun's light. Below the stones, dense trees bordered a smooth-surfaced lake in the bowl-shaped valley.

They rode down into the thicket, dismounted and began setting up a comfortable camp. Cara tied her mare up next to Khoury's gelding while Falin tied her mount at the far end. One-handed, she struggled awkwardly with her saddlebags, and Khoury went to help her.

Cara sidled closer to listen to their conversation, keeping her head down and fiddling with the saddlebags.

"Why don't you let me finish up here?" Khoury said, reaching for her horse's girth.

"I'm fine," Falin said. Cara was surprised there was no growl in her tone.

"You need a bath," he pointed out.

"When I'm done here." She shoved half-heartedly at his shoulder.

"It's an order."

Cara snuck a glance over the saddle. Falin looked ready to argue further but then softened. Exhaustion's purple hue ringed her eyes. "You're probably right."

"Of course I am." His voice was unusually gentle and jealousy flared in Cara. Then Falin grabbed her pack from the saddle and headed to the thin stand of trees.

Khoury untacked and rubbed down Falin's gelding, a thoughtful look on his face. He'd been very attentive to the Huntress since the fight. Cara told herself he was just being contrite but perhaps it was something more.

She'd never forget the look on his face when the rage took over. In that moment, he was the monster she'd seen in his nightmare although today she realized she didn't fear him anymore. Still, what brought on that rage was a mystery she longed to unravel.

Cara finished up with her horse and wandered over to the fire where Archer had just returned with freshly killed squirrel. She plopped down next to Bradan and waited for him to acknowledge her.

"It's good to ride instead of walk," he said.

Cara rubbed at her backside. "I'm not sure that's true," she said making a wry face. He laughed. She caught the shaman's face in her gloved hands and poked at the swelling beneath his left eye. "How are you feeling?"

"I'm good. For an old man."

"You're not old," she said, though she noticed more gray in his beard now than when she first met him. Still, he smiled more often lately, and it was good to see that the worst of his grief was over.

She considered asking him about what Khoury said but decided she didn't care that much. She could only follow her heart. What they thought shouldn't matter. Instead, she asked Bradan about his fighting experience and he happily regaled her with tales of his youth, fighting giants as a young man. When Khoury came to sit by the fire, her attention followed him though she still nodded appropriately at the old shaman.

The captain sat down and took out his whetstone and swords. Smoothing stone over blade, she watched him hone the edge to a bright gleam. The work soothed him. The firelight played over the planes of his face, and she remembered the night in the Keep when she'd been enthralled by his scars. His blunt fingers reminded her of his hands on her waist in the river. Then, as now, watching him kindled something in her. But tonight, she felt something more, a predatory heat and a surety about what she really wanted. Impulsively, she decided that tonight she would finally discover what those couples had really been doing out by the bear pens.

CHAPTER 38
KHOURY

Khoury closed his eyes as he worked the blades one by one. The rhythmic motion, the swish of the stone, untied the knots inside him: The fight, the rage, Cara's concerning power. Behind his eyelids, it was the Huntress who came to mind first. Her anger at him had been justified, but the fact that she just let the matter drop showed how deeply ashamed she was over Rebeka's escape.

Archer had been right; she had excellent weapon skills, the ability to think on her feet, and grace under pressure. But most importantly, she understood there were no rules when life was on the line. All that mattered was surviving. She'd been ready to remove Rebeka as a threat, of that Khoury was sure. And, he would have done the same in her position.

Cara had been wrong to force Rebeka's release. He still didn't know how she'd done it. Did her power extend to coercion? His mind rebelled at the thought.

When confronted, she hadn't given him an answer. She hadn't cringed or apologized. She had met his scrutiny with unexpected resolve and defiance, forcing him to see her as more than the child he'd been telling himself she was. Perhaps that misconception had served him. He didn't want to accept the attraction between them, insisting on seeing her as a child instead.

He glanced up at her, surprised that she was watching him. She didn't drop her eyes either, instead her mouth turned upward in a seductive smile that held promises he wasn't sure she understood.

He tried to see her as a woman with the strength to choose. A woman who would make her own way in the world. Something in his heart shifted. Battle always heated his blood and that smile only compounded his need.

He shook himself. Now was not the time to be swept up in passion. He thought of the cool lake, just the remedy for wayward thoughts. Having finished both blades, he sheathed them and tucked them under his blanket.

The Huntress hadn't returned yet, but the sun was just kissing the edge of the horizon and the air was cooling rapidly. If he wanted to wash the blood and sweat and desire from his body, he'd have to hurry.

"I'm going to the lake," he announced.

Cara's eyes clung to his with uncharacteristic boldness that only heightened his interest. Pushing the intimate thoughts from his mind, he headed to the lake.

When he arrived at the water's edge, he scanned the water for Falin. She was just emerging from the water to his left, climbing onto the flat rocks where her clothes had been washed and laid out to dry. She didn't notice him as he watched her. Her naked body shone wetly in the fading light. In the low light of evening, alone with the forest, she was utterly at peace. The watchful tension she usually carried was gone. Her hair clung wetly to her head and back as she hummed, drying herself with her blanket.

Then she lifted a long strip of cloth and carefully snugged her breasts to her body, hiding her curves under linen and then leather. Her careful attention to dressing drew his gaze to every part of her until finally she wrung the water from her long hair and knotted the strands carelessly at her neck before she gathered up her pack and headed back to camp.

Unsettled by the effect she had on him, he stripped quickly and dove into the chill water, letting the shock of it clear the primal flush from his skin. He swam out from the shore, powerful strokes driving him swiftly through the water. When at last he stopped and turned back, the sun had finally dropped behind the mountains taking the last of the light with it. He strode out of the water in search of his clothes to find Cara waiting for him in the dim half-light.

"What are you doing here?"

"I wanted to kiss you," she said in her simplistic way as she stepped into the ankle deep water.

"Did you?"

She nodded with a smile and stretched up to slide her arms around his neck. "I didn't see your memories today when I healed your arm."

He had noticed that, too.

"I must be getting that control Bradan is always talking about." She smiled at him, mischievous and inviting, and then drew him down to her lips.

He braced himself for the kiss, but there was no aching grief or painful memory in it, only the softness of her lips on his. Her fingers tangled in the hair at the back of his neck, pulling him gently closer. His hands itched to rove over her skin. Instead he placed them firmly on her hips, his fingers wrapping around her curves, fighting the desire to slide her out of her dress. No matter how sure she seemed, he knew she was untouched.

"I've told you before," he murmured against her lips. "This isn't right."

"So you've said." Her voice was playful. "I'm too young, or something." Her hand slid down his chest, provocative fingers tickling his bare skin as they roamed.

His heart pounded with heady anticipation. "Too young to know what's good for you."

"Good for me?" She scoffed. "I don't care what's good for me. I only know what I want." Her hand slid lower. Her boldness shocked him, its naïve seduction breaking through his reserve. His hand cupped her cheek gently though his lips roved over hers with fierce passion. Her eager moan was all the answer he needed. He swept her up in his arms and splashed his way to the grassy shore where he lowered her to the soft ground.

CHAPTER 39
FALIN

When Falin returned from her bath, she felt refreshed but utterly spent. Archer was turning the spit. Bradan had already fallen asleep. Khoury and Cara were missing and she assumed they'd gone to get clean as well though she hadn't seen them at the lake. She laid out her blanket and her pack and dropped to the ground, her mind whirling with the strangeness of the day.

"You okay?" Archer asked, handing her a scorched half of squirrel.

"I'm fine," she said, and strangely enough she was. When she'd checked the stitches at the lake, the wounds had already closed up. And, thankfully, the fingers moved better already. Cara had only touched her for a few moments. The rabbit had far more power than she ever would have believed. Falin yawned widely.

Archer chuckled. "Get some rest. I've got watch."

She smiled weakly at him. After shoving down some meat, she stretched out under her rough blanket. Her mind was weightless and empty as she listened to the popping of the fire. She floated for a while in hazy half-sleep and then she was dreaming...

A warm pair of lips descended on hers. Drowsily she returned the kiss, wondering where the dream would take her. The lips smiled against her mouth, and the familiarity of the accompanying chuckle nudged her toward wakefulness. Confused by the warm weight pressing her to soft ground, she tried to figure out where she was. Languid sleepiness held her in a fog. Someone murmured, but she couldn't make out the words. He kissed her again, slowly and thoroughly, and she became aware of hard-muscled masculine thighs intertwined with hers, drawing her attention to the fact that she was naked.

Alarmed, her mind scrambled to find focus. The kisses shifted to her cheeks and eyelids and when her eyes opened she could just make out Khoury's handsome features in the moonlight.

His eyes wandered over her face like a caress, their smoky blue depths stoking an unfamiliar fire in her; she felt flushed and excited. His hand caressed her curves as she ran her palms over the warm skin of his shoulders and back.

"I have wanted you." His voice was husky as he slipped strong arms underneath her, crushing her to him as his mouth found hers again. His tongue teased hers and she purred, arching up against him, wanting to be closer still.

Encouraged, he shifted his weight lower to kiss her collarbone, her shoulder and down toward her breast. Excitement burned off her drowsiness but her mind was still separate, observant. Desire tingled in her limbs, and her skin beneath his hands was electrically alive. She yearned for the sensations he created. But she felt out of control and the thought that this dream was her master gave rise to sharp anxiety.

As the emotions spiraled upward, their effect terrified her. He made her want him. He made her need him in ways she didn't even understand. She would have followed him anywhere, done anything he asked. And that fact made her rebel against even this delicious servitude.

She told herself to pull away, but her body refused to obey. She wanted to stop, but her hands continued to arouse him as if they had minds of their own. She ached for him to possess her and hated herself for wanting it. When he shifted himself between her legs, her mind cried out for her to jump up and flee.

He paused and she could feel his heart pounding, his restraint tenuous. "Are you sure?"

No! she answered in her mind, relief momentarily easing her fear.

But the word that escaped her lips was, "Yes."

His hands tightened on her hips.

"No!"

Falin bolted upright as her shout echoed against the rocks. Her blanket tangled with her legs, and she almost wept with relief that she wasn't actually naked.

"You okay?" Archer half-stood as he watched her from across the fire.

She nodded and waved him to sit, looking around the fire to reorient herself. Bradan's snores continued unperturbed, and Khoury was nowhere to be seen.

"Nightmare?" Archer asked, leaning against a boulder.

"Something like that." She managed a weak smile. Exhaling slowly, she forced the sensual images from her mind.

She was no stranger to disturbing dreams. She'd had nightmares all her life, always trapped and oftentimes not herself. There was a curiously strong reality about them, and this was undoubtedly one of those dreams. It had been so real that her heart still pounded with longing and her clothes were damp with sweat.

But why Khoury?

She stared at the leaping flames and searched her feelings long and hard only to discover something disappointing—she was attracted to the captain. She reminded herself she was a Huntress and the attraction nothing of consequence, but the swirl of emotions remained. Deeply disturbed, she laid back down to sleep, pulling the blanket around her like armor. Even so, the lure of Khoury's caresses followed her into what fitful rest she found that night.

CHAPTER 40
ARCHER

Archer woke, alert and rested, in the small hours. It was Bradan's watch and the older man was struggling to keep his eyes open. Archer often forgot that the others weren't used to the steady pace or the interrupted sleep.

"Hey, why don't you get some rest," he offered in a quiet voice, startling the older Northerner.

"You need your rest, too." His voice was stiff with pride.

"I'm not tired." Archer folded up his blanket and moved closer to the fire. "I'll wake you in an hour."

Bradan hesitated but in the end weariness won out. "All right," he said around a yawn.

While the shaman settled beneath his blanket, Archer walked the perimeter of camp. He paused by the captain whose arm was tucked around a sleeping Cara and smiled. He couldn't remember the last time Khoury had someone special, and he was mostly glad for it. But choosing her now was ill-advised. Archer had no illusions that a confrontation with Sidonius was inevitable and would cost them dearly. Still, Khoury deserved what happiness he could find while there was still time. Archer wandered back toward the fire and set to re-fletching the best of the looted arrows with the black groundhawk feathers.

When the dawn had chased away all but two lingering stars, Archer woke Bradan and Falin to start breaking down the camp and readying the horses. He let the lovers sleep at least until Falin tripped over her own feet and landed on her wounded hand. Her cursing would have woken the dead.

"Morning," he heard Khoury rumble. He turned to reply but the captain hadn't intended it for him. He watched Khoury pull Cara closer, tucking his nose in her hair.

But then something odd happened. She rolled over and kissed him for the briefest of moments and they leapt apart as if stung.

"I'm sorry," she whispered, scrambling backward. Tears pooled in her eyes. "I'm so sorry." Archer watched her frantically search for her gloves and shove her hands inside.

Khoury scrubbed at his face as if disoriented. "It's okay. It just startled me." He stood up and reached for her. Archer noted her hesitation before letting Khoury pull her into his arms. He kissed the top of her head. "We'll figure it out," he promised.

Archer cleared his throat loudly. "We're nearly ready to go, Captain." The captain nodded but there was a sadness in his eyes that left Archer wondering what had just happened.

The rest of the day passed much like the previous ones. Falin recovered her prickly defiance and even joined the afternoon sparring session. She was a challenging opponent, and Archer liked working with her. They all took turns showing Cara how to wield her staff, but she really had no aptitude for fighting.

Archer silently thanked Rebeka as they mounted up to continue, grateful for commandeered horses. With them, the group traveled farther and faster. Thankfully, there were no signs of Rebeka or any other pursuit.

By the end of the second day, they'd reached the Pass. As the sun set behind them, Archer gazed down on the city of Iolair. The plains stretched out beyond Iolair where it nestled between peaks of the White Mountains. The flatlands were already shrouded in the dusk cast by the mountains' shadow. Rising abruptly up from the gently sloping road, the bold square watchtowers of Iolair shone brightly in the day's last light, their tawny marble stark against the darkening plains beyond.

Archer waited at the top of the rise for Cara to pull up next to him. She stared slack-jawed at the dazzling city ahead, Khoury by her side.

"Beautiful, isn't it?" Khoury said. She nodded, speechless.

"Wait until you see the inside." Archer smiled at Cara's questioning look and clucked his horse forward, leading the way down the widening road.

"They say that the stones were brought from quarries in the Far East," Bradan said, amazing Archer again with his esoteric knowledge of distant places. "The King of Tarantis spared no expense, thinking this would be the crossroads of his great empire."

"This is an empire?" Cara asked.

"No," Bradan said. "He couldn't hold it. At one time, he was at war on three fronts with three different enemies. With each loss, his would-be kingdom shrank."

"But he never relinquished Iolair. He died defending her," Khoury said.

Iolair's main gate in the great golden wall stood open and inviting. Its wooden doors were wide and tall, bleached to the color of flax and banded with bronze wrought into wings.

"The Eagle's Nest, Captain?" Archer asked out of habit.

"Not this time," Khoury said with a quelling glance. "We should head straight to the baron. No telling what Sidonius has been up to."

"Eagle's Nest?" Cara asked with a frown.

"The inn we usually stay at," Archer explained.

Khoury leaned over and took her hand in his. "I've some...history there."

"History?" Cara frowned.

"Nothing important, milady." Khoury teased, bringing her hand to his lips.

Archer almost laughed at the captain's display. The girl had surely stolen his heart. Deciding to let the two of them lead the way, Archer dropped back next to Falin. He caught her predictable eye roll at his presence. He'd checked on her frequently since her injury, much to her overt annoyance. And even though Cara said she'd never worked on Falin's hand, the wounds had nearly healed in the past two days.

"So what do you think?" he asked.

"About what?" she replied with blunt disinterest.

"Iolair." He gestured at the lofty white city with exasperation. "You hadn't seen it before, had you?"

"No." She pretended to be unimpressed, but he noticed her eyes kept returning to the view.

"And…" he prompted, making a clownishly expectant face.

She laughed. "All right. I admit it's beautiful. Breathtaking." She grinned with forced cheer. "Happy now?"

"Yes," he said and then rode next to her in comfortable silence. He'd grown fond of her wry wit and flashes of mood. A sobering thought occurred to him. "You'll be leaving us now, I suppose."

"I swore to bring you to Iolair and we are here," she said softly. "You don't need me anymore."

"You're wrong," he said. "This isn't over."

"I'm sure the captain doesn't need me." Something he didn't understand lurked behind that quiet assertion, but he let it stand. He was determined that he'd convince her to stay somehow.

They passed through the gate as the city finally dipped into darkness. Khoury led them along a wide cobbled street lit by lanterns suspended from poles. Even with night approaching people swarmed the maze of streets. The center of town was governed by a large marble fountain with four carved eagles and eight streets fanning out like the rays of the sun. The captain turned up the northeastern road, which widened as it went, lined with fragrant cedar and statues.

By the time they reached the palace's outer wall, it was full night, and Archer was starving. The open gate welcomed them, and Khoury nodded to the silent guards as they passed.

Farther on was a secondary gate set into a tall hedgerow and beyond that squatted the palace. It wasn't as pretty as the main gate and outlying buildings, but much more practical in a siege with thick granite walls and armored portals. Six guards flanked the entrance, alert but motionless. Surrounding the castle were gardens and fountains and more guards.

Khoury followed the road straight to the steps of the palace. There, stableboys rushed out to hold the reins of his horse as Khoury dismounted. Archer followed suit, and the two of them approached the stair guards while Cara, Falin, and Bradan remained mounted.

"Tell Baron Wallace that Captain Mason Khoury needs to speak with him," Khoury said to the nearest guard.

"Your business?"

"A private matter but of some urgency." Khoury's voice had returned to the clipped aggressive tones Archer was used to.

"He will want to speak with us," Archer added as Khoury turned away from the guard, effectively dismissing the man.

The guard eyed them dubiously then turned and climbed the steps.

"We should be safe enough in here tonight," Khoury murmured to Archer, his eyes resting on Cara.

"Safer than the road." Archer noted Khoury's tension as he scanned the walls and courtyards, but his gaze always came back to Cara. "You think it will begin here?"

"I'm sure of it."

The guard returned, cutting off further conversation. "Baron Wallace sends greetings, Captain Khoury. Please accept his hospitality. This way."

Khoury gestured for Archer to get the others and began up the stairs.

Archer returned to the group. "We stay here tonight."

With grateful sighs, Cara and Bradan slid wearily out of their saddles, grabbed their packs and followed Khoury up the stairs. But

Falin stood frozen, her gelding's reins in a tight fist and her eyes on the castle.

"You coming?" Archer asked.

"Not…tonight," she muttered, staring past him at the massive stone walls. "Someone should stay here. Keep an eye on the horses."

There was no need for that, and he suspected she knew it. Still, he'd never seen her hesitate before. "Falin…"

"See you tomorrow," she said, her eyes daring him to contradict.

"Until morning then."

She turned without a backward glance and followed the stableboys. Then, Archer hurried to the stairs, taking them two at a time to catch up with Khoury near the top.

"The Huntress?" Khoury asked.

"Said she's staying with the horses tonight."

"What?"

Archer could only shrug, and the captain sniffed with annoyance. Then he took Cara's elbow and led them into the palace. The guard led the four travelers to a small library off the main hall where Khoury paced. Cara, however, seemed delighted as she and Bradan browsed the leather bound treasures. Half an hour later, the doors opened to admit a slight gray-haired man Archer recognized as Wallace's right-hand man, Malcolm Cade.

"Captain Khoury." Wallace's advisor shook hands with the captain.

"Cade, you're looking well," Khoury said, formally.

Then Cade noticed Archer and smiled. "Reid! Still on this old badger's payroll, I see."

"Someone has to keep him out of trouble."

"Indeed," Cade said, then his eyes fell on Cara, "though I think you brought the trouble with you." The older man slid up to her and took her hand in both of his. "Since when does Captain Khoury travel in the company of beautiful women?"

Khoury took her hand from Cade's and tucked it possessively into his elbow. "Lady Cara, may I introduce Baron Wallace's chief advisor,

Malcolm Cade."

"My…uh lord," Cara replied with an awkward blush.

"And Chieftain Bradan." Khoury gestured to the Northerner.

"Welcome," Cade said with a smooth smile for all. "Any friend of the captain's is a friend of ours. I hope you enjoy your stay here."

"So, how is Wallace these days?" Archer asked.

"He is in good health, thank you. Iolair has its share of problems but nothing major. He's currently indisposed but will want to see you for a late dinner. Let me show you your rooms where you can wash off the road."

"Excellent." Khoury grinned and patted Cara's hand.

"The food here is very good," Archer whispered to Bradan.

"As long as it isn't squirrel," the shaman said.

"This way." Cade gestured for them to follow and then swooped from the room as quickly as he had entered it.

CHAPTER 41
CARA

Cara was as enthralled by the inner castle as she had been by the outer gates. She let Khoury guide her as she took in every detail. Haughty portraits of Iolair's departed rulers glared down at them while bleached stone busts stared at her from unexpected corners. She marveled at the thick carpets and jeweled tapestries, their warm colors vivid in the generosity of torches that lined the corridors. Cade led them to rooms in the eastern wing on the second floor where two doors opened off each side of a long hallway.

In her room, a hot bath waited in front of the blazing fireplace. She hastily stripped off her worn dress and slid her tired body into the steaming tub. Luxuriating in the scented water, her thoughts drifted back to the lake, and Khoury.

She frowned. The bold temptress who'd thrown herself at the captain that night had disappeared, taking the ability to contain the power with her. The next morning's kiss had brought visions of the same lovely woman, only screaming and bloody. He'd warned her that his first love was dead, but she hadn't bargained on the violence.

Cara slid beneath the water to wash away the vision. At least he'd taken it well; his affection hadn't wavered. But Cara felt his wariness.

How could she blame him? If only she could control her power.

She angrily bumped her head back against the side of the tub. From that angle, she noticed a bar of soap, a comb, and a pitcher waiting nearby. Scowling, Cara lathered herself head to toe with the gritty soap, scrubbing her skin until it glowed. Then she combed her thick pale locks until her arms ached and the comb held enough hair to weave a shirt. She had just noticed the soft towel warming by the mantle when someone knocked.

Probably Khoury coming to tell me to hurry up, she thought.

"Come in," she said, but when the door opened, a mousy woman entered. Cara splashed water everywhere in her hurry to cover herself.

The woman bowed. "I am Nadja," she said, her eyes never leaving the floor.

"Who?"

"Your maid."

"My what?" Cara was confused.

"I'm here to get you dressed for dinner, my lady."

How ridiculous, Cara thought. She didn't need help dressing. "My clothes are right there on the floor. You can go."

Nadja clucked disapprovingly and grabbed the towel from the mantle. "You can't dine with the baron in those." She held up the warm towel, turning her eyes away as Cara stepped from the cooling water. "Baron Wallace has instructed me to dress you appropriately, my lady. If you will just accompany me to the next chamber, we will find a gown that fits."

Cara nodded meekly and followed her through the door not knowing what to expect. After half an hour, Cara was dressed in a tight-bodiced gown of deep-sea blue with a gauzy over tunic of pale blue that matched her eyes and, at Cara's insistence, small white linen gloves. Then Nadja turned her attention to Cara's long hair, lifting it to the top of her head.

"My lady, what happened?" Nadja's face was ashen as she stared at Cara's neck.

"What?"

"I'd swear someone cut your head off." Nadja's finger lightly traced Cara's scar, which apparently completely encircled her neck.

Cara forced a laugh. "Nothing so extreme." Still, her cheeks blazed with embarrassment.

Nadja stared at her a moment longer then, as if she understood, said, "I won't mention it again." She scurried off to an adjoining room, returning in moments with a large necklace bibbed with tiny clusters of gold disks that covered the scar completely. Finally, Nadja braided and twisted Cara's hair into a complicated style that left little of it below her ears.

Cara felt naked as she followed the maid through the twisting halls, the necklace jingling slightly. They approached a pair of wooden doors that opened on silent hinges for them and Nadja stopped, motioning for Cara to enter alone.

Timidly, Cara ventured through the doorway and heard it shut behind her as she stood with her mouth agape. The dining room was even more luxurious than the bedrooms. Fires blazed in two hearths and the stone floors were covered in thick rugs. Tapestries hung on every wall. The chairs even had cushions on them. She took a step forward, trying to take it all in at once.

"Welcome," Cade's voice boomed against the stones making Cara jump. She hadn't noticed the men at the long table in the center of the room. Cade stood to one side. Bradan and Archer were seated, the younger man with his feet up on another chair. Archer grinned and lifted his flagon to her in salute. Across from them was Khoury staring at her, his ale frozen halfway to the table. Then he pushed his chair back and stood up, clumsily sloshing the ale on his hand.

"Cara, you look...beautiful." A hungry look crept into his eyes as his gaze swept over her.

"Thank you," she said, blushing.

He put down his drink and offered her the chair next to him. Before she could take her seat, however, a side door opened. Archer jumped to his feet and Bradan rose. Even Cade stood straighter as a well-dressed man with a hurried frown strode into the room.

"Hello all," he crowed. Cara had expected him to be old like Cade, but he was younger than Khoury, with tousled caramel hair and roguish eyes full of mischief.

"Baron." Khoury bowed his head. Archer, Bradan, and Cade bowed as well. Cara simply stared, drawing the baron's attention. His mouth quirked at her appraisal.

"Mason, you didn't tell me you were bringing friends." The baron's eyes never left Cara. She felt exposed in the low-cut dress.

"I believe I neglected to tell you we were visiting at all, Your Highness." The title fell easily from his lips, but Cara heard amusement in his voice.

"Indeed." Wallace chuckled.

He looked over at Archer. "Reid, good to see you. I hear the giants have been causing trouble up your way again."

"You are well-informed as always," Archer said.

"Your family is faring well, I hope?"

"Well enough," Archer murmured, looking at Bradan.

Khoury cleared his throat. "Wallace, this is the Chieftain of Archer's Clan, Bradan O'Mara."

"My lord," Wallace said, "well met. My sympathies for your troubles."

"The Spirits smile on you, Baron Wallace." Bradan's deep voice rumbled with formality. "Your concern is appreciated."

"What brings you so far from home?"

"A request, Baron. However, I think it best the captain tell you the tale," Bradan said.

"The giant attack is related to why we're here," Khoury said.

"As usual, you get right to business, Mason. But I, for one, am famished so we'll eat first and then you can tell me what favor you think I owe you," the baron said loftily. "And besides, you're being rude, Captain. You've neglected to introduce me to your lady." The baron came around to stand next to Cara who found his brashness strangely charming.

"This is Lady Cara. Cara, Baron Jacob Wallace of Iolair."

"Hello," she said.

"Charmed." Wallace took her hand and placed a light kiss across her knuckles. He met her eyes with a predatory look, then flashed a quick smile and moved to the head of the table. "Now, let's eat." No sooner had he plopped heavily into his chair than servants entered through a door set behind a long tapestry. They brought steaming platters of food and not even the abundance of the Bear Clan could match the baron's table. It was all she could do not to gorge herself as the conversation turned to small talk, primarily led by Cade.

When the baron pushed his own plate away and settled back in his chair with a frothy ale in hand, the other men did likewise, and servants appeared to clear the plates.

"So Khoury," the baron began, "I hope you realize that waging war against giants is not in Iolair's best interests."

Khoury cleared his throat and smiled. "That's not at all why we've come, Wallace."

"It isn't?" Confusion blossomed on Wallace's face. His courtly manner faltered, making him seem younger still.

"No." Khoury looked down into his ale in thought. "Rumor has it you've a Far Isles sorcerer in your court."

The baron stopped mid sip and put his pint down. He wiped his mouth and regarded Khoury with wary eyes. "Rumors are dodgy things."

"Is it true?"

"Perhaps."

Cara thought it was much like a sparring match without swords. But Khoury was losing patience.

"Come on, Jake," he said roughly. "I realize you like to keep your secrets, but you can trust me."

Wallace paused and glanced at Cade, then said, "I admit I owe you much, Khoury. And you and yours have always been faithful. But what do I know of your visitors?"

Archer snorted and leaned toward Khoury, rolling his eyes. "Do you believe this, Captain? Give the man a nice house and suddenly he's as suspicious as a Barakani lord."

Cade bristled with the insult. "Iolair is in a very precarious position, gentlemen."

Wallace held up a hand to silence his advisor. "It's okay, Cade." He leaned toward Archer. "Not suspicious, Reid, just cautious. You'd be surprised how much simpler battles are compared to intrigue."

"You finally understand why I'm only a captain," Khoury said. "As for our companions, the lady and the chieftain are part of this. What we really need is information. From your sorcerer."

"Ah," the baron said, shaking his head vigorously. "Then the answer must be no. Do you know how hard it is to keep a Far Islander? They value anonymity above gold, if you can believe that. If they think you're hiring them out to friends, they scurry back to their little mountain island never to be heard from again. I'm sorry, Khoury, but I can't afford to let you scare mine away."

Khoury met his gaze evenly. "Then I don't believe you'll be able to help us after all. That's really too bad because I liked working with you."

"Wait. What do you mean?"

"Oh, nothing," Khoury said dismissively.

"Yeah," Archer chimed in. "You don't want to get involved and the less you know the better."

Were Khoury and Archer deliberately trying to offend the baron? *Cara wondered.*

She leaned in close to Khoury. "What are you doing?" she hissed. She thought her problems with Sidonius would end in Iolair. But if the baron didn't help them, she would have to keep running.

"We move on to our next best guess." Khoury looked disappointed.

"What?" Cara squeaked. "Where?"

Khoury thought for a long moment. "Barakan is the most likely next choice, right Archer? It's south of here but not too far."

"They're always willing to trade," Archer added.

The baron leaned forward, visibly agitated. "The Captain Khoury I know would never deal with Barakan," he hissed.

"You leave me no choice," Khoury said.

"You're bluffing, Khoury," Wallace asserted. "I know you hate those—what did you call them—ill-gotten venomous backstabbers? Nothing could have changed that. Do you think me so easily played?"

"I do hate Barakan, more than anything. But my sources tell me they have a Far Islander." The mercenary shrugged. "If they have what I need and you're not willing to help me then I will go there." Khoury dabbed his napkin on his lips as if he were finished and ready to leave. Cara began to feel a little sick.

"Wait," Wallace said as Khoury pushed his chair back with a loud screech. "I wouldn't want to see our working relationship suffer. You said you only need information."

"That's right," Khoury replied.

"Perhaps if you tell me what it is you want to know, I'll ask my sorcerer for you."

Khoury paused as if thinking hard, then he looked over at Archer. "I think that'll work, don't you?"

"I don't know, Khoury." Archer frowned. "Perhaps we should just try Barakan. I wouldn't want Wallace to lose his sorcerer because of Lady Cara."

"Lady Cara?" He turned to her. "What does she have to do with giants?"

Flustered, she shrank under the weight of the baron's scrutiny. She felt panic rise as her mind churned with Sidonius's pursuit and what might lay to the south.

"We've recently come from the Black Keep," Khoury said into the silence. "Have you heard of it?"

"There are rumors," the baron said.

"Before her rescue, Lady Cara was a prisoner there. Held by the lord of that Keep, a sorcerer called Sidonius."

Wait, she thought. *I rescued you.*

"So who hired you to find her?" The baron settled back in his chair, sipping his ale. It was clear that Khoury's uncharacteristic grandstanding didn't impress him.

"No one," Khoury admitted.

"Then how did you know she needed rescuing?" Cade asked with a sardonic look. Cara smiled.

"Actually," Archer interjected with humor, directing his comments to the baron. "Embarrassing as it is, Cara rescued us."

At that, the baron put down his drink and broke out laughing.

"She rescued you?" The baron laughed heartily. "Mason Khoury saved by a woman! I'm sorry, old man, but I find that amusing."

Cara felt the urge to chuckle herself but one look at Khoury's displeased expression prevented her from joining the baron. Bradan, however, had no such compassion and laughed along with the young nobleman and Archer.

"Tell me, Lady Cara," said the baron as he wiped his eyes and leaned forward eagerly. "How did you come to rescue the canniest mercenary this side of the Inland Sea?"

Cara looked down, afraid to answer.

"We'd been captured with a group of men and taken to the Black Keep from Telsedan," Archer supplied. Cara looked up at him, and he gestured for her to finish the story.

"My father…I mean Sidonius, takes men from the bordering lands for sacrifices," Cara said as plainly as possible. "When I met the captain and Archer, they were next to die. I couldn't let that happen."

"You say this Sidonius is your father?"

Cara nodded, though it wasn't actually true.

Khoury continued, "The powers he used were obviously from the Far Isles. We were hoping your sorcerer might have some knowledge of him."

"Perhaps. But why do you care? He's in the Keep and you are

here."

"After our escape, we fled to my people for shelter," Archer explained.

"But Father wanted me back. It never occurred to me that he might," she said in a small, sorry voice. "So he sent giants to find me."

"Chieftain?" Wallace looked at Bradan for confirmation.

"Indeed, we escaped a giant raid," Bradan said. "Many died. Those who survived sought refuge elsewhere. I cannot allow them to return until Sidonius is stopped."

"So this sorcerer, Sidonius, sacrifices men on a regular basis and consorts with giants?" Wallace asked carefully.

Cara nodded.

"And you, Khoury, have stolen his only daughter?"

"Yes," Khoury said.

Wallace scrubbed his face with aggravation. "What were you thinking, man? Stealing women is beneath you."

"I asked them to take me with them," Cara interjected. "I couldn't stay there. And after the giants, they were kind enough to help me flee south through Foresthaven to come here."

"Foresthaven!" Wallace eyed the four of them skeptically. "Is this a joke? No man passes through Foresthaven."

"Well, we had a little help there, too," Khoury admitted.

"I'd have you executed for lying if I didn't know you so well," Wallace said.

"Spoken like a true lord-of-the-manor," Archer quipped sourly.

Wallace ignored him. "Any news of the sorcerer since?"

"His agents tried to kill us on the road two days ride west," Bradan supplied.

A pregnant silence hung over the table. The baron's face clouded. "Assassins. Two days' ride from the Eagle's Gate?" Cara sensed his simmering anger as he turned on her. "Many daughters flee their fathers, Lady Cara, but yours seems unusually interested in your return. Why?"

Cara shrank beneath the baron's piercing stare. "I…I don't know," she stammered. How could she explain Sidonius's need of her?

He stared at her hard as if trying to see through a thick fog. "Are you a sorceress?"

Cara didn't know what to say.

"She is a healer, a powerful one," Bradan said. "That's why he wants her."

The baron accepted Bradan's reason without question. "And how does he continue to find you?"

"We're not sure," Khoury said.

"So," the baron said, "he might know she's here?"

Khoury was silent at first, and Cara could feel his reluctance to answer. "Perhaps," he admitted.

Wallace stood up swiftly, his chair clattering to the floor. "What treachery is this?" He pounded the table with his fist. "I trusted you, and you come to my home with an angry sorcerer sniffing at your heels? I can't help you with this mess, Khoury. Friendship be damned! I want you gone within the hour."

Behind him, Cade scowled but placed a calming hand on his lord's arm. "Baron," he soothed, "Captain Khoury would never place us in direct danger. Would you?" The sharp-faced advisor caught Khoury's steady gaze as the baron began to pace, taking deep breaths.

"Of course not." Khoury was calm as if he had been prepared for this storm. "Wallace, I would never risk your position here. It's Cara he's after and, as you said yourself, Far Islanders dislike attention. Whatever he will attempt, it will be covert. If your guards don't intervene, they should be safe."

Baron Wallace walked up behind Cara. His hands gripped the back of her chair. "And what if I took her to him myself? Many fathers pay generous ransoms for the return of their daughters. Perhaps he will assure the safety of my city."

Cara froze in her seat.

"Don't be a fool, Jake," Archer said coolly. "He won't guarantee you anything."

"All I'm asking," Khoury interjected, "is that you find out what your sorcerer knows about Sidonius, if anything. Either way, we will leave Iolair by tomorrow evening."

The baron contemplated Khoury's request for a moment. Cara could see his mind working out his options. "Where will you go?"

"The less you know the better," Khoury said.

Wallace sighed. "I have great affection for you, Khoury, you know that. Everything I have is because of you. But this is troubling. I can't promise anything more than I will think on it. After tomorrow you will leave, and I don't want to see you here again until this mess is settled. Is that clear?"

"Very," Khoury murmured and stood to bow as Baron Wallace strode out the door he had come in. Malcolm scowled at the two mercenaries for a moment, shaking his head and muttering something obscene. Then he followed Wallace.

"That went well," Archer said sarcastically.

"Now what?" Bradan asked.

"We wait for morning."

The doors opened, and Nadja beckoned them to follow. As they wound their way to their rooms, Khoury suddenly ducked into an alcove and pulled Cara along with him. His hands slid around her waist and pulled her against him.

"What are you doing?" she whispered.

"This castle is the safest place we'll be for a while. I don't want to waste it." He pulled her close and kissed her neck under her hair, sending heat to her belly.

"But the visions," she whispered, wanting to feel his lips but afraid of what she'd see.

"You stopped them before."

"And the next day it didn't work."

"I have an idea," he said cautiously as he cradled her face in his hands and leaned down until their lips almost touched. "Trust me?"

She'd seen him at his worst and yet she still wanted him. "Yes," she whispered, closing her eyes.

His lips touched hers gently and her power flowed, tumbling her mind with his memories. A house, music, dancing and over it all the bubbling laughter, but she feared the memories that came next, the screaming and the blood. She tried to stop them, but her power once again refused her request. Then she felt him inhale deeply, gathering his own power like he had in his dream.

He murmured against her lips, his breath mingling with hers. **"Stop."** The word was heavy with power, sibilant and thick. It tingled in her ears and flowed along her tongue.

"Stop the visions," he said, more sure this time. The words were denser, stronger. And the memories obeyed. It felt as if he'd dropped a boulder in the stream of her magic, blocking the flow. Her mind was blissfully silent. She knew nothing but his lips on hers and how his heart pounded beneath her hand.

He tensed and pulled back. "How do you feel?" His voice was tender as he cupped the angle of her jaw, his thumb caressing her cheek. His blue eyes searched hers, for what she wasn't sure.

"I'm free." She almost laughed. Running her fingers through his dark locks, she pulled him closer. He kissed her until she was drunk with it. His hands slid down her hips, then he pulled her up to straddle him, pressing her back against the cool stone wall. Heady with kisses and eagerness, she slid her hands under his shirt, caressing the battle-scarred skin.

He dropped his face away with a chuckle, hands braced against the wall. "We do have rooms, you know. Perhaps we should use one."

"Probably." She felt giddy as he lowered her to her feet. He growled playfully and tugged her dress off her shoulder to kiss the tender skin of her collarbone. Then he stopped, staring at the three vertical lines that were all that remained of her journey wounds. He must not have noticed them in the dark by the lake. But now, his brow furrowed as his thumb traced the parallel scars on her shoulder.

"A long story," she said, "but not one for tonight." She distracted him with a kiss. He slipped an arm around her waist and pulled her back out into the empty hall. She noticed a tapestry across from the alcove that she hadn't noticed earlier. A large beast menaced two children, one defending the other with a small knife. The scene struck a chord in her.

"Wait. Take me to the stables first."

He looked quizzically at the tapestry and then back at her.

"I need to talk to Falin," she explained.

"Can't it wait?"

"What if she's gone tomorrow?"

He ran a frustrated hand through his hair. "Only if you promise to be quick."

She nodded, and he took her by the hand and led her back the way they'd come. Outside, night had swallowed the city leaving only a few souls wandering the streets. Just beyond the tall hedge, Khoury stopped at a large wooden structure that smelled of hay and animals. He opened the door for her and followed her in. "I'll wait for you here."

She stretched up and kissed his cheek, then hurried down the aisle nursing the confidence their passion inspired. Stableboys slept on pallets in the dimly lit aisle. She sensed the familiar minds of their horses near the far end and found the Huntress there as well, lounging on two bales of hay pushed up against the box stall that held her gelding and Khoury's. Falin's armor was propped against the wall, only a sleeveless cotton shirt covered her linen-wrapped torso. The gelding was nuzzling her tangled tresses and a trio of kittens tumbled across her lap.

Cara waited in the shadows, not knowing what to say.

"You've come this far, rabbit. Don't hide now," the Huntress called, not lifting her eyes from the tiger-striped balls of fur attacking her hands.

Cara stepped forward. "Huntress, I…" Again, words failed her.

"You're sorry. I know." Falin's green eyes held unexpected kindness. She was far less imposing without her leathers.

"I was afraid you'd leave before I could—"

"Mend the bridge?"

Cara nodded.

Falin snorted. "Funny, Archer thought I'd leave before morning, too. And I thought the captain was the only one who had no faith in me."

Cara didn't know what to say. The silence lengthened between them. "I shouldn't have stopped you. I just…I vowed there'd be no more death."

Falin laughed. "How could you promise such a thing? It's the nature of things to die."

"But death is wrong."

"Death keeps the balance. Those who cheat death are violating the very life they seek to preserve."

"Then it's killing that's wrong," Cara temporized, crossing her arms with uncharacteristic stubbornness.

Falin pushed the kittens away and stood up with a surprisingly patient smile. "Yet you eat the game I kill."

Cara huffed but had no answer.

"Not all death is bad."

"Yes, it is," Cara said, memories of dust and heat flooding her mind.

"Dying for a reason is far better than living without one," the Huntress said.

"I suppose you're ready to die?" Cara felt anger surge.

"Every time I draw my sword," the Huntress said with such seriousness Cara couldn't meet her gaze. "I was ready to die for you on the hill. Ready to die when I saved your captain."

That, too, had been at Cara's insistence.

Falin touched Cara's arm softly. "But it would have been a death of my own choosing, Sister. And that makes all the difference."

"No, it doesn't." Tears stung her eyes, but Cara refused to let them loose.

Falin walked over to the stall and stroked the flat planes of the gelding's face. "Sorchia used to tell me that promises made while drowning in the dark will turn into the chains that keep you under." Falin's face was almost wistful as she talked about Sorchia.

Cara didn't know what relationship Falin and the priestess had, but it was suddenly clear what Falin risked letting Rebeka go. "Do you think she'll be okay?"

"Who?" Falin turned.

"Sorchia."

The Huntress sat back down on the hay. "Doesn't matter. I can't change it. If anything did happen, I swear by the Thorns that Rebeka will die on my blade." Falin's hands clenched in anger.

"But didn't you just say—"

"I'm not drowning," Falin said. "And even if I was, this is a chain I can live with."

"So you're going home?"

"That depends."

"On?"

"You."

"Do you want me to say I need your help? To grovel?" Cara asked.

"No," Falin said, "what I need is your promise."

"Promise?"

"Never again to come between me and my prey."

So Falin sought the same reassurance Khoury had. Cara could live with that. "I promise."

"Good." Falin smiled and settled back down onto her hay bed. "Now, go find your captain. You've better ways to spend this night than here with me."

CHAPTER 42
KHOURY

"Is there peace?" he asked as Cara tucked herself into his arms though he already knew. Voices carried easily in the quiet stable. That the Huntress treated Cara like a little sister and was willing to face Sidonius earned her his gratitude. Falin was wrong about him though; he did trust her. He trusted her to watch out for Cara if he failed.

Standing in the dim light, Cara clung to him, breathed him in as if fearing there would be no tomorrow. And though he felt the same, he refused to dwell on it. He wrapped his arms around her small frame, savoring the affection that was sure to wound him. Life seldom took pity on unguarded hearts.

"Take me back," she whispered, and he led her out into the night. The captain knew Wallace's castle well having spent a summer and most of an autumn ensuring that the young insurgent ruler had a secure foothold. He was proud of the changes Wallace had wrought. The man was a far better administrator than mercenary.

The captain led Cara to a different hall in the eastern wing. Now that they were in the city proper, the danger of spies was greater but the danger of immediate harm was less. He paused at the door. "Am I invited?"

"I don't think I can unlace this thing without you," she said, her playfulness returning and she slipped through the door with him close behind. "Wait, this isn't my room," she said as he locked the door behind them.

"I know. This is safer."

She frowned at the reminder of her precarious position. "Whatever you think is best," she said, and then began pulling the pins from her hair with nervous frustration. Her efforts did little more than tangle it further.

"Here, let me." He took her hands in his and kissed the tip of each finger. "Trust me. I'll keep you safe." Then he deftly released the plaits and tangles and spread her hair over her shoulders like a pale cape. As he stroked the satiny curtain, she sighed and leaned into him.

Cara wasn't wrong about the laces in her dress and it took far too long to strip her to her shift. He laid her on the bed, banked the fire, and slipped his knife under the pillow before crawling in naked next to her. Though they'd made love once before, he wanted more than consummation. He was hungry for fulfillment, like a last meal before the axe.

He kissed her face, her eyelids, and the end of her nose, making her giggle. Her scent reminded him of rosantia, a humble mountain flower, and the spring waters of Hawk Valley. He drew in his father's voice with a breath and suppressed her magic with soft words, then he pressed his lips to hers, feeling her relax.

Growing up, his talent had always felt like a violation but here, now, his power was a gift. To both of them.

He reveled in the feel of her skin as he slid her shift off, taking time to kiss every inch of her: Fingertips to neck and toes to hips. Emboldened by passion, her hands traveled where they willed, wringing small groans of pleasure from him. Then he heard the sharp intake of breath as she found the scar that wrapped around his right side to his back, the place that birthed his worst nightmares. She hadn't noticed it in the darkness of the lakeside. Fearful of her reaction, he distracted her with artful hands and passionate kisses until they surrendered to each other in the deep of the night.

☙

Khoury woke tangled in pale hair and delicate limbs while the sun still only dreamed of the day. Without waking her, he slipped from the bed and dressed hastily. Slipping out into the hall, he locked her door and headed back to his own room, key in pocket.

Khoury had instructed Archer to go to the Eagle's Nest after their meeting with Wallace. He needed allies and supplies. On the bed were a note and a small sack of coin. When he read it, he smiled. Archer had found Violet as well as Roger Ellis, another trusted Sword and one of Khoury's best tacticians. After the captain's disappearance from Telsedan, the two of them had apparently taken the Swords to honor the arranged commitment to an eastern lord, putting down a minor uprising. Vi reported that casualties were higher than expected but nothing to worry about. She'd released the men on furlough until Khoury's return but a score of cavalry had stayed in Iolair to spend their wages at the summer festival in two weeks. She would meet the captain at the Eagle's Nest sometime that day.

Khoury's shoulders relaxed as he burned the letter. It gave him confidence knowing that he was surrounded by his own. He grabbed his swords and the coin and returned to Cara, grateful that by nightfall he'd be back in armor.

The next time he woke next to her, the sun had burned off the mountain fog and his stomach was grumbling.

"I'm hungry, too," Cara murmured in his arms.

He kissed the top of her head. "Get dressed then, and I'll show you the best pastry vendor in town."

"Not in that thing," she said, gesturing to the laced gown on the floor with a laugh. So Khoury wrapped her in the blanket and led her back to her original room where Nadja had left a practical gown and over tunic on her bed. Bradan and Archer were already gone. Since Archer favored the same vendors Khoury did, he anticipated meeting him over breakfast.

They squinted at the sharp morning sunshine as they wandered the market square. Khoury bought her sweet rolls and hot tea, keeping a sharp eye out for the others.

"Maybe they went to get Falin," Cara suggested, sucking sticky sugar from her fingers.

The stables. He should have thought of that. He led her back up the northeast road toward the palace. The thoroughfare was bustling. About halfway there, he noticed Cara began to turn and look behind them every few steps.

"Something wrong?" he asked.

"I have a bad feeling."

His hand went to his sword. "In what way?"

"I don't know. It's like Father is watching me."

They were almost to the stables when Archer hailed them from the other side of the street. Khoury put his hand to Cara's back and guided her through the crowd. But she stopped midway and whirled around, her body trembling with fear as she peered into the passing faces. He scanned the street himself, looking for the old man.

An alarm began to blare up the street and chaos broke out. Smoke, then flames, rose from the direction of the barn.

"Fire in the stables!" The cry spread quickly through the street. Guards ran to help amid more shouts.

"Fire," Cara murmured, and he knew what she was thinking. She gave a sudden small cry and pressed her hands to her head.

"Cara!"

"Don't you hear him?"

"Who?"

"Sidonius."

"Where?" Khoury asked, turning in a circle. No one looked familiar.

"In my head. I hear him in my head. He's here somewhere."

A throng of people ran toward them buckets in hand and in the press of people, the captain lost her. By the time he saw the hooded figure walking up to Cara, she was too far away.

"Cara, behind you!" he called out, trying to negotiate the throng of people. Nearby, Bradan's bulk also shoved through the crowd toward her, but not before a thick-knuckled hand gripped her shoulder and turned her around. The fear on her face tore at Khoury's heart.

It was Sidonius, except he looked so young the captain barely recognized him. Khoury had no time to ponder the reason before the sorcerer's lips moved and sand landed on Cara's face. She swooned into her father's arms.

Renewed urgency drove Khoury through the thick crowd, but even so he made little headway. Bradan was closer and closing in. With Cara once again in his possession, Sidonius surveyed his pursuit and motioned to someone Khoury couldn't see.

Then Bradan broke free of the crowd near the wall of the far building and rushed to tackle the sorcerer. Sidonius dodged with surprising speed, leaving the chieftain clutching only voluminous robes. But the Northerner was large and strong. He pulled on the fabric with both hands, drawing the sorcerer close, trying to wrest Cara from him. Khoury couldn't believe the sorcerer he'd first seen at the tollhouse had the strength to fend off the bear-like chieftain, but he moved as if a mere child clung to his robes.

Khoury scanned the crowd for Archer and found him on top of a nearby wagon. He thought he saw the Huntress's golden hair in the crowd as well but couldn't be sure. Archer drew his bow and Sidonius turned, using Cara as a shield. The Northerner was undeterred; his eyes never left the sorcerer. Focused on one thing only, he waited for the impossible shot.

Content that Archer was ready to kill, Khoury drew his swords. The crowd gave before his bared steel. He'd nearly broken through to where Bradan still wrestled with the sorcerer when three men accosted the chieftain. Dressed as citizens, they were unarmed. Two of them grabbed Bradan and hurled him into the crowd. The three then turned on Khoury, grabbing for his swords. Khoury was unwilling to kill any of Wallace's people until he noticed their milky, sightless eyes. Another sorcery.

Khoury kicked out at the man on his left arm, freeing his sword. Using it to gut one of his attackers, the man fell to the ground without even a grunt of pain. He hamstrung the next one, who also didn't cry out and continued to claw at him from the ground. Then Bradan rushed in, blood leaking from a bruised cheek and wrapped the last one in a chokehold. Angrier than Khoury had ever seen him, the shaman squeezed until the man's tongue protruded with purple surrender.

Khoury turned his attention back to Sidonius.

"I've seen you before," the sorcerer hissed at him. "At the Keep. You're the troublemaker." He snapped his fingers and a tailed whip made of flames appeared in his hand. He lashed Khoury, catching him off guard.

Fingers of heat slashed at Khoury's face, just missing his eye. He cried out in surprise, hiding his face behind his arm as another blow fell, searing lines around his forearm.

"*Sidonius!*" The familiar voice reverberated off the stone buildings, echoing through the raucous crowd and, for a moment, silence reigned. Khoury looked up to find the Huntress, sword drawn, standing in the alley behind the sorcerer. But when Sidonius turned and she caught sight of him, hesitant dread filled her face.

Khoury heard the hopeful twang of Archer's bow, but the arrow only grazed the side of the sorcerer's head. Khoury charged.

Feeling the tide turning against him, the sorcerer hurried into the alley where the Huntress waited. With a few words and a wave of his arm, a wall of fire sprang up behind him, engulfing Khoury and those next to him in heat and flame. Screams rent the morning.

Pushing the pain aside, the captain steadied himself to press forward. Then, heavy hands on the back of his shirt yanked him from the inferno and tossed him into the nearest horse trough, dousing the flames and his hopes of getting Cara back.

CHAPTER 43
FALIN

Falin had hoped distracting the sorcerer would give Archer the shot he needed, but her plans evaporated when she saw the man's face. She knew him although they'd never actually met. The rheumy gray eyes, the yellowed teeth, the hooked nose—his was the face of her nightmares. And for one stuttering breath, trapped by remembered fear, she could only stand and stare at him.

When she didn't attack, the sorcerer hurried to the waiting horse and tossed the unconscious Cara across the saddlebow. But then he paused and turned to study her.

"Have we met?" he asked, his brows drawn close in puzzlement.

Falin ignored his words instead using the shouts from beyond the fire-wall to focus. She hooked a finger in her bolo.

He's just a man, she reminded herself, *as vulnerable as any other.* And with a determined toss, she sent the bolo spinning at his head.

With a lazy flick of Sidonius's hand, a tongue of fire appeared from his finger to cut the cord midair. The stones clattered harmlessly down the alley.

"I should know you," he mused, his brow furrowed with thought. He circled her, his lips pursed as if he were considering a wild animal.

Irritated, she drew her blade and charged, but he sidestepped the attack with unnaturally smooth grace.

"You have a stout heart," he said, "but I smell your fear."

She swung again. And again he slid away.

"You should fear me," he said.

But Falin wasn't listening. Her only focus was her blade. She swung again, feinting this time and catching a piece of his robe on the redirect with a sharp tearing sound.

He pressed angry lips together. "Enough foolishness," he snapped, sliding a black staff from beneath the saddle flap. He turned and pressed the cold obsidian tip to her chest before she could retreat.

The sun's light paled as if suddenly thrust behind the clouds. Ice crept across her chest and down her arms making her hand too weak to hold her sword. The blade clanged to the cobbles. Then bit by bit her muscles clenched tight, trapping her where she stood.

"I will kill you," she promised through stiffening jaws.

"Such rebellion." He leaned closer, studying her with narrowed eyes. "Irritatingly so."

His face relaxed suddenly, and she noted a smile of discovery. "You…" he said as if the world suddenly made sense. " You were left behind."

The words burrowed like worms into her mind, turning hidden things topside and loosing painful truths: Orphan. Outsider. Unwanted.

Then he uttered something in a guttural tongue that made her chest ache where the staff still pressed. Out of the corner of her eye, she noted black veins running down her arms pulsing with icy pain.

Archer called from across the wall of flame, but she couldn't answer. Couldn't move. Couldn't think beyond the pain that swelled inside her.

"After twenty years," he said, eyeing her like a found trinket, "the puzzle is finally solved. There were two."

She had no idea what he was talking about, but none of it mattered right now. She had to find a way to break free. As she braced herself against whatever magic he had wrought, the pain ran like rope along her limbs, tying her in knots. And when he ordered her to follow in the way a man might call a dog, her limbs jumped to obey.

Shocked, she locked her joints even tighter, resisting the movement.

He frowned. "I said, come." He focused his eyes on the staff and the pressure along her limbs increased.

But she remained where she stood with only the sweat on her face to show for the effort. By sheer force of will alone she managed to say, "No."

Though only a tiny rebellion, it angered him and bright spots of red appeared on his cheeks.

She considered afterward that her rebellion might cost her, but he hadn't been able to leave with Cara yet. The captain and Archer were certainly on their way and any time she could give them was worth it.

"You will obey me, Daughter." He grabbed her arm and pulled.

Daughter? She bristled at that, her anger feeding her strength. But between his hand on her arm and the magic pulling at her like puppet strings, she gave ground inch by inch. The more she fought, the more her limbs screamed in agony.

When she thought she could bear it no longer, a tall man in brown robes stepped untouched through the fiery wall.

"Magus," he hailed. "What trouble is this?" His pleasant voice held a subtle tone of warning.

"Go away," Sidonius barked with impatience. But when he turned to look at the stranger, he froze with a curious look.

"Sidon?" The stranger's voice became hushed and far less formal.

"Therus." Incredulity softened Sidonius's features for the briefest moment. Then he drew himself taller in a haughty stance. "So you finally found the courage to come inland, did you? It took you long enough." Sidonius harrumphed with disdain.

The brown-robed sorcerer's face paled and then hardened. "Don't mistake recognition for permission, Sidon."

"Stand back," Sidonius warned. "And I will leave. Once I've

collected what's mine."

"No! Release the women," Therus said. This time, his voice was strident with authority.

"You think you can stop me, Therus?" Sidonius roared. "You, of all people, should know better."

The brown sorcerer squared his shoulders. "This city is under my protection," he said and began tracing a pattern in the air. Small trails of light lingered behind like colored smoke. Then, with a flick of his wrist, a heavy gust of air pushed her away from Sidonius and his staff.

When the contact broke, the pain vanished. She crumpled to the ground, dizzy with the sudden release. Her stomach heaved.

"Do not cross me, Xantherus!" Sidonius shouted. The tip of his raised staff glowed blue. "Though I loved you once, you will regret it."

It was then that Archer, sword drawn and draped in a wet blanket, jumped through the wall of flame. Seeing the two sorcerers in a standoff, he slid to a halt.

"Get the girl," the brown-robed man said, gesturing to Falin though his eyes never left Sidonius.

Archer sidled to Falin. "You okay?" he whispered.

She nodded weakly as he helped her to her feet.

Then, the man in brown began chanting a lilting kind of tune. A breeze stirred in the alley. Sidonius muttered his own spell and blue flames sprang from his staff. Xantherus mimed a punch and another stronger wall of air flew up the alley. It shoved Sidonius back several feet and snuffed out his staff just as a soaked and sooty Khoury burst into the alley. His shirt was charred and his skin splotched with angry red.

Sidonius retreated to his horse and climbed up behind Cara's limp body. He spared a glance at Falin. "I'll be back for you."

He directed the horse up the alley a dozen feet or so and turned its nose to the wall. Tracing a fiery symbol that lingered like sparks, he cast a handful of stones to the ground. Upon striking the cobbles, they erupted into green flames. Clouds of noxious black smoke stung their eyes and set them all coughing. Falin heard a grinding, the clop of hooves, and then silence.

When she finally could see through the tears, the smoke and flames were gone and Sidonius with them. Archer and Khoury raced to the other end of the alley, swords drawn, but the sorcerer had disappeared.

"No!" Khoury roared with frustration, turning in a circle. "*No!*"

Anguish was etched in the set of his shoulders and the angry quivering of his hands. He hurled curses like she'd never heard, railing at life, luck, and all the powers that be. Then, with a steadying breath he composed himself and returned to them ensconced in a stony calm.

Bradan joined them when the brown-robed man choked out the remaining flames with a wave of his hand. The chieftain was holding a bloody cloth to his temple. He gave the unfamiliar sorcerer a wide berth and a wary nod.

He came over to Falin. "You okay?"

"Yes," she said, already weary of their concern. "I'm fine."

Bradan turned his attention to the ground where Sidonius had tossed the stones, poking a curious toe at what debris remained.

"Bah! You're damn lucky is what you are," the wind wizard groused, pointing a crooked finger at her. "Lucky I showed up."

"And just who might you be?" Khoury asked.

Falin felt his anger, reined in just below the surface.

The old man regarded the captain through squinted eyes. "Not sure it's any of your business," he griped. Falin could hear the captain's teeth grinding.

Bradan's inspection led him to the wall where he crouched down near the sooty outline of a circle that hadn't been there before. Falin noticed him tuck something in his shirt as he stood.

"We need a plan, Captain," Archer said softly.

"Before any of you fools utters another word," the wind wizard said, "know that your enemy has many ears. The street is not safe. Follow me." He turned on his heel and set off for the castle at a long-legged pace.

Khoury wiped off his sword and sheathed it with a graceful sweep before following the old man. Falin joined Archer and Bradan as they fell in step behind. The fire in the stables was nearly out, though smoke still puffed from a charred portion of roof. The sorcerer led them past the front palace stairs through a postern gate into the gardens. The air was thick with the sweet aroma of flowers, warmed by morning sun reflecting off the stone. Tucked behind a vine-covered trellis was a door set into the side of the castle proper.

As the others slipped through into the darkness beyond, Falin hesitated. The scent of stone chilled her blood. Just as she had gathered enough courage to enter, Bradan's head popped back out.

"Coming?"

"Yes." But her momentum was broken. She stared at the darkened doorway.

The chieftain stepped out into the sunshine next to her. "Something wrong?"

"I don't like castles." She schooled her face into an unreadable mask.

"Really?" He seemed surprised by her trepidation.

She eyed the fortress like an enemy. "What did you expect? I've spent my life in the forest." It was a lie but believable enough. In truth, Sidonius's face had brought her nighttime terrors back to life and inside a castle was the last place she wanted to be.

Bradan crossed his arms with a mixture of impatience and skepticism. "You'll want to hear what this sorcerer has to say," he said.

He was right, of course. There would be no escaping to the stables this time. She needed to know what was going on, and it seemed the wind wizard had something to tell them. Pushing her weakness aside, she lifted her chin and strode past Bradan through the squat doorway with far more courage than she felt.

The interior was dark, as she'd expected, but really no darker than the forest at night. Even so, the weight of stone around her made her stomach quiver and her palms sweat. Then the pinched passage opened into a larger hallway with lanterns to light the space. There were paintings and tapestries on the walls, carpets on the floor. She laughed at her own foolishness. This place bore no resemblance to the empty gray hallways of her dreams.

That place wasn't real, she chided herself. The arching beams and stone table existed only in her imagination.

Then how had I recognized Sidonius?

She had no answer.

She and Braden caught up with the rest of the company as they followed the wind wizard to a stairway leading up into the rear tower. He stopped at an ironbound wooden door, uttered something incomprehensible, and drew a symbol on the wood with his finger. A slight breeze wafted across the cramped landing. The door opened. The sorcerer entered first and then beckoned them to join him.

"Please, make yourselves comfortable," he said.

Falin let the others go first, then followed them in. The door closed behind of its own accord. To call the room cluttered was an understatement. It was a small room to begin with. A bunk was set against one wall and four small windows opposite it let in the morning light. Papers, bottles, boxes, and trinkets covered the shelves and tables that filled most of the room.

The wizard crossed the bare stone floor to a desk covered with scrolls and tomes as well as a flask and three cups.

"My name is Xantherus," the brown-robed man said, turning to them. "Baron Wallace has enlisted my services to benefit his people. And as such, I am not for hire...unlike some." Xantherus looked pointedly at the captain whose clenched jaw prevented any retort.

"I am," Xantherus continued, "wholly uninterested in any personal vendetta against others of my kind. The politics of the Far Isles are incredibly complicated. You simple folk could never comprehend the danger of a single misstep. The wrong choice can cost a sorcerer more than his life." The sorcerer's eyes focused on each of them in turn, pausing when he got to Falin.

His regard sent another chill through her.

"We don't want to 'hire' you, as you put it," Khoury said. His contemptuous glance lingered with curiosity on a tome that rested open near his hand. "What we need is information about who or what we're dealing with."

Xantherus crossed to where Khoury stood and snapped the book closed. "I don't know what you mean," he said.

"Sidonius," the captain said.

"In the alley it seemed you knew him," Falin added.

Xantherus frowned. "Indeed I do," he acknowledged with a rueful sigh. "Or did. Still, I cannot help you. I have already jeopardized my position by assisting you as much as I have."

The wizard's eyes returned to Falin and when he took a step closer, her hand instinctively went to her sword. He stopped, hands raised in a peaceful gesture, and smiled. "I will not harm you, child."

Falin spat on the ground. "I am a Huntress of Foresthaven. Not a child." She glared at the old man, feeling her upper lip tighten into a snarl.

He paused, then chuckled and bowed his head. "My mistake. Tell me, Huntress, what did my compatriot say to you?"

Khoury's head whipped around as if struck. "You spoke with him?"

Falin shuddered at the thought that Khoury might think she'd betrayed Cara. "He asked if we'd met. Then he said that I…solved a puzzle." She shook her head in confusion. Nothing he had said made sense other than the comment about being unwanted, and she wasn't about to share that. Then she remembered something else. "But he did call me 'Daughter.'"

Archer and Khoury looked at each other in surprise, but Xantherus was unaffected.

"Is it true, sorcerer?" Falin asked the Islander. "Am I his—" She was so disgusted she couldn't say the word.

"Don't *you* know?" Archer asked.

"No," she admitted, rubbing her face with sooty hands. "I was a foundling. Sorchia never told me my parentage. I always thought it was because she didn't know, but perhaps she was trying to spare me."

"Bah!" Xantherus scoffed. "I am quite positive Sidonius could not be your father." He grabbed the flask from the desk by its slender neck and poured red liquid into a cup. Dark as blood, the faint odor of berries tickled Falin's nose.

"He called Cara his daughter, too," Archer said.

"You mean the girl he took?" The wind wizard took a sip of the wine. "Impossible."

"But she lived with him in the Black Keep," Bradan said.

"The Black Keep, you say?" Xantherus rubbed his chin. "That is interesting. However, it is quite impossible for either girl to be his daughter."

Seeing nothing but skeptical looks, Xantherus continued with exasperation. "A sorcerer's power is greatly diminished by relations with women." He gestured at Falin's lower half, averting his eyes as he did so. He sat at the desk, placing the cup next to the flask, unconsciously straightening the parchments in front of him. "I find it hard to believe he has kept a woman at his side for so many years since they are known to sap a man's power, even at a distance. But Sidonius is certainly celibate, like all practicing members of the Elemental Arts."

For a moment, no one spoke.

"He said he'd be back," Falin said, feeling hot and sick. She looked up at Archer, unable to hide her desperation. "He said I'm next." Suddenly, she couldn't breathe. Her thoughts went fuzzy and the stuffy room felt even smaller. She wobbled to the desk and plunked herself down in a spare chair facing Xantherus, closing her eyes against a wave of vertigo.

"Here, drink this." The sorcerer's voice startled her. When she opened her eyes, he was standing next to her pouring a second drink from the flask. "A bit of wine will set you right." He handed her the ceramic cup, and she stared for a moment at the blood-red liquid inside. Her stomach churned, but she drained the cup in one gulp. The wine burned her throat as it coursed down. It had a wonderful warming effect, and she breathed a bit easier. She closed her eyes again and opened them to find…

She was in a sparsely furnished room with dusty black walls. Blinking bleary eyes, she found herself on a disturbingly familiar pallet, plain wood, no mattress, and the blanket thrown over her was threadbare and gray. Pain pounded in her head. She rose and went to the door. It was locked, not exactly unexpected. Going to the high window, she stretched on tiptoes and looked out. Her heart sank at the endless vista of green tundra to the west and black peaks in the north.

It was like she'd never left. The bolts slid home behind her, and she turned to see the door open. The man from the alley stood there.

"Welcome home, Daughter. I've missed you," he said almost gently.

This wasn't her usual nightmare. This wasn't how it went. And somehow that made it all the more frightening. Her heart raced. As he moved toward her, she retreated until her back pressed to the wall.

Noting her hesitance, he shook his head. "Don't worry. It's not yet time to die. But soon, soon I will have everything I need." He smiled then - a hungry, satisfied smile. "And then this farce can finally end."

Falin gasped and jerked to her feet. The cup in her hand tumbled forgotten to the floor and broke with the sharp crack of shattered porcelain. She still saw the cell and the sorcerer smiling at her. But there was also the ghostly image of the cluttered room. Was someone calling her name? Her breath came in gulps as she swayed on her feet, unbalanced, divided.

Unfamiliar panic inundated her reason. All she could think of was escape. "Help me." Her voice was little more than a strangled cough.

"Get me out!" She stumbled toward the door and bumped into the ghostly desk, which was substantial enough to stop her. Unable to distinguish between the visions and reality, she turned in a circle.

"Falin! Snap out of it!" Khoury's familiar growl snagged her attention; she could see him now though his form wasn't quite clear.

"We have to get out," she said, her arms flailing for a door that wasn't there. She felt him grab her arm, turning her to look at him.

"Calm down," he said, giving her a small shake. "You're okay."

But she could feel the weight of the black stones pressing down on her. She smelled the dust and magic and heat. Trembling in his firm grasp, her eyes darted wildly. "He's coming for me!" Her voice sounded weak to her ears, just like Cara. "Why did I run?" The whining tone grated on her nerves, but she couldn't seem to stop the cascade of emotions.

"Falin, you're safe. I've got you," the captain said.

But she thrashed in his grip. She had to flee. She clenched her hands tightly; her nails driving crescent-moons into her palms and the panic receded a little at the pain. Xantherus's room gained substance, and she could see the cluster of men staring at her. But the other castle threatened to pull her back.

"Hit me," she whispered in a voice that still didn't sound like her own.

"What?" Khoury froze, startled.

She gathered her courage, trying to center herself. "Hit me. Hard," she said firmly, finally sounding like herself again. When she looked at him, she felt the tears on her lashes and hoped he would understand.

In the next instant, he struck her with a sharp slap, whipping her head around. A snarl erupted from her lips as her world narrowed to the spot of pain on her cheek but the anger severed her connection to whatever insanity had sought to claim her.

The captain stood poised to strike again. She held up her hand to stop him. "I'm better now. Thanks."

She didn't notice Xantherus coming up behind her until a gentle breeze caressed her cheek. He muttered in low tones and placed a hand on her forehead. Blessed calm cloaked her frayed nerves.

"A simple protection spell," he said, withdrawing his hand.

"Thank you." Falin took a deep breath and straightened her clothes to cover her embarrassment.

"I don't usually cast on people directly, mind you. Nasty business." The sorcerer shook his head and wiped his hand on his robes in disgust.

"What happened?" Khoury asked, taking a step back as Falin gently rubbed her sore cheek.

"I don't know. One minute I was sitting in that chair and the next, I was somewhere else."

"But you didn't leave," Archer said, his face full of concern.

"I couldn't see you though. I was in a castle, but not this one," she said.

"Did you recognize it?" Bradan asked.

"Yes, I've dreamt of it. Not dreams really—nightmares." She sank back down in the chair, exhausted.

Bradan squatted down in front of her. "You have nightmares?" he asked.

It was shameful that a Huntress would have nightmares. Only children feared their dreams. "Just one. The same one I've had since I was little."

But this one hadn't been exactly that. This one had been different.

"And just now you went there?" he continued. "In your head?"

Falin nodded.

Xantherus watched the interchange with interest and then poured her another cup of wine. She took it with gratitude.

"What are you getting at, Bradan?" Archer dragged another chair over and sat down heavily. Khoury leaned against the desk.

"Cara's back at the Keep," Bradan said.

"What are you talking about?" Khoury's asked, his patience thinner than usual. "By horse it would take more than three days to get there."

"But he didn't go by horse, did he, Xantherus?" There was a note of accusation in Bradan's voice.

"What?" The wind wizard was taken aback.

Bradan stood, took the piece of rubble from his shirt and tossed it on the desk. It wasn't a bit of broken brick as Falin had thought. It was a hunk of crystal, burnt and cracked, inside a setting of iron inscribed with markings.

Xantherus picked up the stone cautiously and rubbed soot from the ruined setting. "*Gerta,*" he read, squinting. "*Kaluzrega gerta.*"

"What does that mean?" Bradan asked.

"This is a gate crystal." The sorcerer's voice held obvious awe. "But that can't be."

"So, Sidonius found a way to go straight from that alley to his Keep?" Archer asked, incredulous.

"No," Xantherus answered quickly. "I know of no magic that could travel so far. It takes three priests of the Dark Guild working together to breach a single wall to access their hidden temple with these. Whatever Sidonius did, he did alone. To think anyone could travel that far in a single spell is—"

"Impossible?" Falin offered.

"Preposterous," Xantherus said hotly, then hesitated. "But, in theory…" He held the blackened crystal to the light, turning it, examining carefully.

"This isn't quartz," he murmured, "which is what the Dark Guild uses so it can't be one of theirs."

He licked his thumb and rubbed soot from the markings. "And see here." He pointed to the markings. "This enchantment shouldn't work. These runes are a melding of two ancient languages from half a world apart."

He inspected the broken crystal so intensely Falin wondered if he'd forgotten the four of them altogether. He finally straightened and looked at the chieftain. "This gate crystal wasn't found or stolen. This was made for a specific purpose." The awe returned to the wizard's voice. "Whoever crafted this was brilliant. And very powerful."

"Then, he could be back at the Keep now," Bradan said.

"Perhaps," Xantherus relented, frowning at the prospect. "With enough magic. But no one has ever wielded that much power."

Falin's stomach churned. "Even if she is there," she said with exasperation, "why would I see her castle?"

"You two are connected," Bradan said.

Displeasure twisted Falin's lips. Sorchia had said something similar to her but Falin hadn't wanted to listen. "No. We can't be connected. I'd never met her before you came to Foresthaven."

"Cara dreamed of a forest and you had nightmares of a deserted castle," Bradan said. "And you recognized Sidonius, didn't you?"

Falin felt the chill hand of fear again. "That still doesn't explain how I got involved." Her voice came out in a squeak.

Now is not the time for weakness, Huntress.

"It would be easy to settle this. Describe this castle," Khoury said, his eyes as steely as the first time she saw them.

"Black. Cold. Dusty. Empty." The two mercenaries nodded as she ticked off her impressions. "Through the window all I can see are black mountains and scrubby plains."

The captain and Archer smiled at each other. "It has to be the same castle." Khoury's face was suddenly eager. He leaned down to the Huntress, his eyes bright. "Can you talk to Cara?"

Was that all he cared about? Falin shoved him angrily away. "I don't see her," Falin groused. "I'm alone with him. Trapped."

"Like Cara was before she rescued us," Archer said.

"Rescued you?" Xantherus asked.

"You didn't know?" Khoury stood up and moved to the wizard, his tone deceptively light. "It seems he has been kidnapping and sacrificing people for some years now."

Xantherus bristled. "What exactly do you mean by that?"

Archer stepped in front of Khoury to forestall any violence. "The captain and I met Cara when we were kidnapped and taken to the

Black Keep. She told me we were to be sacrificed in some ritual. Apparently, Sidonius used it to restore his…energy, his magic. I don't know exactly."

"A ritual to absorb another's power isn't unheard of," Xantherus admitted, "though it would be an extremely rare find."

"Cara helped us escape," Khoury added, "and he's been trying to get her back ever since."

"Her or all of you?" Xantherus asked. "Perhaps he simply is trying to preserve his anonymity."

"Oh, it's not us he's after," Khoury assured him. "Archer and I are little more than cattle. But Cara, she was special enough to collar and track. He came after us with more than the usual assortment of weapons."

"Giants, assassins, fires," Bradan said. "He's very determined."

Xantherus looked shocked though this time he didn't doubt their words. "But why?"

"That is the real question," Bradan said.

"The only thing different about her was that she could survive the ritual," Archer said.

The wind wizard turned to look at him. "She survived this ritual that would have killed you? This draining?"

Archer nodded. "That's what she told me. She would survive but I wouldn't."

This was all new to Falin, and she felt some sympathy for the white-haired woman.

Xantherus eyed the blackened crystal in his hand before tossing it back on the desk. "This is much more serious than I thought," he said.

He murmured to himself as if arguing, then came to a decision.

"Very well," Xantherus said. "It is true, Sidonius and I were once… close, but that was ages ago before his exile."

"Exile?" Khoury asked, grabbing a stool from under a table.

"Patience," the wind wizard admonished. "When Sidonius first came to the Isles, he was young in mind if not years. We roomed together and became fast friends. After a few years, I was apprenticed to Magus Tamiru, in the Court of Air, and he to Magus Urchek of the Court of Fire. Urchek was a truly gentle master considering the other fire sorcerers. He was a traveler and a scholar, fascinated by new magics and ancient legends. Things like temple gate crystals." Xantherus gestured at the blackened crystal.

"He took Sidonius across the sea to lands you've never heard of. Places where gods play and evil things hunt men's souls. Places whose magic Urchek should have left well enough alone."

"You sound like you didn't approve," the captain said.

Xantherus shook his head. "It's not that I didn't approve. But Urchek was a dabbler. Never going deep enough to really understand what he was playing with. As a Magus, his raw power was mediocre at best. Therefore, his failures were disappointing but not really dangerous.

"Sidonius, however, always had a deep well of magic. Add to that the ambition that comes from starting life weak. He should have been taught to be more rigorous. I fear that whatever happened to him in those faraway places was in part Urchek's fault.

"I didn't see him for almost ten years," Xantherus continued. "When he finally did return, he returned alone. Magus Urchek had died. Taken by some foreign disease, or so Sidonius said."

"You didn't believe him?" Bradan asked.

Xantherus shrugged. "Truth or not, who could argue. But Sidon was different after that, haunted almost. He had become nervous, paranoid. He spent all his time poring over tomes and sorting through the chests of relics they had collected. He had no time for anything else. He finally withdrew from the Academy completely and purchased an estate on a small, secluded isle. More stronghold than manor, really. I rarely saw him after that." Xantherus fell silent, staring at the desk and fiddling with whatever his fingers found: a writing quill, the ink jar, a few brown bottles.

"And then what?" the captain asked, startling Xantherus from his musings.

"A few years after he left, ugly rumors began circulating about him. Stories that he had been selling other sorcerers certain commodities. Tame things," he said.

"Tame things?" Falin asked, her strength returning. "You mean horses or dogs?"

Xantherus smiled, a crooked grim-looking thing. "Oh, a few of those at first. Then house servants. But his servants had unquestioned and permanent loyalty. A very important quality to certain Magi. Then more servants, bodyguards, laborers, soldiers. Whatever flesh was required, Sidonius was the man who could get it. No questions asked. Without fuss or chains required.

"Eventually Sidonius began to trade in the black market, providing sacrifices for those who dabbled in the darker arts. At that point, the Academy could no longer look the other way. They sent me to see him, ostensibly a social visit. He must have suspected I was their spy. I asked him about life and work, and eventually we got around to his "business." I flat out asked him how he did it, and he showed me a crystal the color of a sunrise, thin, single-pointed, and nearly as long as my forearm. He called it a 'soul knife.'"

"Soul knife?" Bradan asked, completely enthralled.

"Urchek had found it somewhere west of the Far Isles. He told me the natives had used it to remove mental illness: hallucinations, mania, and the like. But Sidonius said he could remove whatever aspect of the psyche he wished with it. Greed, deceit, even self-preservation."

"The men in the street," Khoury said.

"I suspect they were…altered," Xantherus agreed then he continued his story.

"On my testimony, he was arrested, tried, and found guilty of fostering the dark arts. The Academy banished him from the Isles." The sorcerer scrubbed his face wearily. "A house search was conducted, but we never found the artifact. He disappeared after that.

In fact, most of us assumed he was dead."

"He's pretty spry for a dead guy," Archer said.

"Hard to believe that Sidonius and I are the same age," Xantherus said.

"He looked older when we saw him at the Keep," Khoury said.

"He's gotten younger?" Xantherus paced along an obviously familiar route through the cluttered room as if his mental activity needed a physical outlet. "Still, to soak up and manage enough power to gate himself back to the Keep is almost beyond belief," he said to no one in particular and then stopped to lean against the desk again, the empty wine glass in his hand. "The girl's situation, her survival, hints at something even rarer."

"Rare?" Bradan pressed. "More rare than a soul knife?"

"Sidon talked of many things…creatures I'd never imagined. Scrolls filled with impossible magics." Xantherus stopped and shook his head. "He was unstable. Delusional."

"Sounds like he has accomplished much that is impossible," Bradan said, looking pointedly at the burnt stone on Xantherus's desk.

"True," Xantherus admitted. "But immortality? That is beyond belief even given his talents."

Falin wondered if she'd heard the sorcerer right. Sidonius was trying to make himself immortal? The thought chilled her bones.

CHAPTER 44

KHOURY

The Eagle's Nest was dingy and as crowded as ever. Violet examined the captain with a critical eye, shifted the chewing leaf to her other cheek and said, "You look like shit, no offense."

"Nice to see you, too, Vi," Khoury replied, taking the chair opposite her. After leaving Xantherus, he'd tried to rinse off the soot and even changed his shirt but the scent of scorched hair was tenacious.

Violet's eyes scanned the common room. "Where's Archer?"

Khoury motioned for a drink. "Babysitting. Something's come up."

"A job?" Her voice was low but eager.

He nodded as the maid set a mug down on the table.

She smiled, waiting for him to explain.

"We've got a castle to take."

"A castle."

"Yes. Call the Swords in. Send out word to any others you know of who can meet us on the North Road in the next few days." He took a long drink of the cool yeasty ale and pulled out a hastily written list. "And I'll need these items as well." He pushed it across the table at her.

Vi took it and perused the list as he drank most of the ale, waiting for it to improve his mood. It wasn't working. She frowned thoughtfully and peered at him over the paper. "Why do you want armor for a—"

"Just get it," Khoury snapped, forestalling any discussion. "And no cheap stuff either. I need you to go to Ponston Street, too. Get an assortment; bring it to Wallace's. I don't know what the others will need." He unconsciously patted the cloth-wrapped blade at his belt that he'd retrieved from the treasury. Then he lifted a hefty purse of coin.

His lieutenant nodded. "Okay. By when?"

"Yesterday."

She choked on her drink.

"Problem?" Khoury asked.

"No sir," she replied, pushing away her ale. "Love to sit and chat but it seems I've got things to do. Get the tab, will ya, Captain?" She winked before she strode out into the sunny day.

Khoury squinted against the light. The nugget of fear he'd kept at bay taunted him now. Personal feelings aside, this Far Islander had to be stopped. Such power, unchecked, was dangerous and even now might be beyond the Academy's skill to contain.

Khoury hadn't flinched when Xantherus had talked about immortality. But if that was what Sidonius was up to, Khoury had to kill him and soon. If the sorcerer managed it, it wouldn't be long before the Dunhadrar of Barakan stole it for themselves.

He touched the stinging line beneath his eye.

Even if I get close enough to kill him, Khoury wondered, *what chance do I really have?* He finished the ale but still felt a flutter of fear. He raised his hand to order another, yearning for the heady peace of inebriation. But when the drink arrived, he only stared into the fading foam, despising himself. His father hadn't raised him to be a drunk. Or a coward. Khoury pounded the table with an angry fist. Every enemy had a weakness. He *had* to find it and Xantherus *was* going to help him.

And then, he would find the captain he used to be, that hard man clothed in callous armor, a man with nothing to lose, and he would stop this sorcerer before another soul suffered. He reached into the pouch at his belt and tossed a generous tip on the table. As he stood and scrubbed his face with a smoky hand, he decided on one other thing he'd have to do before addressing his company of men.

CHAPTER 45
FALIN

The captain had instructed them to stay put and stay together, so they gathered in Bradan's room. Archer played a dice game with the chieftain as Falin watched with flagging interest. She was tired and ached to be alone, to wander outside, anything but this confinement. Late in the afternoon, Nadja knocked bringing fresh clothes for the men.

"Come, you must dress for dinner, milady," she said to Falin.

"I'm already dressed."

"That is hardly correct attire for a lady," the maid countered.

Falin bristled. "Who are you calling a lady?"

Bradan couldn't hide his smirk. "She didn't mean it as an insult, Huntress."

"Come," the maid persisted, "I have a very becoming gown for you." She gestured through the door to Cara's room.

"A gown?" Falin glowered at the girl. "Huntresses don't wear… dresses." Her hand found its way to the hilt of her sword.

Archer came over and placed a friendly hand on Falin's shoulder. "Real ladies don't need steel, they have men," he teased.

"I'm not one of your 'courtly' ladies." Falin brushed his hand off with a snarl.

Archer laughed. "No one would confuse you with one of those."

She scowled at his laughter.

Bradan stuffed his humor down long enough to look serious. "Diplomats often must bend to the rules of their hosts, Huntress."

He had a point. Sorchia would have said something like that.

"Just wear the damned thing. You're still the most dangerous woman I know." He punched her on the arm hard enough to show he wasn't coddling her.

"Thanks," she said, hitting him back hard enough to bruise.

A steaming bath of scented water awaited her in Cara's room. Falin decided the trial of wearing a dress might be worth the soak. Soap and towels sat on a nearby stool. She quickly stripped, draping her leathers neatly on a chair, and stepped into the tub. Falin purred in the soothing heat as she closed her eyes and leaned back. Her mind drifted lazily near sleep, though she didn't want to nod off and have another unexpected visit to the Keep.

Last night, Cara had probably lain right here, she thought. And now she's gone.

Falin slid lower, letting the hot water creep up her scalp, soothing her anxiety with the sweet floral scent. It took a while for the warmth to fill her bones and chase away the last residue of the black staff's magic.

In her memory, she pictured the captain howling his frustration in the empty street. She knew he'd try and get Cara back. The question was: Would she help him? She'd promised to bring the girl safely to Iolair, and she had. But Sorchia had intended for Falin to see Cara safely to her unknown destiny.

And my own.

What was it Sorchia said? "...the Mothers have shown her to me in dreams. They want her to claim her destiny, and she can lead you to your own...."

A strange misgiving bloomed inside her heart, but Falin knew her job wasn't done yet. She sighed. She would follow the captain into this storm, though she'd never in her life felt so hesitant to start a fight.

The maid's footsteps crossed the floor. "Shall I coif your hair?" the girl asked, settling down on the stool next to the tub.

Falin just nodded, not sure what exactly she was agreeing to. The maid washed and combed Falin's tangled mane sorely testing the Huntress's limited patience. After much grumbling and swearing from both women, the golden locks were bound back from her face with slender braids and cascaded in waves down her back.

The dress the maid picked was a simple gown of deep green with close sleeves. Falin felt completely naked without her breasts wrapped and the low cut neckline exposed their embarrassingly soft roundness. She rejected the dainty slippers in favor of soft leather boots.

A new argument broke out over her weapon. As Sidonius's next target, Falin was not going anywhere without a blade. She'd even offered to take food in her room, which apparently would insult the baron's hospitality. Her stubbornness won out, and in the end, her hunting knife hung from the thick embroidered belt on her hips.

With all the squabbling the others had already left for dinner, and she hurriedly followed a frustrated Nadja to the dining room—late. Never had she felt so exposed. The men's stares as she entered didn't help. Archer whistled appreciatively and gave her a wolfish grin. She raised an eyebrow and placed her hand on the blade at her belt in warning, crossly determined to take any embarrassment out of his hide at the next sparring.

Next to Archer sat Bradan and next to him was Xantherus. The man at the head of the table she guessed was the baron, a cultured-looking brown-haired noble with a too-easy smile. Behind the baron was a thin man with a hawkish nose and a chronic stoop from leaning over to whisper in the baron's ear, as he did just then.

Then her eyes landed on the man to the baron's right, dressed in a gleaming hauberk of chain covered with a deep-blue tabard bearing silver crossed swords and a running hound. She stared for a moment and blinked. It was the captain, but not the captain she knew.

His face was shaved smooth showing the faint lines of a hundred battles. The lack of a beard accentuated the intensity of his angular features. He had cropped short his wavy dark hair, giving him a stark, predatory look. Black leather gloves hung at his belt, a shining helm sat on the table, and a scowl darkened his brow. Falin's breath caught in her throat as his eyes met hers, the familiar blue depths unfathomable and distantly cold.

She moved toward the table and the baron stood, quickly followed by the other men. "I thought the Lady Cara had been taken," he said with surprise. Falin stopped short. The pregnant silence alerted the baron to his mistake.

"I'm afraid you haven't met the final member of our group," Khoury said. The captain took Falin lightly by the hand, escorting her forward. "Baron Wallace, may I present Huntress Falin of Foresthaven."

She was grateful Khoury hadn't insulted her by using "lady." She bowed formally as a representative of her Sisters, hand covering her heart. "My lord," she said in a smooth but husky tone.

"Forgive my poor eyesight."

"Of course," Falin said with a nod. Khoury sat her next to him, and she noted that the men sat when she did. She risked a glance at Archer sitting across from her. When he gave her an approving nod and glanced at his plate, she surreptitiously sampled the variety of food before her. It was surprisingly good, and she was starving.

"Where were we?" the baron asked, taking a swig of his ale.

"You were just about to give us troops to rescue Lady Cara. As you said, she's been kidnapped, and we're going after her."

Falin closed her eyes, her worst fears confirmed. "Fool," she breathed.

"What?" Khoury demanded, his stare drawing all eyes to her.

"I said you're a fool."

"We *are* going after her," he repeated. Disapproval simmered in his stormy eyes.

She glared right back. "Think before you jump, Captain," she warned, sounding stronger than she felt.

It's not the first time we've disagreed, she chided herself. *If he doesn't like it, Thorns take the motherless bastard.*

"She could be dead already," Falin said, though she knew it was a lie. She could see the meek rabbit locked inside those dark stone walls and felt a stab of pity.

"Khoury," the baron said, shaking his head. "I love you like a brother, but I can't send men to die for the sake of a girl, even your girl."

Khoury put his utensils down with deliberate care. Falin could feel his anger just beneath the surface. "I've done as much for you, haven't I, Jake?"

The baron squirmed in his seat, making Falin wonder what debt he owed.

"Cara aside," Khoury continued, "Sidonius grows in power daily. If not now, then soon, he *will* become a serious threat to all of us. He has giants as allies, a network of information to rival yours, and sorcery that can turn farmers into an army or allow him to step from his Keep straight to your throne room. He may seem distant now, but he will expand his reach, that I promise you. And Iolair lies at the heart of the continent. Eventually, he will come to her."

Xantherus cleared his throat. "I agree with the captain's assessment, Baron. Grant him what you can to stop this threat now."

"You surprise me, Islander," Wallace said. "You don't normally advise action."

"I have already sent word to the Academy in this regard," Xantherus said.

The baron sat back in his chair. "That serious?"

Xantherus turned to Khoury. "Action is required but not haste, Captain. You need not strike immediately. Help from the Academy could turn the tide."

Khoury's face was unreadable. "You don't even know when or if they'll respond. It's possible they'll deny your request entirely."

"He is an exile. The Academy's responsibility is clear," Xantherus sputtered.

"They may not see it that way," Khoury said coolly.

"Wait, Sidonius is an exile?" the baron asked.

It was Xantherus's turn to squirm. "From the Far Isles, yes. Charged with sorcery against the common good and found guilty."

"And your solution was to send him here?" Cade interjected out of turn. He opened his mouth to expound further, but Wallace silenced him with a raised hand.

The baron cleared his throat. "Since Xantherus has advised action, I agree with you, Khoury, sooner is better. However, you know how closely my enemies watch me. I can spare only forty regulars and twenty of my Elite Guard. Any more than that and Iolair may fall before you reach Telsedan. But take whatever siege engines, wagons and horses you need; those items I can spare. Even a small keep can be formidable."

"You are generous, Wallace," Khoury said, then turned to Xantherus. "What else can you tell us?"

"Sidonius was an accomplished fire sorcerer, but clearly he's gone far beyond what he learned at the Academy. I found some old texts concerning the use of 'soul magic.'"

"Soul magic?" Bradan was obviously intrigued.

"Magic involving elements of the persona," Xantherus explained. "Academy sorcerers study only the four elements: fire, earth, air, and water. Every graduate knows incantations of each and has a specialty. But that isn't the only type of magic in the world."

Like Bradan conjuring the fog spirits*, Falin thought.*

"What we saw today with the traveling crystals," the sorcerer said, "is entirely foreign. He must have picked that up on his travels."

"You thought this soul knife of his was important," Bradan prompted.

"You saw his conscripts," Khoury said impatiently. "You've seen what it does."

"But only Sidon knew what happened to the parts that were removed."

"Are you saying we can fix the men he's taken?" Bradan asked.

Falin cursed under her breath. If the men Sidonius was using were not lost, this would be much harder.

"I doubt that's the case," Xantherus scoffed. "But they bring up an interesting line of inquiry. What would happen if you took too much of a person's soul."

At that, Xantherus's eyes locked onto Falin making the hairs on her neck and arms stand up.

"Theory doesn't interest me," Khoury said abruptly. "We've seen his soldiers. What else can we expect?"

Falin saw Xantherus frown at the captain's words. *We're missing the point,* she thought, *but why doesn't Xantherus just say what he thinks?*

"I expect he'll feast himself on energy as he did before today." The wind wizard's tone grew bored. "Any wards or enchantments would be deadly. There's no way to know what other foreign magics he is capable of. He and Urchek were on the road more than they were home, and from what I've seen and heard, no one at the Academy had an inkling of the extent of their inventory. Urchek was such a gentle soul. The most magic he did was to heat his tea."

"Sidonius has larger aspirations, it seems," Bradan said.

Khoury's impatience grew. "From what he'd learned at the Academy, what else could he do?"

Xantherus gave him a quelling stare then said, "He might summon a beast of his specialty."

"Like what?" Archer asked.

"An elemental or a young dragon, perhaps."

At the mention of dragon, the entire hall fell silent. Falin would have paid coin to know what Khoury was thinking now.

"Captain, you can stay another night to prepare," the baron said, obviously shaken by the discussion.

"No. We'll leave tonight as agreed. I'm sure your guard is ready at your call."

"It is probably wisest to go now if you don't wish the Academy's help," Xantherus said.

Was it wisdom, *Falin wondered,* or had the sorcerer tired of Khoury's disdainful inquisition?

"I don't think the Academy *will* help," the captain told the sorcerer.

Not in time to save Cara, *Falin realized.*

"Either way, if I can put a sword through his heart, it will solve the problem. If not, then it will be your mess to cleanup, Magus." With that, Khoury stood.

Falin was about to complain that she'd hardly eaten but there was an angry restlessness within the captain he could barely contain.

"Thank you for your gracious hospitality," he said, bowing to Wallace. "I am in your debt. If I survive, call on me when you have need."

The baron stood and bowed in return as a knot of dread coalesced in Falin's gut.

If I survive....

Khoury spun on a sharp heel and strode for the door with Bradan and Archer scrambling after. Falin followed but when she heard Xantherus excuse himself as well, she waited by the door to find out what exactly he wasn't telling them.

He turned left instead of right, and she followed him a short way up the hall before she caught up to him and grabbed his arm.

A sharp blast of air hit her in the chest, hard enough to knock her back against the wall. The blow felt surprisingly solid for being made of wind. She snarled and drew her knife.

Xantherus turned with a haughty look. "You can't expect to manhandle someone in a deserted hallway and not expect them to react defensively, my dear. Now, put down the blade. I don't want to hurt you."

She frowned. "What aren't you telling us?"

He stared at her for a long moment, his eyes shuttered. "I don't know what you mean."

She wanted to slap him. "You were hinting at something."

"You heard your captain. He wants nothing of my theories." He turned to leave.

"You think I'm involved, don't you?" she blurted out.

He stopped, quietly considering. Then his shoulders softened, and he looked at her. "Yes. I believe you are at the very heart of it all."

"But I met Cara only a few weeks ago, and I don't know anything about the sorcerer."

"Yet you recognized him. Let me pose my question again. If a soul is a thing that can be cut, what happens to the pieces you take away?"

"I don't know." Falin was getting irritated. "What does it matter?

"This girl, she has some kind of power, yes?" Xantherus's voice rose with impatience.

"She's a healer, but—"

"Ah," he said as if it all made sense. "A healer."

Falin sighed and rubbed her eyes. "So?"

"So, let's say that the soul in question has a healing power and Sidonius wanted to cut away everything but the power. Where does that extra go?" The question hung in the hall. "Especially given this particular soul's natural tendency is to fix things."

Fix things. Falin snorted with dry humor. That did sum Cara up fairly well. "You think Sidonius did something to her. With that knife."

"I'm sure of it."

"Okay, he made her meek, but I don't see how this involves me?"

"Don't you?" Xantherus simply looked down at the knife in her hand.

"You think…" A hot flush covered her shoulders and neck. The hair on her head lifted in a chill. "Wait, you think I'm the cut away pieces?"

"It makes sense."

"Except that I grew up in Foresthaven. I didn't appear out of nowhere one day." Her words were quick with anger but not enough to outrun her fear.

"Not if you were an infant when he took you," Xantherus said.

Falin had no words. She herself wasn't a motherly sort, but the thought of that man using his magic on an infant turned her stomach.

"The last time I saw Sidonius was years after he'd been exiled," Xantherus said. "The Academy had been contacted to help with a coup. My services were offered. I had no idea another sorcerer was involved though I should have realized it when I saw the dragon."

"Sidonius," Falin guessed.

Xantherus nodded. "The strange part, the part that made no sense, was that I found Sidon in the nursery."

"You knew?" Falin accused, gripping the hilt of her blade until her knuckles paled.

"No. When I saw him, he was alone. I thought he was hiding from the guard. But he did have the soul knife with him." Xantherus pressed his lips together.

"He stole and magicked a baby, and you just let him get away?" Anger boiled in Falin's gut.

"I had no proof. And he had once been my friend."

As a foundling, she'd always thought she had no parents. Sorchia was the only mother she'd ever known or ever needed. But now, she had to wonder if she had another one, or a father. Had Sidonius stolen Cara and her from them, or had he killed them?

She found that she didn't care. The despair that nipped at her mind now had little to do with being an orphan. It seemed the truth was worse than that.

If Xantherus was right, she was just scraps from someone else's soul.

Falin put a hand to the wall as the floor tipped beneath her. Hot shock washed over her, stealing her air.

"No," she denied it with a snarl, as her heart pounded painfully within her ribs. "No, you're wrong!" She hated Xantherus then, hated him and all the soulless sorcerers of the Far Isles.

Is this what magic does to men? she wondered. The Culling made sense now. The Mothers were truly wise, brutal but wise.

"I know this must be a surprise," he said with easy indifference, reaching out a reassuring hand.

She slapped it away and pointed her knife at him. "Don't touch me, you thornless coward! I'll slit your motherless neck and be glad of it." The hatred she felt demanded blood, but killing him wouldn't stop Sidonius, wouldn't change the past, and wouldn't save Cara. So she scooped up the annoying skirts from around her legs, turned and ran. She didn't know where she was going; she just knew she needed to get away from him. She ran through long hallways, turning randomly left or right hoping for a door to the outside. It hurt trying to wrap her brain around everything.

She was not the little rabbit's cast-off parts; she just couldn't be.

By the time she calmed enough to walk, she was lost. It took almost an hour to find their rooms. Archer and Bradan were waiting for her. Khoury was missing.

"Where'd you go?" Archer asked, noting her sweaty hair and wild eyes.

"Just went for a run. Tired of walls." She plopped down in a chair, wanting to talk about anything to get her mind off Xantherus's wild theories. "So, sixty men from the baron. Is that going to be enough?"

"With Khoury in charge, I've seen miracles," Archer assured her. "Besides, we'll have more than sixty by the time we reach the Keep."

"How?"

"I have a score of riders in Iolair already and Violet sent the call out today," Khoury said from behind her. She turned to see him in the doorway and wondered how long he'd been there.

"Who's Violet?" she asked.

"One of my other lieutenants," Khoury said.

"Best in the business," Archer added with a wry smile. "You'd like her." Then he turned to Khoury. "How many more do you think we'll get?"

"Another fifty to eighty perhaps," Khoury said. "Maybe more with the summer festival coming."

Archer chuckled. "If the great Captain Khoury is asking for swords, they'll come." Archer leaned close to Falin. "They don't even ask why as long as he's in charge."

Was Khoury so well-respected that he had only to ask to be provided with an army?

"Get your things, Falin," Khoury said curtly. "Meet us in my room." With that, he backed out of the room.

Exchanging puzzled looks with the Northerners, Falin went back to Cara's room and gathered the few items that remained. She stowed Cara's packet of medicine in her pack. Then she slipped out of the gown, wrapped her breasts tight, and donned her now-clean leggings and tunic, tucking her totems near her heart.

Once more in familiar armor and having traded braids for her usual knot, she felt more like herself. More able to handle the task required of her. Her destiny was to be Cara's strength. She had nothing else to give any of them. Now, more than ever, there was no room for weakness. Or self-pity.

"Ever a Huntress," she murmured to herself. "By thorn and blade, Cara, I swear I will not fail us."

As she reached for her bow and quiver, the soft green material lying in a heap on the floor caught her eye. She picked it up, running sensitive fingertips over the soft fabric. Without knowing why, she folded the gown and stuffed it in the bottom of the pack, and then headed across the hall.

CHAPTER 46
KHOURY

Khoury didn't turn from the window when he heard the Huntress enter. He'd had to think long and hard about what to do with her, especially since she was Sidonius's next target. He tried to convince himself he wanted her close to use as bait, to bring the sorcerer out. But the image of Sidonius disappearing behind his wall of fire with Cara still haunted the captain. He wouldn't lose the Huntress, too.

At dinner, she implied that she wouldn't join them. He thought about simply asking for her help, but she tended to do the opposite of what he wanted. There was only one way to make sure she cooperated. He took a deep breath and turned, his face like a mountainside.

"Falin, I've decided you should stay behind."

Bradan and Archer stared in shock. Falin looked up at him with short-lived surprise. Then, predictable anger crawled across her features. "What?"

"You should stay in Iolair," he repeated.

"I hadn't said that I was going yet," she said softly.

"Even better."

The blunt dismissal left Falin speechless. Her brow furrowed as if she misunderstood him. "Are you still going after Cara?" she asked.

"Yes. But, like I said, we won't need you." He hadn't expected her to look so hurt.

"You're going to need every possible blade for this," she said, incredulous. "I *can* fight." He had anticipated anger, but this was something else. The pain in her bright eyes was startling. Still, he had started down this path; there was no turning back.

"You're a liability."

"I'm as good with a blade as you!"

"It's too dangerous," he said. That fueled the fire he was seeking, but she still didn't rise to the bait. He'd expected her to yell or lash out at him by now. "Sidonius will be tough, and I don't have time to babysit."

"Captain!" Archer said, coming to stand next to the Huntress. "What is wrong with you?"

Archer's pity did what Khoury's disdain could not. He saw the flush of her cheeks at Archer's intervention. Fury flared in her green eyes, and she spit at their feet. "I don't need a babysitter. I'm *not* Cara."

"But you'd be my responsibility," Khoury said. "I don't want you there."

Archer opened his mouth to speak in her defense but a sharp look from Falin made him think better of it. Her face, when she turned back to the captain, showed the hurt his betrayal had caused.

What happened since the meeting with Wallace? he wondered.

After a moment's thought, she schooled her features back to haughty disdain. Her shoulders relaxed and she crossed her arms, calm as a snake poised to strike. "I don't care what you want, you motherless bastard. I wouldn't dream of sitting this one out."

"Sidonius said you were next," he said. "Do you think it's wise for me to take you straight to him?"

"Wise for *you* to take *me*?" She was indignant, her nostrils flaring and jaw set. "What am I—your dog? You can't *make* me do anything."

That was what he wanted to hear. "I should lock you in the baron's dungeon for your own good." It felt strangely good to argue with her now that her spark had returned.

"Fine. Leave me here," she challenged, "if you dare."

"Following us would be suicide," he snapped.

"Going to the Keep to get Cara is suicide!" Falin shouted. "And this is more about me and her than it is about you. Xantherus said as much."

Khoury wasn't sure what she meant by that, but he was glad she was determined to go. She met his gaze unflinching, refusing to be stared down, and he almost smiled. He had come to like her stubborn contrariness. But he only shook his head with false exasperation. "Fine. Tag along if you wish."

He heard her huff of victory as he went to the chair by the window and retrieved the special item he'd ask Vi to find. His lieutenant had outdone herself. On the chair was a brigantine cuirass for Falin. Far sturdier than her Huntress leathers, it had small plates of iron sewn between pieces of leather. He turned, holding it out to her. "You'd better take this."

Falin looked suspiciously from the chest piece to the captain.

"It's stronger than those leathers of yours," he explained as she took the cuirass with growing interest. "You should have better protection if you insist on coming."

Falin hefted it, testing its weight. Then, she slipped her tunic off over her head, her breasts well-covered by the linen wrap that bound them tight to her ribs. She looked so slender and small that for a moment she reminded him of Cara. An ache of longing shot through him. She settled the new armor over her shoulders. She shifted and bounced and feigned a few attacks, nodding with satisfaction.

The men chose their weapons and when it was Falin's turn, she perused them carefully, choosing only a simple curved short sword, settling for her familiar hunting knife and bow. Then Khoury took the wrapped blade from his belt. It was a family heirloom, having belonged to his mother. Still, it had reminded him of the Huntress when he'd seen it in the treasury. He placed it in her hands without a word.

She unwrapped it carefully, her eyes brightening as she unsheathed the seven-inch barb-tipped dagger, its handle carved with a snarling wolf.

"Thank you," she said with hushed sincerity. Then she gave him a proper Sister salute and slipped the blade into her boot with a satisfied pat. Quick as a flash, she leaned up and planted a quick kiss on the corner of his unsuspecting mouth.

Their eyes met for a brief, awkward moment, then she jumped back. "I forgot something." She left the room and returned in a few moments with the witchwood staff she gifted to Cara. "Now I'm ready."

CHAPTER 47
CARA

Cara woke from dreams of richly colored tapestries and sweet buns to find herself surrounded by black stones as if nothing had changed. An evening gloom was settling over the room, giving it a hint of unreality. The last thing she remembered was breakfast with Khoury. She had no memory of returning to the Keep.

Perhaps her adventures had been only a dream and she would go below and find the red-haired Northerner still imprisoned, his stern captain sparring with thin air.

The idea became so real, it drove her to her feet.

She tripped with a clank of chains and stared in horror at the shackles about her ankles. There was enough length of chain for her to manage a stumbling waddle but little more. The fetters were definitely a change but still the idea that her friends were below clung like a burr. Using her skirts to keep the chains out of the way, she tried the door, thankful it opened. She shuffled her way to the dark stairs and painstakingly hopped down a step at a time. No longer did sentinel torches burn in the halls, and the light from outside didn't penetrate very far into the dusty cloister. From the main floor, she stumbled her way by feel and memory to the stairs that led down to the cells.

Pausing at the pitch-black landing, her heart thudded in her chest. Everything had changed since she'd left, and not for the better.

The whoosh of a candle catching flame startled her and she squinted in the sudden glare, pressing herself back against the wall.

"Still a wanderer, I see." Sidonius's rasp reminded her of empty winds and dead things. He towered over her, one raised fingertip alight like a wick. He looked larger than she recalled. Shadows clung to him like fog. The wrongness she'd always sensed in him had grown. And it hungered for her. Forked tongues of darkness darted out to taste her skin, and she shivered. Her leaving had set something ominous in motion.

"Looking for your friends?" he asked, lifting his hand to let the flickering light tumble down the stairs. Instead of an empty hall, Cara saw bodies pressed together. Not in cells but crowding the entire level. Heads turned at the luminous disturbance, and she gazed in horror on a sea of empty faces and cloudy eyes.

"What have you done?" she whispered.

"What was needed," Sidonius said. He gripped her arm, turning her back toward her tower. She shuffled meekly to the stairs.

"Perhaps I should thank you," he added. "Had you not run away, I would never have found the one thing I still need." Reaching the stairs, he shoved her toward the first step.

"I'm back. What more could you need?" she asked wearily.

"Much, it seems," he said cryptically. "In all the years of failure, the one thing I never questioned was you." In the flickering light, his look of cold disdain shriveled her soul.

What failure was he talking about?

He gestured impatiently for her to go up. "I had no idea all those years ago that I'd be hindering myself. But after seeing her, it was for the best. I'd have killed you both long before fruition had it been otherwise."

He was making no sense, but her curiosity was roused. Who had he seen? She knew how to get answers except the hungry darkness around him gave her the cold shivers. She didn't want to get any closer. All she needed was a speck of courage, the courage to look into him the way she did with the captain. Chained as she was, the stairs demanded all her attention for the moment, and she let him talk.

"I'm certain your soldier will bring her right to me," he continued. "And then…then I will be unstoppable. I will be free."

Wasn't he free already? Free to leave? She'd reached the top and turned to him, using curiosity to light a spark.

Sometimes courage only requires a quick step off the cliff, she told herself and moved before she could reconsider.

"Let them go," she said in a pleading tone. She knew he wouldn't listen but it was a good excuse to put her hand on his arm.

She braced herself for his mind, diving in deep and fast. As icy and shocking as falling into the river at Bear Clan, she felt tainted and queasy as she looked for any memory related to the failures he mentioned. Unlike Khoury or Archer, the sorcerer's visions didn't feel like dreams. They felt like the void she'd fought him in after the giant attack.

One other thing was very clear. The wrongness she'd always felt around him wasn't a wound; it was a being. A dark entity had taken up residence and was growing inside the sorcerer. Not in his body but in his energy, in his soul. How had she not noticed it before?

Had it grown? He'd obviously done the ritual since she'd left or he would have no power at all. Why hadn't it kept the creature in check?

He needs me, she thought. *He chased me all the way to Iolair and even came to get me himself.*

There was no denying that she had something the other sacrifices didn't. How many seers had told her on this journey that she had power. She *was* magic. And only now she realized what a rare and precious gift it was.

Her magic *had* healed the sorcerer and *had* kept the creature at bay. Without her, the darkness grew in power, strengthening its hold over Sidonius. How much of what she sensed was the entity and how much was the man, she couldn't be sure.

She scanned his memories and found the one she wanted. Sidonius had been very young, reckless, arrogant. He tried a spell against his teacher's wishes. Urchek had forbidden it but then again Urchek hadn't understood the pleasure of power. The Magus had tried a counterspell only to have the creature tear him apart and cast him into an otherworldly darkness. Then the dark entity had sliced a hole in Sidonius and crawled inside.

A sharp slap startled her back to reality, making her eyes water.

"Get out of my head!" Sidonius roared and then he struck her again, sending her tumbling backward into the cell. His eyes were wild.

"I see you've learned a new trick, but it won't save you. Or the others." She sensed, rather than saw, the dark shape closing over the sorcerer's head like a cowl. It wanted her but bided its time. "You're lucky I still need you alive."

When he closed the door, she heard the lock click. His footsteps faded into the distance, and the familiar weighty silence descended. She crawled to the door and leaned her head against it as a tear rolled down her cheek in the dark. She was lonelier than she'd ever been. Even Gar was gone. The only sound was the beat of her heart. As she absently listened to its rhythm, she was reminded of Bradan's hut that night, of Ealea's drumming.

The kind gray-haired woman had been one of many souls lost in Cara's selfish bid for freedom. More hot tears flowed, and Cara didn't try to stop them. Her heart ached for company but her loneliness seemed an appropriate penance for risking so many. Despondent and weary, her mind followed the thumping of her heart, and she felt a familiar dizziness. Only half-aware of what she was doing, her mind reached out along unseen threads looking for a friend. She poured her yearning out into the void, but only emptiness returned.

Her isolation was complete, so she slept not knowing what else to do and dreamed of warm fur and black eyes.

CHAPTER 48
KHOURY

Horses and warriors clogged the stable yard though the crowd parted easily for the captain. Archer was heartened by the sight of so many familiar faces, as much a homecoming for him as returning to the Clan.

"There's Archer-boy," Roger Ellis hooted, cuffing Archer on the side of the head and swinging him into a headlock. Archer dropped his pack and swept the other mercenary's feet, dumping him on his backside.

"Save it for the battle, boys," Vi said, skirting the horseplay with exasperation. She signaled to two squires who brought the four horses from Rebeka's cohorts, already tacked up. "All's ready here, Captain. Was the armor what you needed?"

"Indeed," Khoury said, nodding at Falin who was swinging a leg over her gelding.

Vi turned to see her handiwork and Ellis did the same. She nodded with a satisfied smile. "Looks good."

"I'll say," Ellis added with an appreciative whistle.

"Stow it," Khoury reprimanded. "She's a warrior, like Vi." Then he turned on his heel and weaved through the crowd to the wagons that occupied the center of the yard.

"Testy," Ellis grumbled.

Archer opened his mouth to apologize for the captain's behavior but Falin's words came back to him. And instead he said, "That's the Huntress who's working this job with us. Show some respect."

"The captain took on a Huntress?" Vi asked in confusion.

Ellis said, "She doesn't really look like one."

Archer glanced at Falin again. Though the brigantine was a perfect fit, between the blonde hair and the armor, Ellis was right—she didn't look the part anymore. She looked, in her own words, motherless.

What have we done to her? he thought sourly. Taking reins of his horse from the squire, Archer followed the captain.

Khoury climbed on the back of a wagon and surveyed the corps. Twenty Elite Guardsmen, forty regulars, and twenty-two mercenaries gathered in the yard. Extra mounts, a catapult, and two small ballistae waited near the road leading back to the square. When the captain lifted his hands for quiet, the mercenaries cheered instead.

"Where ya been, Captain?" someone shouted from the throng.

"I had a bit of an adventure in the North," he answered to which the men responded with lewd conjecture.

Archer studied Khoury's good-natured façade, searching for the cracks. Cara's capture had hit him hard, and though Archer was eager to tackle the sorcerer, he wondered if the captain's cunning would suffer from the loss.

Khoury shook his head at the men with a forced smile. "Not that kind unfortunately," he called back. The men finally quieted.

"Many of you know me," the captain said, "and most, if not all, know of me. A borderless man, I hold no allegiances except by my own choice and those, subject to change for enough gold." Laughter swept the crowd even as Khoury's mouth twisted with disgust at his own words.

"But today, we are not here for any one lord's cause. No, this is far beyond that. Our very way of life is threatened—by one very powerful man. More than twenty years ago, the Far Isles Academy tried one of their own for dark magic, magic that even they considered immoral.

They tried this Magus and found him guilty. And then Sidonius of the Far Isles, convicted criminal, was exiled. He came here." An angry murmur hummed through the crowd.

"For twenty years, he has lurked in the cold emptiness of the tundra. Twenty years, he has nursed his hate. His web of spies reaches from the Northlands to Iolair and beyond, and he has gathered magic so formidable, the Baron's Islander will not join us.

"I won't lie to you," the captain continued. "I've never met a more dangerous foe. Many will die. Maybe all. Even now, he gathers power from the deaths of innocents, slaughtering us like cattle for his pleasure. He steals the will of good men, making them do his bidding without question.

"I've seen these broken men. They are puppets, and I pity their fate. We cannot save them, but we can stop this Islander. I'm no crusader. You all know I'm not a saint. But some evils cannot be tolerated."

The crowd rumbled in agreement.

"Will you ride with me and finish what the Academy could not? We must put down this rogue, this abomination of avarice and power before he becomes unstoppable. Are you with me?" the captain shouted, lifting his sword above his head and a roar went up from the men. Bridles jingled as horses pranced nervously.

"Onward to the North!" Khoury cried. He jumped down from the wagon and swung up on his horse. Men mounted up, and the sounds of armor and hooves filled the yard.

Falin and Bradan pressed their mounts close to Archer as the throng took on a life of its own and followed Khoury down the road. They cantered out of Iolair, heading east.

The company traveled for two days, east along the dwindling mountain range. They skirted the open plains of Tarantis. The mountains gradually turned into rolling hills, which in turn led to sparsely forested countryside. Then they turned north at a well-marked crossroads. In all that time, there was no sign of resistance or magic. And Archer was pleased to see their numbers swell to almost two hundred warriors as word of Khoury's quest spread.

With so many Swords, tempers frequently ran hot and Archer knew only too well how easily sparked Falin could be. He worried the men would vex her to the point of murder but something had changed in her. It might have been Vi's influence for the two women had become fast friends. But he sensed a brooding. Maybe she felt shame that Cara was taken on her watch or fatigue now that her dreams were troubled by the Black Keep and its master. Regardless, she kept her temper and her counsel to herself. There were a few scuffles but she held her own and claimed respect like any greenie. She pulled her weight and asked no quarter. Eventually even the old-timers grudgingly accepted her.

Archer noticed that Khoury watched her, too. The captain had commented the other night that he planned to assign her to the rearguard with Ellis. But Archer knew the Huntress would want no part of that. Either way, he suspected she was becoming as much a distraction as Cara had been.

As darkness closed in, they came to an old tollhouse that Archer recognized. A chill brushed his shoulders. Here they had been handed over to Sidonius. A crude barrier had been erected across the road but otherwise it looked exactly the same. Khoury called a halt and dismounted. Archer swung a leg over and followed the captain, drawing his sword as he went.

CHAPTER 49
FALIN

Falin watched carefully as Khoury and Archer approached the deserted building with weapons drawn. She scanned the deepening gloom, not liking the feel of the place. No light in the window. No horses in the paddock. No smoke from the chimney. Pulling her sword, she laid it across the pommel. Even her normally placid gelding fidgeted.

The moment Khoury knocked on the door, the ambush was sprung. The door flew open and a man stepped out, thrusting his spear at Khoury, catching the captain in the side. Archer chopped at the man, nearly severing an arm with the great two-handed sword. Chaos broke over the corps as men jumped out at them from all sides, yelling wildly. The horses reared, prancing in surprise.

Struggling to keep her gelding from bolting, Falin realized she'd be better off fighting on foot. She swung her leg over its withers and slid to the ground, running for the tollhouse where Khoury and Archer had disappeared. Above the clank of steel upon steel, Falin heard a fluttering noise. Looking up she saw a flock of pigeons.

"Birds!" she yelled at the top of her lungs. "Khoury!" She jammed her sword point into the damp earth and unslung her bow. The captain burst out of the door just as she loosed her arrow.

Looking up at the fluttering wings, he yelled, "Archer, I need you!"

He turned to the others. "Shoot them. If one gets away…."

She was reaching for her second arrow when Archer emerged. He sheathed his sword, drew his bow and felled two with one shot. The alarm passed down the line of warriors. Men with bows pulled toward the center of the company and began firing into the flock of birds. The other warriors closed ranks and continued to skirmish with their attackers on foot.

'I'm going to find out where they're coming from," Khoury said, racing back into the building.

Falin kept firing arrows at the disappearing shapes in the dying light. The birds seemed to keep coming and all of them were headed north. By now, she was sure one of them had already escaped their range and was on its way.

"It's no use," she said as she shot another and Archer felled two more.

Archer stared at her for a heartbeat, his brow furrowed. "Don't think," he said. "Just shoot."

Chastised, anger welled up inside her. She yanked another arrow from her quiver, set it, pulled, and released. She killed without thought, one after another after another. She barely noticed when Bradan rode up to guard them as they concentrated on clearing the skies.

Khoury emerged from the tollhouse, his face grim. "There were six cages inside. They're all empty now." He peered into the gathering gloom. A few dark specks were fading out of range and she heard him curse.

The combat had broken down into a chaotic melee as the Elite Guardsmen dismounted and attacked on foot. Khoury's small army easily outnumbered Sidonius's lackeys. Soon, all of the attackers were dead and over forty birds littered the road. Falin dropped her weary arm, discouraged and gulping for breath. Archer's face was grim, and Khoury looked into the northern sky one last time and sighed. "So much for surprise," he muttered.

"Probably wouldn't have been much of an advantage," Archer said.

"Still it would have been nice."

CHAPTER 50
KHOURY

Khoury toured the camp as the last light of day faded. They'd lost two Swords in the ambush; eight had been wounded including Khoury, though none seriously. A search of the dilapidated roadhouse had found no more surprises, but Khoury marched the contingent farther east into the woods to camp on a protected hillock. The tents were erected within half an hour. Falin and two other scouts came back with deer and Bradan had ordered all of the pigeons collected, cleaned and cooked as well.

Now mercenaries and Guardsmen drank, ate, and gambled together amicably. Khoury was pleased with how the baron's men and his own Swords were meshing into a single fighting unit. Extra guards had been set around the camp, and Khoury felt fairly certain that they were safe, at least for the night. He was bone tired and ready to sleep.

He wasn't as upset about the birds as the others thought. He realized they probably wouldn't have had the advantage of surprise anyway. His straightforward attack would have been easy to predict. But time was not on his side. He had no idea when Sidonius planned to kill Cara.

Perhaps he already has.

Khoury pushed that thought from his mind as he finished his last turn about the camp. Archer was gambling away money he'd won betting on Falin's sparring matches. Vi was out-drinking some of Wallace's regulars. All was well.

He headed to his tent, hungry, tired and with an ache in his side. He passed Bradan's tent where other injured men were being tended but it was crowded and Khoury didn't feel like talking. He moved his left arm in a circle, testing it and decided he could clean the wound himself. It hurt but didn't feel that serious.

He sat down outside his tent where a small fire blazed within a circle of stones. He should have been pleased with their victory, however incomplete, but instead he felt empty. Even now, doing something he knew was right for the first time in years, discontent followed on the heels of success like a faithful hound. He was weary of fighting.

That thought brought an image of tangled white hair on linen and ice-blue eyes in the morning light. He'd never say it aloud, but he missed her. Pull of magical blood or not, she had worked her way into his life. Sadness seeped into the silence of his solitary camp.

A soft footfall alerted him just before Falin appeared from the dark. She'd already changed from the cuirass to her Huntress leathers and must have been tending the horses. Stray wisps of hay stuck to her clothes and hair. In her hands were two shanks of roasted meat, and she sat down, uninvited, and offered him one. His stomach rumbled.

"Thanks," he said.

She only nodded and ate in silence. The Huntress's quiet presence kept the sadness at bay for which he was grateful though he wondered what had prompted her to seek him out. He had just finished eating when she spoke.

"I didn't want to say anything in front of Xantherus," she said, measuring her words. "I can't help but feel he's—"

"The enemy?" Khoury supplied, sensing a kinship of suspicion.

"Well, not to be wholly trusted," she corrected.

It was splitting hairs but Khoury understood her point. "I think you're right," he said.

Falin remained silent for a long moment, searching for the right words. "When I was younger, Sorchia gave me a rule for fighting magic. I thought it strange at the time, but it might be important."

"And the rule is?" Khoury prompted.

"Simple really: Still the hands, silence the tongue."

Khoury considered those six words carefully as Falin continued.

"You're right that a knife to the heart will kill him. But Sorchia said the real trick was getting past the magic. She said most spells have two components, movement and sound."

"Instead of going straight for the heart," the captain murmured, "we'd be wiser to…"

"…stop the spell first, yes."

"I've seen him use flame without speaking."

Falin's mouth twisted with frustration. "His skill is unprecedented, but…I just thought it might be good to keep in mind. Tomorrow." She shrugged, but he could see her mind still hard at work.

"I appreciate it," he said. "I wouldn't have thought of that." He remembered the fight in Iolair, wondering what he could have done differently.

"Captain," the Huntress said off-handedly, "how long have you been doing this?"

The question startled him. "Sword work? Nearly all my life."

"No family farm or trade to take up?"

"No."

She eyed him skeptically. "But why the sword? Was it for glory?"

"There's no glory in being paid to kill." He sobered at his own words, wondering if Cara was influencing him more than he'd thought.

"But that's what mercenary means, isn't it?" she pointed out with her usual bluntness.

He snorted at the irony.

"Besides, there is glory in victory," she continued.

He paused, considering where her questions were leading. "Don't tell me you want this kind of life." He hadn't intended the disdain that colored his words.

"Maybe I do," she huffed.

"Look, I know you're a good fighter. It's obviously in your blood, but why?" Was he really arguing against what he'd devoted his own life to? Falin was level-headed, almost callous if truth be told. She'd do well as a Sword. But the weight of all the men and women who'd died at his command haunted him. "Why would you want *this*?"

"Why shouldn't I want it?" she challenged, almost angry.

"You could have a better life. In Foresthaven," he said softly.

"No," she said. "You heard Rebeka. I can't go back."

Her confession was a strange and vulnerable offering. Khoury thought that Rebeka had been making empty threats. He hadn't considered that helping them might have cost her so much.

Unshed tears brightened the green of her eyes. "When Rebeka captured you in Foresthaven," she said, staring at the flames, "Sorchia thought it best not to tell the Sisters' Council. Like Bradan, she wanted to help Cara. And I'd always wanted to see the world beyond. But disappearing without a word like that. And the false Culling..." Her voice failed her. She picked a piece of straw from her tunic and angrily threw it in the fire. "They'll assume I deserted." Her nostrils flared with self-loathing. "Of all disgraces, that is the worst. It'll only justify their refusal of my Sisters' oath last year."

She'd never taken the oath? Khoury couldn't understand why they would refuse her. She might be prickly and arrogant but she was tough and fiercely loyal. "Then you're not..."

She forced a grin, though he could see the hurt behind her eyes. "Not officially, no. And they wouldn't have me back now." She cleared her throat and looked expectantly at him. "So, I thought I'd make a good mercenary."

"You would," he agreed reluctantly. "You will."

She stared at the fire for a moment. "I take it home's not an option for you either."

He nodded.

"How come?" She looked up with a raised eyebrow and a hint of challenge.

Oddly enough, he wanted to tell her. His tongue was thick with his secrets, things he hadn't even shared with Archer, and the memories had been restless ever since the Keep. But speaking them wouldn't change the past, so why drag it up?

"Hot-headed good-for-nothing boy, I'm sure you know the type," he said.

She sniffed in disdain. "Coward."

He coughed to hide his discomfort. He knew she was right. And the story was still on his tongue, waiting. She gave him a gentle nudge with her shoulder as if sensing his weakness. The homey scent of hay wafted from her hair.

"Go on," she said.

Her friendly interrogation drew a shadow of a smile that loosened his tongue. "I grew up in Barakan."

Her brow furrowed as if she recognized the name, but she shrugged and motioned for him to continue.

"There isn't a more treacherous place in the world," he said. "Not even the Far Isles, I'd wager.

"My father was a good man and honorable. But that's a dangerous path in the mountains. He…he got in someone's way." Khoury pushed the words out through tight lips. "And they killed him for it. Him and the rest of my family." He kept his eyes on the fire, not wanting to see her pity.

"How old were you?"

"Ten. I had two older brothers." He swallowed, unable to even say their names. "I was there when they were…murdered." His mother had tried to save him and had died for it. But he couldn't tell the Huntress that. He couldn't even think about that. He forced the vision of his mother's blood from his mind.

"I was so angry. I tried to fight. I ran straight in, sword swinging." He chuckled as he pictured himself, a gangling youth against mounted warriors. "But I was too young, too inexperienced. In the end, beaten and nearly dead, I fled…."

His voice tightened to a whisper with the shame of it. "I left them there and never went back. Not even to bury them."

Only crackling flames broke the silence as he waded in the pain of the past until she said, "And the sword work?"

Drawing his mind forward, he remembered how Old Khoury had found him, bleeding and half-dead on that deserted road. "A passing mercenary took me in, helped me heal, taught me to fight better. Where else was I going to go? The man who killed my family was determined to finish the job. There was a price on my head. I guess, after a while, it's just what you do. Besides, I had nothing left to lose."

Her warm hand grasped his forearm. "Mason, I'm truly sorry."

Hearing her use his first name struck a chord, especially since he'd borrowed the old mercenary's last name to keep his past from finding him. "No one else knows, not even Archer."

"A true gift then," she whispered as her hand tightened comfortingly on his arm before she put it back in her lap. "I won't share it. I promise."

She tossed the bones in the fire. "One thing, though. Sorchia used to say that those who have nothing to lose, often have nothing to win either."

Khoury chuckled at how true that was. Though he was well-respected among the Swords, something was missing. Cara's face swam in his mind's eye. "She's a wise one."

"I didn't think so until I left," Falin said with a snort. She shifted away from him suddenly and moved his tabard with tentative fingers, revealing the bent links in his armor.

"Did you know you're bleeding?"

"Only a little."

"Why didn't you go to Bradan?"

"He has enough to do tonight."

Falin slapped him across the thigh in reprimand. "Get in the tent," she commanded imperiously. "We can't have you falling off your horse tomorrow because you're too stupid to have it looked at. I'll go get Bradan." Falin stood up and grabbed his arm.

Khoury waved her off. "Don't bother, it isn't serious."

"It will be when your muscles cramp up tomorrow," Falin argued, tugging on him. He refused to move. She squatted down in front of him. "Fine, I'll get Archer," she threatened in a singsong voice.

Khoury had to laugh. "Okay, okay. *You* can bind it if you must. But don't bother Bradan or Archer with it. They can be such mother hens."

She laughed and rolled her eyes as she helped him into the tent.

CHAPTER 51
FALIN

Inside the tent, Falin watched Khoury drop to his knees on the sleeping blankets, slipping off the blue tabard with his good arm. Her throat was tight after hearing his story. Now she understood why the loss of Cara hit him so hard. She was glad for the distraction of a simple task.

The chain links were distorted, torn at the joint under his arm. As she helped him remove the hauberk, his sharp intake of breath told her it hurt more than he let on. The armor was surprisingly heavy. Falin was impressed that he could fight with all that weight.

She knelt down in front of him, untying the strings at the throat of his bloodied cotton shirt. When she removed it, the tangy scent of sweat mingled with blood sent a warm flush to her face. She examined the wound, his skin smooth under her gentle hands. A large purple bruise ran from his left nipple under his arm toward the edge of his shoulder blade. It was swollen and a small cut oozed blood where the tip had struck. It wasn't deep and the bleeding would stop on its own. She moved his arm in a circle, watching to see if the wound gaped. Then she pressed her palm to his ribs and circled it again with no grinding of broken bones.

"Motion's good. I'd put in a stitch so it doesn't keep opening. You'll be able to fight tomorrow, but it'll hurt."

"It always does," he replied. "Just do what you can." Khoury sat perfectly still as she cleaned the wound.

Shame heated her cheeks that a simple touch and Cara would have healed him already. Xantherus's suggestion that she was Cara's cast off pieces burrowed deep into her bones and robbed her of her pride. Her strength was lost in the riot of emotions that tumbled through her. Threading a small needle from her pouch with thread, she busied herself, closing the wound with a few small stitches and smearing it with one of Cara's ointments.

She looked up to find Khoury watching her curiously. "Thank you," he said, moving his arm gingerly back and forth.

Her restless hands demanded occupation. She retrieved clean bandages from another satchel. Khoury was quiet as she worked, and she wondered what he was thinking.

Maybe I shouldn't have made him talk about his past, she thought. How would I feel if someone killed Sorchia and I just ran? She couldn't imagine carrying that terrible shame, much less confiding it to anyone.

As she leaned over to wind the bandage around his chest, she overbalanced and fell against him. Lifting her head to avoid banging into his chest, she found her face so close to his their breath mingled. Her uncomfortable laugh did little to cover the sudden tension as she gazed into his eyes and put a hand to his chest to right herself.

"Never knew a clumsy Huntress before." His voice rumbled under her hand. The light-heartedness of his smile didn't dim the intensity in his stormy eyes. The firelight flickered over the planes of his cheek, reminding her how he'd kissed her once.

In a dream.

Only, now that she thought about it, it hadn't been a dream at all. The night after Rebeka's attack, she must have been in Cara's mind, sharing their…

She shook the blush from her cheeks but curiosity had taken hold. She didn't think she would return from the Keep. Not as she was now anyway. Unlike the others, she knew she only had now. Why shouldn't she taste that wild passion for herself?

She wrapped his chest snugly, trying to focus only on her task, but her mind kept replaying that fire lit scene.

How would it feel, she wondered, *to lay with him like that?*

A tense excitement curled in her chest at the memory of him kissing her.

After tying off the bandage, she couldn't keep her fingers from lingering on his skin, tracing the scars on his torso and arms, each one a mute testament to his violent life.

"Sorchia used to say our lives are written in our scars." She kept her eyes down, not sure what she wanted from him.

"Again, she's a wise woman," he murmured.

Was there something more in his voice? If there was, she wasn't sure she wanted to know.

Then she found the large, puckered scar that spanned his torso on the right. His breath caught at her touch but he said nothing. Curious, she examined it more closely. She'd never seen so much damage. Underneath the skin, at least three ribs were bulky and deformed. *Broken*, she thought. She followed the stiff scar with questioning fingers around his side to the back. The wound extended all the way to his spine and with some deformity in the bones of his back as well.

"Mothers' love!" she said.

Was this the wound he'd suffered as a boy?

Her finger gently traced the outline of the wound again, and she looked up to find Khoury's eyes searching her face. *What was he expecting to find?*

"It was a long time ago," he said, and then let the silence swallow them.

Needing to break the tension, she slid to the ground next to him and raised the cuff of her legging above her knee. "Well, mine's not big but it's a beauty," she said. A scar ran across her right thigh down to the middle of the calf, it was as wide as his thumb. "I got this trying to beat Rebeka at swords when we were eight. We didn't know where to find the practice swords so we got blades from the smithy." She laughed. "Big mistake."

He reached out a hand to touch her scar but drew back.

"Your turn," she said, pulling the legging back down.

Catching onto her game, Khoury pointed to a through-and-through wound on his right shoulder. "An arrow during my first city siege. Broke it off and fought for half a day. Hurt like a bitch for months."

She examined the wound closely and grinned. Then she lifted the hair off her neck where a burn scar ran from one shoulder up the back of her neck. "I fell backward into the cooking fire. Fighting with Rebeka, again." She laughed.

This time he joined in. They swapped scars for a while—the time when he nearly lost his finger, or when she fell out of a tree. Then Falin pulled her jerkin off her left shoulder.

"These three are from a hunting cat that wouldn't leave the village alone. I got three more across the belly, too. Was lucky it didn't gut me," she continued with bravado.

CHAPTER 52
KHOURY

Khoury froze at the sight of the three scars on Falin's shoulder. Cara had the same scars. His head spun for a moment. How could they have the exact same scars?

"What?" Falin asked, noting his stare. "It wasn't really as close as all that. I knew I'd win."

His tongue was glued to the roof of his mouth. He didn't know what to say. Even without the mystery of her connection to Cara, she seemed different tonight. Approachable. Alluring. He studied her in the lantern's soft glow, her features softened by shared laughter and her eyes bright with something that was neither pity nor disgust.

Then she leaned forward and placed a kiss on his scar. The one that embodied all his shame, all his terrible history. And something inside him wanted to reach out and pull her to him. But he did nothing. Said nothing.

She turned away from his silence and wound the extra bandages neatly, shoving them back in the satchel. Her eyes were focused on her hands, but he noticed the flush of pink on her neck and cheeks.

He'd never mentioned his past to anyone, nor had he ever compared battle scars. Most women shrank from the marks on his skin but, like Violet, Falin knew about battle and courage and death. She'd raised his spirits like another warrior might.

But why the sudden interest, he thought. It wasn't like her, all the talk and the tenderness. The battle at the tollhouse had been furious and short. He wanted to forget the sounds of sword against sword. He desired the feeling of soft strands tangling around his fingers. Did she feel the same need to be touched?

His hands covered hers to stop their busyness. She looked up and, finding him close, impulsively pressed her lips to his. Surprised, he let her kiss him at first. Then he cupped her face with a calloused hand and drew her closer, deepening the kiss himself. Tantalized by her taste, his tongue swept her mouth. Her breath caressed his cheek.

"Falin." His voice came out husky as she playfully kissed the corner of his mouth. "Wait." He pulled back, dropping his hands from her face to her shoulders.

She sighed, closed her eyes and pressed her forehead to his. "Don't worry," she whispered. "I know you love Cara. I just wanted to know…"

She turned her head away and Khoury watched her cheeks redden.

"Know what?" he asked.

Her eyes darkened with purpose as she stroked gentle fingers along the scars on his face. "Know what it feels like…to be touched, to be held."

He grabbed her hand, forcing her to meet his eyes. "Huntress, I…"

"We are kindred spirits, are we not? Warriors know there is only now." Her eyes met his with clear intent. What she was offering was not out of pity or naiveté. She was no love-struck girl.

He was stunned.

"I…am…more than honored, Huntress." His voice was husky with emotion but when he paused to clear his throat, she placed soft fingers across his lips.

"But you will not betray Cara. I understand." The disappointment in her voice wounded him.

"No, it's not that. There are no promises between Cara and me."

She quirked a skeptical eyebrow.

"No spoken promises, at any rate," he clarified, unable to look her in the eye. "I—"

"You're an honorable man, a loyal one. And she is…everything I am not." Her hand lifted his chin so he could meet her rueful eyes. "But Captain, don't fool yourself into believing you have nothing to lose. There are many whose days would darken were you to fall." Her green eyes held more than he'd ever guessed.

Khoury was torn. His father had never strayed from his mother, faithfulness was part of the family code. But need sparked a selfish passion in him. He snagged Falin's hand, pulling it close and pressing a kiss to her palm.

She only asked for now. Surely, a few hours wouldn't be wrong. She stroked his lower lip with her thumb, her eyes following the movement with hunger. Reaching out, he pulled her body roughly to his chest and kissed her with reckless desire. And she met him in equal measure, responding to every touch, echoing every breath. Never pressing further nor holding anything back.

He cursed life's cruelty to send him Falin now. Now, after he had allowed himself to care for Cara, after he had promised to keep her safe. He did love the white-haired woman, enough to die for her. But, here in his arms was someone he never expected. Someone who understood his pain and his rage and the cost of strength. Perhaps because she was a warrior, she touched him in a way that Cara never could. All he desired in that moment was to lose himself, delighting in her strength. To be only Mason.

But he couldn't. Not with the Black Keep looming over them.

"No." His voice was harsh with emotion. "This isn't right."

She moved off him with a soft smile. "You're right, of course. I shouldn't want to ruin that loyalty I admire. Though I must admit to disappointment." She gave him a cheeky grin that only tugged harder at him.

"There will be another man for you," he said, realizing only after he said it what thin comfort that was on the eve of battle.

Falin snorted with dark humor. "In truth, I came here with a completely different offer in mind," she said, retrieving her pouch from the furs where she'd left it. "You know now that my allegiance is wholly yours. I have made no vow to the Sisters of the Haven. Would you claim the Huntress they rejected, Captain? Will you let me swear fealty as your Sword?"

Now her questions made sense. All passion had fled from her eyes. She was no longer his would-be lover, but a warrior wanting a place to belong.

"I think we could make room for you," he teased.

She grinned and pulled a small ceramic pot from her pouch. Inside was a dark creamy substance. The aroma of bitter berries filled his nose.

She knelt before him, placed the pot on the ground, and the wolf-headed dagger made a cut in the pad of her thumb. Blood dripped into the pot, and she mixed it in with fingers that came away covered with a deep-purple dye.

"What's that?" he asked, though his attention was on curly golden tendrils that dangled near her neck.

"Blackthorns, razor berries, and blood. Now, hush." Suddenly serious, she cleared her throat and stared into his eyes.

"I swear by the love of the Old Mothers." She placed three dots of purple on her skin over her heart, below the mountain cat scars.

"And by the hate of the Thorns." She drew a line of purple down the blade of her knife.

"That I will be your sword." Grabbing his right hand palm up, she drew a line from his wrist to his middle finger with a smaller line crossing it.

"And your shield." She picked up his left arm, palm down, and drew the interlocked leaf pattern from her bracers.

"To give you truth, when you are blind." The three dots crested each of his eyebrows.

"And courage when you fear." She drew a rune he didn't recognize over his heart.

"And if the battle is lost." Her voice cracked just a little as she grabbed his left hand and dragged her knife across the pad, then did the same to her own hand.

"I will sing you home with honor." She pressed her palm to his, blood to blood, and kissed their joined hands, placing her forehead to their twined knuckles.

"This, Mason Khoury, is my solemn vow."

He waited until she sat up and he could see her face. "Huntress, your loyalty is an honor I don't yet deserve, but I will endeavor to earn it."

"I will get Cara back for you. That I promise." She hesitated and then kissed him one more time. This time only a gentle touch of lips, full of sadness and longing. He pulled her into his arms, wondering at how right she felt up against him, like they had already been lovers.

She laughed into his lips, pushed away and stood. "I will see you tomorrow." With a heartfelt Sister salute, she ducked out of the tent and into the night.

CHAPTER 53
CARA

Cara watched the layers of clouds scudding past the small window set high up in her room. She pulled the thin blanket closer against the perpetual chill of the Keep. She didn't withstand the cold as easily as she remembered. Over the last few days, she'd sifted through the images she could remember from Sidonius's mind to see if there was anything to help her escape. But there wasn't. A castle in the waves, a crib, an orange crystal point, and rainbow-colored mists were about all she could remember. She wondered if he was mad, or if maybe she was the mad one.

Footsteps in the hall warned her of Sidonius's approach. When the door opened, Cara refused to look at him, keeping her eyes on the sky though she felt the cool darkness that surrounded him even at a distance.

"Today is the day," he said with a cheerful tone.

Suspicion made her heart beat faster. "What do you mean?" Cara had dreaded the punishment she was sure would follow her brazen attempt to read him. Yet he did nothing beyond lock her in her room. Now that he stood before her, larger than life and cloaked with darkness, she knew the end had finally come.

"You'll see." He touched her shackles with his staff and they fell away. Then he motioned her through the door before him and followed, keeping his distance.

Her thoughts turned to Khoury and Sidonius's prediction that he would come. Part of her hoped he wouldn't. She kept the thin blanket wrapped around her shoulders, trying to hide the trembling that shook her slender frame. She told herself it was the cold. Glancing behind, she noted that his weathered face was once again smooth. His thin, bent frame had filled out. Manic energy shot out of his red-rimmed eyes. The oily smile he gave her sent shivers up her spine. And the cloak of dark energy had spread and lengthened.

Cara's heart sat heavy in her chest as she climbed the tower stairs with ponderous steps. Though she had always survived the draining ritual before, she knew she would die today. Absently, Cara gazed out the window that faced south on the final landing.

A cloud of dust caught her eye where the road met sky. "No," she breathed in panic.

"Yes," hissed a voice behind her ear carried on fetid breath. "He rides to your rescue. How touching. Unfortunately, none of you will survive the day." He gestured down in the courtyard near the barn and laughed.

A massive shape was curled up behind the curtain wall, hidden from the outside of the Keep. Cara squinted in the weak light unable to make out what it was. Then she recognized the shape. It was a dragon.

A trap!

Frantic to warn Khoury, she cast about for an escape.

"It's hopeless," Sidonius said with a slow smile that stole the warmth from her body. She stared into his arrogant face and felt her will drain away. How many years had she been helpless before him? Her eyes darted to the window again. But she wasn't that girl anymore. She couldn't escape but maybe there was something else she could do.

She bounced on her toes, wanting more than anything to get away from the darkness that surrounded him.

Anticipating her flight, he caught her arm in an iron grip. "Don't try anything. You've caused me enough trouble already."

He was so close she could smell the dust that pervaded his being. Close enough to touch. She grabbed him, holding tight to his hand and let the memories tumble through her. Strangely, her vision showed her Falin. He hadn't wanted Khoury at all. He was after the Huntress, and she saw again the orange crystal. She was distracted by her own magic as it throbbed with wanting to heal him. How could her magic want that when Cara despised his every breath?

Could he be healed? Could the entity be banished?

This time, Sidonius was prepared for her trick. He tore her hand from his arm and pushed her through the door. The once frail sorcerer sent her careening into the stone altar. Then he entered and closed the door behind him.

CHAPTER 54
KHOURY

The Keep loomed darkly against the pale sky though low clouds hid the sun. Khoury had feared Sidonius would bring storms. Of course, there was still time for that.

Archer rode next to him along with Bradan. And Falin. He'd lost that argument the night before when she'd painted courage on his chest. Then again, it felt right that she should be here with him. She caught his eye from beneath a silver helm and rolled her eyes. It had taken a heated argument and much cajoling by Bradan to get her to wear the damn thing. But if Sidonius knew she was here and wanted her, it was far better she remain inconspicuous. She'd relented finally, mumbling something about not trusting her.

Behind them stretched the company of warriors, almost two hundred and twenty by this morning's count. He wondered briefly how many he would lead home again.

The Keep looked as abandoned as he remembered, but Sidonius would never have let them get this far if he wasn't prepared. Caution was the order of the day. He stopped the corps more than an arrow's flight from the walls. The main gate stood wide open and he could see straight into the empty bailey. His eyes scanned the battlements for movement. The dark castle was quiet as a tomb.

He shifted uncomfortably in the saddle, trying to lessen the ache in his side. Falin had done a good job but the pounding pace they'd set that morning had done him no favors.

"Looks too easy," Bradan said.

"Probably is," Khoury agreed. "Archer, send a spare horse."

Archer galloped back toward the wagon and grabbed one of the extra mounts. Running the animal toward the open door, he slapped the horse's rump and pulled up to let it gallop through alone. Passing unharmed through the doorway, the horse slowed and wandered aimlessly about the bailey beyond the gate.

"I'd expected fire," Khoury grumbled. Though there had been no flaming ward on the main gate, he was sure one guarded the door to the hall. But he had a plan for that.

He signaled for the men to advance. Behind him, the mixed group of the Elite Guardsmen and mercenaries under Wallace's captain, a man by the name of Tolliver, followed on the right. Violet headed up the mercenary forces on the left. The ballistae and catapult trailed the main company with a small rearguard, accompanied by the supply wagons. Ellis was in charge of those.

They trotted to the gate wary of arrows, but none were launched. No sign of catapult or oil. No heads or weapons peeking through the embrasures. Khoury led his men straight into the open bailey where they were flanked by warriors in leather armor. The guards were few in number and not very skilled. Khoury's forces divided to defend the sides while leaving room between to allow more of his horsemen inside the wall. The captain wheeled his horse, shouting directions on both flanks. Beyond the melee, open lawn stretched the length of the stronghold without much in the way of cover. To the right, the bailey ended in sheer mountain cliffs rising upward. To the left, the wall circled around the Keep.

Under the leadership of Tolliver and Violet, half of the warriors dismounted for hand-to-hand. It was an eerie battle. Though swords clanged and horses neighed, their enemy uttered not one word. The fighting spilled from the central gate area to either side as the defenders' lines were broken.

Archer, with Bradan at his side, remained mounted in the center, picking targets out of the turmoil. And Falin, too, with bow in hand, sat atop her horse tucked in behind the Northerners.

Khoury glanced back out through the gate and waved to Ellis who held the siege machines and rearguard in the dead ground beyond the walls.

Khoury had expected greater resistance. Certainly, Sidonius knew he would bring at least a company against the stronghold. For a moment, Khoury wondered if he had been tricked. Perhaps Sidonius and Cara had fled to another hideout.

Falin pulled her horse closer to him as he watched his men clean up the remaining defenders. "What if she's not here?" he murmured.

The Huntress lifted her gaze to the looming towers, her head tilted as if listening. "She's here," she said with eerie surety. She pointed to the defenders as they fell silently before the trained Elite. "Recognize those looks?"

They had the same vacant expressions as the men in Iolair. "Conscripts," he said. These men had all been taken from their homes and bent to Sidonius's will. Renewed anger surged and he itched to get inside the Keep. Then, a shadow fell across the yard.

"Mothers' love," Falin swore beside him, then she bellowed, "Dragon!"

All eyes looked to the sky. A winged serpent soared over the bailey on leathery wings that stretched as wide as five wagons end-to-end. Its armor-plated underbelly gleamed dully. The beast roared so loud the stones of the Keep reverberated with the noise.

At the sight of the monster, Khoury's men fell back, and even he felt a knot of dread. But the wind wizard had warned them. He steadied his horse as best he could and tried to rally his men. The conscripts ignored the serpent and fought on while Khoury's men backpedaled in shock. The alarm spread quickly to the rear where Ellis and his men scrambled to ready the ballistae.

The dragon glided past the outer wall and banked into a lazy loop over the tundra, coming back over the battleground a second time.

The ballistae were ready by the time the dragon neared the large archway. At Ellis's signal, the thunk of the launchers echoed off the stones and the first large steel-headed spear sped past the dragon's nose. As the beast swerved, the second bolt caught it where shoulder met wing. The dragon screamed in pain and dropped heavily out of the air, crashing into a section of wall and landing in the bailey near the gate. A few defenders, as well as some of Khoury's men, were crushed. The beast roared with pain, and its thrashing tail scattered hunks of black stone from the broken wall across the battlefield.

Those still outside the gate drew back out of range, but the wounded dragon lay between Khoury's horsemen and safety. It struggled in the dirt, scraping at its wound. Finally, it managed to break off the shaft with an enormous clawed foot and howled, shaking the black stones once more. The serpent heaved to all fours, hissing angrily. Then it advanced slowly on the men, standing in the center of the bailey.

Khoury did his best to rally them. Archer had dismounted, bow in hand, and was attempting to outflank the beast for a better shot.

Unhurried, the dragon's flat head weaved slowly side to side. It had no fear of the men. Beyond it, Ellis's men were resetting the ballistae. Then the dragon reared back. Its giant mouth opened and took in a rush of air. Khoury knew what it intended.

"Take cover!" he yelled and leapt from his horse to duck behind a nearby piece of wall. Falin rolled over the same bit of rubble and landed on top of him as a jet of flame swept the yard. The captain shifted under her. "You okay?"

She chuckled. "Never better," and pushed off him with a feral grin.

Did nothing dampen her spirits? He could have used a dozen more like her. He peeked over the stone. His men were sprawled across the bailey, all still alive. There were even some horses milling about near the Keep proper. The ground was not even singed.

"Told you he wasn't going to let you burn," the captain said to the Huntress. "He's got bigger things planned."

"Not sure I'd count that as good news," she countered. "Now what?"

"Ellis needs to get that inner door. The catapult should be ready, but the damned dragon's in the way."

The beast sprayed the battleground with another gout of fire. They ducked down behind the blackened rubble, but again it was only a threat. Khoury's men hid behind scattered pieces of battlement, safe for the moment, but they were pinned down. They needed that door opened.

"We need to get the lizard out of the way."

"Okay," Falin said and she stood up.

"Do you have a plan?" he asked.

"Yeah," she said, peeking around the stone, "kind of. When that thing leaves, make sure you hurry up and get that door down. I don't know how long I can hold it."

"Wait, you can't just go out there."

"You just said it won't flame me, remember?"

Khoury's gut tightened. "Sacrificing yourself won't help Cara." His fists clenched, wanting to shake some sense into her.

"She's alive and she's scared, Captain. I can't tell you how I know that, but I do. I promised to help you get her back and that's exactly what I'm going to do." She reached out and laid her hand over his heart, over the symbol she'd traced in her own blood.

Courage, he thought sourly.

Then she unslung her bow and nocked an arrow. Another gush of flame roared over their heads.

"Find us soon. You know how I hate castles." Then she ran out from behind their little bit of rubble.

"Falin, no!"

She turned and winked at him, still only a stone's throw from where he crouched.

As she stood in the bailey, he feared the dragon would notice her, feared letting her out of his sight. The loss of Cara still burned, fueling the magic that came unbidden to his tongue.

"COME BACK," he Commanded her. He'd never cast so powerfully before, but he was more shocked that he'd done so without regard to her desires.

She stared at him quizzically, and he thought she'd obey. Then she shook her head and turned toward the dragon. He hadn't swayed her in the least.

She launched an arrow that struck the beast in the sensitive lining of its nose, assuring herself of its attention. Her next arrow bounced off its eyebrow. The creature rumbled with irritation. Its wings beat hard, lifting up its front end as the chest swelled with air. It was going to breathe again.

She jumped behind a piece of wall just before the gout of flame rushed by. Khoury didn't know where she'd found the horse but the next moment she charged by on horseback across the bailey, away from the gate. The creature took a step toward her but swayed, preparing to flame again.

Then the Huntress did the unthinkable. She pulled the helm from her head and tossed it away. In the hot updraft of wind from the creature's wings, her yellow hair splayed out like a banner.

The dragon gave a cry like a hawk, only deeper and far more terrible. Then, it charged after her. Cursing Falin's stubbornness, Khoury regretted bringing her along. He ran toward his men shouting instructions and waving a signal to Ellis. They had to get that door blown before the dragon returned.

CHAPTER 55
FALIN

The dragon took the bait just like she planned. But as her panicked horse bolted, Falin wondered if maybe she'd been a little hasty. Her mare ran flat out, ears pinned and white-rimmed eyes rolling. The scent of musty leather and soot wafted over them in puffs of hot air as the dragon gained ground. It was faster than she'd have thought with a wounded wing. She sent a quick prayer to the Mothers that Sidonius still wanted her alive, otherwise she was done.

In a burst of wind and pain, the dragon pounced on them, knocking Falin and the horse to the ground. Her bow skittered away across the barren dirt. The serpent crushed the borrowed mare in its talons as Falin rolled to face it, scrambling backward in the dirt. She couldn't get a good angle to pull her sword, so she reached for Khoury's knife as the predatory yellow eyes turned on her. Like a giant cat it crouched, its dark vertical pupils widening at her every move. Before she could scramble to her feet and run, it scooped her up in one front claw. The gaping mouth rushed down at her.

But the bite never came. Long sword-like teeth hovered dangerously close as the dragon roared its frustration. Hot, fetid breath blasted her with drops of saliva. The beast swiveled its long neck to look up at one of the towers, and she felt its rumbling growl.

When it looked down, she threw the small knife hoping it might drop her. The blade missed its eye by a handbreadth. But it stuck in the soft flesh of the corner drawing bloody tears. The beast roared in pain. Its claws tightened, squeezing the breath from her. Her ribs creaked.

The dragon shook its head violently, sending the knife to the dirt. The great beast leapt for the wall of the Keep and with claws and wings climbed to the far tower. Crawling up onto the parapet, the dragon dropped her on the stone platform. Her heart thudded painfully in her chest.

She crawled as far from the angry serpent as possible, gasping for breath. But it was worrying at its own wounds. Her hands went to her aching ribs. She could feel the bones grinding with each tortured breath. The dragon's talons had bent the metal plates inside her cuirass, their sharp edges digging into her body. She struggled out of the twisted armor and fell weakly to the platform, gulping for air and coughing blood.

A man emerged from the hole in the floor of the parapet. He was the man from the street in Iolair. The sorcerer from her nightmares. He said something in a foreign tongue to the dragon. It stared at him with unabashed hate and then launched itself from the tower with a distinctly disgruntled growl.

Sidonius turned to her.

Falin climbed shakily to her feet. Wrapping her arms around her ribcage to soothe the pain of breathing, she coughed again, tasting blood. Hopefully, Khoury had gotten the men into the hall because the dragon had no reason to spare any of them now.

"We meet again," the sorcerer said.

Falin said nothing. He seemed larger inside his black robes, swollen like the bloated carcass of a drowned man she'd once seen.

"You're right," he said into the silence, "there's no time to waste on pleasantries. Come. We have work."

Falin didn't move.

He turned back with a scowl. "It's useless to fight me. Come along."

He was right. Weaponless and badly hurt, she had no hope of winning but something in her resisted. Then, she remembered Cara somewhere inside the black stones, trapped and afraid. Cara needed her, and she'd promised Sorchia and Khoury that she'd keep her safe. So she limped toward the stairs, intending to go peacefully.

That is, until she looked into the yawning dark. A shock of terror froze her in place. *I'm sorry, Cara,* she thought. *I can't wait for Khoury in there.*

When the wizard came up behind her, she sprang at him in desperation. Pain flared in her chest as she latched onto his staff, pulling it toward her to unbalance him as she tried to sweep his feet. But his legs were rooted like a tree in the ground. He dragged her close as if she weighed nothing.

"Fool. You cannot fight me." He grabbed her wrist with fingers far stronger than she would have guessed. The twisting pressure on the small bones brought tears to her eyes, forcing her to release the staff. Then he twisted the arm further, sending pain up into her shoulder. Her knees buckled as the bones ground together, crumbling under the pressure. Pain darkened the edges of her vision.

He turned then and simply dragged her down the stairs by her wrist, each step sending new waves of pain through her crippled arm and crushed ribs.

When they reached the first landing an explosion sounded from below, shaking the stones of the tower. Rage suffused his face, and he cursed. Stalking to the window, he relaxed slightly. Falin saw the dark shadow of the dragon's bulk swoop awkwardly past. "The dragon will finish the slow ones and the guards inside will give me enough time to finish."

"Finish what?" she wheezed. She needed to understand why. Why he had ruined their lives.

"The spell, foolish girl. I can finally finish the spell properly."

He yanked her roughly into a round room with writing on the floor. Cara waited atop a stone alter, chains dangling from her wrists and ankles. Falin's insides quivered with weakness as she recognized the room of her nighttime torment. Her nightmares were finally about to become reality; she knew what came next.

When Cara turned her head, Falin saw she had a blackened eye and wondered what the rabbit could have done to earn it.

Cara gasped at the sight of her. "No, not her. Please, Father. I'll do anything."

Ignoring Cara's pleas, Sidonius tossed the Huntress to the floor in front of him. She glared up at him with defiance, cradling her useless hand against her body.

"What spell are you talking about?" If she was going to die, she needed to know why.

"A kind of healing," he replied. "And the freedom I've desired for longer than you've been alive." He paced the circumference of the room making sure all was in order, adjusting the scroll on the pedestal and situating the crystals with care.

"You mean immortality?"

"Who told you that?" he hissed.

"You cannot change the order of things," she said. "Death is part of life. No one is spared."

"I will be," he said. "I would have been timeless years ago except the spell didn't work. All this time, I thought the incantation was flawed or perhaps I was casting it wrong. That is, until I saw you. Strange your companions never saw the resemblance." He looked back and forth between them, studying them. "It is quite uncanny."

Falin flicked her eyes to Cara's pale face, trying to see the similarity he claimed existed. The one she hoped not to find. Cara was studying her face as well.

"You don't need her," Cara urged. "Let her go."

Falin's heart broke at Cara's words, knowing that if either of them were to survive, it should be Cara—the original.

“Oh, but I do,” Sidonius said, his eyes locked onto Falin’s, his voice hard. “Now, get up there.”

Even as broken as she felt, Falin rebelled. She spat at him and watched the bloody spittle roll down the front of his clothes. When he took a threatening step toward her, she staggered to her feet preparing to meet his onslaught.

“Defiant to a fault.” He sneered and shoved her hard, sending her flying backward and almost onto the altar. “This is exactly why I excised you.” A bout of coughing kept her busy as he lifted her the rest of the way up and tied her wrists and ankles.

CHAPTER 56
KHOURY

Ellis's oil and stone catapult shot was perfect. Khoury stepped over the rubble of the front door. Inside the darkened Keep, he found another knot of Sidonius's bewitched guards. Drawing two swords, the captain attacked the nearest man. His side throbbed with each stroke, but even worse was the gathering fear in his heart. Sidonius had both women; time was running out.

Archer charged in from Khoury's left, sweeping his two-handed sword in a wide arch to force the conscripts back. A guard lunged at Khoury from the right, and he easily parried the strike as Violet charged in between the captain and Archer, swinging her blades in a wide arch. One unfortunate guard was too slow and went to the ground, his belly sliced wide. The three mercenaries forced the guards away from the doorway, opening up more space to bring in men from outside. A third mercenary stepped up, holding two attackers at bay with sword and shield as Bradan slipped in behind Khoury, his mace momentarily useless.

Khoury stabbed another guard and pressed his advantage, using the body to shield him as he slid along the wall toward the rear door. Beyond it was the inner courtyard, the library and the stairs to what had to be Sidonius's private wing of the Keep. Bradan stepped into the hole Khoury left behind and more men came in behind them, escaping the roar of dragonfire in the bailey. Soon Khoury's men had overpowered the small cadre of conscripts.

As they gathered in the hall to press on, the inner door burst open and more guards rushed in. Khoury's men were ready and they held their ground. Gaining control of the doorway, they forced the guards back out into the hall. Khoury kept close to the wall on the right, trying to bypass the guards and get to the tower. Parrying a slash from the nearest man's sword, he kicked an undefended knee and sent the man to the floor. Skewering the guard with one blade, he parried a second who jumped into the opening.

"Archer, Bradan," he shouted, "this way." He jerked his head toward the right as he hugged the wall. Bradan nodded, and he and Archer followed.

Khoury swung his double blades with increasing fury. Every step took too long. Haste quivered in his chest. He had to find them. He rounded the corner, relieved to see the hallway to the stairs was relatively empty. Archer and Bradan were behind him, still embroiled with the main group of guards. Archer called to him to wait, but Khoury pressed on, driven by the urgency in his heart. He hurried up the hall, swinging carelessly at anyone in his way, until he was beyond them, taking the stairs two at a time.

CHAPTER 57
CARA

Excised her? Cara didn't understand what he meant, but a cold dread settled in her bones. Was Falin the "her" Sidonius had rambled about, the one he needed? The one Khoury would bring?

As Sidonius took his place at the pedestal, Cara braced for the pain. Would the forest still be there to soothe her fear, or was that gone too? Surprisingly, Sidonius pulled a crystal wand from within his robes and instead of the guttural chanting began to hum.

What new evil was this?

He admired the gleam of light through the shard with a grim smile. As long as her forearm, its smoky-orange planes tapered to a fine point. She'd seen it before. In his memories.

"The soul knife," Falin said.

How did she know what that was?

Such wondering was cut short as Sidonius wove the wand through the air over them. It glowed with power as his humming grew louder.

Soul knife, Cara thought, struggling to force the pieces into a pattern. Bradan claimed she was missing part of her soul. Had Sidonius done it? And what did Falin know about this? She squirmed, trying to get a hand close to Falin's skin.

"You see, daughters…" Sidonius said, watching the glowing

oranges trails of smoke.

"I'm not your daughter and neither is she." Falin lunged futilely against her bonds. He stepped out of reach without breaking the cadence of his movement, and she dropped back to the stone table with a groan, but not before Cara had shifted her arm closer to the Huntress. She could almost touch Falin's arm.

Sidonius scowled at them, sending a familiar quake of fear through Cara.

"You're right. You were…an unexpected windfall. This ritual requires magical blood. Kidnapping a grown sorcerer would have been far too troublesome."

Sidonius continued moving the crystal, the trails of light lingering like letters in the air.

"When the Barakani Regent hired me to dispose of Prince Gideon and his Corthan wife, the contract required their demise. But it made no provisions for their newborn, a child who would grow into her impressive magical lineage. So, I took the baby. After all, if one is to live forever, a few decades is nothing." Sidonius moved to the head of the table.

"Khoury is coming," Falin whispered as Cara struggled to touch her skin.

She despaired at the once-reassuring words. It was one thing for Father to kill her, but she couldn't bear to think of what he'd do to the captain. She hid her strangled sob behind the pale curtain of her hair, trying in vain to push away the despair that clung to her heart like frost. She had to do something, but she had no strength.

Strength, she thought. *I could borrow some.*

"Let me touch you," she whispered to the Huntress so softly it was little more than a breath. The glowing wand passed over them, and her head swam dizzily. The world shimmered like a dream.

And then Falin shifted, pressing her bare arm into Cara's palm.

She felt the Sister's soothing strength like a balm. She was here to protect Cara. For Khoury's sake. And that influx of courage blunted

Cara's fear and despair. The contact also brought memories. Memories of Sidonius in an alley, of Khoury in battle, Archer with his bow, and of another sorcerer talking about broken souls. She opened her eyes to see green eyes staring back at her, willing her to understand.

This woman wasn't her Sister at all. Falin was the missing piece.

And Sidonius was going to join them into one mind again. And then kill them!

Falin's face faded to hazy shadows and swirling colors, but her thoughts remained. *Without me, you weren't an adequate sacrifice. Once he is done with this spell, he can finally finish the other.*

But it won't fix him, Cara sent back through the growing fog of colors. *Sidonius's soul is nearly gone. Only the darkness will remain and be immortal.*

Then we have to make sure, one way or another, he doesn't finish this spell.

The Huntress's meaning was clear.

CHAPTER 58
FALIN

Fear washed over Falin when Cara touched her and she struggled against the overwhelming tide. Was that how Cara had kept her from killing Rebeka—the power of unfamiliar remorse? She'd known better what to expect this time. Even though she'd lost the room with the table to a panorama of colored mist, she could communicate with Cara without Sidonius knowing. Still tied and weaponless, Falin struggled to find some advantage.

The spell he cast took away her pain, but it wasn't long before she lost all feeling. She was weightless, without a body. She sensed the sorcerer as a heavy, dark presence to her right. Cara was here in the mists with her. Their connection made Cara stronger, but the emotions she threw at Falin felt nearly crippling. Was this how Cara felt all the time? No wonder she was useless.

A memory of Bradan's lectures floated through her mind. He had tried to stress the use of discipline to make her magic work. To control it. If Falin was her strength, then her magic had been flowing unguided, like a sluice without a gate. Perhaps together, they could attack Sidonius with magic. But how?

It was then Falin noticed another presence in the mist. It hovered over the two women, around them. Warm and kind, it seemed to fret over them, eager for restoration, reminding Falin of the Mothers when they'd urged her to save Archer. Was this another fractured part of them? Or was it something else, like the dark presence that inhabited Sidonius? The kind presence paged through her memories as well as Cara's with feather-light fingers, sorting dream and nightmare, castle and woodland, placing images side by side, and replacing chaos with gentle order.

A soul who likes to fix things, Xantherus had said.

But Falin didn't want Cara to know about the kisses she'd shared with the captain, about how she'd offered herself to him. And so, she pushed those memories down and hid them. She was strong enough to keep them out of Cara's awareness. At least for now.

Then Sidonius began a guttural chanting and Falin, whatever part of her remained, was tossed like a ship in a storm. Violent orange light pushed and tugged at her and Cara. Their minds clashed together helter-skelter like lost pages shoved haphazardly into a book and lashed closed. Dreams and memories assaulted her. Landscapes merged and swam, and faces, too. Torn in two directions, she was a dichotomy of views—at once helpless and strong, timid and fierce, magical and physical.

In the midst of the kaleidoscope, Falin recognized a placid pool and the ghost of a black wolf. This time when she looked into the mirroring water, her own face stared back. Boundaries of ego collapsed. She didn't know who she was anymore, victim or Huntress. The kindness enveloped them, trying to mend them into the unity they should have had, searching for common ground they could share.

Together, they clung to a singular thought: Khoury was near and on his way.

CHAPTER 59
KHOURY

He had to find them. And soon. Fear for the women drove Khoury up the stairs, two at a time, until he arrived breathless at the highest tower room. The door stood ajar but his attention was caught by the southern facing window. Below him, the courtyard burned and the dragon paced near the main gate, keeping out of sight of Ellis's guard. Even if he managed to kill Sidonius now, they were trapped within the walls. The charred bodies littering the courtyard attested to the enormity of their losses already.

Forcing his mind to the present, Khoury crept to the door and peeked in. The sorcerer stood near an altar holding a glowing orange wand. Rainbow mists filled the air, swirling at the direction of the wand. But the women were nowhere to be seen. He cursed his luck. Where were they?

Then Sidonius stopped chanting, dropping his arms with a flick of the wand that went suddenly dark. The mists stopped swirling. The colors froze in midair. Wisps melted into rain that dripped onto the altar and where drops fell, they coalesced. Khoury watched in amazement as a body formed. A naked woman with newborn skin and wavy golden hair streaked with white arose from the droplets of color.

"And here you are," Sidonius said, startling Khoury from the mesmerizing sight. "The two are now one."

The sorcerer put the crystal wand in his robes and checked the woman on the altar. He felt for a pulse and eyed her intently. He shook her but she didn't wake. The sorcerer grunted but turned back to the pedestal at the foot of the altar.

Though he'd just seen her materialize from mist, Khoury thought he recognized her face. He couldn't say for sure. What had Sidonius just said? The two are now one. Two meaning Cara and Falin? And now one woman on the altar.

As Khoury's mind struggled with the puzzle, the sorcerer took his position, straightening himself with a satisfied smile. When he started reading from the scroll before him, Khoury felt energy gather in the room. Then Sidonius drew a green stone from beneath his robes. It glowed warmly and a keening, like ghosts in the burial cliffs of home, echoed against the walls. The woman on the table writhed but remained unconscious.

This was Sidonius's plan, make one person of two and then? The ritual Cara had talked about. The one that killed everyone but her. This time, she wouldn't survive.

Memories rose in his mind. Blood on satin. His mother pierced through the heart with the arrow meant for him. Panic nipped at his heels. There was no time for thinking.

Khoury burst into the room, swords drawn. He let anger swell, drawing in the power. It filled his throat with hate and he bellowed, **"SIDONIUS, STOP!"** The sorcerer's chanting ceased and the gathering magic flickered like a candle in the rain.

Khoury could have cheered, but a dark fog rose around the sorcerer, covering him like a cloak. Black tendrils guided the sorcerer's hand to his staff where it leaned against the pedestal. Khoury closed the distance between them but not before the touch of his staff released Sidonius. He deflected Khoury's first attack with the same inhuman speed he'd shown in Iolair. The moment his staff struck metal, the sword shattered and Sidonius began to chant again.

The captain needed to stop the sorcerer, but how?

Falin's words came back to him: *Still the hands, silence the tongue.* He focused all his fear and anger, letting it rise into his throat.

"SILENCE," Khoury intoned. The word reverberated with a strength he didn't realize he had.

Sidonius stared at him. His mouth continued to move but nothing emerged.

Seizing the opportunity, the captain swung his other blade. But another strike from the staff broke the second sword as well.

Then the sorcerer coughed as dark smoke flowed out of his mouth and nose. Again, the captain's hold was broken.

"A Barakani noble," Sidonius said, eyeing Khoury like a prize. "And powerful. Had I but taken you first, I'd be immortal now."

So it was immortality he was after.

"Perfect." Sidonius chuckled. "Whether she will complete it or not, now you are here and my success is assured." Sidonius held Khoury's gaze as he began the incantation again, repeating the guttural words over and over.

The magic gathered more quickly. Something pulled at the center of Khoury's chest. Wielding his broken blades like knives, he attacked again. Sidonius kept chanting as he sidestepped, but not quite fast enough. One blade sliced his cloak down to skin and muscle, and a dark mist, rather than blood, leaked out. Supernatural chill tingled over Khoury's arm where the mist touched him.

There was evil magic here. Magic that made blades useless. Khoury let the power rise again, hoping to stall until Archer arrived. He was sure the Northerner was only a few steps behind.

"SILENCE," he Commanded again, putting as much force behind his words as he could. He'd never had the desire to control others like this, but he desperately needed it now.

Sidonius's chant faltered as he choked to get the words out. The magic waned again, relieving the pressure in Khoury's chest. The captain attacked with the broken blades, hoping for a lucky strike.

Any wound would wear on Sidonius. But with the speed of a striking snake, the sorcerer reached out and grabbed Khoury by the throat.

His long fingers closed, choking off Khoury's air, preventing him from Commanding again. He thrust the captain back, arching him over the altar where the woman lay as still as death. Khoury tried to bring his broken swords up to slice the arm that held him. A single word from the sorcerer and searing pain shot through him, wringing a strangled groan from his closed throat. His swords fell from twitching fingers as electric tongues licked his limbs. The one that dropped from his half-raised arm nicked the woman's arm drawing a single drop of blood.

Khoury thrashed wildly, kicking out, hoping for a soft groin or a knee. But the sorcerer wasn't about to lose hold of him. Sidonius lifted him off the floor with inhuman strength. Khoury's hands tingled and his feet dangled uselessly as his eyes darkened. He could barely hear Sidonius begin chanting again over the blood rushing in his ears.

The incantation wrapped itself around Khoury's heart, his very soul, and dragged him piece by piece toward the swirling vortex that had grown from Sidonius's wound. He fought against the tide, shoring up his will, but tendrils pulled away like gossamer threads disappearing inside Sidonius.

He forced his eyes open, wondering if his sacrifice would save the girl, but she also writhed as smoky tendrils arose from her and stretched toward the sorcerer. Time lost all meaning as little by little he felt himself broken and drawn into the vortex. He clung to life by sheer strength of will, hoping to hear Archer at the door, the whoosh of feathers, the thunk of the arrow. But he heard nothing, and the sorcerer never stopped his chanting. Khoury grew cold; his energy waned. Soon, he'd disappear completely into that darkness and he'd lose everything. He had failed her.

CHAPTER 60
FALIN

When the storm finally passed she returned to herself, bruised but still alive. Her thoughts flitted as lightly as sparrows, unwilling to upset the fragile balance of her awareness. Sensations returned like light at dawn, gradually and yet noticed all at once. She focused on the frigid air kissing her skin and the lumps of fabric beneath her back while the glowing colors faded to the black of closed eyelids. Gratitude swelled as a long breath granted her the feel of air in her nose. She was back.

But not out of danger, she thought.

She felt a tugging in the center of her chest that she recognized as the spell that would transfer her energy to the sorcerer. She couldn't let him win. She needed to fight back but the part of her that had been a hunter was wary of showing too much. Shouts and the scuff of boots on stone nudged their way into her awareness.

Someone was fighting. She kept her face still as she scanned what she could through shuttered eyes.

She recognized the blue tabard that swam into view. But the creature that held him looked nothing like the sorcerer. Above Sidonius's human form, around him, encompassing him was a great ghostly shape, the darkness Cara had sensed in him all along. But now, on the verge of its birth into their world, its malevolent intent buffeted her in waves.

The creature's long hands picked at the glow around the captain and, she noted belatedly, herself. As Khoury tried to attack with his broken swords, Sidonius countered with more magic, and she cringed with sympathetic pain. One of his swords clattered to the altar where she lay. She felt the prick of its edge.

A blade!

She wriggled her wrists ever so slightly, sure that the sorcerer's attention was completely occupied by the struggling captain. She wasn't chained!

Mothers' love! Some luck at last.

She tried not to think about how easily the sorcerer lifted the captain into the air one-handed. Her fingers sought the weapon and slid it into her palm. The pulling in her chest became a pain. She didn't have much time.

The sorcerer was occupied with Khoury, but she needed him to come closer. She'd been badly injured by the dragon, and she had no idea how well she was healed. She felt the third presence trying to mend her, but the vortex within the creature was draining her magic steadily.

Just two more steps and you're mine, she thought.

CHAPTER 61
ARCHER

Cursing Khoury for a fool, Archer raced down the hall after his captain. He sheathed his sword and unslung his bow reaching for an arrow as he ran. An eerie whine floated down the stairs, and he prayed he wasn't too late. He raced up to the final landing where the door stood open and oppressive heat flowed out in waves. Tortured howls echoed off the walls and ghostly black smoke whirled like a tempest about the circular room. There was a woman on an altar in the center, and at her feet was the sight Archer dreaded—Sidonius dangled the limp body of Khoury from one uplifted hand.

An eerie darkness enveloped the two men, translucent but moving as if alive. It made the hair on Archer's neck stand on end. Pushing down the urge to race into the room, Archer backed up to the wall and lifted his bow. He took careful aim, pulling the string to his chin. Forcing calm, he found the silence within his breathing, the space between his own heartbeats. The noise and heat faded from his awareness as he searched for the perfect shot. The tension of the bow felt good in his hand as his eye followed the length of the shaft to his enemy.

Khoury was in the way. From this vantage, he couldn't kill the sorcerer, unless one of them moved. Archer waited for the shot, but as the captain's head fell back, he realized they were out of time.

With icy calm, Archer coughed, risking surprise to create opportunity.

And opportunity came. The sorcerer turned a curious face toward the door, moving Khoury out of his line of sight. In that instant, the bowstring thrummed as one blessed black-feathered arrow sped away.

But Sidonius moved like lightning, stepping forward with a flick of his hand. The door slammed shut in Archer's face just as a breathless Bradan joined him on the landing.

Had the arrow found its mark?

"He's got Khoury," Archer said.

"And the girls?"

"There's at least one woman in there. But Bradan," Archer turned haunted eyes to the shaman, "Sidonius has a dark spirit aiding him."

CHAPTER 62
FALIN

She heard the familiar twang in almost the same instant the sorcerer stepped up to the table. She ignored the slamming door. Sidonius was within reach. Without wasting another minute, she rolled to the side and lunged for him. The pain was gone, but her limbs were clumsy and weak like a newborn colt's. She reached out with her hand to grab his robes, hauled herself close, and thrust the broken blade up under his ribs.

With a hiss like steam, an icy blast of power chilled her hand. Her healing sense burst to her awareness. This was not Sidonius she fought but the incarnate darkness he had once summoned. The creature had been whittling away at him all these years. But now, the ritual didn't feed the sorcerer, instead it strengthened the intruder.

There was no way to kill the sorcerer while the darkness overshadowed him. She had to push the creature back through and close the gap before Sidonius could be killed.

We might be able to save him, a small part of her thought hopefully.

She thrust that foolishness away.

Not knowing how the magic worked, she tried to recall all Bradan had said. She groped for the kind presence she had felt, surely that was the healer in her. Forcing the magic to obey was more difficult. She clung to Sidonius with hands that glowed to her supernatural sight. Liquid gold flowed beneath his skin much like the icy black had trickled into Falin in Iolair. It warmed and strengthened as it went, draining her of what little energy she still possessed. Sheer stubbornness steeled her to the task.

Sidonius's spell took more from Khoury as she resisted. Healing the sorcerer was killing the captain faster, but it couldn't be helped. Sidonius—or rather the dark entity—had to be stopped.

Hold on, Khoury, she thought.

Soon she noticed the vortex shrinking. The darkness encompassing Sidonius shrank also, pulling back from his arms and head. He dropped the now-limp Khoury to the ground and put both hands around her throat as if the darkness sensed her plan.

Then the door behind her opened with a crash. She didn't turn. Her only focus was closing the wound. She recognized the groans of Bradan and Archer as the spell latched onto them, further weakening the pull of the spell on her, and on the captain.

Archer raced over, awkwardly swinging his huge sword, trying not to hit her. Sidonius released one hand to deflect the strike as Bradan chanted his call to the spirits. She felt rather than saw the cool mist gather around their ankles.

With Sidonius still holding her by the neck, she slipped a hand through the torn cloak and laid her fingers over the wound. Her healing power flared as soon as she touched his skin. She drew the edges together, her magic stitching them as simply as stitching Khoury's side. The leaking coldness lessened. The darkness had withdrawn. It was working, though it was exhausting. When the creature had retreated to within the confines of the sorcerer's physical body, it was time.

Wait, said Cara's small voice. *He can be saved.*

You promised, Falin *accused. You promised not to stop me.*

She felt the wide-eyed girl inside her relent. Taking the captain's broken sword in her free hand, she stabbed Sidonius again, this time feeling the warm wetness of blood. Now sure that the darkness was contained, she reached up and slit the sorcerer's throat.

CHAPTER 63
ARCHER

Archer thought he recognized Falin's angry scowl on the woman's face as she slit Sidonius's throat. The sorcerer coughed once in surprise and was dead before he struck the floor. A burst of fetid energy exploded from within the dark robes when he landed, knocking them all backward.

Bradan sat up first, eyes wide with horror as a ghostly squall whipped around him, tugging at his beard and his hair. "Do you feel them?" he breathed at Archer. "Can you hear them?"

Woozily, Archer picked himself up. "Hear who?"

"Every soul he stole," Bradan said. "So many…so many deaths."

The chieftain sounded like Cara. But Archer was more interested in the living. He scanned the room as Bradan climbed unsteadily to his feet. The girl lay unconscious nearby. Bradan listened for her heart and nodded at Archer. She lived.

Archer stepped over the spent body of Sidonius sprawled on the floor where he'd fallen next to the altar. And behind him, near the pedestal, was the captain. Shock shivered through Archer's limbs at the sight of Khoury crumpled on the floor like a discarded shirt.

He hurried to him and rolled Khoury onto his back, searching for signs of life. The captain's neck bore purple-red welts and the blue tint of his lips was a faint echo of the eyes that stared out of his pale face. There was no breath, no heartbeat to be found.

Cold guilt set Archer's heart to pounding as he shook the captain by the shoulders. "Wake up! C'mon, Khoury."

Khoury's limbs flopped like wet rags, laying where they fell.

"No," Archer murmured as the inevitable bumped up against his fading hope. Tension hummed from his chest to his head, making him dizzy and frantic at the same time. "No, you bastard! Why didn't you wait?" Angrily, he gripped the torn blue tabard and shook the captain again hard. But there was no response.

"I was too late," Archer whispered mournfully, then his voice turned hard as he let anger comfort him. He frowned down at his lifeless friend. "You promised me, you bastard. Not to be so reckless."

Bradan laid a fatherly hand on Archer's shoulder, and the anger fled. Tears blurred his sight.

"He promised not to leave me behind."

"No one can promise that," Bradan said, softly. "But I know you were as good a brother to him, as he was to you."

Archer felt lost. What would he do now that Khoury was gone? He had no urge to go back to the Swords without the surly Southerner.

Maura's face swam in his mind, and he ached for home.

The woman who'd killed Sidonius stirred with a moan, interrupting his thoughts. She murmured deliriously as Archer joined Bradan at her side, wiping his damp cheek with an angry hand. There was stark white hair amidst the woman's gold locks.

"Cara?" he asked, but then he thought of her face as she killed Sidonius. "Falin?"

CHAPTER 64
CARA

She heard her name and struggled toward it. A gentle touch on her cheek gave her focus, and the mind followed the senses. She was totally spent, wanting nothing more than a soft bed and sleep. Then someone helped her sit up.

"Falin?"

She groaned, unable to form words around her thick tongue. Her thoughts were blurred. She forced her eyes open.

"It's Bradan, girl."

She recognized the shaman's bearded face. His brown eyes were haggard.

"What…" It was a croak not a word. She coughed to clear the dryness of her throat. "What happened?" Another face came into view with red hair and beard. She knew him, too. "Archer." Relief surged in her heart.

"Who are you?" he asked, and then she noticed the dampness on his haunted face.

Something was wrong. Why didn't he remember her?

Her eyes fell to her hands. Foreign hands, their flesh pink and smooth. She turned them over with horror. Where was the burn from her amulet? Where was Rebeka's revenge across her palm? Only the tiny wine-red drops from a small nick on her arm marred the baby-new skin.

The altar. The darkness.

Snippets of memory returned as Bradan lifted a dress from the dusty stone and helped her into it.

Then she remembered the captain. "Khoury?"

The men were silent. She cast about for the memories. When had she seen him last? Iolair? No. The dragon? No, after that.

She slid her feet under her and pushed to standing with hurried foreboding, slapping at Bradan's offered hand. "We can stand well enough," she snapped, swaying as she sifted through jumbled memories.

He had been here. She remembered his voice—his groans. Her frantic eyes searched the scattered debris. She saw Sidonius's lifeless body and felt neither sorrow nor satisfaction at his end. But next to him was the captain.

"Khoury!" Shock tore the anguished gasp from her lips. She hurried to his side and crumpled to her knees, pressing her palms to his cheeks. "Mason, wake up."

She willed the warmth to flow, like it had for Archer. Where was the healing that had burst awake for the thorn-cursed sorcerer? But she felt nothing. Worse, there was nothing beneath her fingers but cool skin and a terrifying emptiness where Khoury should have been. He was not here.

She could heal the wounded but apparently the dead were beyond her power.

It should have been me, the huntress hought. *I promised to save you for him.*

Archer knelt across from her and reached out to respectfully close the captain's eyelids. "I'm sorry," he said, tawny eyes full of regret.

Falin's heart echoed his pain. She'd failed Khoury more than Archer had.

"It's not your fault," she said. "We did this."

I did this, her inner huntress corrected, knowing it was her bid to push the creature back into its own world that had sacrificed the captain.

Cara blamed herself but blamed Falin more. All she had wanted was to stop the deaths, and now her captain had joined the list of her sins. She missed the feel of his lips on hers, the scent of him on her cloak. Desperate, she took his hand and pressed his palm to her cheek, needing to feel his touch one more time.

He'd been a fixed point around which Cara had revolved from the moment she'd met him in the dungeons below. She traced the faint scar on Khoury's temple, the first one she'd noticed. The coolness of his skin sent a pang of finality through her.

"Mason, damn you," she whispered. "I told you we'd miss you." Sorrow pricked her eyelids but no tears came. "Who's going to pull us out of the river now?"

She grappled with her new reality. She had two memories of everything and each thump of her heart jarred her frail body. She shivered in every fiber.

Then a calm strength flowed through her. The part of her that knew death was part of life stepped up. "First things first," she whispered.

She placed her hand over the rune on the captain's chest. Then, she gripped his left hand in hers, feeling the small scratch she'd left on his palm last night. It pained her to note there was no mirroring wound on her own hand. Her vow was just another thing that had been lost.

She kissed their clasped hands, the scent of smoke and dust and iron branding itself on her soul, and she laid her head on the blue and silver tabard. "And if the battle is lost, I will sing you home with honor."

She took a breath, but her throat was too thick for singing. The more she tried, the closer the tears threatened, and she would not spoil the dirge with weeping. She swore she would fulfill that promise, but not there in the tower.

Behind her, soldiers entered the room. "Archer, the dragon left."

She recognized the voice as Violet's.

"One moment it was breathing fire, the next it flew away. Is the sorcerer dead?"

"Yes," Archer said softly.

Awkward silence filled the space. Then Violet whispered with disbelief, "Is that the Captain?"

"Khoury has fallen." Archer's voice was tight with grief.

Silence followed. "He was a good commander. We're building pyres for the dead. I'll have some men come get him."

They want to burn him? Indignation flared. Her fingers pressed into the rings of his chainmail.

But Archer spoke before she could lash them with her thoughts. "No." His voice broke, escaping control. "He belongs with the Clan. I will take him there for his final rest."

She heard boots leave the room but was too numb to move.

Bradan's strong hands lifted her to her feet. "Come downstairs. Archer will bring Khoury." She leaned into the shaman's solid chest. "And what do we call *you* now?"

She glanced back at Archer as he bent down to put Khoury's body over his shoulder. "We have many names and none. Call us what you will."

CHAPTER 65
ARCHER

Archer found Bradan at the window above the smoky bailey. "We set Khoury up in that room off the hall." Archer's heart was already heavy so he avoided looking down. They'd sustained significant losses and the pyres were stacked taller than his men. But after all he'd seen, Archer knew Khoury had been right—Sidonius needed to be stopped. He lingered next to the older man in silence, remembering a time before Connor's death when they'd been close. Then he noticed the crystal wand in Bradan's hands. As long as a dagger, the chieftain fingered its smooth sides.

"Is that it?" Archer asked.

Bradan lifted sad eyes to Archer and nodded. "I think so."

"So you'll fix them? Put them back the way they were?" Hope lightened his heart but only for a moment.

Bradan pressed his lips together. "I can't."

"With that scroll…."

Bradan stopped him. "It's not that. This is who she was born to be."

"But you can't leave them like this," Archer had no idea how the women would live, stuck inside the same body like that.

"The spirits have decided. She must return to the life that was stolen."

Archer rubbed his eyes with hands that smelled of rosemary and myrrh. It felt as though he'd lost all of them at once. Not just Khoury, but Cara and Falin, too.

The woman they'd found in the tower was disturbingly familiar and yet strange. Her blonde and white-streaked mane was odd enough, but one eye was green and the other icy blue. It was eerie how those mismatched eyes never seemed to meet his gaze even when they looked right at him. The woman had said little to him while they washed Khoury's body, preparing it with herbs and oils. She refused to let him remove the berry stains that adorned the captain's hands, chest and brow. Khoury's forearm was painted with the same thorns that adorned Falin's bracer. And it was Falin's low voice that sang a haunting dirge for the captain in the language she'd used to save Archer from the Thorns. And when she'd finished her song, she sat staring at Khoury's face with eyes so bereft of hope, that for once, Archer hadn't known what to say.

"I hear you found his storehouse," Bradan said, interrupting Archer's thoughts.

"Yes. I'm not sure what to do with it though."

"Destroy it," Bradan said, his words hard as flint.

"What?"

"It's what Khoury died for, isn't it? Keeping the power contained." Bradan looked out over the bailey. He slowly raised the crystal to dangle over the emptiness. Then he whispered a prayer for forgiveness and let it go. The orange wand tumbled, shattering on the rocks below.

Archer knew he'd never get any of them back now. An unexpected wave of sadness choked him. The sorrow of all his losses, past and present, welled up in the hollow left by Khoury's death. Tears flowed, tears he had contained in front of the men. But Bradan was family. Bradan put heavy arms around Archer. The chieftain had always been there for him: The night his mother died, and then Maclan, and even Tarhill. The old shaman had always cared for him.

"It's my fault," Archer whispered, feeling like the boy who'd caused a scene at Maclan's funeral.

"No, it's not."

"Just like Maclan and Connor." Ghosts of his dead past clung to Archer's mind. "Tarhill said—"

"Your father may have blamed you but that doesn't make it your fault. He was a hard man, Reid. And when life isn't kind to men like that, they grow bitter."

"Connor followed me to his death."

Bradan pushed Archer away, forcing him to look at the older man. "No. You followed him to the death he wanted since Maclan's accident."

Archer squeezed his eyes tight, remembering how broken Connor had been after Mac died. Archer had been small consolation to either of them, Connor or his father.

"I know of your father's curse," Bradan said.

"What?" Archer stepped back, shame driving him away from the shaman.

"Do you think I wouldn't wonder why you broke my daughter's heart? The ancestors know all men's secrets."

Archer turned away, feeling guilty. "But he was right, Bradan. A silver tongue and sharp eye is worth very little when leading men. I'm not good enough for her."

Bradan chuckled. "You have yet to actually lead anyone, Reid. You tend to follow."

Archer retreated into sullen silence.

"Would it surprise you to know that my great-grandfather was a bard?"

Archer's eyes widened.

"The best damn chieftain the Clan ever had," Bradan continued. "Your father was wrong. A sword doesn't make you a leader, and neither does blood. You need a kind heart and a strong will. I will tell you one thing. I never had a son, Reid. But if I did, I'd want him to be just like you."

CHAPTER 66
CARA

She floated in and out of dreamless sleep, unwilling to move, not wanting to breathe. Every time she woke, it was as if none of it had happened. Then she'd remember.

She'd helped Archer with Khoury, washing his body, anointing him with oils and herbs and love. They'd dressed him in clean clothes and his armor and laid his weapons with him. Falin sang the Prayer for Homecoming, the song Sisters used to guide the dead to the Mothers. But none of it soothed her sorrow. Every time she'd touched the unnatural empty shell, her heart shriveled further. The haunting lyrics rolled around her head, giving more strength to the sorrow than to her.

She pulled the blankets over her, not wanting to think about the things Sidonius had said.

Get up! yelled a voice in her head, jolting her to sitting. Sudden dizziness darkened the edges of her vision. She lay back down and petulantly pulled the blanket back up.

This isn't helping, rabbit, it prodded. But she didn't want to talk to anyone, least of all Falin.

Go away, she thought as sternly as she could.

You know I can't. And I can't just sit here while you mope. Now get up.

No.

Yes!

Anger suffused her with restless energy and with it came an itchy sensation. Unable to sit still a moment longer, she stood and left the room, roaming her one-time home wrapped in the blanket. The stench of burning flesh still pervaded the Keep. She passed silently through the great hall that was filled with men sleeping scattered on the floor. Stopping to lean against a pillar, she thought back to all the times she'd seen men here, sleeping. At least, these would go home.

It seemed like another life.

It was another life, the Huntress in her head reminded her.

She sighed wearily. How would she live with two voices in her head all the time? It was just another type of prison.

She felt no argument from her other half.

She crossed through the hall on silent feet, not knowing where she was heading but needing something, something to fill the hole in her heart. She padded out into the bailey. The bodies that had escaped the dragon flames had been stacked on funeral pyres and lit. The flames danced high into the night sky. The company had lost more than half its men, adding faceless numbers to Cara's grief. Death was the real enemy.

Death is neither enemy nor friend, her inner warrior chided. *Actions give life value, not the length of it.*

She snorted in defiance. On this point, they would always disagree.

But her rebellious fire was short-lived. The hopelessness of her years in the Keep hung around her heart like chains, casting a pall over her thoughts. So much lost, so many things she wished had been different. They would never be free now. All she wanted was to go back to her cot and try to forget.

But we are alive. Falin's soft voice beat back the dust and the weariness. *And life is hope.*

Hope for what? Cara thought, unable to see past the black walls, unable to think about anything but the dust in the room where Khoury died.

We can choose, Sister. We can choose to turn our backs and hide, or follow where this leads. And I, for one, refuse to hide.

Sister. The word carried with it a warm strength that pushed back the fear. Cara remembered the Huntress waking her for the watch, defending her on the hillside, chastising her in the stable. She could lean on her Sister.

Agreed, she thought to herself. *No hiding.*

The voices went quiet as her path turned toward the open gate. She passed beyond the looming doors out onto the tundra that stretched away under the moonlight. The breeze pushed at her playfully as if recognizing her. Closing her eyes, she lifted her face to it. She'd felt no power since the ritual and wasn't sure if it had disappeared along with everything else, but she reached for the connection she'd felt while locked in the Keep anyway.

Inside her heart, she could sense that the Huntress longed for something, too. The part that had been Cara couldn't tell exactly what Falin yearned for, but it was a deep ache that resonated with her own. And in those heartbeats, when their sorrow was the same and longing united their spirits, they felt something stir.

Energy tingled up the woman's legs as magic reached down into the earth where the feet of the ageless mountains stretched down under the tundra, drawing strength from below. But this energy wasn't for them.

Other ancient energies hummed around them, but they were alien, arising from the Keep's wall. Those stones had been brought from far away. Again, this was something they couldn't use.

The woman sought the forests of the Haven, the pines of Bear Clan. Echoes of the gentler spirits of animals and plants bloomed in her inner eye though only faintly, like a shadow cast by moonlight. These were their power. Familiar things. Warm things.

Before any thought could sap her hope, she allowed the yearning and sorrow and loss of her two selves to merge and sent that out as a call over the tundra.

Please come.

She stood there until she shivered with cold. What she was hoping for she couldn't say.

Finally, the woman walked back into the Keep. They would wait and see what came of it. How long they could stand to wait in this place, they didn't know. Even those who had been her friends were torture to be around.

When Bradan looks at us who does he see? Who does Archer see?

Certainly anyone who had known Falin would think she was acting oddly, no armor, no sword. Could Falin accept being treated as Cara, or could Cara endure the expectations of being Falin?

And who would Khoury have seen?

The question popped into her mind before she could stop it. A startling pang of jealousy stabbed through her as she wondered which woman Khoury had loved best.

She shook her head, chiding herself for even entertaining such a thought. Cara remembered images of Falin's black eye, the captain's sharp words, and even memories from Falin herself of him telling her she wasn't needed. Of course he loved Cara.

But inside her heart there was a thorny wall where the strongest part of her kept secrets. The captain's angular face by firelight, the boyish glee in his stormy eyes when telling tales of battle, the feel of his lips on hers—these treasures Falin buried behind the thorns, too deep for Cara to find.

Their feet took them back into the great hall. Most of the men on the floor were asleep though some stood watch. She passed through silently and out another door, down the hall to a room where the hearth glowed but faintly. On a low makeshift bier lay Khoury. Archer planned to take the body away to the Bear Clan for a proper burial.

Proper burial, Falin scoffed in her mind. *What difference, fire or earth. Either way, he's gone.* Aching loneliness gathered inside her.

She knelt down by the body. A gossamer thread of connection to nature remained, and on it she felt the energy of a home far away.

Drawing upon that connection, she closed her eyes and laid her hands once again on his chest. Before the voice in her head could criticize, she sought the healing she had given Archer in the days before. But the kind presence was silent.

He's gone. We need to accept that.

Cara couldn't fight the voice of reason. Whether her energy was too depleted or whether she had lost that skill was impossible to know, but in either case she still felt nothing. Her hands remained cold.

Tired and discouraged, sleep drew her down into its quicksand embrace, a heavy inexorable descent. She laid her head down on Khoury's broad chest.

...And dreamed she walked through her forest. She felt someone beside her, but when she turned her head she was alone. Nevertheless, the feeling of being shadowed stayed with her as she moved through the brush beneath the unearthly leafy canopy. She came to a stream where a man stood on the far bank. She recognized those cobalt eyes and hailed him, but he wandered off like a lost child.

She splashed through the stream and charged through the trees after him. At every glimpse of silver armor, she called out. Each time she closed in, he faded like a ghost. Finally she collapsed with tears of frustration.

A light drew near, catching her eye. Without a sound, a woman approached wearing shining armor of white metal unlike any she'd seen before. The woman's curly pale hair was unbound and a sword hung at her waist in a scabbard that looked wrapped with vines. She'd seen this woman before. But where?

"You've returned." Relief warmed the spirit's voice. "Now all will be well."

The woman who was Cara and Falin stared at the spirit in disbelief. "What do you mean?" she sniffled.

The spirit noted her tears with surprise. "My child, why are you weeping? Your power is restored. Your path awaits."

The woman snorted with derision. "I have no power," she said. "And there is no path."

The spirit frowned. "Don't you know who you are?"

The woman stood and wiped her face with her hated unmarked hands. "I am a snowflake, nothing more."

For some reason this angered the spirit. "You are mistaken. Your mother gave you a name and a destiny. You are Raenna Alythenine Merrick. And you are my granddaughter."

Raenna Alythenine Merrick?

She'd never heard a name that long before and the thought that she had a mother other than Sorchia sparked her anger.

"I'm just a foundling," she snapped. "And this is a dream."

The spirit softened and moved closer to touch her cheek. She felt a chill breeze on her face. "This is no dream. I've come because you must reclaim your destiny."

"I have no wish for destinies," she muttered, pulling away.

The spirit leaned closer, her radiance almost unbearably bright. "If you do one thing for me…I will grant you a miracle."

The air crackled with a strange potency, and her heart shuddered to a stop. "A miracle?"

"Your captain," the spirit said. "He fell in battle, did he not?"

The woman nodded, afraid to breathe lest she disturb the unreasoning hope that flared to life.

"I know well the weight of such a sorrow," the spirit said. "For all that was lost or gone astray, for all that you've suffered, I can give you one gift, daughter of my daughter. But only one. Choose well what you ask for."

"Khoury will live?" She barely dared to name it but if the spirit had the power to help her….

The spirit nodded, her eyes the glimmering green of sunlit moss.

"Ask anything of me and I'll do it, just save Khoury."

"Be warned, my child. If he lives, he cannot be part of your destiny. You must do this alone."

"Even so. I would do anything to keep him from death," she said, knowing that nothing could keep her from Khoury's side if he were alive.

"Show me." The spirit gestured to her left and there stood Khoury though he didn't appear to see them. "Send him away."

The woman nearly rushed to him, but the spirit was watching her closely. She walked up to him slowly. His haunted face pulled at her. She wanted to touch the angled jaw, soothe his pain and make his stormy eyes laugh. Reaching out a hand, she laid it over his heart. Power glowed around her and shimmered in the forest.

"Khoury," she said and his eyes focused on her then. His lips moved but she couldn't hear his words. He reached for her, his eyes alight with affection and need. But she knew to save him, she must be cold.

"I renounce you," she said, setting her will to the inevitable loss of him. "Now go."

And she must have disappeared from his sight because his face fell as he searched the forest with hungry eyes. He waved frantic hands through where she stood, passing through her as if she were the ghost and not him. Her heart broke, seeing his desperation. She backed away, conscious of the spirit's scrutiny, as he stumbled into the trees where the fog gobbled him up.

"Remember, my child," said the spirit, "love is the root of your power. But you must guard your heart." The spirit reached out then and touched the woman's forehead. Energy shot down her limbs, radiating out her fingers and the top of her head. "The gates are opened to you. Your power awaits your call, but you will need to be strong and focused to wield it.

"And now, Raenna Alythenine, for your task."

"Tell me," the woman said, feeling strong and steady for the first time since the joining.

"Journey south. To Corthantir. There is a castle on the edge of the sea. Find the Ironwood Sword and return it to its rightful owner."

"Is the sword in the castle? And who should have it?" she blurted out. But the spirit woman had already faded away.

CHAPTER 67
KHOURY

He floated in the void after the blast, the emptiness a balm for his pains. The blissful oblivion contained no sound or light or touch. He simply existed, ignoring the urgent thoughts that waited beyond the quiet.

Time had no meaning to him. Shapes appeared, moving around and through him, reminding him what form felt like. If he concentrated, he could sharpen the shadows and paint pictures of places he vaguely remembered from another existence. But as he grew aware, the world took the shape of a round room where shadows wandered. It had an evil chill and dread shuddered through him. Echoes of his past suffering drove him out of the room to a stairway spiraling downward though he didn't remember using the door. He followed the memories backward in time, from the twisting stair to a hallway where his memory sharpened.

He recalled a battle, an urgent quest.

Find her.

The yearning echoed through him, leading him to a great shadowed hall where ghostly fires glowed darkly in the pits. Wraiths wandered around as if a corps of men were camped there, but he couldn't touch them or hear them.

How long he wandered among those familiar shadows, he couldn't say. Eventually sound returned, bringing the low murmur of voices, and with it—haste. He was running out of time.

Find her.

A glow from a room off the hall drew him. When he crossed the threshold, his worldly form returned. The room remained vague and insubstantial, but he had hands and feet again. His blue and silver tabard gleamed over a chain hauberk. More memories returned, bringing strength and hope. Details sharpened but so did his urgency.

In the room, a fire burned darkly in the hearth. A man lay before it, anointed and dressed with funerary care. And there sleeping with her head upon his chest was a young woman who glowed with the warmth of a sunrise.

Her sorrow had drawn him. He'd seen many men die. Perhaps he knew this one. He leaned over to peer at the face, willing the details to emerge. When the fog cleared from his eyes, he recognized the warrior and the shock of it tumbled him forward. He disappeared into a heavy darkness full of pain.

CHAPTER 68
CARA

She woke to sounds of alarm, her dream scattering into hazy pieces. Bradan's voice echoed in the hall, calling for her by both her names. She had fallen asleep on the captain's silver and blue tabard. Her arms tingled painfully, but the chest beneath her hands was as still as stone. Whatever miracle she had hoped to find was nothing more than a dream. He was gone.

She stood to leave, the ruddy firelight flickering over the closed eyes that might only have been sleeping. His skin held a rosy illusion of health. She paused to memorize every line of his dark strong brows and broken nose. Better to remember him in the golden glow of the firelight than with the deathly pallor he'd had in the tower room. She blew him a kiss, afraid to touch his cold flesh and ruin the fire's deception.

"Good-bye, Mason Khoury. We thank you."

Bradan called for her again, and she went into the great hall where the men were camped for the time being. He met her by the long tables.

"Cara," he began. "I mean, Falin—"

She held up a hand. "The spirits say we had a name once. We are called Rae…" But suddenly part of her wasn't sure she should share what she'd heard. It had sounded royal, and she couldn't believe it truly belonged to her.

"Rae?" he asked.

She nodded still unsure, but it would do for now. "What's all the noise about?" Her heart didn't dare to hope.

"There's someone to see you," Bradan said, smiling. He led her to the door where a huge white bear with a torn ear waited for her.

"Gar!" She rushed to him and threw her arms about his neck, burying her face in his warm fur. And she wept. A soothing rumble emanated from somewhere within the furry body, and the bear sat down to wait for her tears to stop.

I can still hear him, she thought, bursting with gratitude that she hadn't lost that. She relaxed into his soothing animal nature, sending him images of the battle and Khoury's death. The black nose pushed at her neck, commiserating with her pain. His simple wordless compassion eased her sorrow as nothing else could.

She heard Bradan behind her and stood, drying her eyes with a sleeve. Turning around, she was glad to see Archer with him.

"In the morning, I'll take you wherever it is you want to go," Bradan said. "But you are always welcome with us."

"Yes," Archer echoed. "Come home with us."

"Thank you, Bradan, Archer." Gar's presence gave her strength. "But we're leaving tonight."

A startled look crossed the older man's face. "But you might need—"

"Yes," she cut him off. "We will need many things. But it is time for you to get back to your own life. Your people wait for you. You already taught Cara everything you know."

"But..." Archer began.

"And Maura has waited far too long for you," she said sternly, punching him lightly on the arm. He nodded, embarrassed.

"Where will you go?" the shaman asked.

"Where the wind takes us," she said not wanting to tell them more.

"If you ever need help, you know how to find me," Bradan offered.

"Yes," she said, "in our dreams." Though she wondered if that power had disappeared as well.

Archer gripped her shoulders and then pulled her into a smothering hug. "Thank you," he said, "both of you. Promise you'll come to see us soon."

She nodded awkwardly. "Perhaps."

She placed a hand on Gar's head and told him to wait. Then she went through the hall and up the stairs with more energy than she felt she had a right to. From the room where she'd been sleeping, she gathered the few things she wanted: Cara's medicine bag, the white staff, Falin's talismans, the green dress, her weapons as well as the wolf-headed dagger that had been Khoury's gift, which Archer had found and returned to her. She threw the small pack over her shoulder and returned to Gar.

"Take care." Bradan hugged her good-bye.

"You too." She squeezed him tightly, blinking back tears. "We just want you to know that we tried our best. For Khoury."

"No one could have helped him," Bradan assured her.

Then she and the bear walked out of the Keep. The moon had set and the night was pitch.

CHAPTER 69
ARCHER

Archer sat in the room where Khoury's body had been laid out, staring at the dancing embers. Bradan sat with him, lost in his own thoughts. A cough startled both men. Archer looked at Bradan who was staring curiously at him. When another wet cough echoed in the empty room, he leapt to his feet. Then Khoury rolled to his side.

"Captain?" Archer reached him first.

"He's alive?" Bradan asked as Archer gently shook the dark-haired warrior. The body beneath his fingers felt more warm than cool. The captain didn't respond, but his chest rose and fell weakly. "He's…he's breathing."

"Breathing?" Bradan whispered, disbelieving. "It can't be."

Archer fell to his knees. "He was dead. There was no heartbeat. I swear it."

"It's a miracle," the shaman said.

"Or Cara," whispered Archer.

How long had she sat with Khoury that night? Had she tried to heal him again?

"Could she have…?"

Both men stared at each other with shock. "We need to find her," Bradan said. He rushed to the door and yelled for the best tracker.

When the young soldier appeared, Archer sent him out to find the woman who had just left in the company of a sledge bear.

They kept trying to rouse Khoury but, despite their best efforts, the mercenary only murmured deliriously. They removed his armor and weapons and wrapped him in warm furs. Bradan coaxed the hearth embers back to life and soon a roaring fire warmed the room. Archer and Bradan both sat with Khoury until the sun rose. Bradan brewed a tincture for him, and the shaman tried to get Khoury to drink a little every time he murmured in his sleep.

When the sun was near its peak in the sky, Khoury still had not opened his eyes, but he was very definitely alive. The good news of Khoury's survival spread quickly through the small contingent of men remaining in the Keep. Since Baron Wallace had agreed to pay the men if Khoury failed to return, Archer decided to send the men to Wallace for their compensation. Khoury was alive but whether he would fully recover remained to be seen. Archer talked to each man in the company and requested that they not say anything about Khoury's condition to the baron or anyone else. Each man promised but in their eyes was the awe that said they'd be unable to keep this gossip to themselves.

"We'll take him to Seal Clan and see what can be done," Bradan said, as he coaxed Khoury to swallow a few sips of water. Archer nodded and left to make arrangements to take horses and the wagon with them.

As the afternoon wore on without news, the men dispersed. The company of Elite Guardsman from Iolair left with the mercenaries who survived. It was nightfall before the tracker returned. And he returned alone.

"I followed the trail," he said as he dropped into a seat by the fire in the great hall. "They turned west across the tundra."

"You found her, then?" Bradan asked eagerly.

"No," the man said. "The tracks disappeared, as if someone had plucked them right from the ground."

Archer felt a suspicious chill. It was too strange.

The tracker continued, "On my way back, I did see someone. You won't believe me but it was a woman. In armor. But it wasn't Violet or Falin. She stopped me near the road at dusk."

"Did she have a bear?" Bradan asked.

"No. But there was something unnatural about her, like a chill in my bones." The man's face was pale. The meeting had spooked him. "She gave me a message. For the captain. Made me memorize it."

"The captain?" Archer felt a cold dread.

"He's delirious," Bradan said.

"I told her that might be the case," the tracker said. "She said to tell him even so."

"This way, then," Archer said, motioning for the young man to follow him. He led him to the small room where Khoury lay murmuring in his sleep.

Obviously discomfited, the tracker gave Archer a pleading look. "Her words exactly, mind you. I'd never speak to the captain like this."

Archer frowned and gestured to the captain. "Go ahead."

The tracker swallowed hard, embarrassment written in every line of his face. He crouched down by the bed and spoke, but the voice that came out was a woman's voice, full of command and derision.

"I see you, Barakani cur. You owe your life to Rowan kindness. But be warned. She is not for likes of you. Do not try to find her, Dunhadrar."

At the last word, the captain's eyes flew open. He grabbed the tracker by his shirtfront. "What did you call me?'

The tracker's face was pale, and he shook his head refusing to answer lest his words not be his own again.

But Khoury's eyes had already lost focus. His grip loosened. "You can't tell me what to do," he said, before he fell back to the bed. "I will find her. I swear I will."

KEEP READING FOR A PREVIEW OF

CALL OF THE HUNTRESS

CORTHAN LEGACY BOOK 2

CALL OF THE HUNTRESS

FALIN

"You wanted to leave as much as I did," Falin bit out. The great white bear next to her flicked an anxious ear at her tone, but continued walking.

I know, but I was wrong. Cara replied. The voice inside Falin's head was petulant. As usual.

Falin sighed and shook her head, letting her hand on the bear's back guide her. She had given up watching where they were going. The tundra stretched out flat and endless and required little in the way of attention. So she gave it none.

"No, you weren't," Falin argued, trying to sound supportive and kind although it galled her.

How do you know?

Falin ground her teeth together. "I just do."

But I miss them, Cara said.

"We promised to do this," she said for what felt like the hundredth time. "You were there."

We should have asked them to help, Cara said.

Falin refused to answer that, trying to let the conversation die from neglect. As far as she was concerned it was too late for that. She wasn't about to turn around and walk back to the Keep when she had no idea how far they had to go to find this damned sword. Bradan and the rest probably wouldn't even be there. It had been over a day and a half since they'd left.

The conversations between them had been like this on and off since they left the Keep. Like longtime foes tied together at the wrist, it seemed she and Cara couldn't help poking at each other. She growled under her breath, trying to control her temper. For now, Cara had given up trying to convince her to go back. Falin sighed with relief. She just needed to be left alone for a while.

She wished again for the solitude of her former life, remembering the thick forest of blackthorn trees with its deep shade and quiet rhythms. As she pictured the purple-black foliage cutting her off from the world she relaxed until it seemed she almost dozed on her feet.

As she walked, her hand unconsciously went to Gar's neck to scratch him and she felt him lean into the touch. His acceptance warmed her.

The sledge bear had come to the Black Keep out of loyalty, summoned by their mutual need. But Falin assumed the bear would see her as an intruder, having been Cara's only family long before she met the men. She tried not to feel jealous of Cara for having had such a steadfast companion growing up.

But Gar had an animal's ability to accept "what is" regardless of what had come before. And he accepted that his human was now this confusing, bickering mass of contradictions. When the argument inside them got heated, he would lean into their hip offering warmth and support.

Falin looked over at Gar and he turned his face to her as if aware of her scrutiny. His bottomless black eyes gazed into hers, radiating a feeling of security and love. She considered him practical, for an animal, and kind. Falin sensed that he would never leave them nor betray them. The thick pelt felt lush between Falin's fingers. His chuffed greeting that morning had been an offer of belonging she sorely needed and his battle-scarred ear marked him as a kindred spirit.

She smiled at him, realizing to her surprise that she loved the beast. Somehow, he had won over her thorny heart. She scratched behind his ear again.

"We're okay," she murmured, hoping it was the truth. She scanned the terrain and only then noticed they were headed into the setting sun. It seemed that while she was arguing with Cara Gar had turned them west.

When had he done that? Falin wondered, angry with herself for not noticing sooner. She nearly commented on it, turned him back south, but the peace she felt at that moment was too precious. Changing direction would be yet another argument.

Cara was content to follow instead of forging her own path, which rankled Falin. The huntress wanted to argue, to insist they should continue south as the spirit from their dream commanded. The one that claimed to be their grandmother. The quest was what mattered right now, their deal. But that would require talking again about the captain. And for all her strength, Falin's heart was too heavy to go there again. For once, she was too tired to fight. And so they followed Gar until nightfall.

In the morning, Gar again directed them west of his own accord and Falin wondered if he might have some knowledge of the road that he hadn't shared with them. Falin quickly realized it would be futile to argue with both of them. The Ironwood Sword had been missing for a long time; she didn't think a few days' delay would change anything. Their grandmother's ghost would have to wait. So she simply followed. For now.

As they trekked west toward the tall snow-covered mountains in the distance, Cara began to make it a habit to withdraw, leaving Falin's head empty of company. Where the other woman went, Falin couldn't guess. The huntress sometimes wondered if the quiet meant Cara's psyche slept. Or perhaps the white-haired girl could escape into the bear's mind. At any rate, Falin was left alone with her thoughts. Which was fine with her.

Her mind often turned to the battle, the dragon, and the Keep, which inevitably led her to think of Khoury. She shuddered at the memory of the emptiness in his body where his spirit should have been. She'd seen death before but this had felt different. She had been as disturbed by the void beneath their hands as Cara had been.

If only they could have healed him.

But the power Cara had wielded prior to their union seemed to have disappeared and Falin wondered if Sidonius had stolen that magic with the spell in the end.

Falin snorted in disgust, trying not to notice the lump in her throat. There hadn't been much of a chance to save the captain to begin with. The huntress knew that no healer on the continent could have saved him. She knew it as a warrior. Knew it was foolish to dwell on such things. And once upon a time she wouldn't have.

Her humorless snort had Gar flicking an anxious ear in her direction.

She petted his head and took a deep breath to loosen the tightness that was gathering in her chest. It had been her choice to risk the captain while driving the darkness back into the sorcerer's body. She knew the spell was killing him.

She wondered now if she had done the right thing.

Memories of his lips on hers teased at her mind, but she stuffed them down in case Cara was listening.

Over the last few days, Falin noticed that she could sift through Cara's memories at will. She wasn't sure if Cara could do the same although the other woman was oblivious to anything that had passed between the huntress and the captain on the road to the Keep.

And Falin intended to keep it that way.

In the silence, she cultivated again the dream-like blackthorn forest she made the first day. It came to her mind readily, like a familiar daydream. She memorized it now, made it her own, this shadowed wood. She surrounded it with imagined thorns, fortifying it with her own strength of will until it was a place Cara could not go. A place where Falin could hide the few precious memories that were hers alone, tokens of her former life like the bag of talismans that hung about her neck. And there she kept those moments of kisses and firelight, the taste of his skin and warmth of his eyes. His laugh.

She conjured a totem in the center of the forest, away from Cara's prying eyes. She made a tribute of blades and stone as a memorial to her heart's longing. Here was where she would keep the desperate hope that the spirit could give them what was promised if they found the sword.

The longing was so shameful she could barely admit it to herself but she allowed herself to feel it as she lingered in that dream-like place, her senses withdrawn from the world around her. Inside her sanctuary of thorns she allowed the hope to rise.

Mason, she prayed to the silence, *come back.*

Just then her toe scuffed over a sharp rock. The brief pain drew her attention back to her surroundings and she pushed down the tender feelings of a moment before. She scanned the lichen-covered ground for more obstacles then lifted her eyes to see gentle folds in the land, the beginning of foothills and the mountains growing closer, the peaks muted blue-grey from mist and cloud. She wondered where Gar was taking them but he seemed sure of his path.

Around her, the steppe bloomed with riotous color although nothing grew higher than her knees. It was beautiful and so different from her forest home. It would have been a glorious sight if her soul hadn't been so overshadowed by loss.

Falin thought of home then and Sorchia.

The huntress she had been was gone as surely as if she'd perished alongside the captain. Although she still breathed, her trials and triumphs, loves and losses had all been swept away in Sidonius's whirlwind of dark magic. Her spirit was all that remained, consigned for the remainder of this life to share this weak body with Cara.

It would have been better to die with the others, she thought sourly as her fingers twirled the strands of Gar's thick pelt. He leaned into her, sensing her distress.

So many had lost their lives in the Black Keep, all at the request of the mercenary captain who risked everything to save the woman he loved. A man as stubborn as a mountain and as faithful as a hound. One she considered a kindred soul. A friend she had grown to … appreciate, only to lose.

His ending had been in honorable sacrifice and how often had Falin espoused the glories of a "good death." Those words were thin comfort to her now, though she'd never admit that to Cara. The stain of regret lingered on her heart. What-if's tumbled through her mind.

What if I'd never followed him to the Black Keep?

What if Khoury had survived instead of me?

What if the soul knife had been recovered?

She frowned with a growl. Second-guessing was a coward's occupation and not one fit for a huntress. She shook her head and pulled herself up straighter, angry at herself for falling into the habit of dwelling on illusions and ghosts.

There was no going back. Likely no miracle to be had for the captain either. She'd sealed her own fate, and Cara's, when she killed Sidonius. He was the only person who knew how to reverse the spell that had trapped them like this.

The hard truth was: the captain was dead and the women were jammed together in one skull. Apparently for good.

Falin had sensed all along that rescuing Cara would require a sacrifice from her. She'd known that fighting the master of the Keep, the dark sorcerer who haunted her nightmares, would cost them dearly. But she'd hoped to be the one to fall. She should have been the one sacrificed. She was, after all, the rabbit's cast off bits of soul, nothing more.

But instead she had saved her timid "sister" and herself in the process. She frowned. It felt like a cowardly and selfish act.

But I didn't do it for myself, Falin thought. *Not even for Cara. I did it because he asked me to, the motherless bastard.*

That Falin hadn't been able to save him as well twisted her insides. She had vowed to be his shield and his sword. A vow she had meant wholeheartedly. And now her promise had come to naught. She'd dishonored herself as a huntress. Bile rose at the thought.

She turned her left hand palm up, fingers rubbing along the heel of her hand for the scar that should be there. But smooth skin covered the place where her blood had mingled with Khoury's the night she'd pledged her sword to him. She clenched and unclenched her hand before her face, studying the slender fingers and soft planes of it, so unlike the strong calloused hands she remembered. This child's hand was hers now. Her once well-muscled frame was frail and thin.

She hated this new body. She was bothered by its weakness but even more disturbed by the absence of the scars which had marked her path through life. Her eyes pricked with forbidden tears as she considered all she had lost.

Perhaps you were the lucky one after all, Captain, she thought. *At least you're not trapped.*

Hopelessness washed through her for a moment, but the huntress in her rebelled at such despair. It was a weakness she would not tolerate.

She scrubbed her face with her baby soft hands, forcing her sorrow down behind the thorns in her mind.

"Ever a huntress," she growled, using the familiar words to whip herself into her former strength. "Quit complaining, woman. You are alive and there are things to be done."

Gar chuffed at the sound of her voice and she offered him the smallest of smiles.

"We're fine."

Cara's sorrow sapped her huntress will, whispering to her in the night, urging her to give up. To fold. To stop striving.

But she'd be thorn-crossed if she let the rabbit's weakness stop her. Falin breathed deeply, reaching for the hidden strength inside, finding it in her bones and muscles and fierce heart. Just like she always had.

So it was only by Falin's force of will they continued their journey. She pushed them to take the next step and the next, each one a choice to seize the life that had been given them no matter how uncomfortable. A choice to follow this fate, however unkind, to wherever it led.

Perhaps the grandmother's task would be worth it in the end. Probably not. But Sorchia had often said, "Roads never end at the place they set out to find."

Oh Sorchia, if only you could see where this thorn-cursed rabbit led me, she thought.

It wasn't that Falin hated Cara. Quite the opposite, she had great sympathy for her weaker half. But the injustice of Sidonius's callous cruelty burned in her chest. He'd done little more than thrust them together, never intending they'd survive the hour. The union might have been easier, if they'd been compatible. But they argued endlessly.

Arguing with a voice in my head, Falin thought wryly, *a sure sign of madness. Or perhaps I'm just the voice she argues with in hers.*

The sorcerer Xantherus had believed the truth was closer to the latter.

She was the spare, and Cara the original.

So she would take care of Cara. She had promised Khoury that much.

When Cara finally surfaced, it felt like someone had stuffed her head with wool, a choked crowded feeling between her ears. Gar was leading them up a sloping hill toward strangely familiar pine forests.

As they crested the rise, Cara's voice lilted through her head, *I remember this place.*

Visions of Captain Khoury, his lieutenant Archer Tarhill, and a sledge drawn by a group of bears that included Gar floated through their mind.

The presence which had joined them during the reuniting spell returned. Falin had come to think of it as the third piece of their soul.

It reminded her of the Mothers, the guardian spirits of Foresthaven, powerful druids who had sacrificed their lives for their families.

The presence had no voice of its own and communicated only in vague feelings and intuitions. Whatever it was, it was intent on bringing the two women to some common ground. As if it wanted to make them whole, to make them the person they were born to be.

To make them into Raenna Alythenine Merrick, if the warrior spirit from her dreams was to be believed.

Falin constantly felt the motherly presence flipping through her memories, sifting, sorting, rearranging. But it could not get past Falin's thorns. Her memories of the captain's kisses and her own desires were safe even from the power of their internal Mother.

Still, when the landscape before them jolted Cara's memories, the magic presence enhanced the images, letting both women relive the journey Cara had taken from the Keep to Archer's northern home, Bear Clan. As they re-experienced them together, the memories became not just Cara's but Falin's too.

She surveyed the slope with new eyes. A river exited the pines here, splitting into two smaller streams flowing south. At the crux of the flow, the ancient stone statue in the likeness of the Clan's bear spirit Borran lay in pieces, smashed by giants' axes. What nostalgia Cara felt, Falin did also. As they stared down at the vale and she remembered meeting Bradan, Chieftain of the Bear Clan, for the first time along with his beloved wife Ealea. The Clan had taken Cara in, given her a place to belong. Something Falin had always longed for as well but never really found. And yet, courtesy of the magical presence, since Cara had felt at home here; Falin did as well.

The huntress frowned, refusing to think of it as true belonging. The memory wasn't hers. It was merely borrowed.

Soon after Cara had settled into life in the Clan, Sidonius had taken his revenge. The story Archer had told Falin in hushed tones by the fire one night now came vividly to life before her inner eyes. Towering warriors swarmed the small Clan. Villagers and bears died. Ealea and her sister-in-law Ingrid were brutally slain right before Cara's eyes.

And now before Falin's eyes, too.

The huntress's hands clenched, longing for her blade, yearning to fight, while Cara longed instead for the company of the old shaman and Archer, sympathetic shoulders to share her tears with.

But they had not chosen to travel with the men to Seal Bay where the rest of the village had fled after the attack. Falin still believed it had been the right choice. If they thought it was hard now between them, being with people who had known them as individuals would surely have driven them mad. Or maybe it was just that Cara might belong there, and the huntress would once again be the outsider.

The empty waterskin slapped her leg as she descended the slope reminding her that they'd need water if they were going to continue. Gar brought them game, but Cara didn't seem to like the thought of eating meat. Although the huntress usually had no qualm about eating her kills, her stomach now roiled at each bite. Perhaps there was something still edible in the village they could take.

Falin felt Cara hesitate at the thought of going into the village.

If not the village, rabbit, then where will we find food? she asked.

TO BE CONTINUED…

AUTHOR'S NOTE

Dear Reader,

Dreamwalker's journey has been long. Very. Very. Long. Epic, in fact. I got the idea for Cara and Falin at the end of high school. Now, over thirty years later, their story is finally published.

And yet, in retrospect, the book you're holding in your hands is a completely different beast than that first story I wrote. The title has changed at least five times, the characters' names nearly as often. The scenery has morphed and shifted with each successive revision and rewrite until only the footings they stand on are recognizable from the original. But more importantly, I took a story originally envisioned with a questionable and definitely Tolkien-esque sense of apocalypse and turned it into a more intimate tale of courage, growth and finding your own path.

They say in writer communities that you should toss out the first stories you finish. When I first heard that, I was offended thinking it meant professional writers considered all early writing 'trash'. Of course, my first draft was trash, and immature, but I still loved it deeply. I didn't disagree in public forums, but I always knew *Quest of the Dreamwalker* would be my exception to the rule. I knew I could write it better given enough time and practice. Something in me didn't want to give up on the heart of Cara's tale. I kept thinking it had something worth saying. And so I stubbornly refused to let it go.

Or maybe, the real truth is that it refused to let me go. You see, I didn't intend to be a writer. I wrote it because the story in my head wanted to be written. And then I put it in a drawer and lived my life. But I never lost these pages. The events relayed here seem as real as memories sometimes. Cara and Falin's story stayed in my head, whispering to me. Sometimes, out of the blue, I'd get ideas for how events could play out better and I'd pull the story out again and redo it, cringing at how bad the previous version was.

Over the years, it's become clear why authors say not to revamp your old stories. There is so much hard work involved in revisiting the stories and bringing them up-to-date with your current skill level and with the culture. Writers do outgrow their stories sometimes. It takes brutal cutting, revamping and even re-envisioning of the text and the plot to make it acceptable to your maturing senses. And the more you grow as a writer in between drafts, the more work needs to be done.

But I'm glad I didn't give up on this one. I still love the story and the characters. They are like family to me after all this time. I'm content knowing I did right by them.

And so, dearest reader, here at the end of this leg of Cara and Falin's journey, I want to thank you for coming this far with me. I'd love to hear what you have to say about this experience: the good, the bad and even the indifferent. Hit me up on my social media to let me know what you think. Or, leave a review if you feel motivated to do so. I appreciate all your input. Thanks again, for taking this journey with me.

Blessings,

Stacy B.

ABOUT THE AUTHOR

A born and bred Jersey girl, Stacy eagerly left the Garden State for college, as was the family tradition. And after graduating from University of Pennsylvania with a psychology degree, she married a Marine and soon developed a distinct fondness for travel, U-Hauls and Southern hospitality. She returned to Jersey after a decade of that nomadic life with two children, a slight addiction to coffee and a hunger to create something of her own. So she began writing fiction, stories styled after the classic sci-fi/fantasy novels of her childhood. She still lives in New Jersey with her two delightful teens, a neurotic dog and a queenly cat. Her favorite things are furry four-legged critters, a good game of backgammon and books that make you forget where you are.